Meet Me at the Art Café

Sue McDonagh

Art Café Series

Where heroes are like chocolate – irresistible!

Published 2020 by Choc Lit Limited
Penrose House, Crawley Drive, Camberley, Surrey GU15 2AB, UK
www.choc-lit.com

A CIP catalogue record for this book is available
from the British Library

ISBN 978-1-78189-288-6

Printed and bound in Great Britain by Clays Ltd, Elcograf S.p.A.

Acknowledgements

My stepson Jack, when little, used to love posing questions along the lines of, 'if there was a fight between a fox with no teeth, and a really old tiger, who would win?'

I'm asking, 'If there was a race between a glacier, and a novel, which one would get there first?' and I'm going to suggest that it's probably the glacier. Writing a novel takes a disproportionately long time.

People like to think that authors sit alone with a laptop or notebook, and eventually out pops a novel. Some days are like that, but mostly, a novel is shaped by people and events who might have no idea that they have had any influence over what you are writing. So here's my chance to say thank you.

For help with the man's point of view and for believing in me always, Allan.

For kicking me forward after my lovely mum died, my wonderful writing friends, Jan, Catherine and Vanessa – the Cursors. And really, we could often spell it with an 'e'.

For eureka 'plot-fixing' moments whilst walking him in the park, thank you to my border terrier Scribble.

For generous and honest feedback – I couldn't do better than Pippa, who runs the chocolate shop in Cowbridge and discusses my characters as if they're real people.

Thanks to my firefighter son, Andrew, for clarifying
up-to-date resuscitation techniques, and to my
always supportive family and friends.

Huge thanks to my motorbike riding friends for
reading and sharing their reviews. You're fab, ladies!

Lastly but by no means least, thank you to the Choc Lit
team, for advice and support, and to my editor, who
helped me to realise the shape of this book and for whom
I have the utmost respect. Thanks almost must go to the
Tasting Panel readers who passed *Meet Me at the Art Café*
and made this possible: Hilary B, Gillian C, August H,
Alma H, Claire W, Melissa B, Barbara B, Sue R, Jo L,
Liz R, Ruth N, Sam E, Gaele H, Dimi E and Melissa C.

Chapter One

The middle-aged couple had been dithering over their order for ages. Lemon drizzle, or toasted teacake? Jo could hardly blame them. Everything looked and tasted wonderful at the Art Café.

Pinning her 'take your time, I have all day' smile on, Jo's eyes slid towards the panoramic windows that gave the café its wonderful view over the beach. Even when the blue-green sea was beginning to rumple into colourless waves, as it was now, blurring the divide between sea and sky on the Gower Peninsula and signalling rain, the coastline was always stunning. Jo could hardly remember a time when she knew nothing about South Wales.

Winter had turned the corner into spring, and there had been a steady flow of trade. Since her boss, Lucy, was poised on the brink of TV stardom, people visited as much in the hope of seeing her, as for the food and drink they were all so proud of.

'Hello? *When* you're ready?' The man rapped on the counter and she jumped. 'Cappuccino and a pot of tea.' Flicking a glance over his shoulder at his wife as she found a table, he muttered, 'And one chocolate fudge cake.'

'Good choice. It's delicious.' Jo smiled. 'Would you like a second plate and fork, sir?'

'I'm not sharing it,' the man said, without a trace of humour, his eyes tracking the cake as she slid it onto the plate. 'She said she didn't want any.'

That hadn't been the message that Jo had understood from their overheard conversation but she clamped her lips together and got on with the order. Her mobile phone, stashed in the pocket of her apron, buzzed just as she turned the steam wand on, spitting scalding water onto her hand.

'Ouch!' Whirling to run the cold tap, she read St Michael's Primary on the screen and fumbled the accept button. Her little boy's school. They never rang.

'Hello, this is Ms Morris,' she whispered. 'Is anything wrong?'

'Our *order* …' the customer reminded her, sharply.

'I'm so sorry, I'll have to call you back. I'm at work,' Jo said hurriedly into the phone, cutting the call. She could barely hear the secretary anyway over the tap and the still steaming nozzle. Despite the woman's habitual peremptory tone.

Despite her stinging hand, she assembled the tea tray with an apologetic smile to the customer – unreciprocated – and returned the call as soon as he'd sat down.

'Everything alright, Jo?' Her other boss, Richard, looked up from the other end of the counter where he was restocking the cake display. The Art Café had brought together his culinary flair and Lucy's artistic talents, resulting in an inviting eating-place where you could also buy gifts and fine art. Both happily settled with their own partners, they made a great team, and Jo loved working for them.

She swallowed, knowing this wouldn't be a popular request, but there was no one else who could go to the school. She was on her own.

'Richard … I'm really sorry,' she began, continuing in a rush, 'you know I wouldn't usually ask but there's been a bit of a … drama at Liam's school. I need to go.'

'You can't just drop everything and leave.' Richard waved his arm at the half-full café. 'Didn't you tell them you were working?'

'I did! I *am* sorry,' Jo repeated, blowing on her burn. 'They've never asked me to go in before. And the secretary won't tell me over the phone.'

'When you've quite finished *chatting* … I asked you for Earl Grey.' It was the man she'd just finished serving, holding up the teapot. 'Have you heard of TripAdvisor?'

Richard sent her a look of exasperation, and Jo, who knew perfectly well that 'the customer was always right', even when he obviously wasn't, turned to make a second pot of tea.

Thankfully, their TripAdvisor ratings were excellent, but Richard and Lucy warned the staff constantly about how much attention customers paid to those sneaky reviews that marked them down for things like, 'The view wasn't as good as promised. It was raining.' Yet another reason why Jo mistrusted social media.

'Please?' she mouthed at Richard. He regarded her steadily for a moment before hitching his head in the direction of the door.

'Go on then. Lucy is coming in this afternoon, and I'll be juggling the school runs myself before I know it,' he told her. 'We'll manage. But I don't envy you cycling over the hills – looks like rain's heading our way.'

'When isn't it?' Jo grinned. 'Thanks, Richard. I'll make the time up.' *Somehow*.

'I'll have another cappuccino too. One that hasn't been slopped all over the saucer,' the customer said in a loud voice. 'And I assume I won't be paying for these.'

Jo gritted her teeth, taking extra care with the hot drinks. What she wouldn't give to just be able to say the words that were threatening to break loose. Nowadays though, she was a whizz at holding her tongue.

'Thank you, sir. I hope these are to your complete satisfaction,' she told him instead, his surprised expression making her laugh inside. 'Have an absolutely lovely day.'

Hurrying out to the loo, she bundled her café uniform into her rucksack and yanked on her stretchy cycling shorts.

Ungainly in her bike shoes with the metal-cleated soles, she slip-skated on the polished tiles past the startled customers, hurdling their bags and piles of coats on her way to collect her bicycle from the storeroom.

Pausing just long enough to plant a quick *thank you* kiss on Richard's surprised cheek – he was such a sweetie and she wouldn't want to upset him for the world – she thrust her arms into the flimsy emergency waterproof jacket which lived in a tiny pouch under her bike seat and scooted away just as slow, fat raindrops plopped onto the pale pavements.

She stood up on the pedals, speeding out of the pretty Welsh seaside town. At first she welcomed the cooling rain, but soon enough the relentless drizzle had seeped through her thin clothes, and she had to pedal hard to stay warm. She tried to guess what the secretary was going to tell her when she got to Liam's school. Why hadn't the woman just told her over the phone?

Only a few more miles to go. Toiling up the steep uphills was rewarded by maximum velocity on the downhills, which she loved. Lying flat over the crossbar to minimise wind resistance, she glanced down at the tiny speedometer which read eighteen … nineteen miles an hour. Twenty miles an hour … the road passed in a blur of eye-stinging drizzle but Jo knew the road well enough to ride it with her eyes closed. She thought … right up until the moment she met the flock of sheep, blocking the lane.

'*Yargh*!' Hauling on the brakes, she swerved for the least woolly gap, heart hammering as she came to a stop without injuring either them or her. She grinned in relief. Pesky creatures. They'd be the youngsters at this time of the year. The older sheep kept to the grassy verges, and if this lot survived long enough then they'd learn to do that too. Better move them on before someone else met them.

Straddling her bike, she yelled and waved her arms to urge them on their way.

Ed wiped his goggles with a gloved hand. They smeared with drizzle almost immediately. He loved this old jalopy, but really it was a summer motorbike, not at all cut out for miserable weather like this. He knew how quickly the weather changed here. Never mind, the shortcut lane was usually quiet. He was just thinking that he hadn't seen another vehicle since he'd turned off the main road as he rounded a left-hand bend ... to be faced with a lane full of skittering sheep.

There was no time to think. Sounding his horn, he braked reflexively and the vintage bike's wheels locked in a long skid. The sheep parted, rolling their eyes at him as they tucked in their tails and scattered. Which just left the long-legged girl on the pedal cycle on his side of the road. Squeezing hard on brakes that were already at their fullest extent, Ed could only watch in horror as the bike slid as if in slow motion along the greasy road. Straight towards her.

Chapter Two

'Are you alright? Hello? Speak to me!'

Lying on her back, winded, eyes closed against the persistent rain, Jo heard the voice as if from a long way off. It sounded panicky, and she wondered who was in trouble. Her cheek was patted with something that smelled like wet dog, and she stared up into a pair of clear grey-green eyes. They were like sea-glass. Bright and translucent, with a dark rim, they seemed to reach into the depths of her soul. Fringed with the blackest, longest eyelashes, set in the face of an angel, and topped off with thick, black hair – and a surprising pair of goggles. So beautiful. Perhaps he *was* an angel. The goggles were an interesting addition though. And the wet dog thing on her face.

As she focussed blearily on the sheep staring down at her over the angel's shoulder, her brain recalibrated and her body propelled itself into a sitting position, startling the sheep into a wild scamper.

'God, those things stink, get them off me.'

The angel sniffed his gloves. 'Do they? Sorry ... I thought you'd knocked yourself out for a minute.'

'Knocked *myself* out? You nearly hit me!'

'I couldn't help it ... you were on my side of the road!'

'Don't talk rubbish! *Your* side of the road?' She swept an arm around her. 'Can you see a white line? This road is *tiny*! There isn't a yours and my side.' Her gaze fell on the twisted wreckage that had once been her pride and joy. 'My bike ... *ohhhh*!'

He at least looked contrite. She focussed on him again, suddenly realising who he was. He was definitely no angel.

'I know who you are. Caramel macchiato double with

extra syrup and cream.' *He was Ed. One of Lucy's biker mates. Handsomest man on the planet. In his own opinion.*

'Huh? Sounds like you might have concussion …'

She struggled to her feet and glared at him, hands on her hips.

'How fast were you going?' she demanded, ignoring the fact that she'd been hurtling downhill a moment earlier. 'My bike is wrecked! And I nearly was too. Thanks to you.'

'I said I was sorry!' Ed unfolded his considerable height and frowned down at her. 'Don't I know you?'

She'd preferred it when she was looking down at him.

'How would I know?' Her grazed palms shook and she felt sick. She could still see him speeding towards her and relived the helpless moment of not quite being able to orchestrate her feet on the pedals before she'd scrambled off at the last minute. Something warm and distinctly sheepy wafted around her. She sniffed her hands before scrubbing them on her shorts. Yuk. Sheep poo. Lucky she'd had her tetanus shot. 'I work in the Art Café,' she muttered, unwillingly.

'Ah.' Ed bent and stood her bike up. 'Better get out of the road before something else comes round this corner and finishes the job.' He shot a glance over his shoulder at her, adding with a nod. 'I do know you. You're Jo.'

Jo glared back at him, still shaken, rather surprised that he knew her name. She wasn't going to give him the satisfaction of knowing his name. Oh, he was polite enough, she supposed, but he was another of that breed of beautiful young men who presumed they'd only have to smile at a girl to get them to drop their panties right there and then.

She'd seen him on the sunny terrace at the café, flirting with the holidaymakers off the beach, zooming in on the skimpily dressed, pretty ones, all taut bodies and salty dreadlocks. Gorgeous Ed, they referred to him in the café.

She squatted now beside her bike, peering in dismay at the

catalogue of broken and bent parts. The rear wheel was bent like a taco.

'For God's sake.' She blew a long, shuddering breath. That could have been her instead of the wheel. Don't keep thinking about it. 'I've got to get to Pengenydd! Like now!'

'Where are you going?'

'St Michael's School.'

'I know it.' He nodded. 'I can give you a lift.'

Jo stared around her.

'How, exactly?'

'This!' Ed gestured to the vintage motorbike.

'You have got to be kidding. I am not getting on that … that thing. It's a deathtrap.'

'I'll ride really slowly.'

'You couldn't have done that earlier?'

'I told you. It was a skid. Bloody lucky to keep her upright.'

'Oh yes,' Jo spat. 'Good for you. You've buggered up my only means of transport, and you're patting yourself on the back. The least you could do is call me a taxi.' As she saw his mouth open, she snapped, 'And don't even think of using that old, "okay, you're a taxi" line on me either.'

'I was going to say that it'll take ages for a taxi to get here. Brenda will be quicker.'

'Brenda?' Jo felt a surge of hope. 'Is she somewhere close by?'

'She's here.' Ed patted the bike, undamaged, even having run over the back wheel of her bicycle. It must be built like a tank.

'And you thought I had concussion …' Jo rubbed her elbows.

'Don't listen to her, Brenda.'

'Brenda.'

'Brenda the BSA! She's old but she's still a goer.'

Jo considered, and then sighed. She didn't have a lot of choice, did she?

'I haven't got a helmet.'

'You're wearing a helmet.'

'Yes, but it's not for a motorbike!'

'Have mine.' He began to unbuckle his chinstrap.

'Oh, don't be ridiculous, mine won't fit you!'

'Maybe not. And pink's not really my colour.' He cocked his head at her appraisingly. 'Anyway, I bet you go faster downhill on that than I do on this, in just your Lycra.'

She shrugged. 'Maybe.' *Definitely*.

'Besides,' he added, 'do you always follow the rules?'

She didn't answer. She did follow the rules. Now. Mostly.

'What am I supposed to do with my bike?'

'Stick it behind a hedge. Who's going to steal it? It's older than I am!'

'Oi! You're one to talk about old.' Jo sent a pointed look at his bike. 'I love my bike. It was my dad's. I'm not leaving it anywhere.' A treasured gift from her father, it was the only thing she had of that time. Tears pricked at the thought of abandoning it in a hedge to the elements. She shivered, wet through.

'Put it over your shoulder then. This will cushion it.' Ed shrugged off his leather jacket and handed it to her. 'Or wheel it next to us? We won't be going that fast, trust me.'

Trust him? She stared at him, now in a short-sleeved white T-shirt, which showed off his muscular arms. So he was going to ride his bike like that. Trust him? Either he was mad or she was, as she didn't see many other options right now. It would take ages to get a taxi here, even if she could afford it. She could make him pay … but he was right, she had been on his side of the road. If she hadn't tried to move the sheep, she'd be at the school by now.

'Keep it. I'll be fine. I don't feel the cold.' Had she really just said that? Was she completely mad? She was freezing! There was just something about him that made her want to do the opposite of what he wanted her to do.

'I don't want us having an accident because you drop your bike.' He held it out to her again and after a brief hesitation she took it.

'Whatever.'

'You get on first, I'll hand you the bike.'

A few minutes later, Jo was perched behind Ed, her crippled bicycle hitched over one shoulder.

'Put your arm round me.'

'Get lost. I'm not one of your blonde bimbos.'

'You can say that again.'

'What does that mean?'

'Look.' Ed twisted so he could see her. 'You're unbalanced enough already. I don't want you falling off the back.'

'You've got a nerve to be calling me unbalanced,' Jo grumbled, but she snaked an arm around his waist anyway and clamped her knees either side of his hips.

'Off we go!' he yelled, and she momentarily closed her eyes and prayed. I *am* mad, she decided. I'm riding a motorbike without a proper helmet, in shorts. Please, *please, no more sheep, and don't let us crash!*

Ed ignored the chilling rain soaking through his T-shirt, and did his best to smooth out his gear changes to give his passenger a less bumpy ride. That old cycle must weigh a ton, and it would be biting into her shoulder by now. But she hadn't complained once.

He grinned to himself, glancing down to see her arm in his jacket encircling his waist. Oh and how hot was she. Long, toned legs and the cutest arse he'd ever seen – and in those figure-hugging shorts he hadn't been able to help seeing it. He'd seen her in the café, of course, but what with the baggy black trousers and apron, plus her way of keeping her head down, she made it easy for anyone to overlook her. Now he'd taken a good look at her, he could see how gorgeous she was. Especially when she was angry, with those bright eyes.

His heart had all but stopped when he'd crunched over her bike. Lucky he'd stayed upright. Bloody sheep. He had no idea what he would have done if she'd stayed on her bike – it could have been catastrophic. Thank God she was quick on her feet ... he didn't even have as much as a sticking plaster with him.

His heart was still thundering at high speed but he couldn't decide if it was the near miss or the feel of her slim, tanned knees gripping his thighs. He had to resist the urge to drop a hand back to stroke one of them. In his thin T-shirt, he could feel the length of her, warm against his back.

It made him think of all sorts of other things that a bloke who already had a girlfriend shouldn't be thinking of. A high-maintenance girlfriend at that. Alexis. Who wouldn't be caught dead on the back of his motorbike. Or anywhere that threatened to mess up her expensive hairdo, come to that.

Okay, she looked great all the time and his mates fancied her, but ... it wasn't enough any more. Probably time for a replacement. Plenty of fish in the sea for her. She wouldn't miss him.

The school was coming up now on the left, and he braked carefully, methodically down-shifting the gears.

'Quick ... stop!' Jo shrieked confusingly in his ear. 'It's Daisy's dad ... Ash! What's he doing here?' She was slithering off one side of his bike but still holding her cycle on the other side.

'Hang on, you'll damage it.' He meant his bike, but she stopped, probably thinking he meant hers. Dismounting, he concentrated on lifting her cycle safely away. She scrambled off and he appreciated once again her long, tanned legs in the shorts.

'Don't let him see me ... he's a copper.' Her eyes darted over his shoulder.

'Have you been a naughty girl?' Ed grinned, turning to wave at his friend. Ash, local police sergeant, and so much more smiley now that he was engaged to the lovely Lucy from the Art Café, wandered over.

'*Nooo*! I'm not wearing a proper helmet. He'll nick me!'

'He didn't see us. Stop panicking.'

'Alright, Ed?' Ash clapped Ed on the shoulder. 'Not exactly the weather for riding in a T-shirt ...'

'No, we were ... um,' Ed began, words deserting him as Ash fixed him with a long stare. 'I mean, I was, er ...'

'I was just checking Ed's pillion seat.' Jo prodded at it with a long finger. 'Very ... um, comfy.' She nodded as if satisfied.

'Hmm.' Ash looked from one to the other and Ed held his breath.

'I have to go. Thank you ... um, for the loan of the jacket,' Jo said, wriggling out of it and handing it back to him.

Taking it and trying not to stare at her lithe body revealed by the wet clothes, a thought struck him.

'How are you going to get home?'

'We'll walk.' She shrugged.

'I can give you a lift, Jo,' Ash said. 'I've just dropped the school guinea pig back. I've got to collect Daisy anyway. I can put your bike in the back of the motor.'

'Thanks, that would be great,' Jo said, relinquishing the handlebars of her crushed steed.

'What happened to that?' Ash asked.

'Sheep,' Jo said, staring levelly at Ed.

'I can collect you!' Ed blurted. What had made him say that? It was fine. He could do it. As long as he rode there like a lunatic and drove back like a madman. And didn't meet Ash on the way. He *should* do it. This was his fault. Mostly.

Ash returned a lifted eyebrow and Ed sent him a meaningful look.

'No thanks, Ed. You've done quite enough already,' Jo said, straight-faced. 'Right. Off to face the lion's den. Cheers.'

Both men watched her neat figure for a moment as it slipped through the code-operated gates, then Ash turned to Ed and said in a stern voice, 'A helmet each please, Ed, next time.'

Ed nodded, not bothering to make any further excuses, and let out a long breath as Ash walked back to his car. God, that was close. He couldn't lose his licence! That would be his job up the swannie for sure.

Next time, though? Now there was a thought …

Chapter Three

God. What an arse. In both senses of the word ... Jo peeped over her shoulder to watch Ed ride away on his old bike, like James Dean. She kneaded her shoulder where the top tube of her pedal cycle had rubbed on the bone, thankful for the loan of the leather jacket.

Yes, alright, he was eye candy. And yes, he'd flirted with her. It might have been ages but she still recognised the signs. But she had no time for a man in her life. Not even one who set her heart racing like Ed had. No. Definitely not. It was just ... what did they call it? Pheromones. A smell or something. And yes, snuggled up behind him, he had smelled good. Not something out of a bottle. Just something ... fresh ... airy. Well, she'd probably left something natural smelling inside that nice jacket of his. Just not as fresh.

And what the hell was she going to do now about her bike? It was the only transport she had. If it hadn't been a case of tit for tat she would have claimed off Ed. Well. She might have. She didn't have a clue how you'd claim for repairs to a bicycle.

She couldn't believe he'd offered her a lift home. No, thank you! Goodness only knew what he'd collect her in – a tractor or something? She knew him well enough to know what coffee he drank when he came into the café, and that he was some sort of bike mechanic. Surely he couldn't be earning much. Not that a rich boyfriend was on her agenda either, she chided herself. Yet there was something about him that commanded attention. People just seemed to do what he asked them to do. Well, she wasn't going to be falling for any of that.

Although she had to admit that the adrenaline junkie part of her had enjoyed the daredevil ride here. It had made her feel, just for a short while, young. Not that she wasn't still young, but being a single mum carried huge responsibilities, and there were times when she felt way older than her twenty-six years.

Anyway. She was going home with Ash, her boss's fiancé and his little daughter Daisy, perfectly safely. Even if Ash did make her feel as if he knew every single rule she'd ever transgressed in her entire life. It wasn't just him. All policemen made her feel like that.

She made her way to the secretary's office, rubbing hopelessly at the patches of dirt that she hoped weren't sheep poo but probably were, and failed to shake off the feeling that she was the pupil. Pale but red-cheeked, Liam leapt off his chair when he saw her, clutching at her legs. She bent and patted his silky brown hair, her heart squeezing with love.

'Don't worry, my little lamb, we'll sort it out,' she crooned. To the thin-lipped secretary she said, 'What happened? Who hit him?'

'Excuse me?' The secretary pursed her mouth. 'I think you'll find that young Liam is at fault here.' She gave a long sniff. 'Still. What can you expect, really?'

'What?' Jo gaped at her in disbelief. 'You said there'd been some sort of a … You mean, Liam *hit* someone?'

'I'll ask his teacher to come down. Please take a seat.'

Jo folded herself onto Liam's child-sized chair, and pulled him onto her lap. Winding his arms about her neck, he pressed his soft, baby cheek against hers and then recoiled.

'You smell, Mummy!'

'Sorry, sweetie. There were these sheep and … ah, hello.' She leapt to her feet, depositing Liam back on the chair.

The reception class teacher was a tall young woman. Her large soft eyes blinked rapidly as they drifted over Jo.

'I … er. He … um,' she began. 'Perhaps Liam would like to go and find a book?'

Liam sent Jo an imploring look, and stayed where he was.

The teacher continued, 'We were discussing what our daddies did at work ...'

Jo's heart sank, and she forced herself to stand straighter.

'... and Liam said that his daddy is never at home because he's ...' the teacher ended on a whisper '... he's an ... astronaut.'

Jo had to lip-read, leaning forward to catch the words. *An astronaut?* The teacher jerked backwards as the agricultural wafts reached her. Dying inside, Jo said in a voice louder than she had intended, 'Yes, and your point is?'

'The other children laughed and, well, Liam kicked them ...' She faded into silence.

The secretary inhaled lengthily through her nose, making her displeasure clear without actually saying anything.

Oh God. Jo's heart bled for her little boy. It made her strong.

'What on earth were you doing discussing sensitive issues like that?' she said, using her haughty, 'talking to grown-ups' voice. 'Surely you must realise that there are many children who ...' *don't have Daddies* '... who come from ... unusual backgrounds? Divorce is very common these days, you know.'

The secretary, who had been pretending to busy herself during their conversation, piped up. 'Not here, it isn't.'

Jo was taken aback.

'You have no children from broken homes here?' she asked.

'Only a few. Death. Not divorce.' Sniff. 'Or not married in the first place ...'

'Well. Lucky you, is all I can say. Not everyone is so fortunate. Be more careful next time, or there will be complaints.' She turned and bent to take Liam's hand.

'Poo, Mummy! You stink!' he cried, pulling his hand away and sealing her humiliation.

The teacher followed her to the door.

'Um, Ms Morris—'

Jo turned. Flicking a look at the secretary, the teacher spoke in her ear. 'Is he in prison? Liam's daddy?'

'No, he bloody isn't!' yelled Jo, reaching out as Liam dodged her hand. How she wanted to shout: *'If you must know, he really is an astronaut!'*

Leaving their shocked expressions behind, she gripped Liam's wrist and hurried out of the office. While Liam collected his coat and bag from the row of pegs outside his classroom, Jo ducked into the cloakroom and bent double over the diminutive sinks, scrubbing at her arms and knees with paper towels. Feeling a little more personable, she went to collect the tag-along bike from the bike shed where she left it every day, and walked as sedately as she could manage out to the car park to wait for Daisy with Ash. At least the rain had stopped for now. Ash was still with his car.

'Another broken bike?' he said, nodding at the tag-along with a smile.

She smiled back. 'It's meant to only have one wheel.' She waggled the front end, where a wheel would be on a normal bike. 'This bit attaches under my saddle. You go everywhere on this, don't you, Liam? Well,' she corrected herself, 'we went everywhere on this before Mummy met a bunch of silly sheep in the road! Say hello, Liam! You know Daisy's daddy, don't you?'

Liam nodded, his face set.

'Hi, Liam.' Ash smiled at the little boy, took the tag-along from her and fitted it carefully into the back of the big estate car with her bicycle. The children would be out in about ten minutes, Jo estimated. So that meant ten minutes of small talk with Ash. A police sergeant. After she'd ridden halfway across the peninsula on a motorbike without a helmet. She swallowed. Sometimes the gap between her past and present telescoped together. But she was a good girl now, she reminded herself.

'You weren't long,' he said. 'Nothing too serious then?'

'No skin broken,' replied Jo, lightly. *Only hearts*.

'You said a bad word, Mummy,' Liam said. 'You said bloody.'

Jo rewound her thoughts and reddened.

'Mmm, yes, sorry, Liam. That was naughty of me. I was … um … provoked.' Jo cleared her throat and avoided Ash's eye. 'But look, we are so lucky to have a lift home for a change! That's nice, isn't it?'

'And tomorrow morning?' asked Ash.

'Oh, fu-udge, yes, I'm so sorry, what a pain!' God, she hated not being independent. She couldn't even get to one of the many car boot sales to find some spares now.

'No problem. It's Lucy's turn to do the school run tomorrow. You can go straight on to work with her.'

'Thanks, that's really kind of you both,' Jo said, earnestly. They *were* kind, and she loved working at the Art Café, but oh, how she hated feeling needy.

'Are you working at the café on Sunday?' Ash asked her, after a moment or two. 'For Lucy's big send-off?' Lucy was heading off to film the pilot for a television series featuring her as a motorcycling artist. It was all they'd been able to talk about in the café for weeks now. The film crew was filming her setting off with her co-presenter, TV Tom, on Sunday.

'We all are, far as I know. All of the part-timers, plus Richard,' she replied. 'I don't know what I'm going to do about Liam now though. I was going to drop him off for a play date, but I'm a bit stuck without my bike.'

'Why don't you bring him with you?' Ash said. 'Daisy will be there … they can amuse each other.'

'Oh, really? Do you think that would be okay?'

'I don't see why not. It's a private party, isn't it? Lucy won't mind. She probably won't even notice, to be honest, her mind will be on other things.'

'Thanks, that would be fab. Wouldn't it, Liam?' She looked down at the little boy who was quietly clutching her hand. Not like him at all. 'You'd like to come to work with Mummy on Sunday, wouldn't you?'

Liam nodded.

'Is Lucy really excited about the trip?' Jo asked Ash.

Ash laughed. 'If the constant packing and repacking is anything to go by, then I'd say excitement is a long way behind nerves right now.'

'It's a really big deal though, isn't it? Being in a TV series? I mean, she's never done anything like it before, has she? And she's pretty much the star, as far as I can see.'

Ash nodded. 'It is a big deal. But TV Tom is the front man, really. He's the experienced one – he's been presenting for years now. The cameras will be on her when she's painting, and on her bike, but she's painted in front of an audience lots of times at demonstrations, and been filmed doing it. It's only the next rung on the ladder.' He smiled. 'She'll wow them, I'm sure. She's amazing!'

Jo glanced over at him. How lovely to have someone like him on your side. He was clearly besotted with Lucy.

'How long is she away for?'

'A month, I'm told. It'll fly by.'

Jo knew Lucy adored eight-year-old Daisy. The little girl had never known her own mother, who'd died in childbirth. The two of them had bonded so quickly, and since Lucy had moved in and become part of their lives, Daisy would miss her terribly, she was sure. A month was a long time in a little girl's life.

'Is Daisy alright about her going?'

'I think so.' Ash nodded, but his expression was troubled. 'She hasn't said very much. But we've got lots of treats and trips planned for her to look forward to.'

Jo nodded, not knowing what to say. Beside her, Liam scuffed his shoes. Ash broke the silence.

'Ed,' he said, looking over at the playground, where there were stirrings of doors opening.

'Mmm?' Jo's eyes whirled around, looking for him, until she realised Ash was talking about him, not to him.

'He's a ... good bloke.'

'Yes?'

'And I trust him with Daisy. Even if she was always going on about going pillion with him.' He rolled his eyes. 'But ... er ...'

Jo turned her attention to him. He looked as if he was struggling with his choice of words.

'He's not renowned for his ... commitment ... to ... um ...' He ground to a halt. 'I feel really disloyal about this, he *is* my mate ... but ...'

'... he has a lot of girlfriends,' Jo supplied.

'Yes,' Ash said, with obvious relief. 'He is single, after all. But, I'm just ... warning you.'

Jo tried for a lighthearted laugh. 'I'm not looking for a boyfriend.' She wasn't. Not at all. And if she was it would be someone organised, educated, reliable and responsible. Like Liam's father ... she sighed. It certainly wouldn't be one like Ed, carefree, immature – she was still cringing about the motorbike ride – and a flirt to boot. She had managed perfectly well until now, and she'd carry on managing. She put the sight of Ed's wet T-shirt out of her mind. Even though it had clung to his well-defined pecs and ... had that been a six-pack under there?

Ash sent her a look that she couldn't quite decipher, but further conversation was impossible as the playground filled with a torrent of overstimulated, overtired children, and Daisy, dark curls escaping her ponytail, ran over and launched herself at her father.

'*Daddeeee*!!'

He swung her round easily. 'Ooh, my back, you're getting too big for this!' he joked, settling her back to earth.

'Hi, Liam!' Daisy high fived the little boy, to Jo's amusement.

'You know each other then?' Ash said.

'I'm Liam's BFP,' Daisy said, importantly, and then pealed with laughter at her father's confused expression. 'Big Friendly Person? To look after the little ones when they first come to school?'

'Crikey,' Ash muttered in an aside to Jo. 'It doesn't seem that long ago that *she* was a "little one".'

Jo nodded, smiling. She had a lump in her throat suddenly, watching Ash with his daughter. She had a lot of things to think about, what with this 'astronaut' business.

And no one to talk it over with.

Ash dropped them off with a cheery wave and when a knock sounded at the door a moment later, she snatched it open with a smile, assuming that she'd left something in the car.

'Oh.' She felt the smile slip as she was confronted by her landlord. 'Mr Evans. It's not time for our inspection, is it?'

'Jo ... Jo ... Jo. What have I told you? Call me Chad.' His small eyes disappeared behind folds of fat as he grinned at her, and she swallowed. 'I just happened to be passing, and I noticed how wonderful the garden is looking now.'

'Er, really? It's just a bit of an allotment ...' She squinted over at the expanse of neat rows that represented weeks of hard digging, and which now housed onions, potatoes, carrots, broad beans and even some asparagus that had been passed on by a neighbouring gardener. It had been a wilderness before. But it wasn't what she'd call a garden. It was her outdoor supermarket, if anything.

'It might be an allotment to you, but it's what we landlords call an "improvement to the property".'

'Oh. Okay. It wasn't a problem. So, if that's all, Mr Evans?'

'Jo. I think you misunderstand me.' He put his foot on the step. 'An improvement to the property means a higher rental value.'

'We've agreed the rent, Mr Evans.'

'For the time being, yes. But there may very well be an increase when the lease is renewed.'

'*Mum-meeee*! I done a poo. Wipe my bum!' Liam's piping voice echoed down to them from the bathroom at the top of the stairs. Jo knew with a sinking heart that if she craned her neck, she'd see him swinging his legs on the toilet, trousers round his ankles. She also knew that there was a window of time in which she could deal with the issue, after which Liam would attempt to deal with it inexpertly himself.

'I do apologise, I'm needed.' Jo stepped back, pushing the door firmly to and meeting the resistance of Chad Evans' foot.

'I'll come in and wait, shall I?' He smiled smoothly at her. 'If there is a problem with the rent, then of course, I'm always happy to come to an … ah … "arrangement" with you.'

'I'm fiiii-nishhhed, *Mum-meeeee*!' Liam's conversational tone became more urgent. 'Wipe my *bu-uuuuum*!'

'Just a minute, sweetie!' Jo called up, and frowned at the landlord. 'An arrangement?'

'Yes. You know.' He raised an eyebrow in a lascivious way, in case Jo hadn't understood him. 'Perhaps, once a week?' As he shuffled his bulk from one foot to another, Jo took the opportunity to push the door closed a little more. 'It would depend on how much assistance you might need. Children are *so* expensive, aren't they?'

22

'Who are you talking to, Mummy?'

'Liam – stay where you are! I said I'll be there in a minute!'

Jo was on the verge of bouncing the door off his fat, sleazy face, when she heard a gossipy Welsh accent call up from the lane, 'Chad Evans! Duw duw, bach, it's been such a long time! Not lost any of that puppy fat, I see. How is your uncle?'

Jo watched as Chad's head whirled round in the direction of the speaker, an effusively coiffed older lady, wearing an orange and pink tunic with lime green trousers. She was like a sunbeam, marching up the path holding a fat bunch of bright yellow daffodils tied with string. She held them out to Jo. 'A little house-warming thingy! Hello! I'm your neighbour, my name's Beryl. I've been away for so long, the garden has run away with itself dreadfully. I think I shall need some advice from you. You've made such a difference here. Just what the place needed, isn't it, Chad?' She turned on Jo's landlord, who wasn't looking quite so sure of himself. Beryl charged on without seeming to breathe. 'After you were living here, it was a proper mess, I have to say, honestly. Good thing your father can't see it. How is old Merve?'

Chad nodded, his piggy eyes darting towards the garden gate. 'Yes, he's … er … good, thanks.'

'Give him my best, won't you? And the family. Or maybe I'll pop over and visit him? Are there visiting times or can we just drop in?'

Jo listened to the seemingly unstoppable monologue whilst aware that there was not a sound from Liam, still upstairs. Either he was as fascinated by their visitor as she was, or he was right now industriously polishing his nether regions with miles of toilet roll.

'Well, I won't interrupt you both, I must go,' Beryl was saying. 'Pilates class to catch up with!'

'No, that's fine … er, Beryl, we don't have anything else to discuss,' Jo said, firmly.

'You must tell me what part of the family you're connected to,' Beryl declared. 'Anyway, I'm sure to see you soon, pop over so we can catch up.' She swirled away in a multi-coloured flurry, propelling Chad out of the gate, to Jo's open-mouthed relief.

'That lady was funny, Mummy.' Liam was still sitting on the loo, his eyes wide. 'Can I go and play with her?'

'Mm, yes lovely, darling,' said a distracted Jo, mulling over the one-sided conversation with Beryl. What part of the family was she connected to? That was an odd question, wasn't it?

Chapter Four

The following morning, Jo and Liam were ready in good time and waiting outside the cottage gate for Lucy and Daisy. After ten minutes, Jo began to think that Lucy had forgotten about them. She was about to ring her mobile, when she heard a car engine and the long Volvo estate appeared at speed around the corner and screeched to a halt at their feet.

Lucy wound the window down.

'Sorry I'm late!' she yelled. 'We had a bit of a "thing" this morning.' Still looking at Jo, she swivelled her eyes towards Daisy, who Jo could see was slumped in the passenger seat with a furious scowl on her face.

'No worries,' Jo said, opening the rear door, helping Liam into the booster seat and buckling him in. 'It's good of you to pick us up. I know it's out of your way.' She climbed in next to Liam. 'Hi, Daisy!'

''Lo.' Daisy sent an uncharacteristic monosyllable over her shoulder and Lucy met Jo's gaze in the rear-view mirror.

'We needed a biscuit tin lid this morning,' Lucy said, chattily as she set off down the lane. 'For a magnetic game, apparently. Who the hell has a biscuit tin lid just lying around at eight in the morning?'

'Ah,' Jo said, with a nod. 'Did you find one?'

'No!' Daisy grumbled.

Lucy rolled her eyes.

'I've got one, if you still need it?' Jo said.

'Oh God, have you?' Lucy jammed on the brakes, and twisted to look at Jo, who nodded. 'Can we have it? I have no idea if you'll get it back, will that be okay?'

'Fine!' Jo hung onto the back of the driver's seat as Lucy

yanked the big car round in the narrow lane and headed back the way they'd come.

'What do you say, Daisy?' Lucy said.

'Thank you, Jo!' Daisy chorused, her face only a bit less grumpy than it had been earlier. It was the work of a moment for Jo to leap out, locate the biscuit tin and jump back into the car.

'I brought the whole thing, just in case,' she said, passing it over to Daisy, who managed a more positive thank you now that she held the tin in her hand.

'Oh, you're a lifesaver, Jo.' Lucy smiled at her in the mirror, and Jo felt a rush of pleasure.

There were no children or parents at the school gates when they arrived. Jo got out to take Liam in. She wanted to explain his lateness to his teacher, but clearly this was a usual state of affairs for Daisy. She jumped out, clutching her biscuit tin, and said crossly, 'Late again. Thanks for nothing.'

'Bye, sweetie!' Lucy said, blowing her a kiss, and smiling sweetly. 'Love you. Have a good day.'

Daisy snorted by way of a reply and stomped up the path towards the school.

Liam's teacher showed no signs of remembering their previous conversation about Liam's parentage, to Jo's relief, and she hurried back out to Lucy, who was slumped in the driving seat. Jo was horrified to see tears running down her face.

'She hates me,' she sobbed, as Jo slid onto the front passenger seat.

'Oh, no … of course she doesn't!' Jo looked around for a tissue, shocked to see her normally cheery and totally in control employer tear-smeared, and … was that pyjamas she could see peeping from the hem of those jeans? And now she was sitting beside her, she could see that Lucy was wearing her slippers …

'She keeps springing things on me just as we're about to leave,' Lucy hiccuped. 'Biscuit tin lids. Fairy Liquid bottles. Obscure ingredients for something they're cooking. Never the day before, when I could do something about it.'

'Aw, she's just testing you, Lucy.' Jo delved into her rucksack and fished out a pack of tissues. She thought about taking one out and then handed the whole lot over instead.

'It's because I'm not her real mum.' Lucy blew her nose noisily and messily.

'No, it isn't,' Jo assured her. 'She's just being horrible. Take no notice. Liam does it to me – it's got nothing to do with you being her stepmum. She's just being snotty.'

'Do you really think so?' Lucy turned a pair of hopeful, red-rimmed brown eyes on her.

'Of course,' Jo said, with more confidence than she felt. How did she know? She was still learning too. But it was making Lucy feel better – and that was what it was about, wasn't it? 'Parenting has to be the hardest job in the world. It's bad enough when you've given birth to them – you've got her at the instant Pain in the Neck stage.' She was relieved when Lucy chuckled.

'Look, will it matter if we're a bit late in today?' Lucy said, to Jo's astonishment.

'You're the boss!'

'Mm. Not that anyone would ever guess. You'll be paid as normal. Only I could do with nipping home and ... er ... getting changed.'

Jo burst out laughing. 'You mean, the pyjamas aren't a fashion statement?'

By the time the two women had got back to Lucy's house, Jo had regaled Lucy with tales of Liam's tantrums and made her laugh until her eyes were running again.

'I don't know how you manage by yourself,' Lucy told her. 'I think you're incredible.'

Jo was taken aback. She didn't *feel* incredible. Mostly, she just felt tired.

Lucy parked beside a beautiful old farmhouse. It was painted a warm yellow and a soft mauve wisteria clung to the sunlit frontage.

Lucy led her around the back over a narrow, cobbled pathway that led into a spacious kitchen, which was as big as Jo's entire house. She breathed in, staring around at the thumb pots of seedlings on the windowsill, the paintings signed 'Daisy' sellotaped to the back of the doors and the fridge, the bright mugs, and the wellington boots lined up by size near the door. Everything about it shouted 'home' and 'love'. Unexpectedly, her eyes pricked with tears.

'Do you want a cuppa?' Lucy asked over her shoulder. 'Help yourself, I'll just be a minute.' She looked down at her slippers. 'A few minutes.'

Jo boiled the kettle and plopped two teabags into mugs. Sitting down at the big scrubbed pine table, she looked round the room again, this time noticing the crockery in the sink, and got up to make herself useful. There was laundry in the machine on a finished cycle, the tumble dryer door stood open with clothes hanging out of it, and by the time Lucy came back into the kitchen, fully made up and wearing smart skinny jeans and heeled boots, Jo had washed-up, folded the dried clothes and was pulling the washing out of the machine, considering what should go in the tumble drier.

'Oh!' Lucy looked horrified. 'You didn't have to do that. But, thank you, I never seem to get on top of it.'

'I don't mind,' said Jo. It was the truth. She didn't. She'd been in that position, lived in relative squalor while baby Liam screamed and didn't sleep and she would have been only too happy for someone to have come round and taken over. Except no one ever had.

The two women worked together, sorting clothes and

sipping tea, and Jo ventured, 'How does Daisy feel about you going off to film?' The film crew were shadowing Lucy as she painted her way up the coast of Wales for the pilot programme. There were plans for the rest of Britain, and possibly abroad if the pilot was a success. Jo could barely imagine doing it herself.

'Glad to see the back of me, I imagine,' Lucy shot back. She made a rueful face and shook her head. 'I'll miss her terribly. I think this is all part of it. She's had no one for so long, and then I turn up and we play Happy Families for a while and now I'm going again. Even though it's temporary. I can't imagine it's easy for her.'

'I'll help in any way I can,' Jo said. She knew the tragic circumstances of Daisy's mother, who had been in a terrible car accident, and died on the operating table even as the surgeons saved the baby Daisy. No wonder poor Ash had been a single dad for as long as he had. He'd adored Daisy's mum. 'She and Liam get on well together, despite the age difference.'

'Yes, Ash mentioned you were bringing Liam on Sunday. Thanks. She probably thinks you're marvellous, conjuring biscuit tin lids out of thin air first thing in the morning!'

'It's my "other" job. I upcycle. I've got loads of stuff that needs repainting or what's the other buzz word? Repurposing!'

'Wow. I'll ring you next time I need something bizarre in the morning.'

Jo exploded with laughter.

'That didn't sound quite so weird inside my head.' Lucy giggled. 'Thanks, Jo, you've made me feel a whole lot better. Right, time to face the day. Richard will be giving me a ticking off if we are any later.'

In the car, on the way to the café, Lucy said thoughtfully, without looking at Jo, 'Ed ...'

'Yes?'

'Don't take this the wrong way ...' Lucy began, 'I mean, y'know, I would! If I didn't already have the most gorgeous man in the world. And if I was about twenty years younger.'

'You're not that old!'

'I so am. Sadly. But anyway ... Ed ...' Lucy persisted. 'He's lovely and everything, but—'

'Don't tell me. He has commitment issues?' Jo said, lightly. 'Ash said.'

'Ah.' Lucy nodded.

'And I'm *really* not looking for a boyfriend.'

Nicola, Richard's wife was at the café when they arrived, their new baby, Jack, on her hip. Lucy squealed with delight as she spotted him, and held out her arms to take him.

'He's all yours.' Nicola smiled, handing the baby over.

Jo watched from the counter as Lucy jiggled Jack on her lap, cooing and snuggling him.

'Ooh, he's so gorgeous. I can't wait to have my own baby,' she said, sniffing his blonde downy head. 'And he smells lovely.'

'You wouldn't say that after one of his poop slicks.' Nicola sipped her coffee with a sigh of pleasure. 'The ones that squish out of the top of his vest.'

'Ew.' Lucy jerked back and made a face. '*Phewee*!' Jack's implacable stare split into an enormous gummy grin. 'Look, I made him laugh. He's so funny, with his serious stare.'

Jo had a sudden flashback to Liam at the same age, his huge, solemn grey eyes fixed on hers, and her heart contracted with love. She'd make everything right for him. She had to.

'He's not a bit like you, Nic,' Lucy was saying. 'But he looks exactly like Richard.'

Jo followed Lucy's gaze as she regarded Richard, watching his baby son with the two women, a smitten look on his face.

'A stumpy, fat version.' Lucy squirted a raspberry into the baby's neck as she spoke and squealed as his chubby hand grabbed at her hair, bringing them eyeball to eyeball.

'Yep.' Nicola nodded. 'No doubting who his father is.'

'*Oi!*' Richard yelled from the kitchen. 'I am here, y'know.'

There was laughter, and Jo thought again how lucky she was to work there. It was like being part of a big friendly family.

A slower day than usual meant that after lunch they all had time to check the plans for the following Sunday. Over coffee and a plate of sandwiches, they confirmed a brunch of simple bloomer cut bacon sandwiches, home-made muffins that could be made in advance and toasted teacakes. All easy to prepare and easy to hold stuff.

Lucy would get changed into her bike leathers, be filmed saying goodbye to everyone, then she would be filmed riding out of the car park on her motorbike, along with TV Tom, the main presenter, who would also be on his own motorbike.

'Are you riding all the way there?' Jo wanted to know.

'I am, yes.' Lucy sucked in a breath. 'Right up to the very top of Wales. Down teeny country lanes and over gravel and tracks. It'll be fine,' she said, in a breezy voice which fooled none of them. Gravel, slippery and perilous, could be a nightmare for motorbikes, and maneuvering required confidence and skill. Jo had overheard the more experienced Nicola advising Lucy enough times to know.

'All packed?' Nicola asked.

Lucy laughed, properly this time.

'Sort of. That is to say, no.' She held out her hands. 'At least I don't have to squeeze everything into my bike panniers – I mean, they are *tiny*! How on earth do girls go touring with them? I could get more in my handbag!'

They all looked at Lucy's Mary Poppins style handbag and laughed.

'I could get more in your handbag than a sixty litre four-wheeled suitcase!' Nicola spluttered. 'Oh, I'm going to miss you, Luce.'

Jo watched, feeling awkward and out of place suddenly as Lucy jumped up and ran around the table to hug Nicola. A brief feeling of loneliness swept over her, and she shook it off with irritation. The companionship she'd felt with Lucy in her kitchen that morning was the nearest she'd come to a proper friendship for a very long time. Friendships required emotional investment, shared confidences. Jo didn't mind people telling her their secrets – after all, she was the best at keeping secrets. But she never returned the favour. Ever. Sometimes, she felt like that crunchy, sweet topping on one of Richard's creme brûlées – just a thin, easily cracked sweet veneer over a whole lot of wobbly stuff beneath.

'It's only three to four weeks, I'll be back before you know it. Just as if it was a holiday.' Lucy cuffed her eyes. 'Just look after the place while I'm gone, okay?'

A flow of customers entered the café and the steady flow kept Jo busy enough to stop her dwelling on anything. Lucy was occupied in the gift section of the café, and Jo cleared the tables, carrying full trays into the kitchen to wash before she left.

Richard was in and out, spacing out the few cakes left in the chiller cabinet so they looked more. He bobbed back into the kitchen where she was busily scrubbing worktops.

'Um ... Ed ...' he began.

'Oh God ... look, I get it!' Jo whirled to face him, hands on hips. 'He's nice but he doesn't do commitment,' she recited. 'But I'm not looking for a boyfriend, okay? End of.'

Richard looked taken aback.

'Er ... no, I was going to say,' he blinked, 'Ed is in the café. Apparently he's giving you a lift home.'

Chapter Five

'Why is he? I thought Lucy …' Jo frowned.

'Lucy's still faffing here. Daisy's having tea with a friend.'

'Oh.' Jo wondered if she'd ever have that support network of friends who collected and fed each other's children. Maybe one day. 'We won't both fit on the back of his bike,' she said, putting a brave face on it.

'*Huh?*' Richard looked perplexed and she didn't explain. In fact, the least said about yesterday's impromptu ride, the better. Several times in the night she'd woken up with a start, panicking about what would have happened to Liam if she'd been badly injured. Where would he go? Her hands prickled with sweat just thinking about it.

'I'll go and find out what's happening,' she said. The sooner she got her bike sorted, the better.

Lucy was now buried in her office cubbyhole, surrounded by order forms and invoices.

'I thought you'd done all that.' Jo tipped her head on one side with a smile.

'Oh – I have! I just keep remembering things that I've forgotten. If you know what I mean.' Lucy raked a hand through her blonde crop, leaving it sticking up like a newly hatched chick. 'Um … sorry about the change of plan. It's just that Ed came in at the same time as Daisy's friend's mum rang, and so I thought …' She shuffled the papers distractedly. 'Is it okay? You don't mind, do you?'

'As long as I don't have to go on the back of that old boneshaker of his again.' Jo grinned. She hesitated for a second. 'We can manage, y'know. While you're away. Shouldn't you be learning lines, or something?'

'Lines? Don't stress me out even more!' Lucy glanced up

and then smiled. 'Go on. Get off with you. You won't be able to mitch off early like this when I'm gone. It'll be all hands on deck to cover the huge amount of work I do here!' Jo's mouth twitched at the word 'mitch'. Another Welsh word added to her vocabulary, it meant to bunk off school or work early and without permission.

Jo hovered a moment, wondering why she couldn't just reach out and hug her employer, like she'd watched Nicola do, easily, a million times. It just wasn't her style. Sometimes, she really wished it was.

'Five minutes!' she called to Ed, who was lounging at a table near the window, staring out to sea. He jerked upright as he saw her and spilled coffee on his white T-shirt. Not always so Mr Cool then, she noted with a private chuckle.

Ed's pickup truck was at the far end of the car park. His proximity beside her in the cab made him weirdly nervous. Which was just stupid, considering that only yesterday she'd had an arm round him wearing nothing but a pair of skinny shorts and a wet T-shirt. He felt hot, prickly and scruffy in his coffee-stained T-shirt.

'Thank you. For the lift.' She waved a hand around the interior. 'And the child seat.'

'No probs. It used to be Daisy's.'

'I hope Lucy didn't bully you into this? You probably had plans, things to do, people to see and all that ...' she tailed off.

'It's fine. I'll sort your bike out as soon as I can,' he said.

'I should think so, too.' Her tone was sharp.

Ed's head jerked in her direction. 'I don't have to, y'know.'

'You hit me. I was stationary,' she pointed out, her eyes meeting his with a challenge.

'You were in my way! And be fair, I did *try* and stop. It's not my fault that there was sheep shit everywhere!'

'Okay. I accept your apology.' She folded her arms. 'You can fix my bike.'

Ed felt his eyebrows shoot upwards. 'How did you do that?'

'What?'

'Make me fixing your bike into your idea, when I'd already volunteered to do it?'

'Dunno.' She shrugged, clearly trying to keep her face straight, and failing. 'It's a gift, I guess … Sorry.'

'No car then?'

'Just the bike. I manage. Usually.'

Casting a sidelong glance at him, she jumped as she met his eye doing the same thing to her. They both laughed.

'You're not from round here, are you?' he said. 'Your accent is a bit of a giveaway.'

'London.'

'What brings you out here to the sticks then?'

'South Wales doesn't feel quite as rural as it did when I first arrived, but I know what you mean. I came for a visit, and never went home!' she said, lightly. 'You've lived here forever, I suppose?'

'Yep. Born and bred, me. I know everyone here. I went to school with most of them!'

'Wow. I can't imagine living my whole life in one place.'

Ed couldn't imagine living in any other place. He glanced at her curiously.

St Michael's Primary appeared, already crowded with parents, mostly mums. Ed dropped her off, leaving in search of somewhere to park.

'I'll meet you back here,' he told her as she clambered out.

Jo noted the heads turning in his direction. There would be tongues wagging, she thought. Local Mystery Mum apparently married to astronaut (or jailbird) seen hanging out with Local Bad Boy. The thought tickled her as she strolled over, early for once, to join the gaggle at the gate.

Sure enough, she was greeted with a flurry of nudged elbows. One or two of the younger mums made comical eyes in Ed's direction and Jo laughed.

'It's just a lift!' she assured them, for once rather enjoying shedding the shrinking violet persona she usually adopted. 'I met some sheep yesterday … and my bike's wrecked.'

'What are you going to do?'

'I couldn't ride on these roads.'

'How do you manage when it rains?'

'How do you do your shopping?'

'I couldn't cycle. I'm too scared of the cars.'

The comments came thick and fast, to Jo's surprise. How could she have thought no one ever noticed her?

'I'm not far from you if you need a lift.'

There were a few of those. People were so kind, she realised. And she'd spent so long avoiding them, feeling as if she didn't deserve their friendship, that she'd missed it. Luckily, the classroom doors opened just then, so no one noticed her wiping her eyes, and if they had, she'd have explained it as a fly. Or hay fever.

Liam shot into the playground like a cork out of a bottle, and Jo was pleased to see him back to his normal self. She'd waited apprehensively last night for further questions about his origins, and, having still not decided exactly how to explain it, had been heartily relieved when nothing had been forthcoming. That wasn't the end of it, she knew her bright little boy well enough to be ready when the questions emerged a little later down the line. He was … processing. She was quite startled that he'd associated astronaut Tim Peake, just returned from his six month long orbit around earth, with his own absent father, although she knew that he thought deeply about things she didn't give him credit for.

'Hey, big guy!' She bent and kissed him, scooping him onto her hip for a hug. Already, his little body was becoming solid with muscles created from constant activity, and just for a second, she mourned the loss of his baby chubbiness. 'How was your day?'

'We did Being Nice to Each Other, because that is Very Important, and ...' Liam squirmed to be put down. 'I was best at Reading and Putting Away, and Jasper is my Best Friend!' He hopped beside her, handing up his bag and coat. She loved how he was so earnest about everything. Hopefully, Jasper was a child, and not the guinea pig or something.

'We have another lift home today,' she told him before he ran ahead to the school gate. 'Not Daisy's Daddy, but Daisy's Daddy's friend,' she added, clumsily. That was a tongue-twister. 'His name is Ed, and he has a big truck!' How was it that that sounded like a euphemism for something else? She shook her head, impatient with herself.

Ed was chatting easily to the gathered parents when they reached him. He was so confident and easy around people, bending to give Liam a casual high five, and keeping up a nonsensical stream of silly questions that had the little boy giggling all the way to the parked truck.

Jo buckled him safely into the child seat, fitted at the front between them.

'I am your chauffeur for the afternoon, sir and madam. Where would you like to be taken?' Ed deadpanned.

'Seagull Cottage, Tre-Cross, SA2 8WY,' Liam returned promptly, to Jo's amazement. Goodness me. He was like a little sponge. She didn't even know he knew that information so thoroughly.

Ed raised his eyebrows. 'Not far from me then!' he said, checking his wing mirrors as the other cars passed. 'I'm surprised I haven't bumped into you sooner.'

'I don't think we move in the same social circles,' Jo said, not really having a clue what circles he moved in, but as she didn't go out, it was a safe bet to assume their circles hadn't overlapped.

'Do you like living out here? It's quite isolated, isn't it?'

She shrugged. 'It's okay. The neighbours are all quite old, but they're friendly enough. They're really into their gardening. Saved me a fortune in veg!'

Ed nodded, his expression thoughtful. 'They've got big gardens, those houses, haven't they?'

'Yes! Enormous … but it wasn't when I first moved in. It was like a jungle – almost to the door. It was only when I started clearing it that I realised how big it was.'

The narrow roads swooped and fell, and Jo fell silent, trying not to watch Ed's muscular arms navigate the big vehicle around the bends.

Between them, Liam piped up, his voice thin and reedy. 'It's very bouncy in here.'

'Yes!' agreed Jo, in a bright tone. 'Bouncy, bouncy! Isn't it fun?'

'No,' whimpered Liam. 'I'm going to be—'

'*Noooo!*' yelled Jo, reaching for the window winder too late as the little boy's vomit bounced off her and dripped onto the floor. Clamping a hand over his mouth, Ed indicated a pile of oily rags behind their seats and Jo, retching, grabbed a handful to mop up the sobbing Liam.

'*Bleurgh*. I gotta stop!' Ed's voice was muffled behind his hand, his eyes watering.

Jo just wanted to get home, but she wanted out of this stinking cab even more. How could one small boy become toxic warfare so quickly? She nodded, edging away from the regurgitated slurry as it slopped back and forth at their feet.

In just a few minutes, Ed steered the truck into the wide gravelled drive of an imposing country manor.

'You live here?' Jo stared up at the stone and stucco house and its endless windows.

'Not quite,' said Ed, turning right into a gravelled courtyard. 'I live there.' He parked directly outside the smaller of two neat cottages, separated from the main house and enclosed by a tall stone wall.

'I want to go home, Mummy,' Liam wailed, his face clammily pale.

'We can walk from here, Ed,' she told him, painfully aware of the fetid lumps in her hair. 'Really … it's only about half a mile across the fields. We've put you to enough trouble already.' She'd have to piggyback Liam for most of it. No matter, she was strong. As long as he wasn't sick in her hair again.

'Let me just clean the cab for you.' She held her hand out for the hosepipe attached to the wall which Ed was unrolling.

'Of course you're not walking!' He held the hosepipe away from her. 'I'd never be able to drink coffee in the café again. Your bosses would kill me.'

Jo could well imagine Lucy giving him a hard time if she found out that Ed had let a sick-covered five-year-old walk half a mile home.

'Okay,' she conceded. 'But I have to clean the cab. Honestly. I'm used to it. You're not.'

'No point in cleaning the cab and then having you stinking it out again. No offence,' he added. 'How about you two helping after you have a shower?'

'What? With the hosepipe?'

'Why didn't I think of that?' Ed grinned. 'No … the shower is just inside the door.'

Jo didn't know whether she was more appalled at the idea of someone else clearing up her son's sick, or using a shower in her grubby condition, in someone else's house. And what exactly were they supposed to wear afterwards?

Ed seemed to read her mind. 'The cottages were designed for the disabled. There are loads of towels – they go in with the laundry for the Big House. I can fetch you some of the temporary clothing from there just for the way home. Liam will be okay in a bath towel or something, won't he? Just for that "half mile home"?'

'Big House?' Jo studied the mansion. How had she not noticed the words 'Nursing Home' at the entrance? It didn't look the way she'd always expected a nursing home to look.

'So, how—? Why—?' she began.

'Mum used to run it,' he cut across her. 'Come on, I'll show you where the shower is.'

Jo chivvied Liam in front of her and followed Ed towards the cottage.

'Mum and Dad live in that one.' Ed pointed towards the much larger cottage, pushing open his front door.

'Goodness me. You're very tidy!' The pale chalky grey tones made Jo feel even more grubby by comparison.

'Cleaners. From the—'

'Big House?' guessed Jo.

He nodded. Turning left into a spacious wet room, he opened a cupboard, where Jo could not only see a stack of clean, fluffy towels, but she could smell their freshness. Her skin crawled and she longed to step into the bliss of a hot shower.

'Oh,' she said, with a deep sigh. She couldn't care less right now if she had to go home in a bath towel too. The thought of being clean was uppermost in her head.

'Thank you. A million times.' She had to stop herself tearing off her disgusting clothes right there and then.

'I'll leave the clothes outside the door. I can't guarantee what they'll be like, mind.'

'It really doesn't matter,' Jo said, with fervour.

'I'll be with the truck. See you in a bit.'

Jo waited a moment to make sure he'd gone and wasn't popping back to tell them something he'd forgotten, and then ran the shower until it was warm and stripped off first Liam, then herself, flinging their soiled clothes onto the floor beneath the hot water.

For a moment she browsed along the bottles of shower gels and shampoos, reading the labels with envy: Molton Brown, L'Occitane, Clinique. A far cry from her supermarket specials. Surely they couldn't all be his? She unscrewed the caps of one or two for a sniff. They were glorious. Some of them must belong to his current girlfriend, whoever she was. She didn't dare use them, and scooped up the thick bar of soap instead. Even that was designer, with its sage green square edges and whiff of rosemary. The whole place reeked of money. He was just a motorbike mechanic, right? Maybe his parents were loaded. Or maybe he was a porn star in his spare time. She chuckled to herself.

Liam's vomit smell rose into the hot steam and holding her breath, Jo soaped him thoroughly, including his hair. Scrubbing herself more vigorously, she ignored the sting as the hot water ran into her cuts and grazes from the day before. She stared longingly at the salon shampoos on the shelves before using the soap in her hair too. Liam poked at the drain with his toes to make the lumpy bits go down and Jo prayed that they hadn't blocked it up.

The room was warm and steamy and Jo wished she didn't have to leave at all.

Ed's knock and yell of 'Housekeeping!' made her jump. Wrapping both of them in the biggest towels she'd ever seen, she wrung out their clothes, took a deep breath and tiptoed to the door, peeping round it for the change of clothes promised by Ed.

She snatched the little pile of clothing off the floor and retreated to investigate. Expecting a flowery housecoat and some Crimplene elasticated trousers at best, she inhaled sharply as she lifted up a silky thick-knit sweater in a deep saffron gold, clearly marked Jaeger on the label. From a nursing home? Although, she mused, thinking about the air of opulence the place gave off, and the smart cars parked outside, she shouldn't really be surprised. There was a pair of soft, stretchy jersey trousers with a label she didn't recognise, and, thoughtfully, a pair of flip-flops, probably Ed's judging by the size of them.

Slipping on the ensemble, and ignoring the fact that she was underwear-less, she wiped the mirror with her towel and stared at her reflection. Quite different from her usual practical jeans and T-shirts, she admitted that she rather liked it.

Tucking her damp hair behind her ears and striking a pose, she said to Liam,

'What d'ya think, big guy?'

'I can see your boobies, Mummy,' Liam said, staring fixedly at her nipples, which she could now see were peeping through the loose weave of the knit. Trust him to notice. Well, her bra was wet, and she didn't have anything else, so she draped a smaller towel over her shoulders letting the ends hang down on each side in the hope that they obscured the pertinent parts, and wound a similar one snugly around Liam's middle. Packing their wet clothes into her cycling jacket and tying the sleeves over it like a handbag, she wrapped Liam into one of the monster bath sheets, scooped him onto her hip, stepped into the oversized flip-flops, took a deep breath and ventured self-consciously into the chilly air.

Ed was winding the hose onto the reel. The truck doors were wide open, there were piles of old rags and torn up towels littered across the ground, and she could have doused herself in every one of those smart bottles of shampoo in Ed's bathroom. No one would be able to detect them against the wall of perfume emanating from the cab, Jo guessed from the armoury of bottles marked 'Interior Clean' and 'Super Valet!'

'*Ta-daaah!*' Ed waved an arm at the cab and then peered at her more closely. 'Clothes okay?'

'Mummy isn't wearing any pants and you can see her boob—' began Liam importantly, in his 'announcer's' voice that Jo recognised of old.

'Ed doesn't want to know that, darling,' she said, hurriedly. 'Shall we play the tidy up

game?' she carried on, tying Liam's shoelaces. 'Then we can go and have some home-made cake!'

'*Mmm.* Home-made cake,' Ed said, with a deep sigh, clearly struggling to keep a straight face.

Recklessly, in a desperate attempt to throw Liam off the subject of her non-existent underwear, Jo said in her 'mummy-voice', 'You can have a slice too, if you're good!'

'I'm always good,' Ed said, with a wink, and Jo frowned at him as she felt her heart lurch in her chest.

'Right!' He grinned, clearly unabashed. 'Let's go! Home-made cake waits for no man!' Handing a spray bottle to Liam to carry, he flung the rest of the cleaning stuff into the bucket sitting in the entrance of the garage, locked up and swung himself into the cab. As she helped Liam in, hampered by his towels like a miniature roman emperor, Jo noticed there was a fat new kitchen roll jammed into the side pocket.

'Nice and slow, please,' she said. 'I don't want to have to use this.' Her eyes signposted the kitchen roll and Ed nodded.

A couple of miles at twenty-two miles an hour felt like an eternity to Jo, alert for any signs of carsickness from Liam. She heaved a sigh of relief as they navigated a sharp bend and Seagull Cottage came into view.

'This brings back some memories,' said Ed, tucking the truck into the lay-by outside her tiny cottage. Jo was already regretting having encouraged him in for cake. She wanted nothing more than a cup of tea, her own clothes, and to crack on with repairing her bike. A hot man was the last thing she wanted, cluttering up her life. She couldn't feel more awkward right now, what with her 'chapel coat peg' nipples threatening to make an appearance, a half-naked son at her heel intent on telling everyone about her lack of underwear and goodness only knew what other revelation, and carelessly handsome Ed, tagging along behind.

'Memories?' She was curious though, despite herself.

'I used to cycle over here to buy sweets.' He nodded at the old post office along the lane a little. 'There used to be a lovely old lady in there. So patient with us kids buying five pence of this and that.'

Jo nodded, barely listening.

Seeing the piles of objects awaiting her attention through Ed's eyes, Jo cringed at how cluttered and messy her house must seem by comparison to his pristine cottage. Little chairs, stools, wooden boxes and bigger pieces occupied every space. High shelves housed tightly lidded jars of mixed paint, tins of white spirit, and bags of various grades of wire wool.

'My upcycling,' she said, by way of explanation.

Hurrying through to the kitchen with her posse in tow, she filled the kettle, poured a tumbler of water for Liam and sliced fruit cake onto plates.

'I'm Batman,' Liam told Ed, in a gruff voice, whirling his bath towel perilously close to the mismatched but lovingly collected porcelain cups and saucers on the counter.

'Liam!' Jo shouted, more sharply than she'd intended. 'Go and put some clothes on please, or no cake.'

The little boy's face fell momentarily, replaced by a wicked glint as he caught the end of his towel-cape and zoomed away, yelling, '*Chaaaarge!*'

'He's made a good recovery,' remarked Ed, sprawling into a chair with an easy grace that made the chair look spindly.

Jo wished he would just go. He made her feel awkward and clumsy, as if he could see right through her single layer of clothes. She folded her arms over her breasts, and said self-consciously, 'I'll just pop up, see how he's doing.'

She looked in on her son, who had exchanged his towels for his Spider-Man outfit, and was piling a selection of Transformer Robots into a basket to take downstairs. Retreating into her own bedroom, she fingered the thick silkiness of the borrowed clothes then quickly stripped off, changing into bra and pants, jeans and an old sweatshirt. Her hair, washed in soap, was promising to be a frizzy cloud and short of rewashing it, was beyond rescue. She squirted a little conditioner on her palms and pulled it through her still damp curls, refusing to acknowledge that she was making even the smallest effort to improve her appearance.

By the time she returned Ed had made the tea and Liam had his toys lined up on the table, surrounding the cake.

'Come and see my den!' he yelled, bounding out of the back door, gripping Ed's sleeve. Jo followed them on autopilot with the tray of tea and cake. Really, it was just like being back at work. She had things to do. She needed to fix her bike, whatever Ed had promised, and a thousand other things. The longer Ed remained, the bigger the contrast between his nonchalant ease and her tensions. His life was an open book, it seemed, as he chatted, while hers was a labyrinth of secrets and papered-over half-truths that she'd carefully hidden with the curtains of an invented life. She found herself more and more guarded in her responses.

The village had accepted Jo and Liam once they'd got beyond the delicate question of Liam's father, which Jo answered with a simple, 'We're not together.' She'd learned a firm half-smile, which seemed to act as a full stop to any further questions. Of course, Jo knew she couldn't hide away forever. But yesterday had brought the past closer to the present than she would have liked – it made her stomach churn, feeling that she wasn't doing justice to Liam. She couldn't bear to think that not only had he been unhappy in school, but it was all her fault. She still needed to think it over, work out how to deal with it. It was bound to come up again.

And instead, she was stuck here with Mr Cool, currently hunched under a tatty garden shelter of old blankets and cardboard, eating her cake and appearing to be fascinated by Liam's collection of treasures. Despite her irritation, her mouth curved into a smile as she watched her son's small quick body, gathering, collecting, building, chattering all the while as Ed nodded.

She couldn't help feeling surprised that he was this relaxed around a small child – and then she remembered that he'd spent a lot of time with Ash and his little girl, Daisy. Recalled Lucy telling her that Daisy used to spend hours in the Vintage Bike Palace with Ed and his dad, collecting nuts and bolts and polishing things.

Just as she'd used to love doing with her dad, before … The memory rose up as if it were yesterday and her throat constricted painfully. He would have been so proud of his grandson. She was sure she hadn't made a sound, but Liam looked up at that moment.

'Come on, Mummy!' he said, through a mouthful of cake. 'There's room for you too!'

Jo sniffed. Bless him, he was such a sweet child. She bent down, preparing to sit.

'Yep, come on, Jo.' Ed nudged his long legs to one side. 'Now you've got your pants on, you can be in our gang.'

Liam pealed with laughter. 'Pants! He said pants, Mummy!'

'You said pants earlier, Liam. You haven't got a monopoly on pants, y'know. We all wear pants.' She nudged him and grinned, then saw his mouth open to refute her statement and said quickly, 'Let's go check on the frog spawn, shall we?'

She jumped up and ran towards the pond, knowing he couldn't resist a chase.

As she had said, the garden was enormous and Jo knew just how lucky she was to have it. Gardening had been her salvation, all those years ago, a way out of the angry jumble of her thoughts – and now a way of meeting the village on new terms, as she discovered.

People found Liam irresistible and would always stop and listen to his little chats over the hedge, and in return they offered seeds, cuttings and advice. Jo knew almost everyone in the village now, at least to wave to, if not by name. Well, all the gardening types who liked children, anyway. No one from her old life would recognise her any more – her body hardened and thinned by digging and physical labour. These days there was more hair and a lot less body.

The wildlife pond lay at the far end of the garden, behind a fence and gate that was kept padlocked. Jo worried about this pond, that Liam would one day be big enough to climb over the gate instead of waiting for her to unlock it. It would either have to be filled in, or made more secure. In the meantime, she'd taken him swimming since he was a baby, ensuring that he was strong and confident in the water, and the pond was shallow.

Muddying his Spider-Man's knees at the edges, he was full of excitement, peering in and poking with his inevitable stick. There were marginal plants, marsh marigolds, irises, reeds and tall variegated bamboos, all donations from nearby ponds.

Liam wasn't at all interested in the plants. He liked the digging and the planting, but mainly he liked the getting dirty, running about and poking with a stick. Jo persevered though, and somewhere in his energetic little boy's brain, she knew he did notice things that grew and moved and chirped.

'This is peaceful. It needs a bench or something,' noted Ed, gazing about him.

Jo nodded. 'It does. Can't afford it though! We bring a couple of chairs out sometimes on sunny days. Or a blanket.'

He was easy to talk to, and he seemed interested, and Jo pointed out plants that she'd persuaded to grow from pitiful specimens on the bargain supermarket shelves.

'Sorry. This must seem awfully dull to you. It's not your thing, is it?' she asked, sure that she hadn't seen much of a garden at his cottage.

He shrugged. 'My grandparents used to have a fab garden, like this. Dad's always been more of a builder, or a fixer-upper. Engines, that sort of thing.'

'Mine too,' Jo said, without thinking. Her eyes widened in panic and she stared straight ahead, willing him not to pick up the thread.

'Last one back does the washing-up, Liam!' she yelled, laughing as he took off, a red and blue blur.

'Looks like we'll be washing-up then,' Ed said, also watching Liam speeding away. 'Your parents, they're …?'

'Dead,' Jo said, quickly. She forced her jaw to remain loose.

'God, I'm sorry. That's … grim. And, er … Liam's dad?'

'Same.' Jo looked away. 'Car accident. All of them.' Even after all this time she crossed her fingers. It wasn't a full-blooded lie. It was as close to the truth as anything was. And it was all she was prepared to give away.

'Bloody hell!' Ed stopped walking, and turned to her, his jaw dropping. 'Bloody hell … that's … that's … I'm sorry. I shouldn't have asked. God.'

Jo drew her lips together. Her heart banged against her ribs and she felt sticky and breathless.

'Is that why you … don't drive?' Ed said, his expression still thunderstruck.

She shrugged. 'Cycling's better for the environment,' she said, flatly. 'Keeps me fit.'

'I should say.'

She flashed him a look. What did he mean by that? There was no time to find out as they were at the back door already.

She made Liam scrambled egg on toast, and Ed showed no signs of wanting to leave. Was she supposed to feed him too, she wondered?

'Will you be there on Sunday?' she asked him. Jo was as excited for Lucy as if she herself was going. She couldn't imagine ever having that kind of life. It seemed a million miles away from her own.

'Of course!' Ed nodded. 'I'll have to get Ash out on some boys nights out, I reckon, while Lucy's away.'

Jo couldn't see Ash enjoying that sort of night out, somehow. He didn't seem the type. Ed, however, did. And she didn't need to be involved with someone like that. Plus, he always seemed to be with a different girl when he came into the café, as everyone had already reminded her. A Bad Boy. She knew about those. And she was a Good Girl, now.

'I'll collect your bike while I'm here. And I've … er … got something for you in the truck,' Ed said, mock-casual. Liam immediately caught his air of mystery and stared at him with goggle eyes.

Ed beckoned them both outside once Liam had finished eating. Jo followed reluctantly, wonkily wheeling her bike out. She did not want to be beholden to this man for another thing.

Liam had scampered after him with excitement written across his face, which made Jo feel even more churlish. Her son had no male influences, and she often felt guilty about that. Sometimes she felt as if she was drowning in guilt.

She rested her bike against the hedge and Ed didn't look at her as he hefted a second bike from the back of the truck, wheeling it to join hers. It was a very classy black and orange mountain bike. But not the usual type of mountain bike. She saw in an instant that it was an all bells and whistles model, with telescopic forks and knobbly tyres, and what she knew to be a very expensive gearing system. And a huge battery, tucked sleekly into the down-tube. It was an electric mountain bike. She'd only read about them. They were the latest thing. You still had to pedal, but a motor helped you up the hills. It would be fantastic, especially with Liam attached to it. It was the next best thing to having a car.

'Alright?' Ed nodded at it without meeting her eye. 'Right size?'

'Erm, yes, but it's—' Her voice was croaky. It was too much. But she was desperate to try it. 'Er ... whose is it?'

'Well, yours – until I've fixed your other one. Want to try it? I think it'll be about right ... here, get on it.' He held the bike out as an invitation and after only a small hesitation, Jo swung her leg over it. The seat probably needed to go up a little but it was, as he said, about right.

'I can't accept this – it's way too expensive for me!' she whispered, her eyes devouring the bike, admiring the polished gear hangers and parts she'd only ever seen in a catalogue. It had to be worth well over a thousand pounds. 'What if I damage it? And whose is it?'

'It's ... mine ...' Ed shrugged, smiling at her. 'Just stay away from those sheep.'

Jo stared up at him, her mouth an 'O'. Clearly it wasn't his – it was far too small for his long legs, but she doubted very much that it was stolen. In her current situation though, she knew she couldn't afford to look a gift horse in the mouth. And she was dying to try it out.

'Th-thank you. Thank you so much. If you're absolutely sure ...?'

'I think it'll fit Liam's tag-a-long – I checked earlier.' After showing her how to charge the battery, Ed turned away and hopped easily into the high cab of the Nissan while Liam watched in awe. 'It was … fun. Thanks for the cake. See you again, Jo. Bye, Spider-Man!'

Liam pulled a Spider-Man pose by way of a farewell, and Jo stared speechlessly after the navy-blue Nissan as it eased onto the narrow lane, her hand lifted, still astride the bike.

'Fancy a spin before bedtime, Liam?'

Chapter Six

Jo, hovering by the café kitchen, couldn't take her eyes off Lucy and Ash leaning into each other, oblivious to the watching crowd. Tearing her gaze away, she brushed a hand over her face and in one fluid movement, hitched her black trousers over her black, Art Café T-shirt and straightened her matching waist apron with its embroidered 'palette of cupcakes' logo. It had been a busy morning. She and Richard had served a brunch breakfast to the many invited guests and film crew. Ash's parents were there – in fact, Babs, his mum, had worked at the café when Lucy had visited her parents abroad, and was poised to do so again while Lucy was away filming.

Jo was a bit intimidated by her – but then, Jo often felt that way about almost everyone. Ed was there, of course, with his dad, Griff. Along with a girl of elfin proportions, who tossed her mane of glossy hair and hung onto Ed's arm.

Ed had tried to introduce her when they'd arrived, and Jo had caught her name – Alexis – but the girl had turned away dismissively, her eyebrows raised at Ed as if to ask why she was having to speak to 'the staff'.

As Jo returned clean crockery to the shelves behind the counter, her eyes wandered over to Ed and Alexis, who were watching Lucy and the film crew. Ed's lean body was stretched casually into a wooden chair, arms folded behind his head. Alexis, in a short skirt with bare, tanned legs and high heels, was standing, chin lifted. Posing. Jo suppressed a grin, but acknowledged that if she had a body like that, then she'd be showing it off too.

Heading back to the kitchen, she was startled to catch her fragmented reflection, made lumpen and shapeless in the polished stainless shelving. It was as if the last five years hadn't happened at all. She marched back into the kitchen, determined to be busy, swallowing with difficulty the lump in her throat that never seemed to be far away.

Following endless retakes, the crew finally packed up inside and it was time for Lucy to leave. The atmosphere altered from the casual chatter of the morning, and Jo watched as if from the wings of a stage performance, as Lucy headed for the loos for the umpteenth time and Daisy pretended to be terribly interested in a noisy and energetic game with Liam. As the crowd drifted into the car park to wave the stars and crew off, Jo ducked back into the kitchen to begin the clearing up process. She had absolutely no desire to be under the all-seeing eye of a camera lense but she could understand the others wanting to be out there. She looked up in surprise to see Ed hovering near the counter, with Alexis, whose body language was saying without any doubt that she wanted to be at the front of the crowd, not hanging about at the back where no one could see her.

Jo saw her chance and ducked beneath the counter, reappearing with a carrier bag containing the borrowed clothes.

'Thanks again for the bike, Ed, I really appreciate it.'

'What bike is this?' Alexis made a head to toe sweep of Jo. 'Motorbike?'

'No!' laughed Jo, through gritted teeth, fighting an urge to check her appearance under Alexis's scrutiny. What was the girl's problem? She wasn't making a play for Ed. Far from it, Alexis was welcome to him. She took a deep breath, resolving to be nicer. 'Bicycle. I fell off mine and Ed's kindly loaned me his spare.'

'What spare?' Alexis turned to Ed, who said easily, 'Yours.'

'You've given my eBike away?' Her look of incredulity morphed into a glare as it reached Jo.

'Loaned,' said Jo and Ed together.

Alexis bristled, painted pout and eyebrows drawn upwards by an invisible string.

'Aw, babe, you don't ride it, do you?' Ed slipped his long arm around the girl's skinny shoulders. 'I did buy it, after all!'

'My ears get cold,' she said, frowning. 'But you could've asked!'

'You don't need it and Jo does. Come on, look on it as your good deed for charity!'

Jo glared at him, slamming the carrier bag on the counter. *Charity*? 'I didn't *ask* for it. I wouldn't have needed it if you hadn't been riding like a lunatic on that stupid old bike that doesn't have any brakes!' she said, the blood roaring in her ears. 'And I don't need anyone's charity, thank you. You can come and collect it as soon as you like.'

'I didn't mean it like that!' Ed spread his long fingers, looking crestfallen.

'What *did* you mean then?' Jo asked, her face hot. She pushed the bag at him. 'And these are yours too.'

'Yes, Ed, explain yourself!' Alexis's tone was brittle. 'And what's in that bag?'

'More "charity".' Jo delved into the bag and held up the silky soft deep yellow sweater. 'From the Nursing Home. I needed a change of clothes and Ed borrowed them for me.'

Alexis snatched the sweater out of her hand and examined it more closely. She rounded on Ed who was, Jo noticed, looking a bit shifty.

'So. Not only do you give my bike away the minute my back's turned,' the girl said, shaking the sweater in his face, 'you give my clothes away too! Jaeger, this is!' She stuffed the sweater back in the bag, slammed it on the counter and stalked away. 'Nursing Home, my arse!' she threw over her shoulder.

Ed looked at Jo with an apologetic expression.

'Ed!' Alexis bounced on her toes near the door to the car park, looking furious.

'Time to go, I reckon.' Jo lifted her eyebrows, just as angry as Alexis.

'Sorry.' Ed lingered near the counter, his hand on the bag of clothes. His mouth opened to speak.

'Come *on*, Ed!' Alexis marched back to them, her pinched face a mask of fury. She put a manicured hand on his sleeve and tugged.

Jo was no psychologist, but Ed's body language was unmistakeable. He stepped smartly back and to Alexis's obvious shock, flicked his arm out of her clutch. She snatched up the carrier bag and stalked to the door, tossing her head.

'I'll see you outside!'

Jo couldn't help thinking it sounded like a threat.

Tipping his head towards her, Ed reached out and lightly touched Jo's arm, his expression questioning. It was a very different gesture to the one Alexis had made to him, and Jo felt warmed by it, despite her determination to hang on to her anger.

'Go and give our Lucy the best send-off ever.' She nodded to the door, knowing she was letting him off the hook.

'Keep the bike. Please. She doesn't ride it. Take no notice.'

She honestly didn't know whether to laugh or cry as she watched him back off reluctantly, his eyes still on hers, turning at the last minute to pull on the door to the car park.

'Take no notice,' said a dry voice nearby. Was that an echo? Jo whipped round to see Ed's dad, Griff, still sitting at one of the tables in the now empty café.

'Oh ... I didn't see you there!' Jo jumped, clutching her hand to her throat. 'Aren't you going out to watch Lucy leave?'

'No. Not feeling too good,' Griff said, rubbing his chest. 'Bolted those bacon rolls a bit quick, I reckon.'

'Can I get you anything?' Jo moved closer to him. An older, still handsome version of Ed, tall and lean, he wore a shock of white hair and a bluer version of those unusual sea-glass eyes. 'Glass of water? Mint tea? It's good for indigestion, I'm told.'

'Water, please.' Griff nodded. 'He's had a … a rough start … Ed,' he continued, sipping the iced water Jo brought back.

Jo was startled. Ed … a rough start? Really? That wasn't the impression she got of him. He seemed to have a rather wonderful life from what she'd seen – plenty of money, nice home, loving parents … Cocking her head to one side, she waited, interested.

Griff continued in a faraway voice. 'Me and Lyn, we thought we'd have a brood of kiddies.' He shook his head and shrugged. 'Lyn just couldn't keep them in, you know?'

Jo nodded, sliding into a chair to listen. There'd be plenty of time to clean up the kitchen.

'And then Ed arrived. He was a bonnie baby. Strong as an ox. Born with all that hair! Came out, very knowing, assessing us all, like he still does.' He gave a dry, papery laugh, and carried on. 'He had all those muscles already, y'know. But …' His eyes met hers, and she stared back, riveted. *But what?*

'Bloody indigestion,' he said. 'I've got some tablets somewhere …' Fishing in his pockets he shook out a little white pill and popped it into his mouth. 'Better,' he nodded, after a moment or two.

Jo could hear the crowd outside cheering, being whooped up for ever more frenzied retakes for the camera.

'You were saying, Griff?'

'Hmm?'

'About Ed? Rough start?'

Griff nodded slowly without answering, rubbing at his neck, his eyes gazing around the café.

'Sounds like a good send-off,' she said, eventually, tipping her head towards the car park and rising to get on with her work.

'I remember Lucy coming in to sell that motorbike of hers, not that long after she won it. Ed persuaded her not to,' Griff said, just as she thought he'd fallen completely silent. 'He took her out on one of our trail bikes, went round our bit of off road track. Bit of fun, you know. Gave her confidence a boost after she made a mess of her lessons.'

'Wow. Just think, she might never have had this chance if she'd given up!' Jo sat down again.

'He's a good lad.' Griff smiled. 'Good hearted. He'd do anything for anyone.'

'I'm sure he would.' Jo thought about the loaned bike, and her mouth curved upwards. *Nutter. It was very generous of him. To loan her his girlfriend's bike ... and her clothes.* A bubble of amusement effervesced in her belly. Honestly, what was he like ...

She craned her neck to stare out of the windows, wondering what Liam was up to, knowing he'd be fine under the steely watch of Ash's parents. Ash himself was planning to take photos of Lucy a bit further down the road, he'd told her earlier.

'You don't have to babysit me,' Griff said, with some asperity. 'I'm fine. Go on.'

'I might just go and peep through the window.' Jo half rose, took two undecided steps, and then whirled around as she heard glass smash to the floor. Griff sagged in his chair and her stomach lurched in horror as she took in his opaque stare and greasily pale face.

Kicking the broken glass aside with her feet, she reached out a shaking hand and shook him gently.

'Griff? Can you hear me?' She bent her head to hear his faint grunt.

No, no, no, this couldn't be happening. Not again.

Get help. She opened her mouth and shouted just as a huge cheer went up outside. One-handedly, she felt for the pulse in his neck, fumbling for her phone with the other.

She knew what this was. Not indigestion. Heart attack.

Her phone slipped out of her suddenly moist hands. She couldn't find a pulse. *Do it properly, girl! One thing at a time, don't panic. Someone will be back in a minute, she could ring, and shout, and ... it would be fine.*

Griff's pulse barely registered under her fiercely probing fingers. No time to lose, she knew. Later, she would wonder how she found the strength to drag him to the floor without giving him a head injury. She got him against the wall, head up, knees bent, maybe that would do it, maybe she wouldn't need to do the whole thing.

'Help!' Her voice echoed back to her. She shouldn't leave him. Grabbing the phone, she made the emergency call, holding on speakerphone, checking as Griff's eyes closed, heard his breathing stop, pulled him into position on his back, measured down the bumpy sternum: one palm, two, linked fingers, then locked her elbows and pumped.

Watched herself as if outside her own eyes as she checked inside his mouth, pinched his nose hard, closed her mouth over his without thinking, smelled the sharp sweaty tang of his skin, prickly round the mouth, recoiled in shock at the so human taste of the now soured bacon roll and coffee – not a plastic dummy, no antiseptic wipes to hand here.

Focus.

One breath, two breaths, and then thirty chest pumps. A third of the depth of the chest. It was harder than she'd expected.

'Nellie the elephant packed her trunk and trundled back to the jungle ...' It was mad, she could hear the song in her head. They used it to get the timing right, otherwise it was too slow to be of any use. How many times had she done this? How many times had she practiced, since that time ...? Twenty-one, twenty-two ....

'You're doing fine,' said the calm tones on her phone. 'Ambulance will be with you in a few minutes.'

A few minutes? How long was that? Breathe, breathe, pump, *Nellie the elephant packed her trunk and trundled back to the jungle, Nellie the elephant packed and took us all on a holiday to Greece that would be brilliant, Oh God, lost count, how many now? Breathe, pump, pump ... horrible crunching sensation under her hands, keep going, keep GOING ... arm muscles screaming, sweat dripping, breathe, pump, pump, pump ...*

'Ew. I couldn't put my mouth on an old man's like that.' The girl's voice floated into her consciousness from somewhere over her shoulder. Where had she come from?

'Thank you, miss, we'll take it from here.' A man. Bright green overalls, and dazzling fluorescence edged into her vision, shifting her firmly to one side. A small warm body cannoned into hers.

'Mummy!' Liam. On her knees, she wrapped her arms around him, eyes closed now but still seeing and hearing. Inhaled his innocence, his very alive-ness, rocked, soothed. Knitted him to her against the world.

'Jo.' A hand on her shoulder. She looked up. Ed. His face stark against the black of his hair. 'I'm going in the ambulance now. I ... I ...' He swallowed. 'Thank you. Thank you.'

She wiped the sweat off her face. Met his eyes as if down a long tunnel, the rest of the world in soft focus. Had no words. Nodded. Submitted herself to helping hands.

And wept.

Chapter Seven

Hunched in the ambulance, Ed pulled his shirt away from his sticky skin, and replayed the last, sickening minutes in his head. The antiseptic smell in the cramped space told his disbelieving head that this was real.

As Lucy had zoomed out of the car park alongside TV Tom, so the motorcycle paramedic had bowled towards them, siren howling, scattering the still waving masses. Puzzled faces all round, and some ragged cheers ... was this part of the filming? A stunt?

Then those terrible, terrible words from the paramedic.

'Heart attack? Café?'

And Ed knew. Scanning the crowd, he *knew*. His feet flew into the café, where they and his own heart stopped at the scene before him.

His dad, on the floor. And Jo, crouched over him, pumping hard on his chest, her mouth working, hair soaked in sweat. *It's not real. It can't be. Why hadn't he noticed his dad wasn't feeling well?* As if from one end of a long dark tunnel, time stood still as he watched Jo breathe into his father, saw her elbows lock, corded arms pushing fiercely downwards. Saw the paramedic readying to take over, fit a defibrillator, and still she pumped, her face ... fierce, determined, he thought afterwards. Absolutely no intention of failing.

He'd wanted to go to her as she'd crumpled to one side, tiny suddenly, deflated.

But as he stood, somehow unable to move, he heard Alexis say something dumb about how disgusting it would be to put your mouth on an old man's, and the part of his brain that was already leaving her clanged shut like a steel door. Stupid girl. The revulsion he felt for her finally propelled him before the throng, to be beside his father.

'Get back! Clear a space!' he yelled. *Dad! Don't die!* 'What can I do? How can I help?'

His eyes locked now on his father's closed lids, willing him alive. He barely remembered the ambulance crew arriving. Was only dimly aware of going to Jo before leaving, hesitating about asking her to come with him, realising she needed help too. Sloughing Alexis off his arm, with her birdlike head on one side, all false sympathy and importance. Stupid girl.

The paramedic nodded at him with a sympathetic smile, monitoring a grey faced Griff with an array of baffling instruments. So calm.

They were always so calm, Ed remembered, the past colliding forcefully with the present. How did they make jokes the way they did? His stomach bucked nauseatingly as the memories flooded back: the sirens wailing rise and fall, hands tucking the waffled primrose yellow blanket around him, checking the buckled straps, holding his hand. He would have died with embarrassment before at the idea of being covered in a sissy yellow blanket and having his hand held at fifteen, by a man. He'd have died if they *hadn't* been there. *Please don't die, Dad.*

When did his dad get old? He looked ... shrunken, lying there. He choked back a sob, remembering his parents fortitude in the face of his own potentially life halting disease. His turn now. His turn to ... he caught himself, about to say *grow a pair*. He almost laughed.

'Which hospital are we going to?'

'Singleton.'

Oh God ... Mum would already be there, working. Not the cardiac ward – she was on obstetrics – but even so. He often wondered how she could bear it there, after losing so many of her own. His parents were incredible. So strong. He had to let her know before she found out. He knew what the hospital jungle drums were like. His thumb hovered over the number. Taking a deep breath, he dialled.

'Could I speak to Nurse Lyn Griffiths, please? It's an emergency.'

The paramedic nodded approval as he hung up. He was amazed at himself: calm, focussed, in charge. His mum, bless her, was made of stern stuff and had crisply informed him that she would meet him as Dad was admitted, but there was no mistaking the break in her voice as she hung up. Together, his parents were a tower of strength ... but apart? Their fortitude had made him whole, and now it was his turn to return that energy in spades.

Edging forward on the slippery bench, he reached out for his dad's hand and squeezed it gently. Remembered the comfort that simple human touch had given him when he needed it. Scanned the face of the man he'd known his whole life, waited and hoped.

Jo sat, dazed, in the café, Liam on her knee, his arms looped round her neck. People hanging about, murmuring. Richard and Nicola were there. Was that Ash? She didn't know. A cup of sweet, milky tea was before her. She hated milk. Never took sugar. Had she done enough? To save him? She visualised him now, in the ambulance. His skin plasticky, grey. Like a chilled chicken. Could still feel him under her fingers, her mouth.

The tea cooled and clouded and she could taste its sticky sweetness in her mouth as she stared at it. She stood suddenly, sliding Liam to his feet.

'Feel sick ...' She ran to the toilets, and threw up, holding onto the sink, her stomach muscles clenching painfully, her legs juddering.

'Oh. Bless you.' A gentle hand rubbed her back. Nicola. Sharp-tongued, scary Nicola, who always seemed to know what to do next, what to say. 'I brought you some bottled water. From the chiller. And a bit of toothpaste? I haven't got a toothbrush, but ...'

Jo took it gratefully, squeezing the minty paste onto her finger and scrubbing at her mouth, trying to expunge the taste.

The taste. She shuddered and dry-retched then splashed her face with cold water. Washed her hands. And then washed them again.

'What can I do for you?' Nicola's quiet voice.

Jo stared past her own haggard reflection in the mirror to Nicola. 'Black tea, please.' She blew her nose on the loo roll Nicola held out. 'Thanks. And no sugar. Can you check on Liam, please?'

'Of course.' Nicola stopped at the door. 'Is there anyone I can call for you?'

Jo shook her head. No one. No one at all. 'I'll be okay.'

'Come over to us for tonight. You shouldn't be on your own.'

Jo considered. 'I might,' she said at last. 'Can I think about it?'

'God, of course you can! You're a hero … heroine, whatever – you can do whatever you like!' Nicola reached out and enveloped her in a strong, bony hug, and stood back. 'Coming out for your tea, or do you want it in here?'

'I'll come out,' Jo said, pasting on a tremulous smile. 'I don't think I can stand up for much longer.'

Nicola hesitated at the door then said, 'I don't think I could have done what you did. You're fantastic.'

Jo returned a bleak smile. 'I'm not. And you could, if you had to. If it was baby Jack. Or Richard.'

'I'm going to learn.' Nicola's face was set. 'Black tea, no sugar. Coming up.'

Liam ran towards her as she tottered from the Ladies.

'Mummy,' he demanded, his piping child's voice cutting through the babble. 'Why were you kissing that man on the floor? Daisy says it means you'll have a baby now. So, can I have a brother?'

The laughter helped. As did several cups of tea and a liberal application of cake all round. Liam wailed, 'But Daisy *said!*' to another round of laughter.

Richard and Nicola had offered her a lift and urged her again to stay over with them, but in the end Jo chose to go home with Liam. Her disconnected lifestyle was a difficult one to shake off after all these years, and she had an urge to do something strenuous and manual. Dig the garden or run to the beach with Liam, then sandpaper the table she'd skip-ratted in preparation for its new life ... anything but to have to dwell on the thoughts that coiled through her brain, now that the memory floodgate had opened.

She really did not want to be sat there like some celebrity, having people gawp at her, revisiting it over and over. No. Best to just get on with something.

They were only being kind, she knew. But once questions began to be asked, things would start to ... well ... emerge. Things she'd buried for years and was more than happy for them to stay that way.

Richard passed over a foil container of lasagne for her as she was leaving, in that diffident way of his, blond eyebrows bright against his blush.

'If you won't come to us, this is the next best thing,' he muttered. 'It'll be defrosted by this evening. Don't forget to eat.' He'd reached over for an awkward hug, substituting it for a knuckled high five that missed both her shoulder and hand. 'Anything you need, just ring us. Okay?'

'Okay.' She swallowed, her voice stuck somewhere halfway down her throat. 'See you tomorrow.' Waved off on the electric mountain bike, Jo felt lifted by a rush of outgoing love from these people she'd known for such a short time.

Chapter Eight

Home stretched out cool and quiet arms. The strenuous effort of pulling Liam uphill, even with the astonishing battery assist that felt just like having her dad push her uphill, warmed her legs and body, and now, drained of emotion and energy, she just wanted to sleep. But little boys needed to run and be busy, and so, changing from cycling shorts to beach shorts, she swung a rucksack full of spades and buckets and some little apples over her shoulder, grasped his plump little brown hand, and headed off on the track to the sea.

There wasn't really a beach as such, on this side of the peninsula. Not like the expanse of soft golden sand and slice of azure sea that the Art Café overlooked. These were salt marshes, bleak in the winter and overgrown in the summer. Grazed by the now famous for their taste salt-marsh sheep and tough little ponies. There were few roads, just some tracks across what used to be military land and Jo loved the sense of solitude there.

She watched now as Liam charged ahead into a landscape dominated by sky, jumping over tussocks and shouting to raise the wading birds. Why did boys always have to be so noisy, she wondered? How her dad would have loved him. She stumbled as those thoughts hit her like a missile, and then tumbled over themselves like one of those old-fashioned flip through photo albums on a wire. A rolodex. Herself as a child with her dad.

It was time. She couldn't push the memories away any longer – it was time to honour them. Make some sense of them. And perhaps, if Griff survived ... perhaps it would have made amends in the tangled story that was her past. She owed her dad those memories, at least. Things would have been so different for her if he'd survived. When he died, so did her life as she'd known it.

As they reached the sea where it lapped untidily against the shoreline, she handed Liam an apple and tucked him into her side on the grassy bank.

'Once upon a time,' she began, looking across the calm turquoise water, 'there was a little girl with sticky up black hair that never went where it was supposed to, no matter how many times it was brushed, or how many clips and bows her mummy put in it. But her daddy loved her just exactly as she was, and never tried to change her.'

'Are there dragons in this story, Mummy?'

'Do you want there to be dragons?'

'Not really.' Liam leaned against her, and nibbled at his apple. 'Sometimes I do. But not today. Who is the little girl?'

'Well, it was me. This is a story about me. Is that okay?'

Liam nodded. 'Okay. I prefer proper stories, really. Out of a book. But it's okay.' He patted her thigh with a sticky hand and she chuckled.

'My daddy used to find things, and then fix them.'

'Like you!' Liam stared at her with his wide eyes.

'Yes, a bit like me, only my daddy fixed things with engines. He was ever so clever. But he did make a bit of a mess.'

'You're messy too.' Liam nodded sagely, and Jo rolled her eyes. How had she ended up with such a tidy child?

'It's called "creativity", actually,' she responded. 'Anyway. I used to help my daddy to fix things in his garage, but Mummy always wanted to take me out. In little dresses. And white socks. *Yuk!*'

'*Yuk*,' agreed Liam, through a mouthful of apple. 'Where is he now, your daddy? Is he in space?'

Oh, why hadn't she foreseen that one coming? 'Erm, well, he sort of is, darling, because he's in heaven now.'

'Is that where the man you were kissing has gone? Only Daisy said—'

'I don't think he's in heaven. I hope he isn't. That would be very sad for Ed, because that man is *his* daddy.' She was beginning to wonder whether this was such a good idea. 'What else did Daisy tell you?'

Liam screwed his face up. 'We-ell ... you were blowing the man up because all the air had gone out of him.'

Jo cocked her head to one side. *Not bad, actually. Even if it did make Griff sound like a deflated airbed.* Helpless giggles threatened.

'But,' Liam persevered, oblivious to her inner struggle, 'then she told me that kissing makes babies. Are you going to have a baby?'

Jo flicked a glance at his worried little face. 'What would you think about that?'

'It would depend ... whether he ate all my Rice Krispies,' Liam decided eventually. 'I think I'd rather have a puppy.'

The giggles finally overtook her. He was priceless, he really was. You couldn't make it up. How blessed she was to have such a wonderful child. She leaned in, shaking with laughter, and squeezed him to her.

'Ow, Mummy, *gerroff* me! I'm still eating, you know,' he said, fixing her with a stern eye. 'Did Richard give you some more cake for us to have tonight?'

'No, he didn't! And if he had, you'd have to run all the way home, because I'm not cycling you up all these hills full of cake, young man!'

'I'm *growing*!' squealed Liam, leaping up and darting away.

He was, too, thought Jo with a pang, as she gave chase to his lightning quick little body. But she'd made a start. It would be easier to broach now, she knew. He was a bright child who thought about things.

And this time she'd be ready for it. Exhaling a long breath, she felt old tensions leave her body, like a reverse form of the Dementors from a Harry Potter film.

She pulled her phone out of the pocket of her jeans and stared at it for a second as Liam zigzagged ahead, making vrooming noises. What was happening with Ed and Griff? Should she ring Richard and see if they'd had any news? Although, they would have rung her, wouldn't they? What if he'd ... gone ... would they let her know? Would they think that might upset her and worry about letting her know? Annoyed with her indecision, she stabbed at the screen.

'Richard ... hi, it's Jo ... yes, no, I'm, *we're* okay, no, honestly.' Richard's voice was a torrent in her ear. 'No, I'm not coming over, we've just had a lovely walk to the sea. I just wanted to ... er, wondered if ... um, how ...?'

The mobile felt hot against her ear as she listened. 'Yes, please pass my number on, that's fine. Okay, right, speak soon. Bye.'

She hung up. Griff was not in space. The Final Frontier. The absurdity of her thoughts made her giggle again. She was losing it. Relief. Shock. Who knew? And now she was seeing things, as she would swear that was Ed strolling down the track towards her. Squeezing her eyes shut, she shook her head and squinted back at the tall figure with the loping gait. Still looked like Ed. She was fixated, surely.

She tugged at her old shorts, feeling self-conscious suddenly. How did he always manage to look as if he'd stepped out of the pages of one of those authentic, retro lifestyle magazines? The moment crystallised in her eye ... soft, tawny light brushing the tips of the long grasses, the little boy skipping ahead on the narrow track, humming, and the tall dark man, white T-shirt beneath his battered leather bike jacket, striding towards her, his downcast profile side lit with gold. Had he seen her? Was he actually looking for her, or had he just come this way for a breath of air, maybe? It wasn't her own personal, private track, and he didn't live that far away.

She hesitated, examining her feelings. This did feel like her own personal, private track. And that tough little knot inside her had grown cross and defensive that she felt cornered on it. There was no way to avoid him now, and it would be plain weird to duck off the track, commando style into the long grasses. Plus, she'd just told Richard to pass on her mobile number to him, so it would make her look even more bonkers to hide from him now.

For goodness' sakes. She was so mixed up. Why couldn't she just be normal, for once? She knew why. He made her ... feel. Feel things that she'd begun to think she'd lost the rights to. And those feelings could lead to ... other things ... that would mean sharing. She'd become good at not sharing. She'd become good at hiding.

As she dithered, his head rose and he lifted a hand in greeting, closing the gap promptly.

'My legs *aaaache*, Mummy,' Liam wailed, his little face turned towards her.

'Shall I?' Ed bent and Jo watched in amazement as her child lifted his arms and allowed this almost stranger to swing him onto his broad shoulders.

'I can see horses!' Liam yelled in excitement, patting Ed's glossy black hair with hands daubed in bits of apple and stick. 'I'm a giant, Mummy!'

'Lovely, darling. Be careful. How's your dad?' There wasn't quite enough room to walk alongside here, and she was forced to bob her head forward to speak, almost tripping over Ed's heels with her toes. Her irritation with Ed grew ... but her annoyance with herself increased more. Liam drummed his heels against Ed's ribs, twisting to see across the marshes.

'Look, Mummy!'

'That's what I came to tell you …' Ed began.

'Don't kick Ed, darling, there's a good boy.' The automatic responses soothed and distracted her, while she waited for Ed to answer.

'Well, he's still with us,' Ed dipped his head to look at her awkwardly around Liam's knees, 'thanks to you. He's in the ITU, wired up, loads of tests … he looks pretty scary.' He shook his head, and Liam squealed, clutching his ears. 'Ow!'

'Careful, Liam!' Jo warned him sternly, torn between wanting him to get down because if anyone was going to be giving him a piggyback it should be her, and wanting him to have a good time. Which he clearly was having.

'*Sorrreeee*, Ed.' Liam patted his ears clumsily, and Ed winced with a grin.

'And they're talking about stents and by-passes and all that stuff.' Ed hoicked Liam up slightly by his armpits, settling him back more comfortably on his shoulders, while Jo tried to suppress a mounting fury that he was somehow taking over her child. 'So, you know, not out of the woods yet. But because of you … all those things are still available.' He halted in his tracks and Jo smacked into his back. 'You're amazing, Jo. You know that?' He yelled suddenly, his face split by a huge grin. 'How do you spell amazing, Liam?'

'Em, ay, zing!' whooped Liam, caught up in the moment. Ed lifted the little boy's arms with his own in a Mexican style salute. 'Yay!' they both cheered, as Ed did a little jig on the track. '*Mayzing!*' they cheered, laughing as the gilded dust motes floated around them. Jo felt her shoulders soften, relax, smile inside at last, as she watched these golden boys dance like lunatics, Liam chanting, 'Mummy's *mayzing!*' between helpless giggles, and Ed swooping his arms aloft and around. She hoped Liam wouldn't piddle on Ed's head.

'I'm pleased.' She smiled. 'Thanks for letting me know.'

'Mummy is having a baby,' announced Liam. 'I think.'

Ed's eyes whirled to meet hers. She shook her head, her mouth sliding into a lopsided grin.

'Because,' insisted Liam, 'Mummy was kissing your daddy ...'

'Oh, that sounds really weird,' Jo snorted, laughter once again threatening to engulf her. Honestly, her insides were going into an emotional meltdown today. She was going to need therapy at this rate.

'... and kissing makes babies!' Liam finished on a triumphant note.

'If only!' Ed whirled Liam around and jogged him up and down, making him squeal.

'And Daisy said ...' Liam wasn't to be deflected '... Mummy will have an egg—'

Ed laughed, a long, rich laugh that boomed up from his chest. Jo stared, open-mouthed, and even Liam stopped. It was a sound of pure joy.

'I think Daisy's getting confused with chickens, Liam.' He wiped his eyes. 'Oh my goodness, you are a proper cheerer-upper, mate, you really are.' He turned to Jo. 'I don't know how to thank you for what you've done.'

'You can fix my bike.' Jo gave him a mock glare.

'I think we can do better than that.' Ed held her gaze and she drowned for a moment in that sea-glass blue green.

'No bloody charity!' she warned.

'Mummy!' Liam's tones were outraged. 'You *swore-d*.'

'No bloody charity,' agreed Ed, unsmiling.

'Oh!' Liam threw his hands in the air. 'That is *unceptabal ahaviour!* I'm a child, you know!'

Jo doubled up with laughter. It was like hearing an echo of herself.

'But seriously, there must be something else I can do for you. To say thank you.'

Jo considered all the things she thought they needed. More money, a car, security, a proper job, the leaky bathroom fixed, a house without a landlord who was intent on getting into her pants, a big brush to whitewash her past. Then she looked at her little boy's strong limbs, his bright, inquiring mind, and knew she had everything, really. She had … enough.

'There is something …' she began.

'Name it.'

'Manure.'

Ed turned an incredulous expression on her. 'You save my dad's life, and the only thing I can give you as a thank you is some shit for the garden?'

'Shit!' said Liam, his mouth and eyes wide. 'Shocking.'

Jo tried not to laugh. 'Now look what you've done.'

'*Oops.*' Ed waggled his eyebrows. 'But really, you want … manure?'

'I can't carry it on my bike. And I'm not talking about that stuff that comes in plastic bags from B&Q, I mean, proper farmyard muck. Good stuff.'

'Shit,' Liam said faintly.

'Liam. That's enough. It's not funny.' The hell it was. He was doing a brilliant job of bursting the tension between them.

'Anyway. This is us.' Jo nodded as her house came into view. 'How did you know where I was, by the way?'

'Beryl told me.'

'Beryl … my neighbour?'

Ed nodded.

'Is there anyone you don't know?' Jo rounded on him with an exasperated eye.

Ed shrugged. 'What can I say? I've lived here a long time!'

'I barely know her!' Jo scuffed the earth beneath her feet.

'She worries about you.'

'What? Why?'

Ed looked skywards with his head on one side, and recited in an 'old lady' cracked falsetto. 'Has she got enough to eat? She's so thin. Does she sleep properly? I've seen her light on in the middle of the night. She's lovely with that little boy of hers, such a nice girl, and digging that garden every hour God gives? It's a paradise now, you know. She even brought my washing in when it rained. And she folds, darns and irons it too. She's such a *lovely* neighbour.' He stopped and looked at her, a half smile on his face.

'What? Darning and ironing? I don't think so.' Jo was taken aback, feeling the blood rush to her face. 'I brought her washing in *once*.' Then she laughed. 'That might have been Beryl herself standing before us. Not. I'm sure she'd kill you on the spot if she heard you.' They strolled companionably towards the road. Ed stooped and let a disappointed Liam onto terra firma.

'I'm *tiiiiiired*, Mummy.'

Jo reached a hand out to the drooping little boy with mixed feelings. Duty and obligation tugged at her unexpectedly … because she wanted to stay and talk to Ed. She straightened up and squared him in the eye.

'No cake today, sorry.'

'*Aw!*' said Ed and Liam in unison. She chuckled.

'No eggs.'

'There's one …' said Liam, hopefully.

'That's your tea,' Jo said. 'With soldiers.'

Liam sent Ed an apologetic face, and Ed made a sad expression that made Jo laugh.

'You two and cake!' Jo looked from one to the other.

'Maybe you should get chickens,' said Ed.

'Like Daisy?' Liam hopped up and down, his tiredness clearly forgotten. 'Can we, Mummy?'

'Liam! I don't have the first idea how to look after a chicken!'

'You look after me, Mummy. I'm probably harder than a chicken.' Liam took her hand and stared into her eyes with an earnest expression.

'Mmm, you're probably right. And it's tea-time, bath and then bed now.' Jo knew she was using him as an excuse to get away from Ed. It wasn't that she wanted to get away from Ed. She just didn't want to face up to how much she *didn't* want to get away from Ed.

'*Awww,*' said a crestfallen Liam. 'Story?'

'Of course. When do we never have a story?'

'Okay.' Ed nodded. 'Well, you have a lot to sort out, and I have to go … get back to Mum. I only stopped to pick up some stuff for her and Dad.'

'Is she staying there tonight?'

'Yes. There's a relatives' bed thing, but I think she's planning on just dozing in the chair.'

'What will you do?'

'Make her go in the relatives' bed thing. I think we'll be fighting over the chair.' Ed's voice was light but his face looked strained suddenly and Jo was surprised by an urge to reach up and smooth the worry from his brows.

She was still staring up into his eyes when he took her face between his long hands and lowered his lips slowly onto hers.

Every rational thought in her mind shouted that she shouldn't be allowing this. On so many counts, this would be the wrong thing to do … he had a girlfriend, he played the field, Liam would get attached to him and then be upset when she was passed over for some other attraction, finally and worse, Ed would find out that she wasn't the person he thought she was.

As her body had other ideas and melted into his, her head tipped back, her eyes closed and she felt nothing but the exquisite, soft firmness of his mouth against hers. She seemed to be made of supple soft silk, flowing towards him. Her hips angled towards him and her hands slipped up his spine over the soft shirt, counting the bumps of his spine, feeling the powerful muscles beneath the flesh on his back.

His thumbs brushed her cheekbones, her chin, her throat, and she felt his arms encircle her urgently, lift her slightly onto tiptoe.

Then another set of arms threw itself around her. Liam. Bless him. Breaking slowly and reluctantly free from Ed's sweet mouth, she rested the side of her face against him and looked down at her son, squeezing them all together in a hug that only a four-year-old would understand. She choked down the lump in her throat.

'Time to go.' She couldn't look up at Ed. Couldn't bear to see the longing there, that she knew would be mirrored in her own face. Stepping firmly back, she pinned a huge smile on.

'Well, wasn't that a lovely way to say goodnight?' She addressed Liam, avoiding Ed's eye. 'What do you say, Liam?'

'Thank you. Goodbye. Night night.' Liam pouted at Ed, who seemed to be having trouble with his posture.

'Yes, er ... Goodnight, Liam.' Ed straightened up with difficulty, tugging his leather jacket across his jeans. 'And ... er ... Jo.'

'Please keep me posted,' Jo said, reaching for Liam's hand and returning reluctantly to Mummy Mode.

'Of course.' Ed jerked a thumb towards his truck. 'I'm off then. Speak soon. Bye both.'

Jo and Liam watched, hand in hand, as Ed swung himself into the cab of the pickup, and waved as he drove away. Her body fizzed from that kiss, and she felt flustered and dizzy. Intimate contact with both father and son – her mouth on theirs – but this last kiss leaving her feeling renewed. She wanted to skip, whooping, back along the track, laughing like a lunatic. But her responsible Mummy brain took over.

Turning to head inside, Jo spotted Beryl in her garden and wandered over.

'I see you met up with Idris then.' Beryl, wearing a kaftan of shimmering jewels over her jeans, waved at her with a smile.

'Idris?' Jo looked puzzled.

'Ed. Idris Griffiths. Proper Welsh name. Means prince or lord or something,' Beryl said, in her lovely lilting dialogue. 'Known him since he was a babby. Funny to think he's my landlord.'

'He's *what*?'

'Well, not exactly him. His family. Lovely they are. It's a trust or something. Isn't he your landlord too? Only I don't remember your cottage going up for sale at all. I would have noticed something like that.'

'Er ...'

'Cause you took over from old Merve, didn't you? Poor old Merve, mun.'

'Is he ...?'

'In a home, you know. Hardly knows himself, he does.'

'Oh.' Jo was relieved that he wasn't dead, even though she'd never met him. The idea of inhabiting a dead man's cottage was just a bit too weird for today.

'Tied, these cottages, you know,' Beryl said, folding her arms across her ample bosom and planting her feet. She nodded firmly. 'Farmworkers. Agricultural.' She rolled the word around her tongue expansively. 'That sort of thing. Why they have such enormous gardens, of course. Lovely job you've done of yours, now. Lovely. And so quickly! Poor old Merve let it go ages ago, and those boys of his were in and out, doing no good at all as far as I could see. Good thing you came. Goodness only knows what it would look like otherwise.'

'So,' said Jo, faintly, 'they've always had these big gardens?

Only, my landlord is trying to charge me more now I've cleared it up. He says I've added value to it, or something. Upped the rates. Something like that.'

'Who's *your* landlord then, my lovely? If it's not the Griffiths?'

Jo screwed her face up involuntarily. Her landlord, Chad Evans, gave her the creeps. She'd felt both relieved and anxious that Beryl had known who he was. There had been something not right at all about that exchange and the way he'd scuttled off as soon as he could. The tiny cottage was in desperate need of modernisation. But it was affordable and she'd already fallen in love with it after the succession of shoddy bedsits and shared flats she'd had to make do with in the past and so she steeled herself to the unpleasant feeling that she was on borrowed time there. Instinct told her that she should keep that information to herself. Find out a bit more.

'I ... can't remember his name,' she said. 'I still can't get to grips with these Welsh names, Beryl. At least I can manage yours.'

'Oh goodness me, my real name isn't Beryl, my lovely! It's Brangwyn! But no one knew how to pronounce it, not even my father, so I ended up as Beryl.' She laughed, her bosom bouncing up and down, to Liam's fascination.

Jo heard her own voice say, 'I'm not actually a Jo. My proper, whole name is Sojourner!' Why on earth had she confessed that? She shrugged. What harm could it do? Old Beryl wasn't likely to be on the internet looking her up, was she? 'It was my mother's idea. It was the name of an activist for women's rights, or something. A heroine.'

'Well, it sounds like she got that right then,' Beryl said, with a nod, hands on hips. 'After what you did today, you've certainly lived up to that name!'

Chapter Nine

Ed was collecting a few things from his parents' cottage, his mind full of Jo and Liam, when Lucy rang.

'Ed! I'm so sorry to hear about your dad, Ash told me. How is he?'

He gave her a swift update, and she replied, 'My goodness, how lucky he was to have our Jo nearby.'

'I know. She was incredible.' He coughed to disguise the choking sensation in his throat as his mind swung back to those awful moments. 'So how was your day? Tell me all about it, you famous TV star you.'

'Hah! Well, I got separated from Tom and the film crew—'

'How did you manage that?' Ed asked.

'Um, the crew had gone ahead and we were pulling out of a garage, and Tom saw a gap and went for it, and, er—'

'You were too slow?'

'No!' Lucy sounded indignant and Ed grinned. 'I ... okay, yes. There was a *huuuuge* lorry coming when it was my turn. Anyway, by the time I got out of the junction, there was a roundabout, and I would have sworn that it was Tom I saw, *miiiles* down the road, in those bright leathers he wears, so I took that exit.'

'Only it turned out not to be him?'

'Hole in one.' Lucy sighed. 'I'd gone a few miles before I realised that though. I was swearing and cursing at him in my helmet for going so fast ...'

'I thought you had helmet comms?'

'We have, but they were out of range. I pulled over as soon as I could, and tried ringing the crew but there was no signal. I didn't have a clue how to get to the B&B, so I went back to the garage, hoping that maybe he would be waiting for me, but he wasn't so I bought a map, and found my own way there.'

'Oh, well, that was top initiative!'

'Mmm, except that they'd all gone back to find me when they realised I was missing, and somehow we all missed each other, and anyway, to cut a long story short, I got to the B&B before they did.' She sounded glum.

'But, that's good, isn't it?'

'No. They were really pissed off with me. Tom was okay, after all, it was his fault, he should've waited for me. But the crew ...'

'Oh, I'm sure they'll be okay with you before long. Buy them a pint. That'll sort it.'

'Yeah, maybe. Hang on, there's someone at the door ...' There were muffled voices, and then Lucy came back on the line. 'Sorry, Ed, gotta go, we're all going to the pub ...' More muffled voices, and then Ed heard TV Tom's voice, 'She's all ours now, mate. Ha haaaa! Yard of Ale!' he chanted. 'Yard of Ale!'

'Lucy ... don't let them bully you into the yard of ale!' Ed almost laughed at himself, coming over all grown-up. 'You're on your bike tomorrow!'

'I'll be *fiiiine*, Ed. Got to go, love to your folks, speak soon!' And she was gone. Ed stared at the phone, smiling at her excitement, before his own world crashed back in on him.

Hospitals at night were never quiet, but there was an impression of other world-ness in the pools of dimmed lights and meaningful beeps. The staff were different too – a sense of purpose, maybe, Ed couldn't decide.

Hooked up to drips and monitors, Griff lay propped on pillows only one shade whiter than he was. None of those things scared Ed. He'd worn them all himself in the past. He could see beyond all that, and it helped now. He'd known people who hadn't felt able to visit him in hospital because they were frightened of all the paraphernalia.

Shifting to sit across the chair, he eased his joints into a more comfortable position. It was warm and his eyelids drooped. At least his mum had gone to get a few hours sleep – he was pleased that he'd persuaded her – on pain of death that she'd be woken if there were any developments. He could sleep tomorrow. There wasn't anything pressing in the Bike Palace that was needed – he'd already texted Ash and asked him to put a note on the gate saying they were closed for the day. He began to think about the workload that would pile up if his dad was out of action for long. He was going to need a plan.

The Vintage Bike Palace had been his father's dream – and when his heart issues were diagnosed, he gave up the family business and opened the Bike Palace. Ed heaved a sigh, thinking about just how much his parents had given up for him over the years. It was payback time – could he take over from his dad? Did he want to? He was fast approaching thirty – and he didn't seem to have a proper career yet.

Having been surrounded by motorbikes all his life it seemed to be a natural progression to go into mechanical engineering – and he really did enjoy the renovating part. It was like a journey into the past, and even as a boy he'd loved the tales of the heroes who'd ridden those old bikes. Lawrence of Arabia. Steve McQueen in *The Great Escape*.

He'd left school with practically no GCSEs. Having missed so much school due to illness, he'd relied on his good looks, popularity and sympathy to mess about during the times he did attend, and consequently had just been funnelled straight into his father's business as an apprentice. His mates, working in offices and call centres, thought he had the luck of the devil, messing about with motorbikes all day.

So now, here he was, at a crossroads of what he was to do with his life. His dad might want to retire – and he could take over – if he wanted to. The trouble was – he wasn't sure it was what he wanted to do forever. Because it had come a bit too easily – and he felt that he should be trying harder at something – something momentous, something worthwhile. What though?

It shocked him to realise how much he was still tied to his parents' goodwill, and he swallowed. Look at Jo – she was more man than he was, a single mum coping without parents, or any family at all, by the look of it. His groin twitched at the memory of that kiss and he crossed his legs hurriedly. God man, it didn't do to be getting a hard-on at the bedside of your seriously ill father.

Now he'd started, he couldn't stop thinking about her. She wasn't like anyone he'd ever met. He corrected himself – not like any other girl he'd ever met. Not actually *girly* – no make-up, for starters. And she seemed to live in shorts – on and off her bike.

How was it he hadn't actually noticed her when she started working at the café? It was her manner, he knew. She just got on with things. She was sensible. What you saw was what you got. No flirting. At least, not with him. Was he really that shallow? He swallowed, unwilling to admit to himself that he probably was. He'd never had to work very hard with women – they just seemed to flock around him. His mates had always reaped the benefits of his admirers – Ed cringed to think how they all hung about watching as the girls danced in the middle when they went clubbing.

It used to be fun … but now … now he wasn't so sure. He was bored with the superficiality of it all. He wanted a relationship – like his parents had – wanted to be part of a team. He'd never admitted it to himself before.

Gazing at his dad brought back the image of Jo, in the

café. She'd saved his dad's life, he marvelled. He wanted to give her something back, had to help her ... more than just some manure for her vegetable plot. He hadn't done a very good job of helping so far, running over her bike – and loaning her Alexis's had backfired – Jo had every right to be angry with him.

Alexis. He was going to have to sort that out – she was so over. He hoped she wouldn't try to visit his dad here. He couldn't dump her at the bedside, could he? What a pain. What had he ever seen in her? That one stolen kiss with Jo had stirred his heart more than the last however many jumps he'd had with Alexis.

Jo. Jo, Jo, Jo Jo Jo – her name was whirling around his head and when he closed his eyes, he saw her walking down that track with little Liam skipping along in front. Those long, tanned legs in those shorts – and all that mad curly hair like a sooty cloud round her head. How poetic. Sooty cloud? Stretching his shoulders, he grimaced at his fancifulness, and yawned, squinting at his watch. Three thirty in the morning.

Coffee. He needed coffee. The chair legs screeched as he jumped up, and he winced at the over loud noise in the silence, tiptoeing out to make amends. Making amends. That was going to be his plan from now on.

Half past four. Jo threw the tangled sheets off her in a fury, and lay, sore-eyed, staring up at the ceiling. Her legs twitched and thrashed – a sure sign of over-tiredness. She'd crawled into bed not long after Liam and for the first few hours had been virtually unconscious.

Then something had woken her, and now every time she closed her eyes, her brain played a film at her. A horror film.

Her dad, her lovely, lovely dad, driving her home from the club she'd begged to be allowed to go to. At 10.30 sharp, no later – and how she'd moaned about that. Ridiculously early, everyone else would be there all night long, she'd asserted. And no drinking? What was that about? She'd be a joke – everyone would be drinking. Did she want to go or not? he'd asked, quietly, not losing his temper in the face of her sulk.

Of course she'd wanted to go. And you know what? It had been pretty rubbish really. Seedy. The other girls pretending they were having such a great time – laughing too loudly, flirting too obviously, hanging onto little bottles of WKD they'd lied to get and chewing at the straws to make them last longer because they didn't have the money to buy more. And the blokes there ... Jo shuddered even now, remembering their watchful faces. If she hadn't made such a big deal about it, she'd have rung her dad and got him to pick her up at eight thirty.

And if she'd done that ... the thing ... and any of the other things ... wouldn't have happened.

But he'd been there at 10.30, right outside the club, to collect her, just as he said he would be. And she'd been humiliated to see him waiting there, with his shabby hatchback, in his baggy brown fleece and the pale denim jeans he was too old to wear. In her opinion. She'd stropped over to him like he was her taxi-driver, with all those bitchy girls catcalling and sniggering, and flung herself into the passenger seat. Slammed the door. She was sixteen, and she knew it all.

What she hadn't known, what she couldn't have known, was that her dad had been having a heart attack all the way to meet her. Had not felt at all well all day, and had still offered to drive her there, to keep her safe, his little girl. And then, on the way home, his big, lovely heart had given out, right there in the driving seat. And at the very last second, he'd turned the wheel so that the old car crashed into the hedges – and not into the traffic. And she hadn't realised –

not one little bit – what was happening, and she'd screamed at him in panic.

'What are you *doing*?' As her body jarred and bounced and she screamed and bit her tongue and muddle from inside the car hit her and her neck whiplashed. She looked over at her dad –and he was just slumped there. In silence. His eyes – not closed – but not looking at her. And she reached over and couldn't get the seat belt off and there was silence but the car was ticking and hissing and she didn't know what to do …

'Daddy!' She shook him, he'd know what to do, he always knew what to do, what was *wrong* with him?

She lay now, drenched in sweat, her teeth gritted, tears pouring down her face, remembering. Remembering the helpless panic that had engulfed her, the terrible sobbing and desperation. Remembering the awful dawning that he'd gone – and she'd done nothing to help.

She couldn't lie there any longer, sleep was gone. The floorboards creaked as she pulled on a soft pair of track pants, T-shirt and sweater, and headed downstairs, yawning.

Standing at the kitchen sink, she filled the kettle sparingly, peering blearily into the pitch-black garden, and seeing only her tousled reflection in the windowpane. Funny, she wasn't at all bothered by the isolation of her rural life. The dark couldn't hurt you. People did.

The kettle boiled and she fidgeted, picking things up, her limbs leaden, sluggish. The little wooden box she'd found recently caught her eye. She was a proper scavenger, discovering treasures in the most unlikely places and bringing them home in her little cycle-towed trailer to be given a new lease of life and sold.

As her tea brewed, she turned the box over in her hands and reached for the wire wool and meths to strip off the years of accumulated muck. She had an idea. But she needed some help.

Slotting the DVD that was never far away into the little TV, she pressed play, turned the volume down to a whisper, pulled on a pair of rubber gloves, and set to work on her latest project – a memory box for Liam. She laid her hands flat on the box, and dropped her shoulders. Who was she kidding? A memory box for her. Her memories of her father. Words, pictures that reminded her of him.

He deserved to be remembered. She'd find a nice lock for it. Maybe change the hinges.

The turquoise sea pictured on the TV sent sunshine into the room, and Jo watched for the millionth time Meryl Streep and Julie Walters in the musical *Mamma Mia!*, and dreamed of the day that she and Liam would have a holiday in Greece, in the sunshine.

And that kiss yesterday? It meant nothing. Nothing. She was not going to be one of Ed Griffith's cast-offs, not her. She was an independent, resourceful woman, mother to a wonderful little boy – and she'd saved a man's life. That counted for something, didn't it?

She didn't give one hoot that anyone watching through the window would have seen her dancing and strutting, holding an old paintbrush as a microphone, dark hair bouncing round her head as she mimed vigorously but soundlessly in deference to soundly sleeping Liam upstairs.

Although later, opening the front door to a dozen eggs on her doorstep, she did wonder.

Chapter Ten

The early cycle ride to deliver Liam to school seemed particularly beautiful that morning. A pale blue sky cradled a lemon sun, and Jo noticed the pinks and soft purples of the early spring flowers tucked under the hedges much more than usual. Despite her lack of sleep, they whizzed up the hills in turbo mode on the electric bike, and she whooped with joy as they hurtled down, grinning as she heard Liam's squeals of delight.

It felt like a new beginning, somehow. She wasn't altogether ready to come to terms with her past, but sitting this morning and jotting down a few words about her childhood memories had calmed the tumultuous thoughts in her head – given her a small sense of peace. And, of course, although she was denying it to herself, and would shout from a rooftop that it meant nothing, that kiss with Ed – it had awoken her body.

She couldn't imagine herself in a relationship with anyone, let alone Ed, but that didn't mean that she didn't occasionally feel lonely, or in need of a hug. So even though she had no intention of allowing anything to develop with Ed – who already had a girlfriend anyway – it had been lovely to feel desired. A huge confidence booster, when she hadn't even known that her confidence had needed boosting in that respect.

She'd become so used to camouflaging herself – practical clothes that did a job and weren't designed to show off her figure helped – that it was a shock to discover that someone had even seen her, remembered her name, let alone fancied her. She smiled now, having taken a little extra time over her hair this morning, tying it into a pretty vintage lace ribbon she'd found in one of her treasures.

Talking of which, next weekend should be a good hunting ground – there were boot sales and barn clearances all the time on the peninsula, and she loved poking around to see what she could find. Liam always came with her, which meant she had to collect purchases later in her cycle-trailer, or arrange to have them dropped off. The eBike would be fantastic for towing the trailer, but she was well enough known in those circles now that someone would offer to deliver if they were passing, and she paid for their time and fuel in cake, which always went down well. She dreamed of a day when she might have her own little van and an upcycling business. When she'd be completely independent.

'Too much dreaming, not enough doing!' she yelled now, laughing as she remembered her dawn sing-a-long with *Mamma Mia!*

That reminded her. When had those eggs arrived? Had to be Ed. Ed the Egg Man. The Egg Man cometh. In her dreams ... Giggles overtook her. Too much time on your own, she told herself, still grinning as she pulled up at the school.

The little knot of parents there looked up and smiled back at her as she dismounted and helped Liam off his tag-along.

'Morning!' they chorused. 'How about you, then, wow!'

'What?' Jo asked, cautiously, disconnecting the tag-along from the bike.

'You! Life saver!' They surged towards her, their voices tumbled together. 'Great stuff! Where did you learn to do that? Have you done it before?'

'How did you know about it already?' Jo asked.

'*Duh!*' There was laughter. 'It's only all over Facebook!'

'And YouTube!'

'Twitter!'

Unsure how to react, Jo bent to deliver a kiss on Liam's pink cheek before he scurried away, merging with the other children beyond the classroom door. His teacher stood, checking them in, and as Liam passed her, she looked up and locating Jo, raised a hand in a chirpy wave. Surprised, Jo fingertip waved back.

'Here's one. Want to see?' A mobile phone was thrust under her nose, and feeling trapped, she squinted at the jerky onscreen video. She caught her breath as she saw herself kneeling beside Griff's inert form, head down, her shock of curly hair bouncing with each compression.

'Here's another one.' Another phone, another video, from a different direction. Jo shrank back, her hands clammy. She swallowed.

'Oh ...' she began, staring down at the forest of screens, all showing a version of yesterday's events. She hadn't even noticed the gathering around her, let alone that they were filming her. 'I ... er ...'

The crowd laughed as one.

'Hah, reluctant hero!'

'Heroine! She's a girl!'

'I know what I meant!'

The excited banter continued as they clustered around her. Out of her depth, Jo didn't have the faintest idea how to reply.

'Pop in for coffee when you're passing.'

'Bring Liam round for a play date next weekend, be lovely to get to know you better. We've got a trampoline in the garden, do you think he'd like to play on it?'

'We're having a coffee morning on Thursday. Can you come?'

The invitations came thick and fast as if each person was trying to outdo the other to be her new best buddy. Eventually, Jo held her hands up.

'Thank you all! But really, I only did what you all would have done, honestly!'

There was a silence.

'I wouldn't have had a clue, if that had been me.' One of the mums, smooth blonde head on one side, regarded her earnestly. There were many murmurs of assent.

'How about I get a course together to teach you?' Jo said, surprising herself, and pleased to see so many nods. 'Okay, I'll keep you posted. Now, I've got to get to work!' She looked over her shoulder at them as she wheeled the tag-along to its home in the cycle shed. 'But thank you. All of you.'

Swinging her leg over the saddle, she pedalled away, waving for the first time. Well, well. How had they known it was her? She didn't really understand social media. She wasn't even on the internet at home – she used the café Wi-Fi to sell her stuff on eBay, and got by on 3G if she had to research anything.

She certainly had no desire to be on Facebook – someone from her past might recognise her and all her carefully guarded secrets would be everywhere. Her stomach lurched horribly at the thought. But her name hadn't been on those videos, had it? Or had it?

Apprehension lent speed to her legs and she arrived at the café before Richard. The sun sparkled off the cobalt sea but Jo was in no mood to appreciate its beauty as she fished out her phone, clicking on the YouTube app she almost never used, unless it was to watch funny films of animals with Liam.

What should she search for? Her fingers fumbled and misspelt and she forced herself to sit on the low wall and slow down. Eventually, the terms: Café Woman Saves Heart Attack Man revealed her in action. Cringing, she watched it all the way through and heaved a sigh of relief. No mention of her name anywhere. Thank goodness.

No one from her past would recognise her from that. It must just be a local thing that the parents found her. Shared as 'Liam's Mum', probably.

Jo had noticed quite early on that she'd lost her own identity. She didn't mind at all, it suited her, and she was proud of it. Her hands shook and feeling exhausted, she leaned back, turning her face to the sun.

'Wow, you're keen!' Richard cast a shadow over her face. She hadn't even realised she'd closed her eyes. 'I wasn't sure you'd be in today.'

'Didn't sleep.' Yawning, Jo rubbed her eyes and then blinked at Richard. 'Really? You mean, I could've had a day off ... paid?'

'*Ooh*, paid? Um ...' Richard looked awkward and Jo managed a weak smile.

'Come on, things to do before the hordes arrive.' She eased herself upright, stretching her legs. 'Heard from Lucy at all?'

'*Oh* yes.' Richard grinned. 'She's okay, but I don't think she's had the greatest start to her adventure. She sends her love, by the way, and told me to tell you that she's proud of you.'

'*Oh!*' Jo felt her face heating with embarrassment as she wheeled her bike into the storeroom, and still yawning, headed off to change into her café uniform.

Jo was rushed off her feet all morning, which kept her tiredness at bay. Mondays weren't usually this busy – there were the regulars: dog walkers sharing their toasted teacakes with their furry friends outside on the terrace, and the little group of mums who downloaded their weekends after dropping their charges at school, but today there'd been a constant stream of customers.

'It'll be the TV publicity, I reckon,' Richard said, when she mentioned it to him as she was washing-up. 'I'd better put an extra order in. Do you need anything?'

'Yes please ... a good fairy delivered a dozen eggs this morning. So I thought I'd make a fruit cake for Ed and his mum.' Jo rinsed plates and stacked them carefully on the drainer. Since Richard had discovered her fruit cake barter system, he let her buy ingredients at trade, which was kind.

He made a googly-eyed face at her now.

'Oo-oh, get you! What happened to, "*I don't need a boyfriend*?"' he said, with a smirk.

Jo turned a reproving expression on him. 'Making a cake does not constitute having a boyfriend.' She shook her head at him. 'I'm just ... returning the compliment.'

'So Ed's your egg fairy?' Richard said, with a laugh. 'He knows everyone around here. He probably got the milkman to deliver them for you.'

Jo blinked. She hadn't thought of that. The café phone rang, making her jump. Spotting a customer ambling towards the counter, she scurried away, wiping her hands.

The young woman at the counter looked just like any one of the walkers that the stunning coastline attracted throughout the year, in her boots and bright jacket. So Jo was completely off guard when the business card proclaiming *Gower News* was slid across the counter, along with a request for a skinny soya latte, and, 'Is Jo Morris in today?'

Jo's mouth dried into sandpaper. Busying herself with the coffee machine, she kept her head down and tossed a fake, cheery, 'No idea. Never met her. I'm just temporary,' over her shoulder. 'Drink in or takeaway?' *Please say takeaway.*

'Drink in, thanks.' The woman, whose name Jo had speed-read on the business card, was Michelle, leaned matily over the counter. 'So – when is Jo next in?'

'No idea,' Jo mumbled. 'Anything else with your coffee?'

'Those cakes look delicious.' Michelle was obviously stalling for time, and Jo fidgeted along with the lengthening queue as she hovered before the chilled cabinet. 'Let me think ...'

'Jo!' yelled Richard, rushing in and slamming a hand on

91

the counter in his excitement. 'You'll never guess – that was the local TV news on the phone, they want to come and film you! Here! In the café!'

'TV?' said someone in the queue. Jo recognised him as the grumpy customer who'd been there the day she'd had the phone call from the school. It seemed a lifetime ago. He was agog now, shoving to get to the front of the queue. 'Are we going to be on telly?'

'So … you *are* Jo!' Michelle said, with a note of triumph. 'I knew it! I recognised you from your videos.' She pulled her phone out and held it in front of her. 'Smile!'

'No!' Jo hid behind her outspread hand. 'No comment.' She turned to Richard, and said firmly to him too, 'No comment.'

'What's she done to be on the telly?' said another voice in the queue.

'Only saved a man's life,' said Richard, importantly.

'A man's wife?' Misheard murmurs spread along the queue.

'What did she do to a man's wife?'

'I always said about her, didn't I?'

'Is that woman from the telly?'

'No. Comment!' Jo held her hands out, feeling trapped and panicky.

'Reluctant Heroine!' announced Michelle, looking at the photo she'd taken and reversing the phone to show Jo. 'I'll just have to use that then.'

'You can't use that!' Jo said, with mounting horror. 'It's awful!'

'Pose for me then. Please? My editor's sent me here to get a story. I can't go back with nothing. I'll have to make it up.'

Richard shimmied up to Jo and hammed a big grin.

'How's that?' he said, imprisoning Jo with his outstretched

arm as Michelle clicked rapidly on her mobile. 'She's fantastic, isn't she? We're very proud of her here. Smile, Jo,' he instructed, through his own stretched smile.

'Maybe I should interview your boss,' Michelle said, her gaze travelling from one to the other.

'Can we get a pot of tea now?' an exasperated voice said from the queue, finding himself shushed by the rest of the queue, who were clearly enjoying being part of the happening news.

'Ooh yes, I was there! I helped!' Richard bobbed up and down like an excited child.

'What did you do?' asked Michelle, her pen poised. Jo, regarding him with a mixture of trepidation and disbelief, wanted to know too.

'Well,' Richard hesitated. 'I ... er ... made sure that people had tea and everything.' He gestured expansively. 'People are in shock after something like that, you know ...'

'Fine!' Jo wriggled out of Richard's grip. If she continued to evade the press they would only hound her. Best to say as little as possible and it would die a natural death. 'What do you want to know? You'll have to wait till I've finished serving though.'

'Mine's a cappuccino and toasted teacake!' said the next person in the queue.

Passing over a few coins, Michelle grabbed her coffee with a grin and retreated to a nearby table. 'I'll just be by here!'

Jo rolled her eyes at the Welsh-ism. 'I'll be there now in a minute,' was another one which had confused her when she'd first moved to Wales. 'By there, and by here,' were other local idioms that always made her smile.

Finally closing her front door behind her later that day, Jo heaved a sigh of relief. Her legs felt leaden. It might not be the smartest house ever, but it was home. Even Liam had been full of questions about her saving Griff's life, which meant they must have been talking about it in school.

The parent trap at the school gates had been even more avid than that morning, but Jo had fended them off with good grace, knowing that the fuss would die down quickly enough if she made little of it and didn't feed their curiosity.

For Liam's sake she'd been pleased to accept play dates for the coming weekend. Even if it meant she'd have to return the favour, which worried her.

She didn't have money to splash and she was sure they'd all have smart houses and she certainly didn't. Whatever would she do with these cosseted children who were driven everywhere and already had the latest i-gadget? She could take them along the sea track – as long as they didn't mind walking and could swim? Or maybe her own garden, which was pretty huge.

Some games if the weather was fine. A picnic, pretend camping – didn't all kids like that? Painting some pebbles, that sort of thing.

Goodness, why was she worrying? They were just kids. Five years old. It would be fine. Liam needed more friends.

Stop fretting before it's even happened, she told herself firmly. She would put the dried fruit to soak in tea for the cakes, do some reading and drawing with Liam and then it would be early to bed. She was dog-tired, and thankful for another of Richard's food parcels for their tea.

Everything looked better when you'd had a good night's sleep.

Chapter Eleven

The fruit cake lay securely cocooned in her saddlebag a couple of days later, and Jo debated where to deliver it. Would Ed be working in the Vintage Bike Palace? Or might he be at home? She decided to try his home first, as it was nearest. And if he wasn't home, maybe there'd be somewhere safe she could leave it for him. She went back into the house and selected one of her own home-made gift tags and a pen, just in case she needed to leave it with a note. The Bike Palace was too far for them both to ride in an evening in any case.

'Come on, Liam,' she called. 'Feeling fit? We're going for a little ride.'

'Where to?'

'Cake delivery!' She buttoned up his red padded jacket and buckled his helmet. 'To Ed's house. Do you remember his house?'

'I had a shower in his house.' Liam nodded. 'After I was sick.'

'That's the one,' Jo said, strapping on her own helmet and lifting Liam onto his seat on the tag-along. 'Let's hope he's in.'

The short journey was barely enough to warm her legs. They could have walked it really, she thought, as the gated entrance came into sight, but she was becoming quite fond of the electric bike, which made mincemeat of the uphills.

'Right turn, Liam!' she yelled over her shoulder, then seeing his arm shoot out, 'Other right!' She laughed as he swapped arms.

'Just checking!' he sang, making her laugh. She unclipped her shoes from the pedals as they began the manoeuvre from tarmac to deep gravel and was just deciding whether to ride or dismount and push the bike as a black hatchback whirled past in a shower of gravel, missing them by inches, and continuing at speed around the corner.

'Bloody hell!' Jo was incensed. What was the matter with people? Bicycles seemed to be a target for motorists these days. With Liam on the back too! She wasn't having it.

'Come on, Liam!' she yelled, standing up on the pedals. 'Push!'

The chunky tyres and motor of the mountain bike made shorter work of the gravel than her road bike would have done and, within moments, Jo pulled up alongside the driver's door of the dark hatchback. She could see the woman driver fiddling with her handbag and then drawing out a lipstick. As she sat up to use the rear-view mirror, she jumped as she caught sight of Jo alongside.

'Get away from my car!' She flapped a hand at Jo. 'You'll scratch it.'

If Jo had been angry before, the gesture made her incandescent. She ducked down to eyeball the woman, realising with a shock that it was Ed's girlfriend. What was her name – Alexis. She tapped on the window.

'Can you actually drive?' she bellowed through the glass. 'Do you realise how close you were to us? You didn't care about scratching *us*!'

Alexis's expression was scornful, but Jo detected a jolt of panic in her eyes.

'You could have knocked my little boy off and killed him. How would that have felt?'

Anger and fear of what could have happened fuelled the torrent of words flowing from Jo's mouth.

'I mean, did you actually look?' She tapped both her eyes, FBI style and aimed her two fingers back at Alexis. 'Or are you in your own "I don't give a shi— er ... *shoot* about anyone" bubble?'

'Well. I couldn't exactly miss you – little Miss Bloody Perfect – on *my* bike!' Alexis cracked the window down a fraction. 'What are you doing here?'

Quelled momentarily by guilt at the 'my bike' reminder, Jo retorted, 'What's it got to do with you?' But she paddled the heavy bike backwards, letting Alexis out.

Squeezing exaggeratedly out of the meagre space Jo had allowed her, Alexis looked down her nose.

'You and your ... your *shorts* can stay away from Ed,' she said, adjusting her figure hugging dress.

My *shorts*? Jo looked down at the garments, mystified.

'He's going to ask me to marry him any day now, and all this will be mine. His family's loaded. Loaded. The old man won't be around for long – even after you and your ... your Miss Hero thing,' Alexis spluttered, 'and Ed will take over.' A small, self-satisfied smirk spread across her face. 'Think of all the Jimmy Choos I'll be able to buy.'

'Hey, Liam!' Ed said, appearing behind Jo. He high-fived the little boy, still perched on his tag-along, and nodded at Jo. 'Lot of noise going on out here. What's up?'

'She said you were loaded,' said Liam, pointing at Alexis. 'What does loaded mean?'

'I didn't! He's lying!' Alexis frowned.

'I'm not lying!' Liam squealed. 'She did say! She did!'

'Actually, we're tenants,' Ed said, shoving his hands into the pockets of his jeans.

'Tenants?' screeched Alexis. 'What are you talking about?'

'We rent it,' Ed spoke patiently, as if he was explaining to a foreigner. Jo almost felt sorry for Alexis, as her expression collapsed. Almost.

'But ...' she stuttered. 'My mum said your family were rolling in it!'

Ed shrugged, holding his hands palm up.

'Rolling in what?' Liam said. Jo shook her head warningly at him.

'You mean … you really are just a … a … bike mechanic?' Alexis shuddered, her eyes wide. 'A grease monkey?'

Ed looked down, scuffing his feet in the gravel.

'Ugh!' Alexis moaned. 'I can't believe I've wasted so much time on you. And I can't bloody stand motorbikes! All that grease and oil! You are so dumped,' she finished, her eyes glittering. 'I'm getting my stuff.' She stomped into the cottage. 'Loser!' she tossed over her shoulder, wobbling on her six-inch heels.

'Well,' said Ed, standing beside Jo and watching Alexis navigate the cobbled path. 'That could have been awkward.'

'Could have been?' Jo stared at him. 'You mean it wasn't?'

Ed chewed his lip. 'She beat me to it,' he said. 'I was just waiting for the right moment. We were getting to the end anyway.'

'Oh? Why – nothing to do with …?' The words spilled out. She gulped, clamping her lips together, her heart jumping, her body betraying her will. She was still standing across the bike, with Liam in his grandstand seat watching events unfold as if it was the TV. Ed crooked his head at her and she looked away, fearing that her thoughts would be written all across her face. Frowning, she said, 'She didn't seem to think so. She thought you were about to propose.'

'Yeah. I caught that bit. I think it was more about the idea of money than real *lurve*.' Ed made a simpering face, placed his hands together praying style and slanted them under his chin. Liam snorted with laughter, even though he couldn't possibly have understood what they were talking about.

'I think it was more about her Jimmy Choo collection, if you ask me.' Jo hurried to help the little boy off his bike. 'We're not stopping. We just popped over to—'

'We bringed you a fruit cake, Ed,' said Liam, importantly. 'Can I get it out, Mummy?'

'Brought,' corrected Jo. 'Yes. Be careful not to drop it!'

'Wow, thank you!' Ed bent to take the foil wrapped parcel, proffered by Liam like one of the Three Kings. 'Did you help to make it?'

Liam nodded with his whole body. 'It's to say thank you for the eggs, Mummy said.'

'You're very welcome.' Ed nodded. 'But you didn't have to. I'm the one in your debt.'

Jo seemed glued into place, held by his gaze.

'How's your dad doing?' she managed, finally.

Ed's mouth drew a straight line. 'They're stabilising him and still deciding about surgery options. He'll be in for a while, I reckon.'

Jo didn't know what to say. Everything sounded like a superficial platitude.

'Wow,' she said at last. 'Lots to think about.'

'Mmm, I should say.' Ed's eyebrows rose and fell in acknowledgement. 'But at least he's still with us. Want a cuppa? I'd better go and check on ...' He nodded at the open door of the cottage.

'Hah. In case she's stealing your family heirlooms,' Jo deadpanned. 'Look, it's obviously not a good time, we'll go.'

'No!' Ed almost shouted. 'No. She'll be gone in a minute. She didn't have that much stuff here. I'd like you to stay. Would you like some juice, Liam?'

Talk about blackmail. Jo's anger with Alexis fizzled out as the girl appeared at the door, her make-up smeared, carrying a couple of bulging bin liners. She shook them in Jo's face.

'At least you can't "borrow" my stuff any more either!' she shouted. 'My clothes, my bike and now my boyfriend. Bitch!'

Jo stood, unmoved. She'd been called worse.

'I don't need a boyfriend,' she stated.

'*Whatev*,' snarled Alexis. 'Well, you're bloody welcome to him. The most boring, stinking boyfriend I've ever had!' She marched to her car.

'But she still wanted to marry me,' murmured Ed, his face impassive.

'Oily, stinky, greasy, boring and broke,' Jo said, out of the side of her mouth, watching Alexis heave her bin liners into the boot. 'Not much of a catch then.' Her grin slanted up her face.

Alexis slammed her door, reversed and took off in a spray of gravel.

'There'll be more gravel left now she's not visiting,' observed Ed. 'Look, it's a lovely evening – want to come down to the beach? Make sandcastles? Maybe have chips and ice cream or something?'

'Can we, Mummy?' Liam made puppy dog eyes.

Jo hesitated, torn between wanting to go and not looking as if she was available to slot into Alexis's freshly vacated spot. Or maybe he was just being friendly? Yeah right ... if that kiss that her body still remembered was anything to go by ...

His proximity loosened her resolve in every way.

'It's a school night,' she said, weakly. 'And Liam's had his tea ...' *And I don't have a penny on me for chips and ice cream!*

'Aww!' Liam looked crushed. She made a decision.

'Oh, okay,' she said. 'As long as we're back before Liam's bedtime.'

It was a matter of moments before he was in the driving seat and they were bowling – at a sedate pace with due respect to Liam's dodgy gastric system – towards one of Gower's southern beaches.

'Are we going to Caswell Bay?' Jo asked, watching the

scenery pass, her eyes alight with enthusiasm. 'It's my favourite beach.'

It was his favourite too. Smaller than some of the others, it was more of a cove than a huge windswept beach, with rock pools and surf and sand, perfect for kite flying and sandcastles. Ed owned all the necessary accoutrements for those activities and more, and seeing his eagerness to hunt them out of his garage, Jo had laughed that they were going as much for his benefit as theirs. She was probably right, and Ed was glad that he'd suggested the little trip. It was a welcome break from the stale air of the hospital. The sun was beginning to lower but it was still warm – a perfect spring evening.

She let out a happy sigh as Ed turned into the huge car park across the road to the beach.

'Alright?' he said, tipping his head towards her.

'I love it here,' she said.

'Can we build a sandcastle?' Liam was round-eyed with excitement. 'With a moat?' He sniffed the air. 'Can I have chips? Please, Mummy?'

Ed smiled at the little boy's energy, watching Jo keeping a tight grip of his hand as he jogged on the spot, eyes on the sea. He pulled a bag of beach toys out of the boot and locked up.

'I bet I can build a bigger sandcastle than you two!' Jo yelled, grabbing the hood of Liam's jacket and checking the traffic as they crossed the road. Her long, toned legs loped over the packed sand towards the sea, and Ed jogged behind with his burden of buckets, spades and paper flags.

She looked like an Instagram photograph, he thought, with the sea breeze whipping her dark hair into curls, teasing it free of its ponytail and catching the light. Liam's little legs thundered in pursuit and she slowed down, skipping in circles to let him catch up. Ed booted a brightly-coloured plastic football towards her, and she ran for it as he galloped in front, scooping a giggling Liam to swing from his outstretched arms.

'Get it, Liam!' he whooped, holding the little boy over the ball like a Subbuteo player and aiming a kick with him. Liam missed hopelessly, and Jo stepped in neatly, swiping the ball from beneath them and dribbling it towards the sea.

'Oi!' yelled Ed. 'Referee!'

Jo turned and flicked the ball up, caught it on her knee and juggled it on alternate knees for a few moments before lobbing it gently to her son.

Liam took a mighty swipe, missed the ball and tumbled backwards. Ed saw his face start to crumple as Jo ran over to him and swept him straight up.

'And here comes David Liam Beckham, mightiest footie warrior of the twenty-first century,' she intoned, TV presenter style. 'And despite massive injuries, he carries on without so much as a single complaint.' She 'pretend-cheered,' and planted a big kiss on his pink cheeks before setting him down. 'Okay, big guy?'

'A bit ouchy.' He nodded. 'Sandcastles now, please.'

Jo sat him on the sand, pulled off his shoes and socks and rolled up his jeans. He held his hand out for a bucket and spade, and zoomed towards the wet sand.

'I'm making a moat!'

'Don't go in the sea!' shouted Jo.

'I won't!' Liam's voice came back, ragged by the wind.

'You're pretty nifty with that football,' Ed said, falling into step as they jogged in Liam's little footprints.

'Hidden depths, me,' Jo said.

'I get the impression there's a lot more to you than meets the eye.'

'Me? Nah,' Jo said, quickly. 'What you see is what you get. Last one to the sea's a big fat pollock,' she shouted, lengthening her stride and pumping her arms.

Ed was slow off the mark, transfixed by her muscular bottom as she flew across the beach. He beat her, but only just. Bent over, he gulped for air, as Liam excavated industrial quantities of sand at his feet.

'You need to get a push bike instead of that old jalopy of yours,' Jo said, grinning at him. She threw him a spade. 'Come on, let's do Liam proud with a sand palace to beat all sand palaces.'

'It's a *castle*, Mummy,' said Liam, from behind a spray of sand. 'And you're standing in my moat.'

Ed laughed. 'You have ace comic timing, young man!'

Hot salty chips eaten out of a paper bag had never tasted so good. They sat with their backs against sun-warmed rocks and blew on their fingers, dangling the long chips in the air to cool them before burning their tongues on them anyway.

'I sort of forget about coming here,' Ed said, watching the sun slip behind the navy blue cliffs in a bath of apricot and pink streaked with purple. 'Thanks for reminding me.'

'No, thank *you*, it's been a lovely outing.' Jo jumped suddenly as Liam's ice cream plopped onto her warm bare knee and tumbled messily down her shin before sinking into the sand.

'Li-am!' she began, and they both turned to see the little boy's head nodding, his pudgy hand outstretched and smeared with ice cream. '*Aw*, bless,' she said, holding her chips between her knees as she reached into her pockets, bringing out a little packet of baby wipes.

'*Oops*.' Ed hunkered forward, taking a wipe and blotting the creamy blobs off her skin as she attended to Liam. Her smooth warm skin sent a wave of heat through him and he hurriedly scrubbed the wipe away in case she thought he was being a bit fresh.

'Sorry, Jo. I've worn the little guy out.' He had forgotten just how quickly small children tired, now that Daisy was so much older.

'It's been lovely. We've really enjoyed it.' Snuggling a slightly cleaner Liam onto her lap, Jo blew on a chip before popping it into her mouth. 'Thanks, Ed.'

'*FangyouwEd*,' Liam mumbled, leaning against her, his eyes tight shut. 'S'lovely.'

'You're welcome, mate.' Finishing the last of his chips, Ed groaned as he pushed himself upright and dropped his greasy chip wrapper into a bin, lifting his knees exaggeratedly.

'God, I thought I was fit!'

'Kids are better than any gym!' Jo laughed. 'I'll loan him to you.'

'Any time.' Ed nodded. 'Are you finishing those chips?'

'Too right!' Jo turned her body away, shielding the chips from his questing fingers. 'I'm going to need some chip fuelled energy tomorrow, cycling this young man up the hills! He'll be good for nothing.'

'Sorry. Too much?'

'Nah. He's tough. And nearly five now.' She looked down at her almost asleep son, ice cream faintly daubed around his smooth cheeks and rosebud mouth, and Ed swallowed at the pride he could see in her expression. Despite the chips, his stomach felt hollow.

Jo's eyelids slipped shut on the way home in the warm cab of Ed's truck. She took a deep breath to wake herself up. She couldn't remember feeling this relaxed, warm and ... yes, safe. It was him. Ed. He exuded an air of 'anything's possible', that she couldn't help being drawn to. But every time her heart opened a crack, a door in her mind clanged shut.

He might seem safe, but he wasn't. He was fickle. He couldn't be relied on ... and God knew, if she was going to have the boyfriend that she insisted she didn't need or want, it was going to be someone responsible and reliable. Ed would dump her once he was bored, and she'd be the one left heartbroken and lonely, not him, with his millions of mates and close family. Not to mention all his family money. There was no way he was a tenant in that cottage. He'd lied to give Alexis the elbow, that was obvious.

And there was the whole issue of her housing to consider. Was Ed … or at least, his family … her landlord? She had to know. Or did she? The more she thought about that conversation with Chad and Beryl, the more she worried that Chad was pulling a fast one. And what would that mean for her? She was almost startled to hear her own voice fill the silence in the cab as her cottage came into view.

'What's this all about, Ed?'

He flicked her a startled look.

'What do you want it to be about?' he said, a half smile playing around his mouth. She pressed her lips together but the words escaped.

'You're not "just a grease monkey", are you?'

'I should think not!' Ed said, smiling. 'Bike restoration is a skilled job!'

'I meant,' Jo pushed on, despite her inner voice screaming at her to stop talking *now*, 'Alexis wasn't completely wrong, was she?'

Ed was silent.

'Beryl told me that your family are her landlords.'

He chewed his lip, checking his mirror as he pulled over outside the cottage.

'And,' Jo gulped – *better to be leading the charge than cannon fodder* – 'and she thinks that your family own Seagull Cottage too.' She couldn't bring herself to say 'my house'. She needed to distance herself. 'Do you?'

'I don't have anything to do with that side of the business.'

Concentrating on parking, Ed shook his head. 'I never have. That's always been Dad's thing.'

'But …' Jo paused. She'd gone far enough. He didn't know. And now she'd alerted him and he might just make an effort to look it up. And she might be out on her ear. Might lose the house … with its leaky bathroom, mouldy ceilings, ancient kitchen and … fabulous garden, allotment, sea track …

Why couldn't she just keep her big mouth shut? Cross with herself, she blurted,

'Well, if it *is* yours – your family's, whatever – you should all be ashamed of yourselves, leaving an old man to live in it! It's barely habitable! There's mould on all the ceilings upstairs! It's only because Liam and I are so fit that we haven't come down with something!'

'An old man?' Ed frowned at her in confusion, his hands drumming the steering wheel.

'Yes! The old man who lived there before me! He's in a nursing home … didn't you know?'

'I don't know what you're talking about …' Ed lifted his hands, frowning. 'Dad runs the lets. It's not my business.'

'Yeah. You said. Maybe it should be.' Was it a fair comment? Her mouth seemed to have bypassed her brain, in its usual way. She was in self-destruct mode – as if she was giving him permission to retaliate. As if she didn't deserve whatever it was he was offering and so she was pushing him away before he could wreak havoc on her careful life. It was mad. Irrational.

The tension was broken by Liam clattering awake, blinking and mewing like a kitten.

'What?' he mumbled, bleary.

'Time for bed, baby.' Jo attempted a smile, but was sure it was a ghastly grimace. She was so angry. With herself, with Ed, with her situation … everything. It had been a wonderful evening, and she'd ruined it. Her and her big mouth.

Now she'd be worrying and waiting for the eviction notice. It all made sense, didn't it, just as she'd always suspected, if she was honest with herself. Chad was a fake landlord, subletting his father's rented house, trying for a fast buck at her expense. The nerve of the man! And trying to make it seem as if he was doing her a favour, the sleazebag.

She sighed. Better start looking around for accommodation. Goodbye allotment, hello window box. If she was lucky. She sniffed back the impending tears. Nothing to be gained by feeling sorry for herself.

Ed stood lifting and dropping his hands as she awkwardly hefted the grumbling and half-asleep little boy out of the truck. The skin on her legs goose-pimpled and she shivered.

'Okay,' he said. She couldn't see his expression in the dusk. 'Right then. See you.'

Hating herself, she marched into the cold, dark cottage, and clicked the front door shut with all the intention of a fully charged slam.

Chapter Twelve

Ed and his mum had long run out of things to say, and sat silently in the cramped, dimly lit space either side of Griff and his beeping, hissing bed, as the air mattress inflated and deflated like a living, breathing thing. The staff arrived, checked the monitors and drips and bags, nodded a smile at them and moved onto the next patient. He was tired just watching their constant rounds. They waited to see what the consultant would advise today.

'Mum,' he hesitated for a moment, then, 'Seagull Cottage. Opposite the sea track ... do you know it?'

Lyn frowned thoughtfully. 'Seagull Cottage ... isn't that old Merve?'

'Merve the *Sweeeeeerrrrve* ...' Griff's long, low murmur took them both by surprise. His eyes were still closed, his mouth slightly open. If they hadn't both heard it, Ed would've thought he was dreaming. His dad was listening to them.

Staring at his father in astonishment, he met his mother's eye and smiled. As Griff's announcement of Merve the Swerrrrve echoed round his brain, the smile became a grin, and suddenly the pair of them were convulsed with silent, helpless laughter.

'Merve the *Sweeerrrve* ...' mimicked Ed under his breath, his shoulders shaking with mirth. He squeezed his father's hand gently, careful to avoid the drip. 'Morning, Dad. You always did know how to make an entrance, you old bugger.'

Wiping her eyes, his mother stooped over the bed and kissed Griff on the cheek, pushing back his shock of white hair.

'Morning, my lovely,' she told him, a smile in her voice. 'Good to have you back. Now stop eavesdropping on us and get some sleep.' Settling back into the chair, she turned back to Ed. 'So … Seagull Cottage? Merve?'

With difficulty, Ed suppressed the powerful urge to burst into childish giggles again, plucked a tissue from the box near the bed and blew his nose. His voice was squeaky when he spoke.

'Yes. Only it's not Merve …' His body shuddered with laughter. God, he'd never be able to say the name Merve again at this rate. Whatever was wrong with him? Get a grip, man. 'It's Jo. She's living there.'

'Is she a relative of … Merve's?' His mother grinned at him, knowingly, her eyebrows raised. He'd always been a shocking giggler under stress, collapsing into inappropriate mirth in churches and solemn occasions.

'I don't think so. I'm not entirely sure.'

'Does she have family locally?'

Ed shook his head. 'No. Her family were all killed in a car crash.'

Lyn sat back, shaking her head. 'Goodness, that's tragic. Poor girl.'

'As far as I know, she's on her own. Single mum.'

'You like her.' It wasn't a question. His mum always could see right through him.

'I do. She's … different.' *And beautiful. And passionate.*

'What she did … for your dad. That's pretty special. Not many people can do that.' Lyn nodded, her eyes tearing up. Years of nursing had made her a tough nut to crack, Ed knew.

'She *is* pretty special. She tore a strip off me the other day.'

'Oh? Doesn't sound like your usual type of girl …' Lyn regarded him, her head cocked.

Ed made a rueful face. 'She's not.'

'I'd like to meet her. Tell her thank you.'

'I asked her if I could give her something to say thank you, the other day, when I nipped home?' Ed smiled as he remembered. 'She said she wanted some manure for the allotment.'

Lyn's eyebrows rose in astonishment.

'I think we can do better than that!'

'That's what I said. Anyway. It got me thinking ...' Ed sat up straight. He'd been mulling it over since Jo had ripped into him, and he'd realised that his father had let things slide. How many other of their properties were in need of attention? 'It's time I took over the business. Give Dad a proper retirement.'

Lyn nodded thoughtfully. 'Yes. Good idea.'

'I need to go and visit Merve the Swerve first. And find out who Jo's "landlord" is.'

Chapter Thirteen

The letter that Jo was dreading appeared on the doormat along with the dark clouds that morning several days after that evening on the beach with Ed. Liam toyed with his breakfast as she turned the hand-delivered envelope marked Griffiths Associates over and over.

Hand delivered. The final insult. If it was good news, wouldn't Ed have called with it? Or had she totally ruined their fragile friendship with her outburst? She hadn't seen or heard from him since, and she hadn't felt brave enough to contact him directly, telling herself that he had a lot to deal with, hospital visiting and everything.

Was this it then? Goodbye Seagull Cottage? Gulping back her fears, she looked at the rain lashing against the kitchen window, put the envelope on the table and went to collect their waterproofs from the hook in the hallway.

'Why can't we have a car like everyone else?' grouched Liam, picking up on her mood.

Tight-lipped and heavy hearted, Jo zipped him into his bright waterproofs, and wished they did too. She would have to return the electric bike too, just as she'd fallen in love with it. Collecting her backpack from the back of the kitchen chair, she stuffed the letter into it, taking satisfaction in crumpling the thick envelope. She needed to be with someone when she read it. She couldn't face it alone.

It burned through her rucksack as she cycled through the saturated roads to the café after dropping Liam off. Acknowledging that the mountain bike was so much better at coping with the gravel-strewn roads than her elderly road bike, she nevertheless cursed ever having met Ed. This might never have happened. She could have dealt with the sleazy landlord. Eventually. She swore hideously, head down, her tears mingling with the slashing downpour.

Arriving bedraggled and wan at the café, Richard put a steaming mug of coffee in front of her.

'You've got ten minutes before the hordes arrive, sheltering from the rain,' he warned her. 'Get this down you.'

Jo burst into tears.

'What? It's only a cup of coffee!' Richard looked stricken. He handed her a roll of blue paper towel, and she tore a sheet off and blew her nose on it. Dragging the envelope out of her dripping rucksack, she flapped it at Richard.

'I can't bear to open it,' she stuttered with a fresh burst of tears. 'It's an eviction notice. It has to be.' Hiccups punctuated her explanation of her last conversation with Ed.

Slitting the top of the envelope with a table knife, Richard unfolded the letter as Jo blew her nose vigorously.

'Your phone's ringing,' he said.

She fished the phone out of her bag and pressed accept without looking at the screen.

'So ... have you decided where you're going to live?' Ed said.

'How could you, Ed?' yelled Jo, in a choking sob. 'After what I did for you!'

'Jo ... no ... listen,' Richard held his hand up, waving the letter under her nose. 'It's good news! Look! Read it!'

'What?' Jo sniffed. Rubbing at her tear-swollen eyes she squinted at the printed word.

'Give me the phone a minute.' Richard reached a hand out, and spoke into it. 'Hi, Ed ... get back to you in a minute ... not quite herself this morning ...'

Flattening the paper, Jo read and re-read the letter with growing incredulity.

'Give me that phone,' she instructed into Richard's wide grin. Taking a big gulp of her coffee and blowing her nose again, she pressed Return Call.

'Ed!' she yelled. 'I'm so sorry … I feel like a complete fool. Thank you! I'll get back to you a bit later, okay?'

'*Phew,*' Ed said, in her ear, 'you had me worried for a minute! Speak to you later.'

Slumping back in her chair, arms hanging loosely, Jo blinked at Richard.

'Blimey,' she said, shaking her head slowly. 'Helluva week this is turning out to be. I *am* moving out, but for a …'

'… total re-furb!' said Richard, still grinning at her. 'Only what you deserve, of course.'

'Did you know his family own half the Gower?'

'*Mmm.*' Richard collected their mugs. 'You saved the life of the most influential man on Gower, and you wonder why people want to interview you …'

'I'm beginning to understand that.' Jo looked up with the glimmer of a smile. 'Anyway. Can't sit around here being famous and amazing and all that. Work to do!'

She leapt up, feeling more energised than she had in a very long time. Every customer that morning was treated to an especially dazzling smile.

She was flustered to find Ed sitting at a table in his trademark leather jacket, after the lunchtime rush.

'Thought I'd meet you here. Wondered, like, if you might want a lift,' he said, watching her carefully as if she was a wild animal of uncertain temperament. 'Discuss what happens next, maybe.'

'Oh, Ed.' Blushing to the roots of her hair, she stared down at him. 'I'm so sorry. I was awful … I shouldn't have said those things.'

Ed held up a hand. 'Oh, you should have,' he said. 'It was a wake-up call, trust me.'

'And what about my, my "other" landlord?' She'd been thinking about him all morning.

'Chad Evans? Hah.' He snorted a laugh and then looked serious. 'Any chance of a coffee? I'm as dry as a bone, after sitting in that hospital.'

Returning with his usual coffee, plus a glass of water, she said, 'How is Griff?'

'Getting along okay. He'll probably be home in a few days.' He drank thirstily, emptying the glass. 'I went to visit Merve.'

'Oh! How is *he*?'

'Physically, he's strong as an ox. Mentally though ...' Ed's mouth compressed into a sad smile. 'He thought I was dad.'

'You are similar though.'

'*Hmm*. So I drew a bit of a blank about who your "landlord" was – and I'm sitting there drinking tea with Merve while he's rambling on about the old days, and Beryl shows up!'

'*Ok-aaay ...*'

'And she mentioned about seeing one of Merve's sons on the doorstep, the other day, looking a bit shifty. Chad Evans.'

Jo looked down and fiddled with her apron, her hands suddenly clammy.

'I did a bit of digging, and found his address, and went to have a little chat with him. And it turns out that Chad was charging you more than Merve's rent, and pocketing the rest. Merve was on a peppercorn rent after all these years. I remember him always being one of these gruff types who always refuses help, and I suppose as Dad became unwell, he kind of slipped under the radar. It's not good, and on Dad's behalf, I apologise.'

'Chad Evans.' Jo shuddered. 'Cheeky git. He kept threatening to put the rent up. And if I couldn't pay, then he gave me other "options". He's a sleazebag.' Her hand leapt to her throat. 'He's not going to start coming round and giving me grief because I dobbed him in, is he?'

'First of all, you didn't "dob him in", and secondly, he wouldn't bloody dare, as I reported him to the police. Ash says they'll probably decide it's a civil matter, because we aren't out of pocket, but Evans doesn't know that. I told him if I see him within a mile of Seagull Cottage I'll get an injunction out against him.' He took a deep breath and sent her a serious look. 'And if he ever comes anywhere near you, and threatens you or Liam in any way, then you ring me and I will knock his bloody block off, slimy fat weasel that he is.'

Jo blinked as he sat up straight, his shoulders wide, his long fingers spread. He was so mild and jokey, it was a bit of a shock to see him in, well, adult mode. Her stomach fluttered. It definitely suited him.

He sat forward and sipped his coffee. 'Although I almost feel sorry for him. If he turned up at your doorstep right now, I think he'd suffer a worse fate at your hands.'

Jo laughed, hurrying away to serve a customer with a spring in her step. Her shoulders felt loose and relaxed, and the fact that she noticed it spoke volumes. Ed had finished his coffee by the time she returned. Flicking the menu out of its holder on the table, he flipped it in his hands restlessly.

'I'm taking over the family business.'

'The motorbikes?' That didn't surprise her. Richard had filled her in on The Vintage Bike Palace, Griff's business where Ed worked. Where she'd thought he was 'just a mechanic'.

'The property rentals.' He slotted the menu back into position and met her eyes. 'And that brings me to a tricky issue.'

'What?' Jo felt her hands grow sticky again. This was it, wasn't it? The rent would be going up. She'd never be able to afford an increase. Unless it was only a very small one. And after doing the house up, it wouldn't be small, surely. How had she not thought about that earlier? What a fool she'd been, skipping around as if she didn't have a care in the world. She tried to recall the wording on the letter. No mention of the rent at all …

'What?' said Ed.

'What's the tricky issue?' She willed her voice to remain steady but it betrayed her.

'Ah … well, the houses are tied … they're for agricultural tenancy.'

Mounting dread churned Jo's stomach.

'Yes, Beryl told me.'

'Well, it goes back to the days when we farmed. But we don't now … we own land but it's all contracted out or goes with the farms, so it's not entirely relevant to Seagull Cottage. Basically,' he paused and Jo wanted to shake the words out of him, 'basically, you have to be employed by Griffiths Associates to fulfil the terms of the tenancy.'

'But I'm not employed by—'

'No, I know. But,' Ed cleared his throat, 'Mum and I have decided that Dad won't be going back to work at the Bike Palace – at least, not full time.' Ed drew in the little puddle of condensation on the table left by the glass and Jo bit back a nervous urge to wipe it up. 'I mean, he can come and play with things if he wants to, but no pressure. He's been doing it already for far too long, and—'

'Ed, stop!' Jo interrupted, frowning, her mind racing ahead and trying to join the dots. Her, working at the Vintage Bike Palace? 'I don't know a thing about motorbikes!' She paused and then added, 'I don't even like them! Sorry …'

Ed laughed. 'I know. But I really need a hand in the office. Everything's gone to pot … honestly, there's stuff everywhere!' He ran a hand through his thick black hair, leaving it sticking up in all directions. It suited him, she thought, irrelevantly, as Ed continued, the words tumbling over themselves now. 'I've got people leaving phone messages about bikes they need servicing, the bike school has left bikes that need repairing … and Dad and I had booked a stand at a Classic Bike Show which is coming up soon. I hate to admit it, but I can't manage on my own.'

He rubbed his hands across his face and Jo could see how tired he was. 'What do you reckon? I mean, you're good with junk – not that our stuff is junk, and your stuff isn't junk either,' he corrected himself hurriedly, 'but y'know, it's old, and you seem to like old stuff …' He trailed off, fixing her with an imploring expression.

'Is this by way of an interview?' Jo checked there were no customers waiting at the counter or tables to be cleared and slid into a seat at the table. 'How many hours are you talking about?' she continued, leaning forward, elbows on the table. 'Am I still working here? Or for you? What about Liam? And how much?'

'Oh God, I dunno!' Ed grimaced. 'I've never had to do this before!'

'How about you take me to your office, and show me what needs doing,' Jo said. 'I'll get my coat.'

Ed, Jo and Liam stood in the chilly and cluttered Vintage Bike Palace. Seeing the building suddenly through Jo's eyes, Ed rushed round, putting on lights, ripping bikini-girl posters off the walls and straightening the teetering piles of paper and magazines on the counter.

'Wow!' said Liam, struggling to escape his mother's tight grip. 'Cool!'

Ed watched as Jo stared around her, sniffing the air. It stank of old oil. The flickering fluorescent tubes cast a dismal, cold light over the random bits of engine and tyres everywhere. It really was a mess. He'd never noticed before.

'My bike …' She pointed at her disabled bicycle, leaning against the wall with boxes propping up its rear forks, chain drooping from the front chainwheel. He'd had no time to do anything with it, he recalled guiltily. 'How on earth do you find anything in here?' She swivelled, taking it all in.

'It's not usually this cold,' Ed said, plugging in an elderly oil filled radiator that gave off an instant smell of burning dust. 'But I haven't been in much, and the main heating is off, well … it's the old oil that we burn and, that's that smell and—'

'How do you invoice?' Jo said, cutting across him. 'That's the stuff you want me to do, right?'

'We just write things in here,' Ed pulled a printed book towards him and turned it to show her, 'and then the customer pays, and it goes in here.' He rattled the tin box he'd retrieved from beneath the counter.

'You don't use a computer? Or a till?'

Ed shook his head. 'I've got a laptop. But we don't use it for sales or anything.' He caught himself shuffling his feet and stopped.

'Do you accept cards?'

'Nope. Cash or cheques.'

'And how do you do your accounts?'

Ed shrugged. 'Everything goes in there.' He indicated a grubby pile of paper in a box with a Harley chainwheel on top.

'What's that for?' Jo leaned over to inspect it.

'Stops everything flying away when the doors are open.'

'Oh … er, so what will you be wanting me to do? The accounts, VAT, invoicing, reminders, website – do you *have* a website?'

Ed's jaw dropped. 'How do you know about all this stuff?'

'I did a business degree.'

'I've barely got a GCSE!' Ed admitted. 'Have you really got a degree?'

'Yes. No. Sort of,' said Jo, with a shrug that once again

made him wonder about her and all the things he didn't yet know. 'I used to work in a shop.' Her eyes travelled about her. 'You could do with a better system, I reckon.'

'It is a bit of a mess, I suppose.' Ed surveyed the building as if he'd never seen it before.

'Does it always look like this? I'm not the tidiest person in the world but it makes my car boot finds look positively finicky!'

'Not this bad,' Ed admitted. 'But it'll tidy up! Liam can help, can't you, mate?' He grinned at the little boy's eager nod.

'Liam isn't going anywhere near this lot.' Jo ignored her son's pouting lip. 'Something might fall on him! Is that,' she pointed, 'a hole in the floor there?'

Ed followed her gaze. 'It's the old inspection pit. But it's got scaffolding boards over it!'

'And you want my son to help you ...' She glared at him.

'We can put a ladder in there, in case the little guy falls in.' Ed's mouth tweaked upwards. 'It'll be fine.' His smile slipped as he saw her face. 'I was just joki— I didn't mean ... Sorry.'

'So ...' Jo stepped carefully towards the back of the counter. 'If I don't work here, I don't get the tenancy. Is that about it?'

'You make it sound like blackmail! It's only because the terms of the lease say that...'

Jo took a deep breath. 'Right then. Let's get tidying, and you can explain what everything is as we go along.'

'What ... now?'

'Do you want me to do this or not?'

'Only I was meant to be going to the pub with my mates ...'

'You're going to be late then. There's one last thing.'

'What's that?' Ed looked wary.

'No funny stuff. I'm not one of your bimbos, not an Alexis replacement or anything like that. We're friends, and that's it. Okay?'

'Okay,' said Ed, slowly. Just friends? His reputation had gone before him. It had to be that, because there had been no doubting her response to that kiss. She wasn't giving him any time to mull it over.

'Right. Do you have a kettle in this, this ...' she flung an arm out '... man cave?'

'We've got a rest room back here, with a kettle and a microwave.' Ed pointed.

'God, I don't know if I really want to look back there. Is it tidier than here?'

'Er ... there might be some unwashed cups and stuff.'

Jo rolled her eyes.

'Sounds like I'd better start in there then. I've brought some sandwiches for Liam. And some cake.' Ed's eyes brightened, and she added, 'Liam gets his tea now ... you have to earn it!' A glimmer of a smile lightened her face. 'And we're going to need music. Loud music!' she shouted over her shoulder as she made her way towards the rest room.

'*Eww!*' She yelled over the radio. 'And rubber gloves!'

A few hours later The Vintage Bike Palace, whilst not exactly living up to its stately aspirations, was now at least a bit more organised, and Jo was satisfied that you could drink out of the mugs without getting botulism.

They'd agreed an hourly rate, that Ed would collect both of them after school and she'd work there for a couple of hours or so a day, on whatever days they agreed. Liam was ecstatic at the idea of 'having a job' there, as Ed had put it. He'd tirelessly sorted nuts and screws into jars that evening, whilst they'd scrubbed and sang. It was a tired little boy whose head nodded now, beside them on his car seat.

'So. We need to rehouse you while we gut Seagull Cottage and make it habitable,' Ed said.

'Yes. I read that.' *Eventually*, she thought guiltily, recalling her earlier outburst. Dear me. She really needed to think before she spoke. 'What are my options?'

'We could put you up in one of our empty rentals, we've got some little flats you could use ... but they're a bit of a distance for you to cycle,' Ed said, glancing across at her.

'I've got an idea,' said Jo. There was the allotment to think about, and so much *stuff* in the house – she couldn't imagine where it would all go if she had to move into a flat again.

It would be like the old days. A memory of carrying baby Liam, shopping and her bike up three flights of stairs flashed across her mind. She hadn't been able to put any of them down for fear of someone stealing them.

'Yep, me too.' He grinned. 'You and Liam could move in with me!'

Jo visualised his man-pad. A clutter free zone ... even his bike magazines had been stacked in a neat pile. Not a good idea. No. Not to mention the obvious implications ...

'No,' she said, firmly. She shook her head. 'You'd hate us inside a week, trust me. I'm messy, and Liam would make a den out of everything in your house.'

Ed pretended to muse, head on one side. His eyes flicked towards her. 'Could be fun ...'

'No.' She was immovable. 'But how about I have a caravan in the garden? There's bags of room, I'll still be able to cycle Liam to everything like I do now, and I can look after my allotment. You can pick up one of those static caravans quite cheaply ... and sell it on when I've moved back in. It's probably cheaper than putting me up in one of your rentals.'

'A caravan?' Ed looked aghast 'Won't you be cold?'

Jo laughed. 'Ed, the draught has been whistling through

the cracks in the windows for half a year now. I reckon a caravan would be quite cosy by comparison!'

'Oh. Is it really that bad?'

'Yes, but it was exactly what I needed, when I needed it.' She nodded. 'The place I was in before was *waaaaay* worse.'

'Right, I reckon we could manage that. You okay to move out as soon as we can get a caravan installed?'

'Hell yeah!' Jo's eyes shone bright with excitement. 'I should say. I'll start packing tonight!'

'Are you on speed or something?' Ed sent her an astonished glance. 'I am wrecked after clearing the Bike Palace tonight!'

'Hah … cycling and a small child. I told you, way better than any gym!' Jo laughed.

'I'm not going to be able to keep up with you, am I?' Ed crinkled his eyes at her. 'You're gonna be a slave driver when I'm at work, I know it!'

'Someone has to be!' Jo tutted, with a smile. 'You blokes turn feral without a woman around.'

'You've got a nerve, after admitting how messy you are!'

Parking outside the cottage, Ed switched off the engine and turned to her. Unbuckling the sleeping Liam, Jo avoided Ed's gaze. She was already regretting her decree of 'no funny stuff', as every nerve in her body wanted to have funny stuff with him that very minute. She steeled herself. It was for the best. This was about security. Long-term, and all that. She sighed silently. Ed fished in the inside pocket of his leather jacket, and brought out a small packet.

'This is for you,' he said, handing it to her. 'I thought I'd give it to you in person. Save any other misunderstandings.'

Jo fingered the white envelope. It was not too thick, not written on, no clues as to what it was.

'It won't bite!' Ed drummed the steering wheel. 'Open it!'

Eyeing him, she ripped it open and stared down at the

contents. It was a rent book. She opened it, scanning the information – her name, Seagull Cottage as the address, the Griffiths as the landlords, and blocks of legal looking jargon.

On the first page, though, was today's date and then in thick black pen across the next few pages, the words 'Nothing to Pay Until Further Notice'.

Her eyes misted over as she stared at the solid words and she couldn't stop a fat tear plopping onto the page. She wiped it away quickly. A warm, modern house, and financial security. It was like winning the lottery.

'Thank you.' She stared down at the little book, swallowing the lump in her throat with difficulty. An enormous grin spread across her face.

'I can afford my own manure now.'

Chapter Fourteen

The caravan arrived on the back of an enormous lorry, and was winched over the hedge and into place on levelling blocks. Jo kept a tight hold of Liam's little hand as he twisted and hopped with excitement.

'Ooh, there's lovely for you, my duck!' Beryl said from beside her. 'Maybe they'll be doing mine next!'

Jo waggled her head and made a non-committal mumble. Ed had told her not to tell Beryl about their 'arrangement', 'Otherwise she'll be on at me for free rent!' he'd said. She liked Beryl and hated adding to her battery of lies, but agreed that it was just between them.

'We're camping!' Liam piped up.

'You are indeed, young man,' Beryl agreed. 'Very cosy.' Her eyes swept the length and breadth of the caravan, now jockeying into position. 'Very, very cosy … you're surely not having all your possessions in there with you now, are you?'

'Hah, no.' Jo laughed. 'There wouldn't be room for us! I've got a storage facility for all my junk, thank goodness.'

'What will you be doing about showering and all that, the two of you?' Her voice lowered to a prim mime when she got to 'showering and all that', and Jo suppressed a giggle.

'There'll be all mod cons, Beryl,' Jo assured her, crossing her fingers that there would be.

'Well,' said Beryl, pursing her lips. 'If you need to use my bathroom, then just let me know.'

'Oh, that's really nice of you, Beryl!'

'And I'll make sure that I have my rent adjusted accordingly,' Beryl continued, without missing a beat, her eyes crinkling to show that she was joking. Possibly. 'What's that thing for?' She pointed at what looked like a flat pack shed that was being offloaded behind the house.

Jo shrugged. 'I have no idea. Maybe it's a potting shed – that would be fab!'

'It's probably your outside toilet,' Beryl said, with a wink. 'With a dug out hole inside.'

'*Ew*,' said Jo.

'Wow!' said Liam.

With the caravan levelled and steadied, Jo slumped finally that evening into the surprisingly cosy corner sofa. Liam snored gently in his little bedroom despite his complaint that it was still light out, and Jo jumped at the light tap on the door. It echoed around the caravan. Feeling weirdly vulnerable in a way she never had in the cottage, she peered nervously out of the window, then hurried to open the door.

'Beryl! Are you okay?'

'Oh goodness me, yes, I'm fine,' Beryl said, peering wide-eyed around Jo. 'I brought you this. It's sort of a housewarming, isn't it?' She held up a bottle of Prosecco. 'Have you got glasses? I can go and get some if you like?'

She seemed determined to come in and, to her own surprise, Jo stood back and let her.

'*Er*, thank you,' she said.

'*Ooh*,' said Beryl, staring round the little kitchen area. 'It's like a Wendy house, isn't it? Like being on a ship ... you know, a place for everything and everything in its place!'

'I suppose so ...'

'Right, so ... let's get this open, shall we?'

'I don't really drink, Beryl ...'

'Well, no point wasting it, I'll have to drink it,' Beryl said, opening a cupboard and pulling out a tumbler with a worn Spider-Man logo on. 'I've brought some nibbles, too!'

She produced a giant pack of Kettle Chips and a gigantic bar of Dairy Milk chocolate.

'Now then,' she said, groaning a little as she bent to acquaint herself with the interiors of Jo's cupboards. 'Let's find a bowl for these.'

It seemed rude not to help. Jo reached up and brought down a rather lovely porcelain bowl she'd found at yet another car boot sale or other and, after a rummage, a small wine glass, which she swapped with Beryl's tumbler.

'If you don't mind, lovely,' Beryl said, ripping open the crisps and pouring them into the bowl, 'I'll hang on to the tumbler. I can get more in it. Seeing as you're not a drinker …'

She bustled towards the lounge area at the end of the caravan, tugged a couple of cushions up and, like magic, a table appeared.

Jo was astonished. 'How did you know about that?'

'Me and my Les used to go on holiday in one of these. They're all the same inside. Or thereabouts. Now then, tea towel. Let's get this fizz open!'

Her mouth an O, Jo spectated as Beryl popped the cork on the Prosecco, obediently holding her little glass beneath the froth as Beryl whooped and giggled.

'Iechyd da! Cheers!'

'Iechyd da,' repeated Jo. It sounded like yacky dar, meant good health or cheers and it was one of the growing number of Welsh phrases she'd picked up. She sipped the wine and jumped as the bubbles fizzed up her nose. It was pleasantly dry – not at all the sickly sweet drink she had been expecting.

'Like it?' Beryl's blue eyes sparkled. She'd already emptied half her glass, Jo noticed. 'You'll be onto a bigger glass soon, I'm betting.'

Setting the glass down and pushing it out of reach, Jo took a few crisps and sat back.

'So, tell me about these holidays with Les,' she said.

Everyone liked to talk about themselves. Which meant she didn't have to talk about herself.

'Oh, it was fun when the boys were little. Like your Liam. All they need is a bit of sand, and sunshine, and some sea to paddle in and they're happy. Not like the kids today with all their phones and gadgets.' She tutted, and drained her glass. 'But it's abroad for me now Les's gone. That's where I've been this winter. You can't beat it. Proper sunshine and sangria for me and the girls!'

'Girls?' prompted Jo.

'Golden Girls, we are!' Beryl gurgled with laughter. 'I went to school with most of them. All our men gone ... now it's time to have some proper fun!'

'Are your sons close by?' Jo knew nothing about her neighbour, she realised. Her determination to stand on her own two feet brought with it isolation and she'd missed this kind of casual camaraderie. She'd have to be careful with the alcohol though. It was a tongue loosener.

'Not really.' Beryl's face fell a little. 'Still, roots and wings, eh? One's in Australia, and the other's in America. Clever lads, both of them. My grandson works for NASA, you know!'

'Wow!' Jo didn't have to pretend to be impressed. 'Have you visited them?'

'Ah.' Beryl topped up their glasses. 'Drink up, girl. I'll be finishing this off by myself at this rate. Les wouldn't fly, bless him. And it's a bloomin' long boat ride. So I've not managed Australia yet, but I've been to the States – I go for Christmas every year, you know.' She glowed with pride. 'Lovely house they have. Huge.'

'Wouldn't you like to move over there?'

'Uh-huh.' Beryl shook her head, thrusting a handful of crisps into her mouth. 'I couldn't take the heat, ducks. I love Wales. I know it rains all the bloody time like, but it's what

I'm used to.' She laughed, dusting off the little bits of crisps that littered her bosom. 'You been abroad?'

'Nope.' Jo took a longer sip. Mm. It really was rather nice. Beryl topped her glass up immediately. 'Can't afford it.' She shrugged.

'Where would you go, if you had the choice?'

'Greece,' Jo said straightaway. She sighed. 'I'd love to see all those colours ... the way they paint everything in that blue. And bright geraniums in old paint pots and olive trees and donkeys ...' She looked down into her glass. 'Oh. My wine seems to have evaporated!'

'It does that,' giggled Beryl, the perfect host. 'But it's Sunday tomorrow! Nothing to get up for, is there? Have a lie in for once. Too busy you are, by half!'

'I was going to do a barn sale tomorrow,' Jo murmured half-heartedly.

Beryl didn't seem to have heard her. Jo wondered if she'd said it aloud or whether it was just in her head. She should have a cup of peppermint tea or something now. Stop drinking.

'Greece is lovely. And the food, *mmm!* But Spain is nice. And Portugal.' Beryl had begun to tick them off on her fingers. 'Turkey, Italy ... now that was an interesting holiday. Those eye-tie men. *Oooh!*'

Jo listened as Beryl recounted tales of her holidays. She really was very entertaining.

'In fact, I've still got some of that Limoncello from our skiing holiday. Shall we try it?'

Jo didn't know if she was more surprised that Beryl skied, or that she seemed to be unaffected by the almost entire bottle of Prosecco as she skipped out of the caravan, returning a moment later with several strangely shaped bottles, each containing a luridly coloured liquid, and some tiny shot glasses.

Beryl slopped a little into a glass and held it out. 'Try this one. We bought this from a little shop in the mountains …' She rambled on about snow-capped mountains and hunky ski guides and Jo curled up on the sofa, sipped the liqueur and listened sleepily.

She watched her hand reach out for more chocolate and was surprised to see that it had all gone. 'And this one's an orange liqueur,' Beryl was saying. 'Oranges and lemons, said the bells of Saint something or other,' she sang, wiping the spilled drips off her sleeve. 'It's ever so nice with a bit of lemonade or something. Have you got any lemonade?'

'No,' Jo said, with an effort. 'We have council house pop. Tap water.'

'Just have to neck it down straight then.'

''Kay.' Jo giggled. 'S'luvly,' she slurred, taking a big gulp. '*Yuk*.'

'I remember,' said Beryl, twirling her shot glass, 'when we were …'

Jo leaned back, warm and cosy, and let Beryl's tale wash over her.

'*Mummee!* I wee-ed the bed!'

Jo winced as the shrill voice pierced her head. Who was that? Who'd wee-ed the bed? She turned over, buried her head into the pillow and reached for the duvet. Several seconds of patting around her body revealed that there was no duvet. Must've fallen off, she thought, blearily.

'*Mummeee!* My pyjamas are all wet! And my bed's all wet. I'm co-old. Get *uuuuup!*'

Jo felt the solid and damp little body slump on her at the same time that a hammer drill started up in her head.

Chapter Fifteen

Fuzzy memories returned of last night. Oh God. Easing herself painfully to a sitting position with Liam still draped miserably over her, she blinked around at her bedroom. Except – she wasn't in her bedroom. She was still in the lounge of the caravan. Her pillow was one of the velour cushions. And what was that on the other side – a pile of clothes ... oh God. Was that Beryl?

A memory of last night seeped back into her brain, and she groaned. This was exactly why she didn't drink. First, it meant you felt like shit the next day. Second, it meant you felt like shit the next day. And you had a wide-awake ... and bed wetting four-year-old to deal with. She couldn't blame Liam. For all she knew, he'd woken in the night and called her and she, drunken bum that she'd been, hadn't heard him. She scrubbed her palms up and down her cheeks, feeling ashamed. First night in the van, she was bladdered, Beryl had passed out, and her bright, intelligent four-year-old had wet the bed. Way to go. Trailer trash, that's what she was.

What had she told Beryl about herself last night? Beryl had been very free with information that Jo would never have guessed at. Even feeling as ropey as she did, she couldn't help smiling at Beryl's energy and zest for life. Even if she had got Jo paralytic on slops of leftover holiday liqueurs. She clutched her head, remembering swigging recklessly one sickly drink after the other. *Bleurgh*.

Staggering upright with Liam attached to her like a damp koala, Jo ricocheted off the walls on the way to Liam's tiny bedroom, noticing the chaos of bottles in the kitchen. Dragging the bedding into the passageway, she pulled open a drawer and found clean pants and T-shirt for Liam.

'Okay, Super Spidey,' she said, dredging up the still sober inner Mum that was in there somewhere, 'nice hot shower for you and clean clothes. We'll pop this lot in the washing machine, and Bob's yer uncle. Okay?'

Liam nodded, a dubious expression on his face. 'Who's Bob?' he asked, shivering.

Jo turned on the shower, peering at the controls and deciding which way was hot. The water remained stubbornly freezing no matter which way she turned.

'Damn!' she muttered, after a couple of frustrating minutes that left her nearly as damp as her son from the spray. 'I mean … durn … Liam. I'll boil a kettle. We'll pretend we're camping.' *We blimmin' well ARE camping! And I'm not enjoying it. Do people actually do this for holidays? For fun?*

'A miners wash,' said Beryl, from the sofa at the front of the caravan. 'Miners used to wash at the sink.'

'Beryl.' Water overflowed from the kettle spout and squirted Jo and Liam. 'There's no hot water, for some reason. Perhaps you should go home now.' Setting the kettle to boil, she blotted her sopping jeans with a tea towel.

'Have you turned on the gas?'

'Gas?' A faint memory returned from the overwhelming list of instructions Jo had read on the document accompanying delivery of the caravan.

'Yes, and the auxiliary pump? And turned on the water heater?'

Jo's head was thumping. Defeated, she slumped onto the nearest seat, yelping as it gave way and deposited her upside down in its cavernous innards.

'Lots of storage in these vans.' Beryl snorted with laughter, and held out a helping hand. 'I think you just found some under that seat.'

'Bloody … er … flipping thing!' Jo bent and slammed the

seat cushion back into position, then lifted it and peered underneath. Beryl was right, of course. There was a gaping hole that ran beneath the entire sofa length. She thought of all the spare bedding in black bin liners, buried under a mountain of other black bin liners in a temporary storage shed in the garden, and sighed. Most of that would have fitted under the sofas. No worries … she'd have this lot washed and dried in no time. She was too late for the barn sale anyway.

'*Mummeeee*,' whined Liam. 'I'm co-old … and I'm *hungreeeeeee*!'

'Right.' Jo leapt up, ignoring the stabbing headache. It was her own fault, all this, and she'd just have to sort it. 'Let's get you washed and changed first. And then we'll sort some breakfast.' She filled the kettle and switched it on.

'Do you want bacon sandwiches?' said Beryl.

'Yes, please!' Liam's voice was muffled behind the pyjama top his mother was currently pulling over his head, but there was no doubting his enthusiasm. Jo swallowed down the bitter bile rising in her throat at the thought of food.

'Not for me, thanks.' Her voice sounded quavery and weak. How did Beryl manage to look so perky?

'Bit of toast and some tea for you, Jo?'

Flannelling a shivering Liam with hot water and soap, Jo nodded. 'Thanks, Beryl, that's really kind of you. Shall we come over to you?'

'Go on then.' Beryl nodded. Halfway out of the door, she said, 'Bring that mucky washing over too as you've no hot water yet. Can't see the lad suffer.'

He wasn't suffering until you turned up and got me smashed! At once Jo felt ashamed. It wasn't Beryl's fault she'd got drunk. She hadn't *had* to drink. She could have stuck to her guns and had a cup of tea and left Beryl to it. Kneeling, she gathered Liam in the bath towel and pulled him towards her, planting a kiss on his scowl.

'Sorry, sweetie,' she told him. 'Mummy just needs an aspirin and everything will be fine. Now, where did I put all your clean clothes?'

Beryl's cottage was a revelation. The exact reverse of Seagull Cottage, except that it was warm, decorated, and had no leaks and draughty gaps. Jo was dazzled by the bright red sofa set against a brilliant jade green wall. She took in the mosaic lamps and colourful throws and rugs, guessing that they came from Beryl's trips abroad. Beside Beryl, she felt like a dowdy sparrow.

'Will our house look like this, Mummy?'

'Nearly, sweetie,' she promised, thinking that she would have to spruce up her furniture if it wasn't to look absolutely grotty in the newly-painted house. Goodness. She was becoming house-proud. She sent a silent Thank You to Ed and his family – thanks to them, she'd have some spare cash to make the house that bit nicer. It was the first time she'd lived anywhere long enough to feel proud of it. Had she done the right thing, fending Ed off the way she had? It was too late to worry about that – it was done now. She'd made the decision to protect herself and Liam. If Ed acted true to form and dumped her, she'd be faced with working with her ex-boyfriend, and landlord. No. Best to be friends. She didn't need a boyfriend, she repeated the well worn mantra.

Unshowered, she felt grubby and like a homeless person, pitching up with the urine soaked bedding. Beryl, commanding operations like the matriarch she clearly was, was grilling bacon by the stove and directing Liam to set the table. Hawk-eyed for sharp knives that he might decide to investigate, Jo stuffed the duvet cover and sheet into the smart washing machine and followed Beryl's instructions to locate the correct programme.

Her plans for the day dissolved. Liam wanted to play board games and Beryl was only too pleased to oblige.

'My grandsons are such a long way away,' she explained. 'This reminds me of them.'

'Can I leave him with you while I go and sort out the van?' Jo asked. 'Would you mind?'

Their engrossed concentration as they assembled Buckaroo was answer enough. 'You know where I am if you need me,' she said, reluctant to leave the calm, homely warmth of Beryl's kitchen. 'Okay, I'm going …'

Back in the van, she boiled the kettle for a strong coffee, unearthed the folder of instructions, and set about familiarising herself with what was going to be her home for the next month or more.

An hour or so later, her head felt clearer, the van was cleaner and fresher, Liam's bed waited to be remade and the space beneath the sofas was occupied by spare towels and duvets, lugged out of the storage shed in the garden.

She was thrilled when hot water cascaded from the showerhead and kitchen tap. Restlessly, she stared round at the pristine van, shut the door on it and marched round to her neighbour.

'Oh, we were just about to watch *Finding Nemo*,' Beryl said. 'I thought you might want a bit of a nap or something, after last night?'

'Oh!' *What a cheek! She was fine!* 'Actually, I was thinking of going for a quick bike ride. There's a barn sale I wanted to check out. Might still be stuff there …'

'You mentioned that last night.' Beryl slotted the DVD into the side of the huge television. 'Go on then. We'll be fine!'

Jo hesitated. Liam was already wearing a goggle-eyed expression, and the film hadn't even started.

'Sorry, Beryl … I meant, Liam is coming with me.'

'*Aww-wwer!*' Liam slumped in his seat with an injured expression. 'I want to watch the fi-ilm!' Tears started in his eyes.

'It's a lovely day, Liam,' Jo glanced outside at the beginnings of the faint mizzle and continued hurriedly before he noticed, 'and I need your help to find all the best bargains. And you can take a torch!'

Liam brightened as Beryl sagged.

'When we come back, perhaps Beryl will let you watch *Finding Nemo*?'

'Maybe Beryl wants to come to the barn sale too!' Liam said.

Jo felt guilty. It hadn't even occurred to her that she might want to go too.

'Goodness me, no thank you!' Beryl said. 'Poking around in a grotty old barn – all those cobwebs and giant spiders? I've seen *American Pickers* on Sky. That's as close as I'm getting to the inside of a barn.' She shuddered. 'You come back later and we can watch a bit of Nemo. You'll be nice and exercised then. Not so fidgety.' She winked up at Jo, who realised belatedly that it was Beryl who was in need of that nap. She smiled gratefully back at the older lady, as Liam heaved himself sorrowfully off the sofa.

Chapter Sixteen

The bike was her saviour, Jo thought, as she powered through the remains of her hangover. It wasn't a terrific day weather-wise but the lack of tourists this early in the season kept the roads quiet – if a little greasy – and both Jo and Liam were wearing decent waterproofs.

The rhythmic exercise soothed her anxious brain, and she noticed herself smiling as she gazed over the hedges into fields grazed by placid sheep and energetic late lambs.

Her mind turned towards thinking through what needed to be done at The Vintage Bike Palace. She was surprised to find that she rather enjoyed working there, despite her sneer when she'd first laid eyes on Ed's bike. It *had* just run over her beloved pushbike, though, she told herself.

The vintage motorcycles owed more than a passing glance to a pedal cycle, with their stripped down frames and spoked wheels. Although she was still drawn to the purity of the bicycle, with its burnished and machined parts shaped to perfectly perform the task of aiding propulsion by legwork only, she was beginning to understand the attraction of the engineering that had moved bicycles into motor-bicycles. They felt familiar – and she was getting to know their inner parts, although Ed had taken a huge and schoolboy delight in asking her to google a Left Handed Screwdriver for a Bonneville, and to ring up a parts company asking for a Long Stand.

Liam loved it in there, importantly finding things and sorting without ever getting bored, and she and Ed worked well as a team. There was more though. It reminded her of her dad. Different engine bits, but same smell, same disarray. Same blokey posters, same casual indifference to hygiene. He would have loved it in there.

She could imagine him, sorting, drawing around the shapes of tools to hang up, 'so you always know where to find them for next time' he used to tell her. It had been her job, identifying those tools and putting them exactly in place.

Her eyes prickled from the sharp memory. She could almost smell his rolling tobacco. Liam loved the Bike Palace already, always keen to get in amongst it all. Definitely got his granddad's genes. Sort of. However that worked.

The barn sale was still open, although there were no other buyers there.

'Okay to have a look round?' Jo asked the frazzled looking woman who seemed to be in charge.

'Go ahead,' she said. 'It's my father-in-law's place. Well, my late father-in-law, you know what I mean. So much stuff! And muggins here ends up having to sort it, as usual.' She sighed and Jo made a sympathetic noise. 'I'll just get my coat and I'll show you round.'

'No running off,' Jo told Liam as they waited. 'We're not far from the road, okay?'

Liam made an exaggerated affirmation. 'I *know*, Mummy!'

Grinning at his little boy version of a teenager, Jo rummaged in her rucksack and handed over his torch, loving his delight.

'See what you can find!'

It was a shame that these old farmhouses ended up like this, she thought. This could be wonderful with the right people in – there was land, a lovely farmhouse with lots of light, and all these barns would make brilliant workshops, she thought longingly.

'This is the biggest barn,' said the woman, who introduced herself as Kirsty.

'I'm looking for small stuff – chairs, small tables, stools, chests, lamps – anything I can upcycle,' Jo explained.

'Good luck. I don't think there's much left after this

morning, but everything must go. We are selling and have nowhere to store anything.'

She was right. There wasn't much left except big ugly pieces of furniture that Jo couldn't do anything with, particularly with no storage room at the moment.

When she came out, the drizzle had become a downpour, and Kirsty shivered.

'Does it always rain here?' she said, picking daintily across the slippery mud and knee high weeds to the next barn.

Jo sympathised with her. It was just how she'd felt when she'd first arrived in Wales. 'It does feel like that, doesn't it?' She laughed. 'It's lovely when the sun shines though. Where are you from?'

'Guildford. My husband has had to work,' said Kirsty. 'You?'

'London.' Jo avoided the husband question. 'Been here for a few years now. Couldn't go back to London now. I love it here.'

'It's so … rural though, isn't it? I couldn't cope with it. Thank God Costa's has arrived. I couldn't even get a decent coffee when we used to visit.' She made a face, and Jo was compelled to tell her about the Art Café, overlooking the golden sands, with fantastic coffee, legendary cakes and great artwork. 'Our boss is being filmed for a TV series at the moment,' she finished, proudly.

'I'll make a point of dropping in,' promised Kirsty, with a smile.

The second barn was crammed with what looked like old tools, sacks and an ancient tractor.

'Find me, Mummy!'

'One, two, three … ready or not, here I come!' said Jo, poking about amongst the paraphernalia, brushing aside ancient cobwebs and the tangles of briar which entwined the archaic contents into a living chain. Kirsty perched near the entrance on an upturned box and watched them.

'You're not looking!' Liam peeped from behind the tractor, flashing the torch beam into her face.

'Ow, Liam! What have I told you about doing that?' Jo blinked. 'Shine it on *things*, not in people's eyes!'

'You didn't even look for me.' Liam trudged out, all misery.

'I promise to look in the next one,' said Jo. 'There *is* a next one, isn't there?' she asked Kirsty.

'Sadly, yes.' Kirsty hauled herself to her feet. 'Last one.'

Liam skipped away as soon as the door was creaked open.

'No hiding underneath anything!' warned Jo, staring around her and tracking his progress by the flicker of his torch beam. A few tatty and broken farm tools, some machinery and tractor type body parts – too modern to have any interest or value.

Kirsty perched fastidiously on an elderly chaise longue.

'Sorry,' she wrapped her arms around her. 'Said there wasn't much left.'

Jo considered the chaise longue longingly before dismissing it. No storage space. And nowhere to even do it up, for now.

'Come on, Liam,' she called. 'Let's go.'

Her voice echoed back, with not even a giggle from Liam to indicate that he was hiding from her.

'Li-am!' She squinted into the dim recesses. 'Okay … one two three here I come!' She made her way over towards the back of the barn.

'Am I warm?' She peeped behind a steel cabinet … nothing. She stared round … there wasn't really anywhere else that a little boy could hide. Was there? Why hadn't she kept an eye on him? He was only four. She always treated him older than his years because he was so bright. Oh God, supposing something had happened to him?

'Liam!' she shouted, beginning to panic. 'Liam! Come out now, please. Liam!'

Kirsty got up, alerted by Jo's tone. 'Liam!' she called. 'Come out, there's a good boy!'

Jo had squeezed to the back of the barn, frantically searching beneath anything that looked as if it might have toppled over. She felt sick.

'LIAM!' she shrieked. 'Where are you?'

'I'm in here, Mummy!' came a small, muffled voice.

Jo stared in the direction of the voice. She could see nothing.

'Liam …' she shouted, mustering the remaining shred of her nerves, 'I can't see you. You have to hide where I can see you.' It sounded illogical even as she said it.

There was a creak, a door opened at the back of the barn, and slowly, like a cheap horror film, the small body appeared around it. Jo heaved a sigh of relief.

'Where's that?' said Kirsty. 'I didn't know there was anywhere behind there!'

'Mummy,' Liam beckoned her urgently. 'I've found something!' His eyes were like saucers. 'You have to see it!'

'What is it?' Jo's heart sank. A dead dog? An equally dead cat? He was fascinated by dead things, and she'd often had to overcome her revulsion to inspect his finds.

'Follow me!' Liam stage whispered, and pulled the little door open just far enough for him to squeeze in. Jo followed, and after a brief hesitation, so did Kirsty.

Had she not been working in the Vintage Bike Palace, Jo wouldn't have recognised it for what it was.

'Clever boy!' She caught his arm and steadied the torch onto his find.

Tucked away behind the main barn, was a space about eight feet deep, extending along most of its width. Propped up against the wall, and partly wrapped in tarpaulin, was the main frame of a vintage motorbike, together with a heavily rusted pair of wire spoked wheels, complete with tyres.

Jo fished her phone from beneath her waterproofs, clicked off a few shots and texted them to Ed. She ran her hands over the engine parts. They were smoothly engineered, which indicated that it had been a quality machine. But the thing that would tell her what make it was – the petrol tank – was missing.

Her phone pinged.

Where is it?

She texted her location.

Coming over now

'Is this for sale?' Jo said to Kirsty.

'It's all for sale,' Kirsty said, with a shrug.

'Before I start digging it all out – how much?' Jo stared around the cavernous space. What else might there be lurking in there? 'I've got a tenner in my pocket …'

'I think it's worth more than a tenner!'

'You've got more than that, Mummy.' Liam looked up at Kirsty, nodding earnestly. 'She's got more than that.'

'There's no tank,' Jo said to Kirsty, raising her eyebrows at Liam. 'It's impossible to tell what it is.'

'What do you want it for?' Kirsty looked curious.

Jo paused for only an instant. 'I want to give it to a friend. To say thank you.'

'You want to give this pile of junk as a thank you?'

'As a project.' She felt her cheeks heat despite her attempt at nonchalance. 'A do-er upper.'

'Just a friend?' Kirsty said, knowingly.

'Yes,' said Jo. 'He's been very good to us. And I wanted to say thank you.'

Kirsty considered. 'Right. Whatever you can find … it's yours for a hundred quid.'

'Fifty.'

'Seventy-five.'

'Sixty.'

'Fine. I'm freezing. I'll be in the house. Happy hunting!'

Ed was there in a flash. He spotted Jo and Liam outside the barn, guarding their treasure and could hardly believe that Jo had thought of this. Not a single other woman he knew, apart from his mum, would have considered it worth even a passing mention.

'I finded it!' Liam jigged with excitement, urging him on.

'Well done, Liam!' Ed shook the little boy's hand. 'What is it?'

'It might be nothing,' Jo warned, leading the way inside.

'And you've dragged me out of a nice warm pub for nothing!' Ed teased.

'You hadn't been drinking, had you?' Jo said. 'I should've asked!' She opened a little hidden door.

'No, lucky for you!' Ed chuckled in her footsteps, craning his neck to see what they'd found. 'I've got something for you too. It's on it's way.' He could hardly wait to see Liam's face when he delivered his surprise.

'What is it?'

'Aha!'

Pulling a torch out of his pocket, he stooped over the bike frame, rubbing at the rusted areas in silence, his heart starting to beat faster as each part revealed itself. Jo waited beside him in silence, watching him.

'Sorry, I don't know anything, not really. It's probably just a common old bike, isn't it? Just left to rust in a barn.'

'Hang on. Let's just see if we can find the rest of it, and the petrol tank.' Ed squeezed further into the back of the barn, picking over the rubble with all the finesse of an archaeologist, selecting an object and turning it over in his hands, before placing it carefully to one side.

'Is this a bit?' Liam held up a screw.

'No, mate.' Ed considered it seriously. 'Put it in here for

now.' He searched around him and handed the little boy a plastic dish. 'Keep looking though.'

The three of them hunted for the tank. Ed sifted through the piles of machinery. At regular intervals, Liam rushed over with a find, demanding of Ed, 'Is this anything?' He studied each proffering on the small upturned palm, occasionally declaring it a rim rod or a brake pin or other such invented term. Everything went in the dish 'for safekeeping'. Liam was delighted, grubbing around with his little torch.

The afternoon was darkening with the onset of heavier rain, and still no tank.

'We've looked everywhere. There's no tank. Or if there is, it's not in here.' Ed raked dusty fingers through hair draped with cobwebs.

'Hah. You look just like your dad all of a sudden!' Jo laughed. 'So why would someone take the tank off?'

Ed shrugged. 'Loads of reasons. It had a leak, or needed repairing, who knows.'

'Is it still worth buying?' she said, her eyes anxious.

'Oh aye. I'd need to properly look at it, but I reckon you've got yourself a nice little collectors piece there.'

'It's yours now.' She shoved her hands into her jacket pocket, looking embarrassed. 'I bought it.'

'Mummy's spent all her money on it,' Liam told him. 'For you. To say thank you.'

'Wow.'

'Liam!' Jo cleared her throat. 'Yes. I've bought it. Well, I've agreed a price …'

'How much?'

'Sixty quid.'

'Really? Thank you – both of you!' Ed swallowed, feeling suddenly quite choked up. It was possibly the best thing anyone had ever bought him. It wasn't the value, so much, although once restored that would be considerable, it was the fact that she knew that he would want it. Barn finds like this were the stuff of magazine articles.

'Only, er, you'll have to pay for some of it yourself.' She looked up at him, sideways. 'Got twenty quid handy?'

'Bargain!' He fished the notes out of his wallet and handed them to her. It was all he could do not to kiss her. Even so, he paused to watch her neat figure as she marched, straight-backed, over to the farmhouse to pay her dues.

Jo looked around her with interest as she ducked into the low doorway which opened into a huge kitchen, complete with dresser, and a vast open range. It was like stepping back in time. She wouldn't have been surprised to see a smelly Labrador snoring beside the fireside. Kirsty followed her gaze around the room.

'Ghastly, isn't it? It needs a total re-furb – fabulous new kitchen, get rid of all this junk. Big job for someone though. They'd probably just gut the place. That's what I'd do.'

Jo blinked. How sad. All this history and life, just to be wiped away. She hoped that the new owner would have a bit more sensitivity. 'We couldn't find the tank in the barn anywhere,' she said, handing over the cash. 'Ed thinks it may well be in the house, perhaps it went for repair or something, if you could keep an eye out for it?'

'Sure.' Kirsty held out the lined pad and Jo wrote her mobile number down. 'There's still the attic to do. I expect that'll be my job, too.'

'Good luck. If you need a hand, let me know. I'll bring over some coffee and cake.'

'Thanks!' Kirsty said in surprise. 'I might just do that!' She came out with Jo to watch the bits of bike being ferried away. Hauling it out to the truck, along with all the boxes of bits and pieces was back breaking, and they were just in time to see Ed arching his back and stretching. Liam conveyed his finds with deep reverence.

'It's blimmin freezing out here!' Kirsty grumbled.

'Give us a hand carrying this lot,' puffed Ed. 'You'll soon warm up.'

Kirsty sent Jo a twitch of her eyebrows that said, unmistakably, '*Phwoar*'.

'*Friend?*' she mouthed and Jo nodded firmly, hiding a smile. Ed had that effect on every single woman who came into contact with him.

Kirsty peered into the tatty boxes as they were loaded.

'I think I should be paying you for getting rid of this lot!'

'Don't let me stop you!' Jo laughed. 'I'll be back with that coffee and cake soonest, to play hunt the tank. Bye!'

Swinging into Ed's cab, with Liam between them, all of them covered in cobwebs and grime, the pickup full of her bicycle and vintage motorbike, Jo felt like a family of wheeler dealer gypsies, and grinned, waving out of the window to Kirsty, incongruous in the steady rain in her office coat.

Chapter Seventeen

'That farmhouse is amazing,' Jo told him, in the truck. 'Enormous kitchen – like the whole of Seagull Cottage downstairs!'

'*Mmm*, there are still those original stone Gower cottages around.'

'I never even thought about decorating or doing somewhere up before. I was just grateful for somewhere to live. But since you've started on the cottage – I don't know, you've made me think. I can see the possibilities.'

Ed sent her a sidelong glance. 'What would you do in that farmhouse then?'

'Well, I do love all 'that old stuff", as you pointed out before,' Jo said, slowly. 'Kirsty was all about a new owner gutting it and modernising, and I can see that it would need a decent cooker and fridge and all that … but,' she blew out, 'there was a fabulous big wooden table and dresser. And rocking chair. I expect it's all sold now though. That sort of stuff goes for a fortune.' She thought for a moment longer. 'And I really like those soft greys that you've got in your cottage. They'd look great with lighting to accentuate the exposed stonework …'

'… and a vintage motorbike, hung on the wall as a feature piece,' Ed added without missing a beat.

Jo laughed. 'Did you always want to fix bikes?' She yawned. Liam wasn't at all sleepy, Ed noticed, his bright eyes following scenery made mosaic by the rain-spattered windscreen. He could hardly believe that they'd found that bike. And he couldn't imagine a single one of his girlfriends ever considering buying it for him. Jo was one in a million. And she wasn't even his girlfriend. More's the pity. He'd agreed that they'd be 'friends' but oh, he was finding it difficult. Seeing her most days, getting to know her, and little Liam, who was just adorable … he swallowed a sigh.

'I was always good with my hands …' he said, glancing sidelong at her. Predictably, she rolled her eyes. 'No, but,' he continued, grinning, 'I always liked fixing things. And Dad always had a project bike on the go.' He jerked his head towards the rear of the pickup. 'Just like that one! And he got me helping. Took my mind off …' he paused, not yet ready to dredge up his secrets '… things.'

Jo was silent for a moment. It was one of the things he liked most about her. She really did seem to listen to him. Not just yatter on for the sake of it.

'Things?' she prompted.

'I didn't do very well in school.' Ed blew out his cheeks. It was close enough to the truth. 'I messed about, and I paid for it.'

'I like my school,' said Liam, clearly listening to every word as usual.

'You're a very clever young man,' said Ed.

'You're clever,' Jo said to Ed. 'Exams don't mean everything.'

'I suppose. Anyway … Dad took early retirement and set up the Bike Palace and sort of funnelled me into it, straight from school. And there I've been ever since.'

'You like it though, don't you?'

'I think I do …' He sighed. 'But just lately … I've been wondering.' He swivelled his head and their eyes met just for a moment. 'I'm wondering if there isn't something more meaningful that I should be doing.'

Jo's brow creased. 'I know what you mean. I feel as if I'm kind of living day to day. Surviving. I wanted to be a teacher.'

'You'd be a lovely teacher, Mummy!'

'Yep, I reckon you'd have been a great teacher. What would you have taught?'

'Well, I would have liked to teach Primary. And maths.'

'*Eep!*' Ed said, grimacing. 'My utterly worst subject. I'm hopeless at maths.'

'I'm getting that impression from your paperwork.' Jo grinned.

'What is maths?' asked Liam.

'Counting.'

'I'm good at counting. And abc. A,B,C,D ...' He recited the alphabet at top speed.

'You are very clever. You're my little genie-mouse, you are.' Jo reached an arm round him and squeezed him.

'You've done that,' said Ed, nodding at Liam. 'Parenting. That's huge.'

'You've got loads of patience,' said Jo. 'You'd be a great dad.'

Ed remained silent, staring at the road ahead. He swallowed, struggling for something to say, some way of changing the subject.

'So how was the first night in the caravan?' he heard his voice, bright and forced.

'I weed the bed!' said Liam.

'Oh.'

'And Mummy had a party with Aunty Beryl! I could hear her laughing. Really loud.' Liam pouted, for all the world like a Victorian parent.

'My word,' said Ed, faintly. 'It sounds like quite a party. I'm sorry I missed it.' He was.

'You could come tonight,' said Liam. 'Couldn't he, Mummy? We can have another party. We could watch ... um ...' he thought for a moment '... your film!'

'I'm sure Ed has better things to do tonight than watch ... er ...'

'What?'

Liam was straight in. '*Mamma Mia!*'

'What's that then?'

'You don't know *Mamma Mia!*?' squealed Liam. 'Mummy! He doesn't—'

'Do you still want a job in the Vintage Bike Palace, young man?' said Ed, gravely.

Liam clutched his sides, shrieking with laughter.

'Overtired,' murmured Jo with a smile.

'Obviously, I have to see this film. My education will not be complete, according to Sir Liam, without having seen it.'

'We're having pasta carbonara ... want to eat too? It's just a simple—'

'Fab! Shall we stop off for wine?' Ed couldn't imagine anything nicer than an evening with his two favourite people.

'No! No. No wine.' Jo shook her head.

'So that's a no to wine then.' Ed laughed.

They pulled up outside Seagull Cottage, and Jo left to unload the cycle and tag-along, which was being stored in the old porch. Jo was relieved that she'd had a cleaning spree earlier ... had it only been that morning? Her stomach was turning somersaults at the idea of entertaining Ed in the close confines of the caravan, but was sure that Liam would distract both of them.

'Welcome to my ... our ... er ... *your* ... humble abode!' she said, opening the door to him. 'Make yourself at home. I'm just going to nip over and tell Beryl we're back, she's probably wondering what happened to us.'

'Come and see my toys, Ed!' Liam tugged at his sleeve.

Jo left, remembering with a sigh that all of her son's bedding was currently in Beryl's washing machine. His bedroom probably looked like a refugee camp.

Beryl, bless her, had the duvet cover dried and folded, and

was reading the Sunday newspaper and knitting something vast, complicated and colourful.

'Thank you so much, Beryl!' said Jo, spotting the clean bedding.

'Blanket's in the tumble drier now,' said Beryl, following her pattern instructions through a pair of snazzy multicoloured glasses.

'And, er ... Ed's here. We're having a pasta carbonara tonight, early, and watching a film,' Jo said in a rush. 'Would you like to join us?'

The words sounded alien in her mouth yet it was strangely easy to invite everyone into the caravan, where it had never been easy at all in Seagull Cottage. The caravan felt temporary, and like a grown up Wendy house and Jo felt, for the first time in a very long time – settled. With extra money ... due to not paying rent and having an extra job.

'*Ooh*, that sounds lovely! Will you have enough food for two extras?' Beryl leapt up, discarding her knitting and peering into the biggest refrigerator Jo had ever seen. 'I've got garlic bread, some nice cheese, salad. How's that?'

'Beryl, you're a star. But you don't have to bring your own food, honestly.'

Ignoring her, Beryl shovelled her supplies into a wicker basket and scooped the dry washing under the other arm.

'I'll pop back for the rest,' Beryl said, ambiguously, just as Jo was covertly checking the basket for alcohol. She wasn't sure her liver could take another session like last night. 'I'm sure I've got a cheesecake in the freezer that we could have for pud. I do love a party!'

Rescuing Ed from the depths of the sofa storage which now contained the overflow of Liam's toys, and announcing Beryl's arrival, Jo took the DVD out of its box and slotted it into the back of the TV screen, which for once looked the right size for its surroundings.

'Singing is obligatory,' she asserted.

'*Ooh*, I love Abba, I do!' Beryl said.

Uncoiling from the sofa, Ed stood to greet them, and stretched, filling the entire space of the caravan, or so it seemed to Jo. 'Abba?' he said. 'Do you know all the words, Liam?'

Liam nodded with enthusiasm. 'Course I do!'

'Does everyone know this film except me?' said Ed, collapsing back onto the sofa.

'Yes!' they chorused, shushing him as the film began.

It really was like a party, Jo thought. She'd never had people round for dinner. She only just had enough plates ... all mismatched, as was the cutlery.

'Wow. This is a better oven than I've got in the house!' She switched it on for Beryl's garlic bread.

'For now,' Ed said, with a wink, from beneath a mountain of action toys.

'*Oops.*' Jo assembled the ingredients on the worktop. 'Porridge for breakfast tomorrow, Liam. That's all the eggs gone again!'

'Told you. Chickens are the way to go,' said Ed.

'We used to keep chickens,' said Beryl, a reminiscent smile on her face.

'We. Are. Not. Having. Chickens.'

'*Awwww!*' said Liam.

The food was simple but delicious, and plentiful despite Jo fretting that she hadn't made enough. There was something wonderful and spontaneous about sitting on sofas around the table at the front of the caravan. Liam was perched on two cushions, and had insisted on sitting beside Ed, his new best friend.

Jo wished she had some tea lights, to soften the dazzling spotlights, but the brilliantly enhanced colour palette of the film was casting its own glow. She wouldn't usually let Liam eat in front of the TV, but this felt like a special occasion.

'Is this like being on holiday?' Liam asked, beaming around at everyone and spooning pasta into his mouth.

'It is!' Jo reached across to wipe his face. 'This is our holiday! We have the seaside, sunshine – sometimes – a holiday caravan, and good friends.' She swallowed, looking round the table. 'What else could we possibly need?'

'Wine,' said Beryl.

'Ice cream!' said Liam.

They all looked at Ed.

'Nothing else at all,' he said, meeting Jo's gaze. 'This is perfect.'

Jo's heart stopped beating for a second in the silence that followed.

'Cheers!' Liam wrapped sticky fingers round the Spider-Man tumbler that Beryl had used the previous evening, and waved it. Jo glanced at Beryl. Where had he learned that, she wondered, as if she didn't know.

'Cheers!' They clinked glasses with him.

'This definitely needs a glass of wine,' Beryl said. 'I'll pop over and get it. Back in a mo.' She was up and gone before Jo could protest.

'There's no stopping her, is there?' Ed grinned.

'Aunty Beryl is The Flash,' said Liam, through a mouthful of pasta. 'Ooh, I love this bit!' He bobbed extravagantly to the music, spreading pasta sauce as Beryl burst back through the door loaded down with cheesecake, cream, Liam's washed and dried blanket – and wine.

Getting up to relieve Beryl of her load, Jo was astounded to notice how relaxed she felt and … at home. Safe. Not alone. It wasn't a sensation she was used to. Stealing a glance back at Ed, she was startled to see him looking back at her with a speculative expression. She rushed to make Liam's bed.

Passers-by might have been startled to hear the enthusiastic rendition of Abba's 'Super Trooper', which it turned out, even Ed knew. Jo was sure she could feel the van rocking as they all lent a hand washing and drying up to the music, turned up as loudly as the little set could manage.

Ed twirled Beryl around in the tiny lounge, and Liam demanded to be twirled too. Dishcloth in hand, Jo stepped back, telling herself she was content to spectate. *Just friends. No funny business.*

'Come on, Mummy!' Liam ran and clutched her hand, dragging her into the inner circle. 'Dance!'

The four of them linked arms in the confined space and swayed to the music, singing gustily. Jo smiled, looking round at them all. Beryl's cheeks were flushed from wine and exertion, Liam's ears were pink and his hair was damp, Ed was off-key and making the words up, but everyone looked happy.

Why had she never done this before?

The words of the songs seemed to have more resonance than ever, she thought, as she sang to 'Take a Chance on Me'. Should she take a chance? What was the worst that could happen, really? They could both have some fun … and if it didn't last, well, so what? They didn't have to fall out, did they?

The thoughts churned round her head, as the music stopped and they sank back onto the sofas to watch the final scenes.

'Has it finished?' Ed asked.

'*Noooo!*' Liam pinned him down, by now sitting not beside him, but on him, like a large and boisterous dog. 'This is the bestest bit!'

Ed pealed with laughter as Pierce Brosnan strutted on stage wearing a skin tight and spangled flare-bottomed suit and stacked heels.

'I'll never be able to watch him as James Bond ever again!' He put his hands over his eyes, and a giggling Liam prised his fingers apart. 'Honestly, he can't sing, he can't dance, whatever made him do this film?'

'I think he's lovely,' Beryl said, a dreamy smile on her face.

'I do too.' Jo chuckled at Ed's look of horror. 'Shows he doesn't take himself too seriously. Doesn't care what people think. A real man.'

The film faded out leaving Amanda Seyfried singing over the credits.

'Bedtime, Liam my lovely!'

'*Awwww*.' Liam's ears ... his tiredness barometer ... were bright pink. 'Can Ed read me a story?'

Jo's heart lurched. She should have foreseen this. As 'just friends', everything would be fine ... *She did not need a boyfriend*, she told herself, for the millionth time. Did she? 'I think that depends on Ed, sweetie.'

'I should go,' Ed said, to an even longer '*Awwww!*' from Liam. Jo struggled between disappointment and relief. If he was really boyfriend material, he would have stayed to read the story, wouldn't he? 'Thank you, Liam, for my motorbike. It is the best present I ever had.' He reached down and shook the little boy's hand. 'And I've been meaning to say, Jo, Mum wants to meet you. Is Thursday evening okay? For tea?'

'Er ... tea? Is that tea the drink, or tea the dinner?' Jo was gabbling she knew, but – meeting his mum? What was that about?

'Tea the dinner.'

'What about Liam?'

'Sorry, I can't babysit Thursday,' said Beryl, 'It's my Drone Club night.'

Jo's brain did a double take. Drone? As in the PG Wodehouse comedies she used to read as a little girl? Or …

'I didn't know you kept bees, Beryl!'

'I don't.' Beryl looked puzzled.

'Mum wants to meet Liam too,' Ed said.

'What am I supposed to wear?' Jo felt really flustered now.

'It's tea the dinner with my mum, not the Queen.'

Jo mentally walked through her wardrobe. Shorts for cycling, shorts for the beach, shorts for digging the allotment. Maybe Alexis had had a point about the shorts. A couple of baggy pairs of jeans. That was about it. She couldn't remember the last time she had to go somewhere smart. And if Ed's mum's house was anything like his, then it would be very smart.

'It's not an interview!' Ed shrugged. 'She just wants to say thank you.'

'You've already done that!' Jo gestured around the caravan and outside at the huge pile of manure that he had had delivered a few days earlier.

'You'll be working at the Bike Palace anyway … we'll leave a bit earlier to give you time to change and I'll come and collect you.' Ed nodded. 'Thanks for tonight. I really enjoyed it.' He bent and pecked her on the cheek, and then straightened up. 'Even if you've ruined James Bond for me. You will never, ever, catch me in an outfit like that. Ever.' He smiled round at them all. 'See you tomorrow. Goodnight!'

Chapter Eighteen

The caravan seemed empty when he'd gone, even though there were still three of them in there.

'What a nice young man,' said Beryl.

'*Mm*,' Jo said, non-committal, although her heart was banging like a drum after that chaste kiss on the cheek. 'Let's get your jim jams on, big boy, now you have a nice clean bed again.'

'Can Aunty Beryl read me a story?'

'That depends on Aunty Beryl,' said Jo. 'And on how quickly you get into your pyjamas and brush your teeth!'

Beryl poured herself another glass of wine and settled back. 'I'll still be here,' she said.

Once Liam was settled – which seemed to take an eternity – and Beryl had read him a story, Jo made herself a cup of peppermint tea and sat in the lounge opposite Beryl.

'So,' Beryl said. 'What are you going to wear? He's asked you to meet his mother! That's very telling …' She waggled her eyebrows and sipped her wine.

'It's not what you think. We're just … friends.'

Beryl peered at her over her glass and said nothing.

'I can't get involved with him, Beryl!'

'Who said anything about getting involved? Just shag him! Live a little!'

'Beryl!'

'What?' She shrugged. 'He obviously fancies you! No bloke is going to sit in a caravan with a kid crawling all over him and watch a chick film if they're not trying to get into your pants. I'm telling you now.'

'I've told him we can only be friends.'

'Well … un-tell him! For goodness' sakes, what's the problem?'

'He's not reliable. He's a commitment-phobe.'

'Say all the girls he's dumped … because he's just not into them?'

'I don't want Liam to get attached to him – and then he dumps me. And that means he's dumped Liam too. Plus, I work for him now. And Liam comes with me. It's too complicated.'

'Yes. I can see that.' Beryl picked her wine glass up and put it down, untouched. 'So you're going to just give up on it. In case it goes wrong. You can't use Liam as an excuse forever. They're not little for long. He'll be living his own life … and you'll be left on your own.'

'*Ouch*. I suppose. But,' Jo eyed Beryl's glass, and sipped her tea, 'there are other things.'

'Spill then.' Beryl got up and brought back the tiny wine glass from the night before. 'There's only a little bit left in the bottle. Go on. You look like you need it. I'm telling you, girl, my life would make your hair curl … not that it needs it!'

They laughed. Jo drained her teacup and stared at the wine in the little glass.

'If Ed knew about my life, he wouldn't want to be with me anyway.'

'He's no angel.'

'He thinks I am though.'

'Did you shoot someone?'

'No.'

'Well, how bad can it be?'

'Pretty bad.' Jo took a deep breath. 'My dad died when I was a teenager. Of a heart attack.'

'Ed told me that. He said it was a car crash.'

Ed had told her? Jo frowned and then shook her head. It didn't matter. 'He was driving.'

'I don't understand.' Beryl leaned forward. 'That wasn't your fault, was it?'

'Maybe not. Sort of. But I kind of went off the rails afterwards.'

Jo chewed her lip and stared at the carpet. It *had* been her fault. She would never stop feeling guilty about making her dad drive. And she'd been a prize bitch. More like her mother than she wanted to admit to.

'That doesn't surprise me. Death of a parent is shocking at any age, but to be that young. Didn't you tell Ed that they all died in the crash, including Liam's father?'

Jo raised her eyes, gazed unseeingly at Beryl and dully recited the line she'd used for so long. 'The crash is what killed my father ... and was the end of my family.' It still wasn't quite the truth, but it had been so long since Jo had actually said it out loud.

'O-kay,' said Beryl. 'Maybe we need more wine.'

'No. No wine.' Jo got up, putting a hand out to steady herself. 'I'll make some more tea. Do you want tea?'

'Got any coffee?'

'De-caff.' Jo slopped water into the kettle.

'It'll do. I can pretend.' Beryl stood up. 'Let me do it. You look more sloshed than I do, and you haven't drunk a drop.'

Sinking back onto the sofa, Jo hugged the warm mug into her lap.

'Don't feel you have to tell me anything, Jo, love.' Her neighbour tipped her head at her. 'But sometimes it helps to hear your own voice talking through it.'

Where to start? She'd only told some of this to the psychologists. Did she want to tell it all over again? And yet, somehow, the words seemed to be tumbling out of her mouth of their own accord.

'I never got on with my mum like I did with my dad.'

'Daddy's girl?'

Jo exhaled through her nose, a kind of sad laugh. She nodded. 'I should say. He used to fix things. Engines, that sort of thing. Always had a project on the go. I used to help him, in the garage. Only, the projects didn't always stay in the garage.' She laughed properly, remembering. 'They migrated into the kitchen, to be washed. And then seemed to spread themselves round the house. In boxes, and old towels.'

'I bet your mum loved that.'

Jo shook her head. 'Not a bit. There was that, plus the fact that Dad let me eat whatever I liked.' Jo smiled. 'And Mum didn't.'

'None of that sounds so terrible. Perfectly normal, if you ask me.'

Jo nodded. 'I guess. I was a plump child – always eating chocolate digestives in the garage with Dad. And I turned into a fat teenager. Mum thought I was gross.'

Beryl shook her head. 'And yet, look at you! There's not an ounce of flesh on you!'

'*Mm.*' Jo stared down at herself. 'Mum was always really thin, proper glam. Liked parties, going out, dressing up, that sort of thing.'

'And your dad didn't?'

'Got it in one. She couldn't understand why I'd rather be in the garage in overalls than getting dressed up. I know why now … it was camouflage. I didn't have to expose myself to ridicule … the fat girl.'

'Aw, puppy fat, they used to call that. But you look lovely now. You could knock spots off any model!' Beryl's smile was kind, but Jo couldn't accept the compliment.

'After Dad died, Mum …' she swallowed '… she brought a boyfriend round.'

'*Oh.* I suppose, people react to bereavement in different ways, and maybe your mum was lonely?'

'What, by replacing my dad straight away?'

'How soon?'

'I don't know … a couple of months?'

'Goodness.'

'Yeah. I didn't like him. He didn't think much of me either. I was horrible to him – and her. Cow … she must've picked him up from the pub or something. I reckon she was seeing him before Dad died. She was always in there, with her mates, all done up.'

'Bless you. That must've been very hard on you.'

Jo sucked air between her teeth, remembering. 'I went from top student – I'd always planned to go to uni – to bottom of the class school rebel. Piercings, dyed and part-shaved hair, ugly clothes, the works. I actually really enjoyed it. It was the first time I'd ever really chosen my own clothes!' She grimaced. 'Apparently, it was my "cry for help".' She made her fingers indicate the speech marks to show that she still didn't quite believe it. As far as she was concerned, it was more of a visceral shriek of anguish at the world. Nothing as faint and mewling as a cry for help.

'Did you have tattoos?' Beryl leaned forward, suddenly eager.

'No. Only because I couldn't afford it!' A quirk tugged Jo's mouth up at one side at Beryl's disappointment. 'Is it something you fancy then?'

Beryl nodded. 'I will one of these days. I'll have to be careful to make sure it doesn't look like something else as my skin sags though.' She winked. 'Go on, ducks.'

Staring into her empty teacup, Jo said, 'Oh, I got in with a proper rough crowd. I was the original angry girl. Drugs – I never took any, but I did smoke – various things.' She shook her head. 'Theft – some not so petty. General hooli behaviour. I'm not proud of it. And if Liam ever did anything like that, I'd be devastated. But Mum didn't even notice.'

'Surely just dealing with your dad's death in an immature way? I'm still not shocked.' Beryl smiled.

'Well, that's something!' Jo rubbed her hands over her face, and forced a bleak smile. 'But, after the ... the ... *worst thing*, she came to visit me – where I was living, and she said to me ...' She scrubbed her hands up and down her jeaned thighs, the raw emotion threatening even now to unbalance her. 'She said, "I don't know why you're so upset about him. He wasn't even your proper dad."' Tears spilled onto her jeans and her agitated hands reached up to knuckle them away.

'What did she mean by that?' Beryl frowned.

'My "proper",' Jo made the universal speech mark sign with her fingers, 'biological father was some random bloke in a pub.'

'Oh.' Beryl's expression was full of compassion.

'And my real dad, who wasn't my "proper dad" according to her,' she carried on, still furious, 'he knew Mum was pregnant with me. And married her anyway. He was worth ten dozen of her,' she finished, angrily. 'He would have adored Liam. And I still miss him. Every. Single. Day.' She leapt up, grabbing their mugs and striding the short distance to the kitchen.

Beryl followed more slowly. 'Does it really matter, what happened then?' she said, reaching for a tea towel as Jo crashed the mugs around in the sink. 'What matters is what you do now. Who you are ... now. And as far as I can see, you're a really good person, Jo. None of what you just told me was your fault, anyway. It sounds as if it was all really badly handled. You should have had counselling, really.' The tea towel squeaked inside the mug as she dried it. 'You're a fantastic Mum. Liam is a credit to you. Did you know, he pleased and thank-you-ed the whole time he was with me. He's a delightful, bright little boy. And if that doesn't say everything about the person you are, I don't know what does.'

Beryl's words whirled around Jo's head. Did the past really matter? It had mattered to her ... impossible to get over it. She just assumed that everyone else would feel the same as she did. Would judge her.

But she'd glossed over the thing ... the worst thing, and Beryl hadn't picked up on it. Or maybe she had and didn't want to bring it up. Faster and faster, her thoughts circled, like a tornado in her head.

'So ... what are you going to wear on Thursday night?' Beryl looked over her shoulder as she put the dried mugs away. 'Probably not your compulsory shorts, I'd say.' She swept a glance over Jo and added, 'And those jeans ... did they ever actually fit you?'

'What? They're practical – and I have exactly no time at all to go shopping ... even if I had the money. Which I don't,' Jo said. 'It's these or nothing.'

'I'm sure Ed will appreciate the nothing part.' Beryl laughed. 'But you've got great legs ... why not go for a mini or something?' She gazed at Jo thoughtfully. 'Back in a bit.'

She disappeared into the night, leaving Jo restless in the van. Padding into her little bedroom, she opened the wardrobe door and peered inside at her sparse collection of clothing, trying to think creatively. Beryl returned with an armful of garments, to find her tossing everything onto the bed.

'I don't wear any of this lot,' Jo said. 'No idea what made me buy most of it. Look at this!' She shook a black blazer at Beryl. 'Maybe I thought I was going to work in an office or something!'

'Don't chuck it, you never know. Right, how's this for an idea?' Beryl laid a pair of leggings, a couple of shirts, a fringed and tiered dress and a long cardigan on the bed.

Jo picked up one of the oversized shirts and held it against her. It was a gorgeous emerald green.

'Aha. Beautiful colour on you.' Beryl nodded with approval. 'So ... put that cobalt tiered dress on first ... I bought it for the colour, but it never looked right over my boobs.' She worked busily on her model, pulling here and tweaking there. 'Belt the shirt round that tiny waist of yours.' She steered Jo towards the mirror. 'What do you think? You could wear it with leggings, or tights, or bare legs.'

'Wow.' Jo stared at herself. Her legs seemed to go on forever. She would never have thought of putting those items together, the colours sang like jewels. The emerald green made her hair look lustrous.

'But maybe a bit too dressy for "tea the dinner",' Beryl said. 'Try tucking half the front of that shirt into your baggy jeans, pull them down to sit on your hips, stick a belt on them and roll them up. We'll pretend they're boyfriend jeans, and not just jeans that don't fit you. We could rip 'em up a bit, sharpen up the look.' She winked. '*Ooh*, and fling that black blazer over the top, across your shoulders. Awesome, girl!'

'I can't turn up with ripped jeans! Besides, I'll get cold knees.'

'How old are you?' Beryl laughed. 'You can be too practical, y'know.'

Jo was beginning to feel as if they'd fallen into one of those old/young body swap films from years ago. *Freaky Friday. Big.*

'Where did you learn all this, Beryl?' Jo admired herself in the mirror. She looked ... young.

'Hah. Pinterest! You can find anything on the internet. Plus, I'm choosy about who I spend my time with. So many retired people my own age,' Beryl was still rummaging, 'all they want to do is moan about everything. Their pills, their knees, the news. God, they can't half moan.'

'I could do with lessons from you, I think.' Jo smiled back at her. 'Maybe you could come shopping with me next time I go!'

'What about shoes?'

'Hmm. I have cycling shoes, beach shoes, allotment boots ...'

'Daps?'

'What?' Another Welsh word that had bewildered her all those years ago. 'Oh, you mean trainers?'

'Yes, but plimsoll type trainers?' Beryl was on her hands and knees in Jo's wardrobe and pulled out a pair of tatty navy blue trainers.

'I was going to chuck those.' Jo coloured. 'They're ancient ... but they're really comfy.'

'They'd look perfect with that get up. Dress it down a bit. Make it edgy.' Beryl waved them in the air. 'You just need a bit of imagination. And you've got the figure, and the hair, to carry it off.'

'I don't look at myself,' Jo said.

'Well, you should,' Beryl said, firmly. 'Ed certainly does.'

Chapter Nineteen

The week had whizzed by and it seemed no time at all to Jo as she waited for Ed to collect her and Liam that Thursday. She tugged self-consciously at her clothes, her hair, and checked her appearance in the reflections in the caravan windows every few minutes. She couldn't remember the last time she'd made any kind of an effort with her clothes. There just hadn't seemed to be any point in it. And although tonight wasn't a date or anything, she'd rather enjoyed trying things on and being creative with her look. Beryl had made it fun.

She'd finally settled on a simple white vest top, tucked into the belted baggy jeans, topped off with the blazer jacket, sleeves pushed casually up.

'Young and interesting, but not like you're trying too hard,' pronounced Beryl, appraising her real life dressing up doll with a critical eye. 'That vest thing is way too big though. Don't lean forward or you'll give Griff another heart attack.' Griff had been sent home from the hospital earlier in the week.

'What am I going to do about it now?' Jo panicked. 'I haven't got anything else!'

'Got a needle and thread?'

'Yes, but goodness only knows where it is …' Jo swept a hopeful gaze around her temporary home as if it might materialise just by thinking about it.

'I can pop home and get mine.' Beryl started for the door.

'There's no time!' Jo whirled around the small space. 'What about this?' She held up the mini stapler she used to keep her accounts in order.

Beryl tutted and rolled her eyes. 'You won't be able to take the jacket off,' she warned.

'Whatever. Better that than have my boobs fall out as I reach for the salt and pepper.' Jo snorted a giggle as her vest was yanked in and stapled at the back. She wriggled her shoulder blades experimentally. 'It'll do.'

'Jewellery?'

'My watch.' She cocked an eye in Beryl's direction, sensing her about to suggest something wild and colourful from her own collection and bent to pull a small velour covered box from the depths of her wardrobe. She opened it, snaked the delicate gold chain into her palm and with a deep breath, held it up to her neck.

'Perfect.' Beryl nodded. 'That's lovely, actually. Simple but classy.'

'My dad gave it to me.' Jo met Beryl's eye as she fastened it. She hadn't worn it for years. The memories it conjured had been too painful. But since she'd talked about it the other night, it felt … doable. As was allowing Beryl to dress her up. Tonight was not a big night. She wasn't looking to impress anyone. It was more of an awakening of a sort of pride in herself.

'Hair … up or down?' asked Beryl.

'God, I can't do up,' grumbled Jo. 'It falls out! Too curly, too slippery, I don't know. I can only do tied back. Or loose.'

'What about a loose tie back?'

'That makes me sound like a curtain.' Jo pinned her neighbour with a jaundiced eye.

Beryl wasn't to be put off. Smoothing and brushing Jo's lustrous curly mane, she held it at the nape of her neck and flipped Jo's scrunchy band around it, pulling it down from her head and then teasing it out gently so that loose strands framed Jo's face. 'What do you think?' she handed Jo a little mirror, so she could inspect the back. 'I could tie it with a nice ribbon. If you had such a thing …?' Jo got up to rummage in her bedroom and returned with a selection of vintage lace ribbons, which she handed to Beryl. 'Perfect, thank you.'

'S'okay, I s'pose.' Jo pretended to pout before her reflection, teenager style, turning this way and that so she could see it from each angle. She smiled. 'You could do this for a living, y'know, Beryl. A wardrobe consultant or something. I bet there's a demand for it.'

Beryl blushed. 'Make-up next?' she asked.

'No.' Jo was firm. 'I don't do make-up. Actually, I don't even have any make-up, and I don't have the money for make-up, so that's that.' Her jaw jutted and she frowned, reminded of her mother's insistence on never leaving the house without full make-up.

'Well, you could get away with the natural look,' observed Beryl, 'as long as you don't glare like that at everyone. What about a bit of mascara? Or lippie? It would make all the difference.'

No amount of wheedling on Beryl's part could persuade Jo into make-up.

'I hate that pasty, unformed look on women when they don't have make-up on, after you get used to seeing them "with their faces on".'

'Well. At least you have lovely skin.' Beryl put her hands on her hips. 'And a good colour. All that cycling and digging, I expect.'

'Thank you.'

'Just you make sure you don't get all weathered looking,' Beryl added with raised eyebrows and a disapproving expression. 'Even young skins need some moisturiser.'

Jo threw up her hands. 'Enough already! I've got some baby lotion. Will that do? Look at the time! Ed will be here any minute. Thank you, Beryl. You're a marvel.'

Hearing Ed's pickup arrive, she kissed Beryl's soft cheek, slicked a little Vaseline on her lips despite her anti-make-up pronouncement of moments before, and called Liam away from his digger trucks.

Ed had dropped Jo and Liam off earlier with reluctance, wishing he'd brought a change of clothes with him so that he could just enjoy their company for that little bit longer. The Bike Palace was such a welcoming place to be when they were both in it. Not only was it cleaner and tidier, but Jo was a genius at re-arranging stock so that people actually saw it, and he enjoyed seeing her chatting to the customers, becoming a little more knowledgeable almost daily.

Despite her assertion that she didn't like motorbikes, he'd spotted her smoothing a hand over the paintwork of the vintage bikes ranged in rows as she flicked a duster over them, and browsing through the occasional *Classic Bike* magazine. In her customary T-shirts and shorts, curly hair tied back and freckles she was the friendly 'girl next door' face of their business, and together with little Liam, were unbeatable at charming customers who'd come in to find that Ed was once again behind with their orders. There was no doubt that he was finding it hard without his dad, but Jo was definitely helping. Even if she did give him a hard time about being disorganised once the customer had left, now smiling. He took it from her when he knew he'd accept that kind of bollocking from no one else except his dad.

He would have loved to have read Liam his bedtime story the other night. He'd felt privileged that the little boy had asked him, but he'd also been aware of Jo's sharp eyes on him. He knew what she'd been thinking, that he was treating Liam like an entertaining novelty that he'd drop when he got bored. He could hardly blame her. He'd brought that reputation on himself – almost coveted it. It protected him, from girls who got too attached, so when the inevitable happened and he broke up with them, no one could say they hadn't seen it coming.

He pulled up outside Seagull Cottage, and caught himself checking his reflection in the driver's mirror. *Get a grip, man!* He told himself. *It's not a date!* Laughing at himself, he strode towards the caravan. Liam had his nose pressed to a window, presumably as early warning signal, and Ed approached at a crouch, leaping up with a loud '*Boo!*' and laughing uncontrollably as Liam shrieked. He could hear the little boy's excited voice as he knocked on the door. His jaw dropped as the door opened to reveal a goddess within. It was Jo, but not at all the Jo he'd become accustomed to. This Jo was a glossier version, somehow, and his eye was drawn to the slim gold chain around her slender neck.

'You look – stunning!' And not at all girl next door. She opened her mouth to reply just as Liam cannoned into him.

'Do I look stunning too?' he demanded.

'Very handsome,' agreed Ed, returning his fierce hug with a gentle squeeze. Jo smiled at him over Liam's head and Ed found himself grinning back like a fool. Was this what it felt like to be a parent? Part of a loving relationship? He banished the thought. Jo had made her position quite clear, and he had to respect that. Or risk losing her friendship, which he valued.

Unless he could change her mind about him. Could he do that?

Even though she now saw Ed almost every day, he was never in anything but his habitual battered leather jacket and T-shirt. Riding the short distance to his parents' house in the cab of the pickup, Jo felt like a stranger beside him, in his indigo slim fit Super Dry shirt, cuffs rolled back to reveal his muscular and tanned forearms. Even his jeans were smart, in a darker blue. She was glad she hadn't let Beryl slash her jeans. Her mother would be proud, as if that was any recommendation. What had happened to the girl with the piercings and attitude? She'd become a responsible mum, that's what. A glance at Liam beside her showed him unnaturally quiet in his best outfit – charcoal grey cargo pants, white T-shirt with checked overshirt.

'Should I have brought something?' In a sudden panic, Jo turned to Ed as they crossed his drive towards his parents' house. 'A cake? Flowers?'

Ed took her hand and squeezed it gently without saying anything. It was most unexpected, and unnerved her just at the moment the front door opened and a slim, older woman with a trendily spiky haircut burst out of it.

'You must be Jo … I've been so looking forward to meeting you! I'm Lyn.' There was a moment when Jo thought she was going to be hugged, and then a hand shot forward and she found her hand pumped enthusiastically. 'And this handsome young man must be Liam. How are you? We have lasagne for tea. Do you like lasagne?'

Liam nodded, his round eyes flicking from Jo to Lyn.

'I think I do. What is it?'

'Bogies and snails in sheets of glue,' said Ed with a wink, just as Lyn began to explain.

A horrified Jo, visualising Liam refusing food and making a scene, was about to correct him but Liam giggled.

'No it's not. You're silly, Ed.'

'You said snot,' said Ed. 'You said, "No it's snot." That's what you said.' He nodded with a serious face and Liam pealed with laughter again.

'Ed! Liam! I'm so sorry, Lyn …'

'Ed. Now, then. Leading poor Liam into bad ways,' chided Lyn, herding them into the large cottage.

Ed made a fake nose-picking gesture at Liam and Jo tried not to laugh.

The hall opened up into a lounge with big comfortable sofas. Upholstered mostly in cream, with a pale terracotta pattern. Jo tightened her grip on her son's hand. The carpet was also cream. Not exactly child friendly. Jo hoped the dining room was not similarly decorated. She was so busy stressing over the possibility of Liam redecorating with pasta sauce, that she failed to see Griff in a high backed chair beside the fireplace. Her face flamed as she remembered the last time she'd seen him and she had absolutely no idea what to say to him. As he began to struggle out of the chair though, she rushed towards him.

'Please, don't get up!' She cringed as she heard herself say, 'I don't want to have to do mouth to mouth on you again! I mean ... um ... You're looking ... er ...'

'Scrawny,' supplied Lyn, eyeing him with her hands on her hips. 'But at least he's home, and alive ... thanks to you, Jo.' This time she did envelop Jo in a strong, wiry hug. 'We are indebted to you. What you did ...'

As Jo stalled in a fluster of indecision, Liam looked up at Ed and said, 'I'm glad your daddy isn't in space.'

Laughter broke the ice, and Jo's offer to help in the kitchen was waved away.

'Go and chat to Griff. He wants to know what's happening in the Bike Palace since he's been away!'

As Lyn bustled into the kitchen, Ed and Jo sat side by side on the squashy sofas, closest to Griff, Liam perched between them. She was shocked by Griff's appearance. His tall frame looked ... well ... deflated. The memory of his ribs crunching beneath her pumping hands made her feel suddenly nauseous. Ed was in full flow about bike stuff and she extracted herself from the clutches of the sofa and headed for the kitchen for a glass of water, pulling her vest away from her skin.

'Sorry, the heating's turned up for Griff. Bless him, he's feeling the cold at the moment. Seems so strange for him ... he was never one for having the heating on,' Lyn said. 'Too early for a glass of wine, I suppose?'

'It is for me. Liam would have to put me to bed instead of the other way around.' Jo smiled, sipping her water. It was cooler in the kitchen, despite the heat from the oven.

'He seems like a very grown up little boy.' Lyn threw a salad together in a big colourful bowl. 'Ed is very fond of him.'

'He's very good with children. Very natural. Gets right down to their level.' She was thinking about him teasing Liam about the lasagna, which had broken the ice straight away.

'Mmm, he does.' Lyn shook her head, her mouth tightening. Jo frowned. What had she said? Ed's Mum didn't think that she was taking advantage of Ed, did she?

'Shall I take this in?' She held out her hand for the salad bowl. 'Anything else?'

After a moment's hesitation, Lyn loaded her up with cutlery with a smile.

'Take no notice of me. It's not up to me … he should tell you himself.'

Puzzled, Jo followed Lyn's directions to the dining room, mercifully tiled in a soft charcoal flooring that looked wipe-cleanable. There was a bowl of spring flowers on the runner that covered the farmhouse table, and what looked to her like an antique chandelier hanging low over it. She liked the mix of old and new in there … one of the walls was painted a deep grey, whilst the others were a soft grey or white. There was a huge clock on the dark wall, made of metal – just the numbers and the hands. It looked fantastic, and Jo found herself decorating Seagull Cottage in her head. She'd never allowed herself to fantasise about that kind of permanence, and surprised herself by how excited she felt about it.

'I wondered where you'd got to.' It was Ed, laden down with a dish of hot lasagne that looked as if it could feed an army. He placed it centrally on the runner, left and returned moments later with a jug of water and tumblers.

'Oh, I could have brought that in …' She turned guiltily to see Liam carefully bearing a basket of sliced baguettes at head height. 'Shall I pop that on here, sweetie?'

'No, I can manage,' Ed deadpanned, as Griff was helped in by Lyn.

Eventually, the meal was apportioned, a cushion was found to raise Liam, and Jo began to relax at last, whilst cutting up Liam's food and keeping a beady eye on him. Conversation batted across the table, flitting from Lyn's work at the hospital, work at Seagull Cottage, to the Bike Palace, while Jo joined in, amazing herself at how much she now knew.

Liam interjected happily about 'helping Ed' at the Bike Palace, until Lyn and Ed cleared the plates and returned with dessert. Nearly full, Jo was relieved to see that it was a simple fruit salad.

Liam was picking through his fruit to Jo's consternation, when she became aware of Lyn and Griff sharing a look and a conversation in lowered tones.

'I think she'll do very well, don't you, darling?'

'She might not want to do it, Lyn. It's not everyone's cup of tea.'

Jo leaned forward. 'What might I not want to do?'

'It's a motorbike show,' said Lyn, taking the lead. 'A classic bike show.'

'Okaay … I have no idea what that is.' A vague memory surfaced, of Ed telling her that it was booked.

'In Nottingham. For three days. We'd put you up in a hotel. And pay you. Of course.'

Jo shook her head, confused now. 'What am I doing? What about Liam? And … are we all going? What sort of show is it?' Finally, she put both her hands flat on the table, and said, 'Right, tell me properly.'

They did. Afterwards, she said to Lyn, 'Maybe I will have that glass of wine after all.'

Chapter Twenty

'So, mainly, we put the renovated BSA on the stand,' explained Lyn, as Jo sipped her wine, 'which dates back to the ...'

'Late nineteen fifties,' supplied Jo, to her own astonishment. Where had that knowledge been hiding in her brain? She liked the BSA Gold Star vintage motorbike though, with its lustrous silver tank. It was her favourite, she always whisked any dust away as she passed. There was a romance about it. She could imagine it being ridden by some daredevil in a flat hat and goggles.

'Yes!' Lyn shot a complicit smile towards Ed and Griff. 'And beside it, we put a tatty, non-renovated version. As a before and after comparison.' Jo nodded, and Lyn carried on quickly, flicking her eyes up at Jo. 'And ... er ... you and Ed will be dressed in forties mode.'

'*Uh-uh*.' Jo nodded, then looked up in astonishment as she rewound that in her head. 'D'you what?' She sounded very London, suddenly.

'Griff and I usually do the shows, and Ed carries on at the Bike Palace after helping us set up. But this year ...'

'Yes, I got that bit ... but ... what was that about dressing up?' Jo glared at Ed's grinning face. 'Forties style? Even Ed? And ... what about Liam?'

'Liam would look fantastic in a flat cap, long shorts and braces. What do you think, Liam?' Lyn tipped her head at the little boy. 'Want to help Ed and Mummy sell some motorbikes?'

Liam nodded enthusiastically, although Jo was sure that he'd agree to anything that had Ed and motorbikes in it.

'What would I have to wear?' she asked, cautiously, rather

wishing that Beryl was there. She'd be full of enthusiasm at the idea of fancy dress, Jo was sure. 'Land girl costume? I could totally do Land girl.' Dungarees and practical stuff. She could only hope.

'I've actually got one or two forties style dresses. You could try them on!' Lyn was on her feet, all enthusiasm and Jo followed more slowly. Dresses? When was the last time she wore a dress? And that would mean doing her hair. It sounded like a lot of fuss to sell an old bike or two.

'How do you keep this house so clean when you're all into bikes?' she asked, as they climbed the stairs.

'Easy.' Lyn glanced over her shoulder. 'I don't let them in.' She chuckled. 'Not really. When the cottages were renovated, we had a changing room and shower fitted out where the garage meets the house. That way, all the mess stays out there. Ed has a shower just inside his front door.'

'I know,' said Jo, before she could stop herself. Lyn sent her an enquiring look but made no comment, and Jo found herself having to explain the whole embarrassing incident.

'Poor Liam, bless his soul.' Lyn looked sympathetic, leading Jo into a bedroom, kitted out with hanging rails, upon which hung garment bags.

'Right, now, let's see.' Lyn riffled through them until she found what she was looking for. Unzipping the bag, she pulled out a dress and held it up. It was a deep red with tiny polka dots.

Jo fingered the crisp material, holding it against her before a full-length mirror. It was the most girly item of clothing she'd ever encountered, with puff sleeves, a high sweetheart neckline and a full skirt swirling from the tiny, belted waist. The little girl inside her suddenly longed to try it on.

'It's a tea dress,' explained Lyn. 'Maybe a bit short for you though. You're taller than me. Try it though, you never know.'

Jo was about to strip off there and then until she remembered that she was stapled into her vest. She couldn't let Lyn see her like that. As her face reddened to the same shade as the dress she said, 'Could I try it at home? Would you mind?'

Lyn looked disappointed but said, 'Of course! I'll pop it back into the bag. Try this one too.' She bundled another over her arm, and Jo caught sight of a deep blue material with a rose pattern.

'What do I do about shoes?'

'Mary Janes, a peep toe, something like that,' said Lyn. Jo stared at her as if she was speaking a foreign language. What on earth was a Mary Jane? 'But what ever you wear, it'll have to be comfortable – you'll be on your feet all day. You've got lovely long legs – you could probably get away with a pair of plimsolls like those. Only newer.' She nodded down to Jo's tatty shoes, and Jo cringed. 'We'll pay, of course!' Lyn added in a hurry, probably misreading Jo's expression of horror.

'What will I actually be doing on the stand?' Jo asked. Her heart was beginning to thud, as the warm glow of the wine wore off and she realised the enormity of what she was taking on. It would mean not only doing her hair, but wearing make-up and a dress and tights – the forties was a glamorous era, despite, or perhaps because of the war. It meant, above all, being noticed. Which was something she'd spent most of her adult life avoiding.

'There'll be more bikes on show for sale, and then bike bits, partial engines, that sort of thing, and I expect people will want to ask about the renovations. That's what we're selling – Ed's renovating talents.'

Jo swallowed. 'What will you do if I can't do it?'

Lyn shrugged. 'Well, either I'll have to get a nurse or something for Griff and go myself, or we'll have to cancel it. We won't get our money back now, it's too late for that. But don't let that pressurise you. It's a big ask, I know.' She tipped her head on one side and raked Jo's doubtful face. 'What do you think, really?'

Had the heating been turned up again? Jo felt faint and sticky under Lyn's gaze.

'It's not that I don't want to do it,' she said, slowly. 'I'm scared that I won't remember things and I'll be useless and let you all down.'

'Oh well, that's not going to happen, is it?' said Lyn, in a brisk voice, looping the garment bags over her arm and heading for the stairs. 'Ed wouldn't have suggested you if he didn't think you could do it.'

Jo felt much happier, until Lyn threw a mischievous aside over her shoulder just as they entered the lounge, 'That, and none of his mates would look any good in a dress ...'

Liam, Ed and Griff were in deep conversation around the fire as they entered.

'Mummy! You look just the same!' Liam sounded disappointed, obviously having been primed by Ed to expect her to be twirling her way downstairs in a posh frock. 'I'm going to have a uniform too!'

'Lovely, darling!' said Jo, in her bright, 'It's nearly bedtime voice'. A thought struck her. 'One thing I didn't ask, when is this show?'

'Next month,' said Ed.

Jo breathed out in relief. 'Oh, so I've got plenty of time to learn everything and get my outfits sorted.'

'Well, when I say, next month,' said Ed, not quite meeting her eye, 'I mean in two weeks time.'

'So ... not this weekend, but ...'

'The weekend after that.' He nodded.

'That's not two weeks!' Jo's voice was shrill. 'That's ten days! Ed! How long were you going to leave it before you asked me?'

He wriggled, looking for all the world like a bigger version of Liam when he was caught out.

'I thought I could do it on my own. Until I started talking it over with Mum and Dad.'

Jo plopped onto the sofa. After a moment, in which four pairs of eyes regarded her hopefully, she said, 'So, you'd better start telling me everything I'm meant to be doing. I am not looking like an idiot on that stand. And by the way, where's your outfit, Ed?'

'Cup of tea first, I think,' said Lyn, firmly. 'And don't go terrifying Jo with a whole load of stuff, Ed.'

'She doesn't scare easily, I reckon,' Ed said. 'But she knows loads already. The next thing will be to actually get her on a motorbike.'

'No, thank you!' said Jo. 'I am very happy with my battery powered version, as it happens!' But a tiny bead of curiosity was bubbling inside her. Those vintage motorbikes didn't look nearly as scary as the great big things she saw Ash, Lucy and Nicola riding. They looked more like motorised bicycles. Maybe one day she'd get Ed to show her how to ride it. Maybe.

'Oh! That reminds me!' Ed looked mysterious. 'I've got something for you.'

'For me?' Liam's eyes were bright.

'We-ell ... Both of you, actually. Back in a mo.' He returned with a child-sized pedal cycle, BMX style.

'Wow!' yelled Liam, rushing to it. 'Is it for me, Ed?'

Ed nodded. 'It is!'

'Ed! It looks new!' Jo helped Liam clamber on to it. It was overwhelming, all this gift giving.

'It's second hand. One of my mates passed it on from his little boy. I've got the stabilisers for it too.' Ed nodded. 'It's got proper gears and everything. I thought, as he was already pedalling behind you ...'

'I love it!' Liam shouted, making everyone laugh. 'Please can I keep it? Please thank you please thank you please thank you please ...'

'Yes! Of course you can keep it.' Jo laughed. 'Very naughty of you, Ed, but thank you. It is time he learned to ride his own bike.'

'Can I have a go now?' Liam gazed pleadingly at Jo and Ed in turn.

'Oh, why not?' said Jo with a laugh, after Ed turned an identical gaze onto her.

They trooped into the back garden, and Jo watched Ed bend like a hairpin to push a wobbly and giggling Liam endlessly up and down. She wasn't sure who was enjoying it most.

'You have to pedal, mate,' Ed puffed. 'Is this what you do behind your mum's bike?'

'Yes!' said Liam, the unspoken but very obvious 'of course!' making them all laugh.

'Don't be cheeky, Liam. Time to go soon.' Jo caught Ed's eye and tapped her watch. 'It's bedtime.'

'I'm not tired!' squeaked an outraged Liam.

'I am!' Ed eased his long frame upright and rotated his shoulders. 'Now I know how miners must've felt.'

'You can play on it again, Liam,' Jo said. 'But sleep makes you big and strong.'

'Like Ed?' Liam twisted on the saddle to inspect his hero, and Ed pulled a muscle-man pose.

Jo's stomach somersaulted. 'Yes. Just like Ed.' She turned to Lyn and Griff. 'Thanks for feeding us, it was lovely to meet you. I'm really excited about the show. Thank you for involving us.'

'Pop over any time,' said Griff, adding with a sidelong grin at Lyn, 'I'm always up for a bit of good-looking company.'

'Ew, Dad.' Ed paused at the door. 'You've had quite enough one on one lip action from Jo!'

'What's lip action?' Liam said, unerringly seeing an excuse to stay for longer. Encumbered by her dress bags, Jo ushered him gently from the house, turning impulsively to hug Lyn and Griff while Ed and Liam put the bike in the back of the pickup.

'Thunderbirds are GO!' Ed said to Liam, buckling him into his booster seat. 'The Three Musketeers! Yay!'

'You pair.' Jo chuckled, watching Liam's little arm pump the air in imitation of Ed. It felt great to have something to look forward to – even if it was scaring the pants off her at the same time. She was determined to give it her best shot.

Ed pulled up outside Seagull Cottage, and walked them both to the caravan door, which Jo found rather endearing. It was still early really, and light, and Liam whined in his over-tired voice about having to go to bed and wanting to ride his new bike, which was to live in the shed beside hers.

'If you get your pj's on really quickly, how about I tell you a story?' said Ed, in a light, offhand voice.

Jo was taken aback, remembering what Beryl had said about him fancying her earlier. Somehow, in his parents' house, he'd been his usual friendly self and it had all been businesslike, but in close proximity to him, her skin tingled and she couldn't quite get her breath.

'Is that okay?' Ed said to her. 'I should have asked first, I suppose, but I thought it might get him to bed earlier.'

'No, it's fine. Fine! If you're sure? I mean, you don't want to nip off to the pub with your mates?' Jo was gabbling, she knew.

Ed opened his mouth to reply as Liam scampered back wearing his pyjama bottoms, and carrying a book and his top. Jo looked at his solid little body with pride. He was utterly perfect.

'This one,' he demanded, scrambling up and pulling his top over his head as Ed folded himself onto the low sofa. Ed opened the book.

'The Story of ...' he began, and then stopped. Jo could see him reading ahead. He began to laugh, that deep rich chuckle they'd heard the day he'd met them on the sea path. Liam giggled along with him.

'Read it!'

'It's all about poo!' Ed said, nudging him. 'You're obsessed with poo!'

'All children are.' Jo grinned. 'Cup of tea?'

Ed nodded, took a deep breath, and read, making all the different voices for each animal.

'Again!' said Liam, as the story came to an end.

'Another time,' said Ed, straight-faced. 'And only if you go to bed right now this minute.' Jo was impressed when Liam didn't argue. Either he was really tired or Ed had sounded like he meant it.

After Jo supervised the teeth cleaning and last wee, she tucked the little boy up and kissed him goodnight. It had been lovely to watch him enjoying the story ... to share, just for a little while, some of the responsibility. To think that she'd been almost jealous of the attention he paid Ed not that long ago. Her stomach churned ... would he leave now? Stay? Try to kiss her? Or just chat, while her body and newly woken libido fretted like a dog at the end of a leash. She really wished she didn't fancy him – it would make life so much simpler.

'I've made some more tea,' Ed whispered, as she quietly pulled the door to. She liked to be able to hear Liam if he woke and needed the loo again.

'Thanks.' She sat opposite him on the U-shaped sofa. 'So. Tell me everything.'

'What kind of everything?' Ed was still, watchful, a slight frown creasing his forehead, and Jo had the distinct impression that they were talking at cross purposes.

'Where are we going? Where are we staying? I want times,

dates, catering arrangements … er … transport?' She noticed him relaxing, losing that frown. He was hiding something, she knew. But what? He outlined the hotel – separate rooms, obviously – that there would be catering onsite at the show and plenty of places for them to eat after. They'd have an early start, and travel in the rented long wheelbase Transit, which would be towing everything they needed for the stand.

'I can't help you move the bikes,' warned Jo. 'I'm scared I'll drop one.'

'I can do all that,' said Ed, waving an airy hand. 'But, honestly, it's all about confidence. I'll show you.'

'*Hmm*.'

'Anyway, you'd have no problems with your muscles. They're nearly as big as mine.' He winked, sliding across to sit beside her, and enclosing her bicep with his hand. It was a physical shock.

'*Oi*!' she said, failing completely to throw him off, not that she wanted to, and succumbing to the inevitable glow of warmth that drew her body towards his. She felt a hand on the nape of her neck and closed her eyes as he lowered his lips onto hers.

'Ouch! What the hell … something's bitten me!' He jerked backwards and Jo leapt up. Bitten him? What … a flea? In the caravan? Ugh.

'What is it?'

'On your back.' He reached out to lift her jacket just as she remembered and pushed him away. He looked perplexed, reaching again to find out. 'You got teeth back there?'

'*Nooo*.' She whirled away, embarrassed, and then relented, fearing his imagination might invent something worse than a few staples. 'Oh God, okay. Look.' She lifted her jacket and turned to show him. He shouted with laughter. 'Sssh! You'll wake Liam up!'

The moment was lost. They were back in friends mode

and Jo didn't know whether to be relieved or disappointed as he strode casually out of the door an awkward ten minutes later. She could scream. Mostly at her own lack of will. He was a man, after all. He was primed to try it on, wasn't he? She'd told him no funny business, and yet her determination to see it through was dwindling. It was all she could do not to open the door and call him back in.

Ed didn't want to go home. He wanted to stay right where he'd been until a few minutes ago until those ridiculous staples had made him stop and look at what he was doing. He could still feel her lips beneath his. Unable to straighten his thoughts out, he drummed his fingers on the steering wheel with frustration, then pulled over to get his phone out, sent a few texts and headed back over the Gower to the Mumbles to meet his mates.

'Pint?' His friend Stu was already in the snug, and several inches down his pint. Mind, he only lived a mile away, so he was walking. 'How's your dad?'

'Yeah, go on then. Just the one.' Ed nodded. 'He's coming on okay, thanks.' Propping up the bar, they talked about the rugby as Cled and Lloyd joined them. Ed began to relax. They didn't meet up as often as they used to, the other three had steady partners and Cled had a second baby on the way.

'So I hear you dumped Alexis.' Lloyd thrust his fingers into a packet of beef crisps. 'Who's on your radar now?'

'She dumped me, as it happens.' Ed sipped his pint.

The three men laughed. 'Course she did, mate. You probably drove her to it. So?'

'I might have a break from women.' Ed grinned at the chorus of catcalls this provoked. 'I could!'

'No you bloody couldn't.' Cled sat back, crossing an ankle over his knee. 'Come on, who's the lucky girl? The missus won't let me come home until I've got the full SP.'

'What does that actually mean, the SP?' Stu nudged his pint along the table, making tracks in the condensation.

The ridiculous conversation that resulted from this idle enquiry diverted attention from Ed and he wasn't sure whether to be grateful or not. Blokes didn't discuss private stuff. It was sport, cars, bikes, jobs. Maybe holidays. Women, in an abstract sense. Not relationships, as such. Or maybe that was just him, as Cled had plenty to say about his little girl and impending new baby. He checked his phone constantly, and Ed felt envious.

'Who's the bird working at the Bike Palace now?' Stu asked. 'She's fit. I would.'

''Cause she's got a pulse?' Lloyd laughed.

Ed frowned. 'All right, all right, that'll do. She saved Dad's life, as it happens.'

'And have you given her her reward?' Stu eyed him with a grin. 'Has she been Edded?'

'Bedded, more like,' Lloyd said.

'Don't talk about her like that.'

'Oh-oh – somebody's tired,' Stu slurred, and Ed looked at the empty pint glasses lined up at his elbow. 'She's got a kid too, hasn't she? She's a MILF.' He shrugged his eyebrows obscenely and Ed had to focus on unclenching his fists.

'Christ, Stu, you're a tosser when you've had a few,' Cled said, following Ed's gaze. 'Come on, I'll give you a lift home.' He jiggled his car keys. 'Ed, mate, she seems nice. Go for it. What's the worst that can happen?'

'She could dump him,' said Stu, swaying. 'Like all the others. Haha.'

'Well,' said Cled, 'try not to be an arse then. She's already got one child, she doesn't need you behaving like one. If you really like her, either don't get involved, or treat her properly.'

Cled's words whirled around Ed's brain while his mouth talked about motorbikes with Lloyd until closing time.

Chapter Twenty-One

The buzzing of her mobile sent Jo scurrying to find it, hoping and dreading that it might be Ed changing his mind.

'How did it go? I just happened to hear Ed's truck leave and—'

'Oh! Beryl! What are you up to?' She cringed, hearing the false note of brightness in her voice.

'I was just watching *Death in Paradise*. Did it all go okay?'

'Ye-es, but I'm … er … I'm going to need some help, Beryl. Quite soon.'

'Really?'

Jo couldn't miss the note of excitement in her neighbour's voice. 'I've got the kettle on,' she said, smiling, 'and there's some cake …'

'I'll just pop this on record … and I'll be over.'

'Oh, thank you, I'll see you in a—' Jo found herself talking to a dead phone, and was pouring boiling water into mugs as the caravan door was knocked.

Beryl's eyes were round as Jo related the tale of her 'tea the dinner' with the Griffiths family. She laughed.

'So … you haven't even tried the dresses on yet!' Jo shook her head, her expression glum, which made Beryl laugh even more.

'I almost did … but then I remembered the staples.'

'I'm sure she wouldn't have minded.'

'No, probably not. But I minded, Beryl! I really need to earn some proper money. I'm fed up with charity shop finds.' She shook her head and slumped back in her seat.

'Feeling sorry for yourself gets you nowhere, young lady. Let's have a look at these frocks, come on.'

Chivvied on, Jo unzipped the garment bags and shook the dresses out.

'Get it on, then!' Beryl urged. 'I would've loved to wear something like that.'

'Didn't you, then?'

'How old do you think I am?' Beryl looked outraged and Jo had to cover her blushes by slipping the dress over her head. She was quite sure it wouldn't fit. It looked tiny, and that was another reason why she'd been reluctant to try it on in front of Lyn. But Beryl was so positive about everything, she was sure that there'd be an alteration that could be done to make it fit. She was mortified that she'd offended her. How old was she? Definitely over sixty. Oh, so that made her only born in the fifties. No wonder she'd made a face ...

The smooth material swished against her legs, as different as could be to her usual jeans and shorts. She reached behind to assess the gap in the zip, and was surprised to feel that there wasn't one as she contorted herself to close it.

'Wow.' Beryl nodded her approval. 'Nice.'

'Really? Is it too short though?'

'It's a tiny bit short,' Beryl said, after a considering pause. 'But you can take it. You've got great legs, girl. Have you got anything to wear with it?'

'Like what?'

'Jacket? Cardigan, bag, shoes, seamed stockings?' Beryl ticked them off on her fingers, and added, 'Hat?'

'No. None of the above. That's why I need your help.' Jo looked imploring. 'You've seen my shoe collection! Ed's mum said something about plimsolls, like mine only newer, and Mary Janes? Whatever they are ...'

'Right. I'm sure we can find something to suit shoe and bag-wise, maybe even a hat, with a bit of tweaking.'

'Oh and I need to dress Liam up too!'

'He'll be easier, really.' Beryl made a thinking face. 'A flat cap, little tweed jacket and waistcoat maybe, cut a pair of trousers down, and some long socks and boots.'

'I don't have any of that. Not a thing. And certainly nothing I want to start cutting up.'

'Looks like we need a trip round the charity shops and flea markets. And I need to get my trusty Singer sewing machine out of storage!'

'I knew you'd know what to do.' Jo hugged her carefully, feeling the breadth of her shoulders strain against the material of the dress. 'Seamed stockings though?' She shook her head. 'I don't think so. Wearing a dress feels like a big enough step!'

'I'm sure they'll be good for sales ...' Beryl winked, chuckling at Jo's reaction. 'We'll have to get our skates on ... there's not much time.'

Jo felt her stomach lurch. 'I know! And I'm going to be spending the money I've saved on rent on buying stuff I'll never use again!'

'Why don't you ask the Griffiths for an allowance? I'm sure they'll be fine about that ... they're putting you up and paying you anyway, aren't they? They surely can't expect you to have to buy one-off stuff.'

'*Mm*, yes, Lyn did mention something about paying for it when we were talking about shoes. *Phew*, that's a relief.'

Expecting Jo to be apprehensive about the impending bike show, Ed was surprised and pleased to find her so excited when he came to collect her from her shift at the café. She bombarded him with questions that had occurred to her since he'd seen her. Her eyes were bright.

'You won't leave me on my own on the stand, will you? What if someone wants to buy something? What if I don't know what they're talking about? What if I sell something I'm not supposed to?'

'You're right,' said Ed, keeping his face straight. 'You're fired. I'm not taking you.'

Jo sat back in shock, scrutinising his implacable expression, before knuckling him hard on the shoulder.

'You're so mean,' she huffed at his grinning face. 'I'm going shopping for Liam's outfit at the weekend! I'm just scared in case I let you down.'

'Jo.' Ed threw her a pensive glance from the driver's seat. 'You could never let me down.'

'Oh.' Jo chewed her lip.

She'd made him think though, as usual, as they drove to collect Liam, and once at the Bike Palace he began a thorough rundown of the stock they would take and how he would like enquiries regarding renovations to be handled, until Jo threw up her hands.

'Stop! I need to write this stuff down so I can remember it. And,' she tapped the counter, 'have you got photos of the renovations you've already done?'

'Loads!' Ed nodded.

'Where are they?'

'In there.' He indicated his laptop, half-hidden under a heap of bike magazines. 'Somewhere …' He had the decency to look embarrassed, caught out in his still disorganised chaos. He had so much to do these days, between the bikes and tenancies. No wonder his dad hadn't been able to keep up with it.

Jo broke into his reverie. 'How about one of those photo books to show your customers what you can do?'

'Nice touch. Have we got time?'

'I could Google it first … and then see if I can find the photos and pull it all together. But we'll need the internet to upload it. Or …' she paused, pulling out her mobile and he watched over her shoulder as she thumbed to the browser page, 'don't some of the big supermarkets do them? Hang on, wow, I've found one that will deliver in five days.'

'What are you waiting for then?' He opened his laptop. 'Let's have a look. I think they're under "Bike Stuff". Dad took most of them.'

They stood shoulder to shoulder, poring over the screen as Ed clicked on one album after another, revealing hundreds of vintage motorbikes in various forms. Some she recognised, but many were a complete mystery to her.

'How am I going to write about them?' She hooked her hair behind her ears, frowning. 'Maybe this wasn't such a great idea after all ... and it needs to go in as soon as possible otherwise it won't be back in time.'

He rested a hand on the counter and thought for a moment. 'Are you free tonight?'

'I don't have the internet,' she said.

How did she always seem to know what he was thinking? 'No, but I do.'

'And I have Liam.' They looked to where the little boy was sitting, absorbed in polishing a collection of Very Important bits and pieces with some old rags.

'You could both sleep over ...' He held his breath, and tried to look casual.

Jo straightened up, chewing her lip as she contemplated the glowing screen.

'It's tempting. But we've never had a sleepover,' she said after a long pause. 'We'd have to collect all his paraphernalia, and mine, and he might not settle, and I'll end up sorting him out instead of the photo book.'

'Or he might be absolutely fine,' Ed said, trying for a positive spin. 'And I could cook us some tea and you could work all night.'

'Wow, you make it sound so inviting! Not.' She laughed.

'I have wine. And beer ...'

'And I really wouldn't get anything done.' Jo bent back

over the screen. 'How about a compromise? I'll work at yours tonight, if you don't mind dropping us back afterwards?'

'Done. No one's due in now, let's pack up early, and crack on with it.'

'Oh, by the way, can you let your mum know that the dresses fit? I just need to get accessories and Liam's outfit. Beryl's coming with me tomorrow.'

Ed smacked his palm against his forehead. 'I forgot to say! Mum said to give you some cash for anything you need to buy, and to tell you about a shop that does all that stuff.' He fished out a piece of paper on which was scribbled an address. 'She says the girl who runs it is really helpful. I think she's expecting you.'

'Have you got your outfit sorted out?'

He shrugged. 'More or less.'

'What does that mean?' She put her hands on her hips, her expression all suspicion. 'I had better not be the only one making a fool of myself!'

He grinned at her. He just loved to tease her. 'I just … can't decide which one.'

'You can show me when we get to yours,' she said and winked.

'In your dreams!' He snorted. 'You wouldn't let me see yours, so I'm not showing you mine.'

'Your what?' asked Liam, looking up from his polishing.

'Nothing important, big guy! I'm just being silly. Coming over to mine for something to eat tonight while your mum does some work?'

'Yes, please!' Liam leapt to his feet, with one of his whole body nods, and harangued them to hurry as they locked up.

'Slave-driver!' Ed swept him up and fed him into the front of the pickup. 'There's no slacking with you around, is there!'

'Let's go!' said Liam.

He scampered into Ed's cottage, observing loudly that he'd

had a shower in 'there' and 'I poked all my sick down the holes!'

'*Oi*, you … vom-boy! What do you want to eat?' demanded Ed, switching the huge TV on and scrolling to *CBeebies*. Eyes glued to the screen, Liam backed onto the sofa and sat down without answering.

'What culinary delight are you preparing?' Jo asked.

'Beans on toast, cheese on toast, cheese on beans on toast,' said Ed. 'Or takeaway.'

'What happened to: "I'll cook us some tea?" Beans on toast isn't cooking!' Jo cast him a reproving glance.

'I can fry an egg? Egg on beans on cheese on toast? Or a bacon sandwich.'

'Nothing with veg? Or salad?'

Ed pulled a face. 'Don't be disgusting.'

'Scrambled egg on toast, Liam?' Jo said, enunciating slowly and carefully.

'*Uh*,' said Liam, never taking his eyes from the cinematic screen.

'Scrambled brains for Liam,' said Ed, cheerfully. 'What about you, Jo?'

'I was going to say beans on toast,' she said, 'but, actually, I'd love a bacon sandwich. Have you really got bacon?'

'Course I have!' said Ed, making a face that said that he hadn't. 'Back in a mo …' His mum would have some. Or he could nip down to the supermarket if she didn't. He crashed out of the front door.

'Bring back some salad!' called Jo with a grin, settling the laptop on her knee. The laptop connected instantly to the internet, and she began to assemble the photographs she recognised into an album.

His photo library loaded as she clicked on one of the photos, and after a moment's hesitation, curiosity overtook her and she scrolled quickly through, telling herself she was only looking for bike pics. He was being very trusting, handing over his laptop. She didn't want to abuse that trust. Hurrying past the more recent selfies of him and a posing Alexis sent the page spinning to a date marked fifteen years earlier.

Peering more closely, she recognised Ed as a teenager, but only just. Dressed identically to a bunch of his hoody clad mates, and squashed alongside them on a sofa, he looked gaunt and pale. Slowly, she clicked on the photo before that one, identifying Ed on a chair beside a hospital bed, thumb up and a cheery grin on his thin face, a beanie pulled down to his eyebrows. Was that someone else's bed? Or his …?

Alert for sounds of Ed's return, she swiped right, poring over the photos that showed him on a skateboard, a bicycle, playing football … always surrounded by mates whose healthy physiques only seemed to make Ed's appear even more meagre by contrast. Illness? Anorexia? Just one of life's thin people? The front door clicked, and feeling guilty, she hurried to close the photo library.

Quickly typing BSA Gold Star and variations on that theme into the search bar brought up a stack of photos that she recognised as the one they would be featuring on the stand, and she was completely absorbed in her task when Ed popped his head round the door, allowing a succulent waft of bacon into the room.

'Tea? Coffee? Coke? Beer?'

Looking up at his solidly built physique reassured her, and she smiled up at him. 'Tea, please. Liam will have water. Or milk?'

They ate on their laps. Liam shovelled his scrambled egg approximately into his face whilst his eyes were glued to the television and Jo dropped bits of her own sandwich trying to keep an eye on where his food was going. This was why she didn't let him eat in front of the TV at home, she thought, trying to keep a lid on her irritation. He was enjoying himself, doing no harm, a little treat didn't hurt, she told herself. And Ed hadn't noticed. She had nothing to prove to anyone.

It was exhausting.

Ice cream followed for Liam, and then Ed set up his Wii, and Jo retreated as far as possible to concentrate. Liam laughed uproariously and she feared for the pale grey carpet. It looked like so much fun that she felt quite left out as she began to upload photos to the template provided.

She'd decided to use a beautiful photo of the completed bike on the cover, with a little insert showing its original condition. She left a page blank between the photo entries so she and Ed could add the words, and tried to vary the layout. It was looking good. Despite the racket going on at the other end of the room.

Her motherly instinct told her when Liam was flagging, and she stood and stretched, suggesting a nice, quiet cartoon or something to Ed. Liam would probably fall asleep, and she could just lift him straight into bed.

Bringing them another mug of tea, Ed hunkered down beside her, and Jo's brain turned to mush at his proximity. Slightly sweaty after his exertions with Liam, he smelled faintly of something expensive that Jo didn't know. She had no idea about perfume or after-shave, couldn't afford it and stayed away from it. But there was something warm and smoky about this smell.

'This was a box of bits, really, when we started on it,' he said, pointing now at the screen, his arm brushing her shoulder. 'Here ... this picture. I thought Dad was being super-ambitious!'

Jo began to type his words as he spoke. It would surely be more interesting to a reader than a long-winded, dry account of the renovation.

'We scoured the bike jumbles, online sales and collectors backyards until we got all the bits. It took months and months. A real labour of love.'

'It's beautiful,' Jo said. 'I think it's my favourite.'

'Mine too!'

Adding the words took ages and several more mugs of tea, until Jo stood and stretched and declared a time out. Liam was serenely asleep, with a cosy blanket thrown over him.

'Beryl and I are shopping on Sunday … bits and pieces for our fancy dress. I hope Liam won't be bored to death.'

'I'm free all day. How about if I take him out? We'd have a whale of a time. I mean, he would. That's what I meant.' Ed's expression was eager. Her heart leapt and she wasn't at all sure whether she was pleased or scared by his offer. She swallowed, and took a deep breath.

'Really? You want to spend the whole day with a four-year-old?'

'Be fair. He's not just any four-year-old. He's Captain Fantastic! It'll be a laugh!' He added hurriedly, glancing at her expression, 'And obviously I'd feed him and everything. Pie and a pint will do him, won't it? Or fill him full of Smarties?'

'You are not having my son and—'

'I'm only joking, Jo. I know how to feed him. I've watched you often enough. Whole foods, low sugar, no junk. There's a deli that does a kid's takeaway. I might even eat one myself.' He grinned. 'And that leaves you and Beryl to shop till you drop. We've got our phones so we can keep in touch if anything happens. Not that anything will happen, of course.'

He'd obviously thought it through. She wasn't sure who was more surprised, her or Ed, to hear her words, 'Okay, why not? Thank you!'

Her cherished child, and she'd trusted him to Ed. But one

look at them together was enough to know that they'd both have fun.

Ed delivered Jo and a dozy Liam with a sense of euphoria. The words had been out of his mouth before he'd thought it over, and even now he'd had time to think about it, he was still glad he'd offered to have Liam for the day. And not a little surprised that Jo had agreed! Liam was so precious to her – it had to mean something that she'd entrusted him to Ed's care. It was a chance to have a great day with the little boy, and also to show Jo that he could be responsible.

He was beginning to deeply regret his well-earned reputation. It had been fun up until now, but since he'd met Jo, he wanted ... well, he glanced over at the two of them, Liam leaning into Jo, head lolling, and he wanted to be better. For them. For her. And he was still having fun – just a different kind. Deeper. More satisfying.

He'd have a word with his mate Cled, and find out what little kids liked doing these days. Although after spending so much time with Liam, he had a pretty good idea already – but he wanted to give him a day to remember.

Chapter Twenty-Two

Saturday was a bitty, disjointed sort of day. In a morning beset with soft but relentless rain, Jo and Liam scoured the local charity shops for a tweed cap which would fit him and not fall over his eyes too much, and something which could stand in as a jacket, or tank-top, or pullover. Liam was tired and whiney, and Jo wisely cut the trip short very quickly after finding the cap. She'd have to sort out the other stuff later.

Back home, the builders were back and forth and Liam seemed determined to get under their feet until Jo felt frazzled and irritable herself, as she tried to write down all the nagging tasks that whirled around her head. Priding herself on her usual organisational skills, Jo wrote everything down to keep track … and what with things for Liam, the café, shopping, and the bike show, her little notebook was a mass of scribbles and crossings out. The stickers Liam didn't use were pressed into service, leaving her notes sprinkled with Mr Men, space rockets and dinosaurs.

Liam interrupted with incessant 'Look, Mummy' this, and 'Mummy, can I?' that, until finally she gave up. The sun had decided to make an appearance at last and getting the eBike and tagalong out again, they headed off to the towering Oystermouth Castle, overlooking the shimmering expanse of Mumbles Bay. After a sulk about not being allowed to use his new bike, Liam perked up enormously, hiding round corners and making her pretend-jump as he leapt out at her, giggling.

Taking advantage of his improved mood, Jo made a game of visiting the few charity shops in the High Street, and managed to find a little tweed jacket, to her delight. It looked as if it was probably a little girl's originally, but she was sure that Beryl would work wonders on it. There was also an almost new little boy's rucksack that she pounced on for him, thinking of the following weekend. It was blue with a big yellow paw-print and they both fell instantly in love with it.

As they cycled home Liam sang at the top of his voice and pointed over the hedges at the new lambs as they scampered and played.

'I could have ridden my new bike, Mummy. Couldn't I? It wasn't that far, really.'

'That's because I was towing you, sweetheart!' Jo called back to him over her shoulder. 'Maybe when Ed has put stabilisers on it for you, we can go for some little rides. And you can see better over the hedges at the lambs on this, can't you? You'd be ever so low down on your own bike.'

Jo felt exhausted. It would help if she actually slept these days.

With Ed and his parents showing such faith in her, she was determined to do her best – even though her stomach churned every time her mind touched on the bike show weekend. It was undeniably exciting – a break from the commonplace activities of their lives as it had been for so long – the ordered, reliable rut, which for years had given Jo some much needed peace. Since meeting Ed, everything in her life had been shaken up and nothing had settled back to where it used to be. And although it was thrilling, it scared Jo – because of that feeling that she couldn't quite rely on it. That it might at any moment be yanked away from her. Her nights were peppered with fears that she'd mess up, and Ed would be disappointed in her. In daylight, she could rationalise it, but at night, the fears assailed her.

As her legs churned rhythmically round on the pedal cycle, to a backdrop of Liam singing a collection of mis-remembered nursery rhymes to the wrong tunes, Jo took a deep breath, sucking in the tangy salty sea scent, which was never far away anywhere on the peninsula. She noticed the yellow and blue wild flowers garlanding the hedges, and she felt thankful. For her's and Liam's strong legs, for a life that was unfolding before her – a safe, warm house, and two jobs.

All she had to do was to put her big girl's pants on, and do her best.

Ed tapped a tune on the caravan windows as he passed each one early the following morning, sending Liam into overdrive. The little boy's excited voice could be heard from outside the van, and Ed chuckled to himself. He was looking forward to the day as much as Liam and, more to the point, he wanted to show Jo that he could be trusted.

'He's here! Mummy! He's here!' Liam opened the caravan door, running on the spot as Ed climbed the steps.

Jo stuffed another spare pair of underpants into the little bag of clothing she'd set aside to give Ed, and smiled at them both.

'Where are we going?' Liam demanded. 'I've got a new rucksack, look!' He dangled the blue bag with its yellow paw print at arm's length.

'Wow, it's a Jack Wolfskin!' said Ed, inspecting the bag. 'Look at you, designer-dude!'

'I've put some spare clothes in this carrier in case he needs them.' Jo looked at Ed with a meaningful eye. 'And there's a sliced apple, raisins and a little banana in this plastic box in case he needs a snack. If he's grouchy, feed him.' She laughed at Ed's expression. 'Remind him to drink his water, please.' She lowered her voice, and continued, 'He can use the toilet by himself, but don't wait for him to ask, or you'll need more than this bag of clothes. He just doesn't like to think he might be missing something, so he tends to hang on till it's too late. And he might need some help bum wiping if he has a poo. I've put a loo roll in ... and wet wipes.'

Ed made a horrified face and Jo chuckled. 'You did offer ...'

'We'll manage,' said Ed, looking down at Liam. 'Won't we, mate?'

'Now, you've got my mobile number ... sorry, I know I'm fussing.' Jo opened the rucksack again to look inside. Ed waited patiently, understanding how difficult this was for her. 'He'll eat anything, but if you value your car upholstery I'd go steady on the ice cream and sweets.'

'Check.' Ed nodded.

'Chips,' said Liam, listening with a wise look on his little face.

'There are shoes and wellies in the bag, in case you want to go paddling or whatever. What have you got planned?'

'Go-karting first,' said Ed, promptly, 'and then maybe the outdoor trampolines, depending on the weather, and then the adventure playground and mini-golf place along the seafront if he's still got any energy left.'

'*Wow.*' Jo looked impressed, and Ed hoped she was. He'd confirmed all this with Cled. 'Liam will have a wonderful day! I almost wish I was going along too.' Ed wished that too. Maybe another time. 'Sounds like you've put a lot of thought into this! Can I suggest you maybe do the trampoline first? Or at least before lunch?'

'Good thinking.' Ed nodded. 'Daisy used to love the trampolines. Haven't had a chance to try the go-karts yet!'

'You're an old hand at this, I keep forgetting,' Jo said. 'If I wasn't looking forward to my day out with Beryl, I'd be feeling quite left out. Go-karting sounds brilliant. Well, enjoy yourselves, boys, and I'll see you both later!'

'What time do you want him back?'

Jo shrugged. 'Look, Ed, I trust you ... the shops shut at four on a Sunday, but if you're having a good time, just bring him back when you're done. He's got bags of energy, as you know, but if he gets tired, hole up in a café or something. He soon perks up after a break or some food. Little boys are little engines … they need refuelling!'

They looked over to where Liam was 'practicing headstands' on the sofa at the front of the caravan, which amounted to him bent like a hairpin with his head on the carpet. 'You will watch him, won't you? He's like Billy Whizz, one minute he's there, next minute he's gone. Don't let him out of your sight …'

'I will watch him, Jo, I promise. Have a good day with Beryl.' Ed gently prised the bag of spare clothes from her clutches and peered inside. 'Crikey, Liam. Is it just one day, or are we going on holiday?'

'Holiday!' yelled Liam. 'Let's go!'

'Bye, sweetie.' Jo bent to squeeze him and Ed felt for her as the little boy wriggled impatiently away. 'Have a lovely day, and be good for Ed!'

'Love you!' she called to their departing backs, Ed holding firmly onto the skipping Liam's hand.

'Love you too!' Ed threw over his shoulder with a cheeky grin. 'Right, c'mon, Liam! Let's go paint the town red!'

'I didn't bring my colouring pencils with me. I need to go back!' The little boy's hand twisted in his but Ed kept a steady hold.

'It's a figure of speech, mate. Paint the town red means to have a good time.'

'Oh. Okay. Yay!' Liam yelled. 'Let's go and colour in!'

Jo's stomach flipped back and forth and she was still standing, hand half raised outside the caravan after they'd disappeared down the lane, as Beryl bustled into sight.

'Ready?'

'*Oh!*' Jo blinked at Beryl. 'Yes! Just …'

'He'll be fine.' Beryl looked down the lane. 'They'll have a great time … you know they will.'

'Yes. Yes, I know.' Jo nodded, swallowing. 'I'll just get my stuff, and I'll be there.'

In no time at all, Beryl was parking near the Swansea Bay Marina.

'Free all day Sunday,' she said, gathering her coat and bag. 'Come on, let's hit the shops first and then stop for coffee.'

The older woman's energy was infectious, and Jo enjoyed relinquishing the lead role for once as Beryl marched her to shops that Jo didn't even know existed.

They bought long grey socks and a skinny tweedy tie for Liam, plus a soft grey jersey shirt that looked just like the old woollen shirts of the forties. Jo had decided that he could wear his school shoes, even though they were modern velcro trainers, but Beryl was determined to find him something that would pass for a hobnail boot. Stopping for coffee an hour later, Jo texted Ed to see how they were getting on.

'Oh, look, Beryl!' Jo turned the phone screen to show the photo of Liam, wearing a helmet and goggles and overalls, beside a miniature go-kart. 'Isn't that cute? I'd never have thought about taking him there. I probably couldn't have afforded it anyway, to be honest.'

'He's a good egg, that young man,' said Beryl, nodding. 'We'll go to the dress shop that his mum recommended next, but can we just pop into the flea market here and hunt down a pair of kiddies boots?'

Fuelled by coffee and an enormous salted caramel muffin, Jo humoured her, sure that they were never going to find what they were looking for at a price she could afford.

But Beryl was unstoppable. She dived into the heaps of old footwear and had the stallholder searching too. Triumphantly waving a pair of the tattiest old boots ever aloft, she haggled the price down like a pro. A seasoned bargain hunter herself,

Jo decided she'd met her match, although the boots looked in shocking condition and she wasn't at all sure she wanted to put them on Liam's feet. She always saved and bought new for him ... other stuff, coats and jeans, whatever, she'd happily buy 'pre-loved', but feet needed to be properly fitted. Goodness only knew where these had been. They looked a hundred years old. Which was exactly the point, she supposed.

Outside, Beryl took the boots out of their brown paper bag and inspected them with pride. Jo didn't have the heart to tell her that they were ghastly. It was one thing to pick up an old cabinet or bit of furniture and do it up to sell, but quite another to clothe her son in hideous junk.

'They look awful now, I know,' Beryl said, turning one of the little boots over in her hands, 'but look, a good scrub, and then a few layers of dubbin, and they'll look brilliant.'

Jo picked the other one up, pulling back the tongue to look inside. It was cobwebby and dusty, but the leather was smooth and uncracked, showing that it had been looked after. They might clean up, after all. And Liam would only be wearing them for a short time.

'Where's this place you've been told about?' Beryl asked.

Jo pulled out the piece of paper Ed had written the address on and they both squinted over it.

'It's not in the main shopping centre,' said Beryl, pulling out her iPhone, and keying in the address. 'But that's not really a surprise. Probably a cheaper location.'

Jo watched her with admiration as she held the phone aloft. 'Come on!' she said, lining up her phone with the street. 'This way. It's a bit of a trek, but we need to walk those muffins off.'

Vintage Rose, as the sign proclaimed it to be, looked tiny from the outside, with a single window onto the slightly shabby backstreet, but as Beryl bustled in, Jo could see that the shop was much larger. She'd been expecting a fusty place, packed rails, and a case of rummaging to find what you wanted, but this was like stepping straight into the forties – glamour called from the full-length ornate mirrors and glittering chandeliers, the beaded necklaces draped from elegant dresses on padded satin hangers. There were hats on tall stands, patent leather belts, and polished leather court shoes displayed prettily on boxes alongside.

This was no flea market like the one where they'd bought Liam's hobnail boots. It truly was a boutique. Jo sniffed the distinct scent of roses and spotted the little dishes of potpourri dotted about the gleaming surfaces, and the tiny pink scented soaps and bath bombs shaped as roses. On the counter stood a bowl of fat pink roses.

'Good morning,' said a light voice.

Jo whirled round. '*Oh*! Good morning!' She'd been so busy staring round the shop she hadn't even noticed anyone in there. The voice belonged to a tiny girl who looked as if she'd stepped straight out of the forties herself. With her dark curly hair clipped up at one side and falling in luxurious waves to her shoulders, she was wearing a deep red dress with a V-wrapped neckline and tightly cinched waist. Jo caught sight of herself in one of the full-length mirrors … in her jeans, vest and blazer outfit she looked smarter than usual, but still somehow unfinished. She hated that she was making comparisons – it took time and money to look smart, and she didn't have either of those luxuries.

'Lovely shop,' she said to the girl. Beryl had already made her way to the back of the shop and was busy riffling through the displays, while Jo was rooted to the spot at the front, running the satiny fabrics of scarves and blouses through her fingers and trying to see the prices without making it look obvious.

'Can I help you with anything?'

'No, thanks, I—' began Jo, at the same time as Beryl said, 'Yes, please. We're looking for a jacket or cardigan for a dress similar to this, in a ten, possibly smaller. And shoes ... and a bag.'

Flicking over one of the dainty price tickets and reading it with horror, Jo tried desperately to catch Beryl's eye. She couldn't, wouldn't commit to spending on things she didn't need, just for this dratted bike show. She should have asked Ed for some money. Why hadn't she?

'Is it for a particular occasion?' the girl asked. 'A tea dance or something? Hen party?'

'Goodness me, what a lovely idea!' Beryl said.

'Yes, afternoon teas are very popular with hens! And dressing up does make it special – lovely photos too, perfect for social media,' said the tiny girl.

'It's for a vintage bike show,' Jo blurted. 'I'm working on one of the stands, and I have to be dressed in the same period as the motorbikes.'

'*Oh*! Are you Jo, by any chance?'

'I am, yes ...'

'How nice to meet you. I'm Marjorie.' She held out a childlike hand and Jo shook it, feeling her own hand enclose Marjorie's completely. She felt gigantic beside her. 'Lyn rang me – she said you'd be coming in. She said to give you this.' Reaching behind the counter, she lifted out a rose pink tissue envelope and handed it to the puzzled Jo.

The envelope was sealed at the point with a tiny rosebud, and Jo slid her fingernail beneath it, reluctant to rip it.

'Open it, girl!' said Beryl, at her shoulder.

Jo drew out the contents and stared at it. The pink edged stiff card inscribed with flowing script told her that it was a gift voucher, to the tune of £200.

'*Wow*!' said Beryl. 'How lovely.'

Marjorie smiled.

'Lyn told me what she thought you probably needed to buy, and I told her how much it might be.'

'But … that's such a lot of money!' Jo stared at the voucher, swallowing down the lump in her throat. How kind of Lyn and Griff. 'I can't possibly accept it.'

'Don't worry, you don't have to spend it all. I can refund the difference to her.'

Jo reached out and turned over the nearest price ticket, and then another, adding up in her head. Eventually she nodded.

'Thank you!' she said. 'I was really worried about it. How nice of her. And you!'

'So,' Marjorie tipped her head and appraised Jo. 'What kind of look are you after?'

Jo looked nonplussed, as Beryl said, 'Glamorous, groomed, sexy.'

'Oh, really, no, I was thinking, er …' Jo said, flustered. She couldn't really say she'd been thinking 'cheap'. In price, of course. Not morals.

'No problem,' Marjorie said with a smile. 'So, you have a dress already, I understand?'

'Yes, but it's a bit short …'

Marjorie turned to Beryl, who nodded.

'It is, but she's got great legs. I know it's not exactly the right period to have your knees on show, but …'

'Well, actually, the thirties had the skirt to calf length and the forties brought them up to the knee, so you'd be fine. You're happy with it otherwise?'

Jo nodded, but couldn't prevent her eyes from straying towards the racks of dresses. What was happening to her? She was a shorts and jeans girl through and through … and yet, she was becoming bewitched by the rose petals and scents of this shop.

'That is pretty, isn't it?' said Marjorie, following Jo's gaze and lifting the exquisite dress off the rail. 'Very Rita

Hayworth. Why don't you try it on, and then we can accessorise more easily with the bag and bits and bobs.'

Jo allowed herself to be chivvied into the changing room, with its soft lighting, pink brocade stool and heavy jacquard curtains in grey, threaded through with metallic pink. The effect was like walking onto a Hollywood set. Jo found herself imagining how her upcycled pieces would look photographed against this kind of backdrop.

It was sumptuous … and gave the impression of luxury, whilst actually probably not that expensive to do. It was just about having a vision, she realised, conjuring up the newly renovated Seagull Cottage, and indulging in a little daydream about having a bedroom like this changing room. With a bit less pink. And maybe some soft, warm greys.

'Need a hand?' Beryl called through the curtain after a few moments.

'Nope, I'm good, thanks.' Jo wriggled the zip closed and inspected her reflection. Her jauntily patterned ankle socks jarred horribly with the pretty blown rose pattern on cream fabric. 'Are there any tights I could borrow? Or buy?'

Beryl returned in seconds and handed a pair of nude tights to her through the curtain. Once she'd carefully pulled them on, the mirror showed her a complete stranger. She tugged her hair out of its band and held it up at the side, like Marjorie's.

'Come on! Let the dog see the rabbit!' Beryl urged.

Tentatively, Jo stepped through the curtains. Marjorie clapped and Beryl gave a wide smile, dabbing at her eyes.

'Beryl, you softie! It's not a wedding dress!' Jo laughed. 'Could you help me find a cardy, please, and some shoes? I'll bloody freeze if I have to wear just this at the show.'

'*Tut*,' said Beryl, heading off to riffle through the racks. 'You can take the girl out of London, but you can't take London out of the girl.'

Jo laughed, and then stopped. Had she told Beryl that

she came from London? She shrugged. She probably had. Yes, didn't she usually say something like she'd arrived for a visit and never went home? And her London accent was a giveaway, of course, although it was much softer now.

She didn't like any of the cardigans, declaring them 'mumsy' and Marjorie steered her instead to a dark velvet nipped in jacket with shoulder pads. The bag – not vintage, but a reasonable imitation and affordable – was easy. Not so the shoes. Jo had bigger feet than most of the tiny shoes in Marjorie's collections – or if they fitted, they were toweringly high.

'I'll break my neck in these,' she complained. 'Didn't they ever wear flatties?'

'*Hmm.*' Marjorie paced her shop, and Jo couldn't help noticing her petite feet, surely not much bigger than Liam's. She wanted to hide hers.

'We need to sort your hair out too,' said Beryl, lounging in a velour armchair, upholstered in the inevitable pink.

'How about these?' Marjorie had returned from the depths of her stock room, a pair of what looked like leather bowling shoes with a small heel in her hands. They were cobalt blue.

'That's more like it!' Jo snatched them up, ignoring Beryl's sad expression. 'I love them! God, I hope they fit …'

'Glass of Prosecco, ladies?' Marjorie said, as Jo pulled the shoes on in an ungainly fashion.

'Is it pink?' said Jo, lacing the first shoe.

Marjorie's laugh tinkled merrily, as she offered them crystal glasses on a silver tray, and opened the bottle of fizz. 'Of course! You had to ask?'

'*Oh*, just a little one,' said Beryl. 'I'm driving.'

'God, I'd better not spill any on this dress.' Holding the glass carefully away from her, Jo sipped hers from a distance. 'I'd have to add to Lyn's voucher for this!'

'It does look lovely on you,' Marjorie nodded. 'I heard you mention your hair, would you like some tips?'

Jo sank onto a second chair, upholstered in grey. With pink arms. 'Go on then. I'm not promising that I'll manage to do it, mind.'

'*Oh*, but you have to! It's the little things that make all the difference.' Marjorie moved Jo to a chair before a mirror lit with lamps all the way round, and then began to brush and backcomb, pinning here and clipping there.

'Backcombing!' Jo grumbled. It reminded her of her mother. 'Doesn't that split your hair?'

'Do it with the brush, and don't be vicious,' said Marjorie. 'Look. What do you think?'

'*Oh*. I wish that was me,' Beryl said with a deep sigh. 'You look like a film star, Jo.'

'Hah. If only.' Jo laughed, but, secretly, she was delighted with the way she looked. She pushed the thought away. This was a one-off. It would only make her want a way of life that she didn't have the rights to.

'So ... just make-up now.' Marjorie regarded her with a proprietorial air. 'It had a minimal look in the forties, really, just about definition.' Jo heaved a sigh of relief, until Marjorie added, 'But the lipstick was everything. Crimson. Or coral. You've got lippie though ... everyone's got lippie, haven't they ...?'

'*Pah*. Not unless you count Vaseline as lipstick,' said Beryl, twirling her pink Prosecco. 'And that doesn't come in red.'

They both inspected Jo until she wilted before them.

'Oh ... *ok-aay*! Do your worst.' She submitted as Marjorie covered her with a huge silky gown to protect the dress and fluffed her with face powder from a huge pink puff. Defining her brows with a pencil, she teased, 'Do you actually own any tweezers, Jo?' and from a case of brushes which any artist would be proud of, made up her eyes and then mascara-ed layer after layer until Jo's eyes were watering. Finally, lipstick was painted carefully within the lines that Marjorie drew, and then Jo was invited to view the results.

'*Wow.*' Beryl was open-mouthed. 'Me next!'

Jo leaned into the mirror and stared at herself. This really wasn't her at all. Not one little bit. It was a beautiful woman who might have been a distant cousin. When she said that, Marjorie and Beryl laughed.

'That's the real you! It's just that the make-up is helping you to see yourself,' said Marjorie. She glanced down at the delicate gold watch on her birdlike wrist. 'Goodness me, look at the time! I'm actually closed!'

Guilt leapt in Jo's chest – she hadn't given a thought to Liam and Ed. In the little changing cubicle she wriggled out of the beautiful dress, hung it up reluctantly with a feeling of sadness and carefully stepped out of the tights. The afternoon had flown, and to her surprise, she'd completely enjoyed herself. Perhaps she should spend a little more time on her appearance, every now and again.

Marjorie was totting up Jo's purchases at her antique and baroque till, and Jo held her breath, her heart hammering. Suddenly, she wanted to leave right away, ring Ed and see if everything was okay. She felt hot and slightly sick. It must be the Prosecco, on an empty stomach. That would be it.

'A fair bit to go back to Lyn from her voucher,' said Marjorie. 'I haven't charged you for the hair and make-up tutorial, but I'd recommend you buy some make-up, honestly, Jo. There's this little set here.' She pushed the palette towards Jo, who deliberated for only a moment beneath Beryl's steady gaze before agreeing.

'Hairpins? Clips?' Marjorie asked. Those went in the bag too.

'That dress,' said Marjorie. Jo edged towards the door, anxious to leave, guilty now that she'd only just remembered

Liam and Ed. 'It looked fabulous on you ... now, I know there's not quite enough money left on the voucher, but it's nearly enough, and I was thinking ... if you could put some cards and brochures out on the stand to advertise my shop ... and some photos of you while you're there that I could use ... then ...'

'I'm sure we can do that.' Jo eyed her, trying not to hope. She shouldn't hope.

'Then I think we have a deal,' said Marjorie, hooking the beautiful dress off the hanger and laying it on the counter to wrap it in tissue.

Jo swallowed. It was truly the most stunning dress she'd ever owned, and she wanted to cry. She sniffed. 'Thank you so much,' she whispered.

Beryl handed her a tissue and said, 'You can keep it at my house until yours is done.'

'Oh God, yes, please.' She turned to Marjorie with a self-deprecating laugh. 'I'm trailer trash at the moment.'

'No, she isn't,' said Beryl, with a tut. 'She'll have the most fabulous cottage very soon, but she's having to be minimal about possessions just now.'

They left with a pile of business cards and brochures and hugs all round, both of them slightly breathless and giggly from the combined effects of the pink fizz and the sense of having participated in a performance of some sort.

'I can't believe it's gone four,' said Jo, as they hurried back towards the car park. Jostling her purchases, she checked her phone. 'No messages from Ed ... I hope they're okay.'

'Boys day out ... they'll be enjoying themselves.' Beryl squinted up at the road name. 'Was it this way? I don't think I can carry my phone and these bags.'

'I think I should ring, make sure,' Jo said, following Beryl without attending at all to their location. Hooking the bags into her elbow, she found Ed's number and rang it. There was no answer.

'He might just be out of signal. Don't panic,' Beryl said. 'I think it's this way. Yes. This is it.'

'No, it's me. I haven't got a signal.' Jo trotted behind, staring at the little screen. 'Stupid thing.' She slid the phone into the pocket of her jeans. If it rang, she'd feel it buzz, and wouldn't have to hunt through her bag. Settling the shopping more evenly on her arms, she looked up at the buildings. 'Wasn't it this way, Beryl? There's a sign for the Marina there,' she gestured with her head.

'Oh, yes, I was just testing you,' Beryl puffed and they both laughed, jogging across the traffic lights as they turned red. 'Jaywalking now! You're such a bad influence on me!'

As they reached the pavement, Jo's phone buzzed in her pocket. Fumbling to answer it, one of the bags slid to the ground – the one containing the dress. She shrieked into the phone, '*Agh!* Yes?'

'What?' said Ed's voice. 'Are you okay?'

'Me? Yes … I'm ringing about you? Are you okay?'

'I'm ringing you, Jo.'

'Oh.' Jo took a breath. 'Sorry. Yes, of course you are. So … is everything okay? How's Liam? Have you had a lovely day? We've had a fabulous day, we—'

'We're at the hospital, Jo—'

Chapter Twenty-Three

'You're what?' Jo shouted into the phone. 'Hospital? Which hospital?'

'Singleton. Down the road.'

'Wh-what? Why? Is Liam okay? What's happened?' Her fingers felt nerveless and she had to squeeze the phone in case she dropped it. Why had she left Liam with this idiot? To go shopping? For goodness' sakes! She'd never forgive herself. Never.

'He's ...' The phone crackled and Jo found herself screaming into a dead line. She clicked return call, and listened as it rang without being answered, then just as she dragged all the bags together intending to run for the car park, it rang again.

'Ed!' She shrieked into it. 'Just tell me ... is Liam okay?'

'He's ... mumble mumble ... I ... mumble ...' Ed's voice crackled.

'We're on our way!' Shoving the phone in her pocket she turned to Beryl. 'Hospital ... Liam ...' Her voice cracked as her throat closed with panic and fear.

Beryl put her fingers to her mouth and whistled shrilly. To Jo's astonishment, a taxi appeared from nowhere and cruised to a halt beside them.

'Car park, quickly,' Beryl said, bundling Jo in with all her bags and climbing in after her.

'Yep, which car park's that then, love?' The taxi driver craned his head to look at her.

'*Er* ... the one on the Marina! Quick!'

The taxi swung into the traffic and Beryl patted Jo's hand. 'We'll be there in no time. It's only up the road. What did Ed actually say?'

'Nothing,' Jo said. Feeling sick, she fumbled with the door panel knobs, trying to wind the window down and realising there wasn't a winder. 'The line went dead. Both times. Oh God, Beryl …' She turned wide, frightened eyes on the older woman.

Beryl reached across her and opened the window.

'Deep breaths. You don't know anything yet … stop expecting the worst. Look. Here's the car park … and there's my car. We'll be there now in a minute.'

She passed the few coins to the driver, who said, 'Hope everything's okay,' before driving off.

Nothing could go fast enough for Jo. She wanted to scream at Beryl, who seemed to be taking an eternity to stow the bags, switch on the engine, clip on her seat belt, check the mirror, pull away. She felt that if she jumped out, she could run there faster – be at Liam's bedside, comfort his bruised, battered body. She imagined him in the bed – had he been run over? And she hadn't been there for him. What had happened? What?

Sweat trickled in the small of her back and she clawed again at the door for some fresh air.

'I'll open the window from here,' said Beryl, her calmness piercing Jo's fog of fear. 'There's the hospital … just need to turn right at the traffic lights, and it's just by there, look. Goodness me, I used to be in and out of here all the time with my boys.' She manoeuvred the car around the buildings, driving right up to the door. 'Minor Injuries … that's where they'll be. Used to be Casualty, *pah*, another casualty of the National Health. I'll park and come and find you. You go. It'll be fine, really.'

Even though her legs almost gave way climbing out of the car, Jo marched through the double doors of the hospital, a determined set to her jaw, the mother bear searching for her wounded cub. Her gaze raked the waiting room as she approached the desk.

'Hello ... I believe my son Liam has been brought here. Is he—'

'Do you have any ID?' said the receptionist.

Jo stared at her. What did she have? She didn't even have a passport! 'I've got this ...' She opened her wallet and showed her bank debit card, 'He came in with Ed ... *er* ... Idris Griffiths?'

'Ah. Yes, they're both booked in ... Liam is in the Children's Ward,' she pointed, 'and Mr Griffiths is—'

Jo barely listened before running in the direction she'd given.

Liam was at a little table, colouring in.

'Mummy!' Liam called to her. 'It's my mummy,' he told the young nurse beside him.

'Liam?' Jo's eyes scanned him more fiercely than any machine. 'Are ... are you okay? Is he okay? What's this on his face?' She ran her hands over him as she hugged him, checking him over.

'*Ouch*, Mummy. That hurt!'

'What did? What hurt, baby?' She looked over at the nurse. 'What happened?'

'Bit of a black eye ... you can see the bruising starting to come out here.' The nurse pointed it out. 'He's been checked for concussion ...'

'Concussion?' Jo gaped. 'What exactly happened? And ...' Her head swivelled around the ward. 'Where's Ed?'

'His daddy?

'His—? *Er* ... yes ... his ... *er* ... Daddy ...'

'He's in the Treatment Room,' said the nurse. 'There's no other damage. Liam's such a brave boy, aren't you, sweetheart?'

'I am,' said Liam, proudly.

Jo wanted to scream. She said, in her 'just tell Mummy everything and it will all be okay' voice, 'Darling, what happened just before you came here?'

'Well,' said Liam, going back to his colouring and not meeting her eye, 'I flied, and Daddy catched me.'

'Caught,' corrected Jo, before she could stop herself. 'You ... you "flied"? What does that mean?' And then, "Daddy?" She stood up and looked around. 'How long will Ed be? Why is he in the Treatment Room? Where IS the Treatment Room?'

'I had to leave him in there.' Liam crayoned on.

'How long ago? Is Liam ready to leave?' Jo had a terrible feeling of foreboding, now that she'd seen her son in one piece.

'I'll get the doctor to come and have a chat with you.'

Beryl was leafing through ancient magazines in the packed Waiting Room, as Jo flopped onto the chair beside her, hefting Liam onto her lap.

'Ah ... so Liam's okay then!' Beryl smiled at them both. 'One down, one to go! What's happened?'

Jo shrugged in frustration. 'Apparently Ed's in the Treatment Room. All Liam says is that he flew and Ed caught him ... whatever that means. And Liam has a bit of a black eye.' She explained what the Paediatric Doctor had told her.

'Goodness me,' said Beryl, looking Liam over more closely. 'Well, a Boys Day Out isn't complete without a black eye.'

It felt like an eternity before the double doors swung open, and Ed appeared, beside him a young nurse who was looking up at him with the adoring expression which was inevitably worn by every female within close proximity of him. What was more unusual though, was the sling holding his arm across his chest ... and the paleness of his face. Dislodging Liam, Jo leapt to her feet.

'Ed ... oh my God ... what on earth happened? Sit down. Are you sure you're alright to come home?' Jo guided him to a chair and she and Beryl flanked him.

'Sorry, Jo, I'm so, so sorry.' His voice was so small she had to lean in to hear. He put a hand out to keep her away from his dressed arm. 'Mum's on her way to collect us ... well, me, now you're here, Liam can go home with you.'

'Your poor mum!' As if she didn't have enough to contend with right now.

He glanced over at her, a look so full of intensity that she recoiled. 'I know.' He nodded.

'I can take you home, no need to get your mum out,' Beryl said from his other side. 'Can you tell us what happened?'

Jo noticed that Liam was leaning against Beryl, fiddling with a crayon.

'Monkey rings,' said Ed.

'Uh-oh,' said Beryl, with a sidelong look at Liam.

'Liam, you're not allowed on the monkey rings, you know that,' Jo said, seeing that the crayon was suddenly the most important and interesting item in Liam's world. 'What did you do?'

'I can do it on myself. I can!' pouted the little boy, flinging the crayon onto the shiny floor, where it broke into pieces. There were tuts from the full Waiting Room.

'And you believed him?' Jo winced, visualising the scene. 'Oh, Ed, you numpty. What have you done to yourself?'

'Dislocated my shoulder.'

'Ouch,' said Jo and Beryl together with feeling. 'Poor you!'

Liam began to cry. Beryl lifted him onto her lap, where he burrowed his head into her shoulder, avoiding Jo's gaze.

'I don't know,' said Beryl, rubbing the little boy's back. 'Ed is the one who gets hurt, and you're the one who's crying!'

'It was an accident,' said Ed. 'Could've happened to anyone.'

'I'll ring your mum and let her know we'll take you home,' said Jo, dialling as she spoke. 'So, what actually happened?' She swivelled towards him as the phone rang in her ear.

'We'd had a fab day – karting – Liam was brilliant. He's got no fear!'

'No, I know.' Jo rolled her eyes with a glimmer of a smile, as the phone was answered. Briefly she caught Lyn up to speed, making light of it, understanding somehow that it was what Ed needed. He nodded, a little colour coming back into his face, she presumed as the painkillers kicked in. She hung up the phone. 'And then?'

'Well, he ate a huge burger and chips, and I thought that trampolining might not be a good idea …'

'Good call.'

'So – we went on the beach, kicked a ball round, played crazy golf …'

'Sounds lovely.'

'… and then he saw the adventure playground. He went onto everything – no problem – he scared the pants off me a few times climbing onto the space thing, like a giant ball made out of connectors or something … and I'm standing underneath waiting to catch him, and he says,' Ed lowered his voice, and continued in a Liam impersonation, '"I do it on myself, okay, Ed? I do it on myself," and he gives me this fierce look every time I'm helping him – because he's only four, right? And he goes onto something else, and then, God, then I looked away for a nanosecond, and he's stepped into space onto a fireman's pole thing …'

'Yeah, he does that to me too,' said Jo, with a wry grin, visualising the scene with feeling.

'So, I make a game of helping him slide down that, and he's cross with me for helping.' He glanced over to where Liam was snuggled into Beryl's shoulder. 'I don't want to grass him up or anything …'

'You're not. But I don't want him to do it to me next time we're there!'

'He runs over to the monkey rings. They're a bit bloody

high, I reckon and I tell him that, without the "bloody", but course, he's scampering up the climbing frame thing and I'm telling him to get down because I can suddenly see what he's thinking of and he reaches out and grips the first one and I'm underneath waiting to catch him … but he manages the first one, and then the second, amazing! And he's swinging to get the next one and then he just … goes! And course, I'm underneath, so I catch him, no problem, but as I do I kind of trip and I twist and hold him away from me so I don't fall on top of him and I fall right on my shoulder instead.'

'Ouch, bloody hell, Ed.' Jo's mouth twisted in sympathy. 'That was very naughty of him though, not to do as he was told. I'm so sorry.'

'Don't be cross with him. He just wanted to show me what he could do.' He grinned at her. 'He's so strong, Jo! I tell you, give him a year and he'll be flying across those rings. He should be doing gymnastics. If I hadn't tripped, we'd probably still be there and you'd still be shopping.'

'I'd already bought half the shop anyway, so don't worry about that. I've got the most fabulous outfit for the show—' She clapped a hand over her mouth, stricken, as her brain joined the dots. 'How long will you be in that?' She pointed at his sling.

'Yeah, I've already thought about that,' Ed said, slumping into the hard chair and wincing. 'I can take this off after a couple of days, they said, but no heavy lifting for a good few weeks. I don't know what to do about the show. I can't possibly leave it all to you – we'll have to cancel. What a state, father and son, the dynamic duo! Not.'

'We-ell,' Jo thought quickly. 'Could you ring the organisers and see if anyone could help set up the stand once you're there? You've got loads of mates to help you load and unload at this end. And,' she took a breath, 'I'm strong. You know I am. I can help. I can put the gazebo up and I'm sure I can move those bikes about. You've told me often enough that it's just about confidence and technique.'

Beryl leaned forward, Liam still curled onto her lap. 'Do you feel well enough to leave now, Ed? I can bring the car a bit nearer for you.'

'Where's your car?' Jo said to Ed as Beryl left, leaving a grumpy and tear-stained Liam half lying across Jo.

'Car park.' He jerked his head towards the exit. 'I'll get a mate to collect it for me.'

'How did you get it here?'

'Drove. Superhuman, me.' He attempted a grin, but his grey face showed how much pain he was still in, and Jo wondered how on earth he'd managed to get them both there safely.

'Ye-es … just that the car seat is in it. For Liam. So we can all get home. Can I have the key?'

'Shame you can't drive,' said Ed, handing it over after an awkward tussle with his pockets. Jo almost offered to get them, just as she would have had he been Liam, but stopped herself just in time.

'I can drive,' she said.

'But you said … you said you don't drive.'

'I said, I don't.' She shrugged. 'That doesn't mean I can't.' Fingering the keys, she said, 'Will your insurance cover me?'

Ed nodded, appraising her. 'How long ago did you drive?'

'Five, nearly six years … mostly tractors. And trucks.'

'But you passed your test, right?'

'Course. It's like riding a bike, right?' She stood up, holding tightly to a tired and grizzly Liam's hand. He was clingy and unsettled, and she inspected the reddened area around his eye, which was changing colour. He'd been lucky, at least he wasn't concussed, but she'd keep a special watch on it. It could have been so much worse. 'I'll get the car seat. Shall we get a bit of fresh air, baby?' she said to Liam.

'Wanna stay wiv Ed,' said Liam, transferring his allegiance and leaning against Ed's leg.

Ed nodded, and her heart hammered as she headed towards the car park.

Thank goodness Beryl had been around, she was so calming. Poor Ed. She felt so sorry for him. He'd really come off worst. She couldn't blame him, not really. The same thing had so nearly happened to her. You only had to blink, take your eye off them for a moment. And being on your own ... it was so hard. Having to be 'on duty' all the time, every single second of the day.

The last couple of weeks since she'd met Ed had changed her life so much – but she was still that single mum on alert for danger. It was exhausting but it had made her tough. Resilient. And brave.

Beryl's car was already outside the glass doors, and Jo climbed in, explaining about the car seat. Beryl drove round to Ed's blue Nissan truck, easy to spot, parked wonkily nose in across two spots.

'I'm going to drive it back,' she told Beryl, drawing in a shaky breath.

Beryl blinked. 'You are full of surprises.' She nodded with a smile. 'Do you want any help?'

'No thanks, I'll manage,' Jo said, hoping that she would. Her heart was already hammering. 'Honestly. I'll be fine.'

'How about I take Liam home with me?' said Beryl. 'He could probably do with a bit of peace and quiet after his exciting day out. You get that other young man home. Ring me if you need a lift back.'

'Thanks, Beryl.' Jo squeezed the older woman's arm and planted a kiss on her soft cheek. 'You're better than a mum to me, you are. I've had the best day.' She chuckled quietly as she fitted the booster seat into Beryl's car. 'Apart from this last bit, obviously.'

'What doesn't kill you, makes you stronger.' Beryl winked, and moved her car out of the way.

Jo clambered into the unaccustomed front seat of the truck, adjusting it and the mirror. She felt sick for the second time that day – and then a bubble of excitement popped in her stomach. Driving again!

Right, now then. Reverse. Where the hell was reverse on this thing? Her nerve almost failed as she pushed and pulled and wiggled the gear stick with no luck. At the last minute, she remembered something from her truck driving days and pushed it into first gear with the clutch down, revved a bit, took it back to neutral and then felt it slip into reverse with ease. Phew. Inching out of the parking space, she gave Beryl – who'd stopped to make sure she was okay, bless her – a thumbs up with a confidence she was barely feeling. Wincing as she ground the gears into first she drove at a snail's pace to the pick-up point, with Beryl tailing her.

'Respect!' Ed nodded at her as he emerged from the hospital entrance. Liam was peeled without complaint from him and perked up when he saw that he was going in Beryl's car, waving jauntily at them from the front seat. Motherhood was a thankless task, she thought with a chuckle.

'Are you sure about this?' she said to Ed, buckling his seat belt carefully around his sling. Leaning across him did funny things to her tummy. His face was so close. She could just turn her head and her lips would meet his and …

'Drugs have kicked in!' he said, cheerfully. 'Get on with it. I'm feeling no pain!'

The sky was pinky blue, reflected in the sea as they cruised along the wide Swansea Boulevard. It was a beautiful evening, but Ed felt nothing but remorse for wrecking the day.

Beside him, Jo hunched over the wheel. He felt sorry for her, and guilt washed over him again. He tried for comedy, making pretend pained faces as she over-revved and crunched the gears.

'You can take over any time,' she told him, her face set and focussed.

'No, no, it's fine. You're doing brilliantly.' Ed shrank into his seat with a pretend scared face. He couldn't help teasing her though. It wouldn't take her long to get into the swing of it, if she could just relax a bit. 'You can go faster than twenty miles an hour, you know.'

'Is there an ejector button on here anywhere?' She huffed. 'This is payback for damaging my son.'

'I think it was him that damaged me, actually.'

She gave a snorted laugh. 'Price of honorary parenthood.'

Ed fell silent, staring over the turquoise sea. She was right there.

'He called you daddy.'

'Aw bless, did he?' Ed's head whipped round to stare at her and winced with the sudden movement. God, that had hurt. So, Liam had called him daddy? But that was … well, that was phenomenal! Wasn't it? It meant that the little boy trusted him, that he was a role model in his life, it was marvellous! Ed felt a surge of pride that he was held in such esteem. He'd never ever thought he'd have that title, it was … wow … wait till he told Cled. He looked at Jo, and the beam on his face fell as he saw her dark expression. She didn't look at all happy. Was it the car? Was it … the 'daddy' thing? He felt as if he was skating across a thinly iced pond. 'I … I never asked him to do that, Jo. I haven't spent the whole day telling everyone I'm his dad! I wouldn't do that!'

Jo's shoulders sagged. She shot him a swift glance, and he couldn't fathom what her expression meant.

'I suppose it was the nurses. Making assumptions. He just

picked up on it.' Her slim fingers on the wheel spread like the wings of a dove. 'He really likes you. But … I don't want him to be confused.' Her voice was sharp and she fell silent.

'No.' Ed slumped back in his seat. 'I get that.' He didn't get it. Not at all. And he didn't know how to ask her without somehow editing himself out of their lives.

Maybe they were better off without him. She'd told him no funny business right at the beginning and, to be fair, she hadn't really given him the slightest encouragement, romantically. Joining them for a meal, watching that silly film, that was a mate's thing, wasn't it? He heaved a sigh, and rubbed at his shoulder to disguise it. Maybe he ought to back off.

Could he, though? He thought back over the day he'd had, with Liam chatting non-stop. It had been such fun, right up until the accident. Even then, even through that shocking pain, his first thought had been for the little boy. He'd been so devastated at Ed's obvious agony, bless him. In short, Ed had felt just like a parent. Responsible. He wasn't used to feeling like that. And he'd liked how it felt.

As for Jo. He slid a sideways glance at her now, concentrating on her driving. His stomach clenched as he watched the long muscles of her lean legs moving beneath her jeans. He couldn't even begin to put into words how he felt about her – his body was doing all the talking. He wasn't at all sure that he could back off now.

Chapter Twenty-Four

'So.' Lyn's expression was despondent. 'That's that then.' They sat in the kitchen, around a pot of tea and a plate of biscuits that only Ed was eating. 'I suppose we might get some money back. On medical grounds. What with Griff, and now you.' She looked Ed over as if he was a teenager who'd fallen out of a tree.

'Nope.' Ed sipped his tea, awkward with his left hand. 'We're doing it. Jo's going to drive the van up.' He couldn't let them down, not after everything they'd done for him.

'O-kaaay ...' Lyn's eyes widened.

Griff appraised Jo with a glimmer of a smile. 'I didn't think Jo drove ...'

'Me neither,' said Ed, sandwiching two biscuits together and dunking them in his tea. 'But she does. Tractors and trucks!'

Jo stared at the table and fiddled with a coaster. She looked miles away. Ed thought she was probably wondering how Liam was. Or was it still the 'daddy' thing? He swallowed, feeling his stomach lurch.

'How will you get on with moving the bikes, Jo?' Lyn said. Griff leaned forward. He was looking much more like his old self, Ed noted with relief.

'I'll teach her,' he said.

'I can do that,' said Griff.

'You most certainly will not,' Lyn said. 'Neither of you is in any fit state. I'll do it. And I'll show her how not to use brute strength.' She looked over at Jo, and smiled. 'It's all about technique.'

'I hope so,' Jo said. 'Does that include the BSA Gold Star?'

Ed gulped at the thought of the most valuable bike in the

collection smashing to the tiled floor. He looked away so that Jo wouldn't see his doubt.

'Oh, by the way, what did you think of Marjorie at Vintage Rose?' his mum asked Jo.

Her face flamed. 'Oh my goodness, I'm so sorry … I should have thanked you for your voucher, Lyn!' She jumped up and ran round the table to give her a hug. Ed was astounded to see her so demonstrative. The only other person he'd seen her hug was Liam. And Beryl.

Lyn waved a hand. 'Don't worry. I think you've had a lot on your mind! Did you find anything suitable?'

'Oh, I should say! Isn't she lovely? We had the best time … and I bought the most utterly beautiful dress.' As Jo described her purchases to Lyn, Ed and Griff exchanged rolled eyes. She laughed. 'This is all your fault, Ed Griffiths. I'd still be in my shorts if it wasn't for this show.'

'Oh now, would that be so bad?' Griff pondered to Ed. Both women laughed as they hammed their response.

'The apple doesn't fall far from the tree,' Lyn said. 'Where is the dress? Can I see it?'

'Drat!' Jo clapped her hands to her cheeks. 'It's in the back of Beryl's car. She's hanging it up for me until the show. I don't have anywhere to hang it in the caravan.'

'Maybe I could run you home and sneak a peek?'

'Mum! It's only a dress …' Ed would never get this fascination with shopping.

'I didn't mean right now! Obviously.' Lyn made a face at her son. 'Anyway, we need to schedule the bike moving lessons. We'll start with the dirt bikes,' she said to Jo. 'They get thrown about anyway, so it won't matter if you drop them.'

Ed and his dad passed a hand over their eyes in simultaneous horror.

'We'll put blankets down,' said Lyn, ignoring them. 'It's all about balance and confidence.'

'That's what Ed says.' So he wasn't quite persona non grata then. He took heart from that.

'Right, well, the Bike Palace will have to be closed this week.' Lyn cleared their mugs as she spoke. 'You two are as much use as chocolate tea strainers. The dirt bikes are in the garage, so how are you fixed for tomorrow evening, Jo?'

'Early?' said Jo. 'Liam …'

'Oh, you can bring Liam. I'll do fish fingers.'

'I love fish fingers!' said Jo.

'With chips?' Ed hoped.

'In your dreams,' Lyn snorted. 'New potatoes and salad.'

'Perfect,' said Jo.

'Oh joy,' said Griff, his mouth quirking up at the side to show that he was only teasing.

Jo chuckled. It was a nice sound.

'Talking of Liam,' she said, 'I'd better make tracks. Thank you for having him today,' she told Ed. 'I'm sorry it ended the way it did.'

'I enjoyed it. Really,' Ed said. He cursed himself for his lack of words, wishing he could say aloud what was whirling round in his brain. If he could only unravel his own thoughts.

Jo sent him a searching look, as if she was trying to decide something about him. 'I'll see you tomorrow, Lyn. Half four?'

Lyn nodded. 'You'll be a bike moving pro in no time.' She stood up. 'I'll run you home.'

'Jo.' Ed dangled the Nissan keys from his forefinger. 'Take the truck. It's insured for employees.'

'Wow. Really?'

'Yep.' He nodded, and added with a smile. 'You need the practice.'

Lyn walked her to the door, leaving him with his dad.

'She's a good 'un,' said Griff, his eyes on the door the two women had just walked through. There was a long silence, and once again Ed felt like a naughty teenager. 'You be careful.'

'I'll be sure to rest it,' Ed said, deliberately misunderstanding his dad. 'We can't both be out of action for too long.' Griff rested his clear gaze on him for a long moment.

'It's a bit of a novelty, with the lad,' he said, eventually. 'But he's not a toy, y'know, that you can put back in the cupboard.'

Ed blinked. He opened his mouth to protest and then shut it again. Was this what *everyone* thought of him? Maybe Jo was better off without him.

'Thanks so much for everything, Jo. You're a breath of fresh air, compared to … well, some of the er … girls that he's, er … brought round.' She added quickly, 'We owe you such a lot. I just wanted to say thank you for being a good friend to Ed.'

'He's been very good to me. To us. Liam adores him.'

'He's very fond of you. Both of you.'

'The feeling's mutual!'

'But?'

Jo took a deep breath, feeling the metal keys warm in her hand.

'I've been … let down before.' Her tone was hesitant. 'I can't commit and then …' She shrugged. 'I can't do that to Liam. Do you know what I mean?'

Lyn nodded. 'Heaven knows, he doesn't have the best track record. But he's got a good heart.' She swallowed. 'I'm biased, I know. But don't write him off. He … he has his reasons.'

Jo rubbed a hand over her forehead, suddenly exasperated and exhausted with trying to read between the lines.

'What are his reasons?'

'I can't tell you. He'd kill me. Just—' She stopped. 'Listen to me. I sound like a meddling old matchmaker here. Ignore me. See you tomorrow, and bring your muscles!'

'What happened to "technique over brute strength"?'

227

'Pah. That's just for them.' Lyn jerked her head behind her. 'They don't need to be reminded that we're stronger than they are right now. How do you think they'd cope with childbirth?'

They laughed, friends again, and hugged a goodbye.

'Don't forget that dress!' Lyn called, as she closed the door.

Jo was there on time the following day, her confidence high from having driven a little more. It was like never having been away, and felt wonderful. Liam sat beside her like a little prince gazing over his kingdom. He kept up a running commentary of 'red means stop, green means go', 'turn right, my friend lives down there'.

There was a motorbike parked outside Lyn and Griff's cottage, and Lyn emerged piled high with blankets as Jo parked. After the now customary hug, Lyn shooed Liam indoors. 'Griff has something for you,' she told him and faced Jo with a businesslike hands on hips. There was no sign of Ed. Jo couldn't decide whether she felt relieved, disappointed, or worried.

Worry won.

'Ed not coming to lend his words of wisdom?'

'Doesn't look like it.' Lyn smiled. 'I think he's going out later anyway.'

After twenty minutes of not quite mastering the bike-pushing technique, Jo felt sweaty and cross with herself. Was he watching her out of the window? She'd watched him wheel bikes around as if they were pedal cycles in the Bike Palace. What was wrong with her? If she leaned the bike against her, it refused to go where it was supposed to, and if she stood it upright, she pulled her back muscles trying not to let it overbalance the other way. She couldn't do it. She was going to have to pull out of this show. She'd make a total idiot of herself, and drop the most expensive bike in the world.

'It's just about finding the centre of gravity,' said Lyn. 'It doesn't matter if you drop it. Well, not this one, anyway.'

'Don't they come with stabilisers?' puffed Jo. Lyn had made a sort of course for her by leaving flowerpots on the ground. Jo was either wildly off or knocked them over. If the bike went where it was supposed to, it was by mistake. And this was one of the lightweight bikes …

'Try not to care about it,' said Lyn. 'Look.' She took over the handlebars, and wheeled it round the course as if she was leading a pony. 'Once it's rolling, it's easy.'

'I can do this,' Jo told herself, glaring down at the machine, just as a black 4x4 rumbled into the drive.

'Hi, Lloyd!' Lyn called, lifting an arm as the driver climbed out.

'Hi, Lyn! Is he ready?'

'I am,' Ed said.

Jo risked a glance up to see Ed at the door of his cottage, looking heroic and handsome in his sling and a smart navy shirt. As her thoughts wavered, so did her hands, and the bike fell slowly away from her, just as she knew it had wanted to do from the beginning.

'Shitting buggering thing!' she yelled, trying to hang on to the heavy machine as it tore at her bicep muscles.

'Charming,' said a familiar voice. As the bike crunched to the tarmac, Jo looked up to see Alexis slink out of the back seat of the huge vehicle and simper on high heels towards Ed's front door. 'Ed! Oh, you poor thing, look at you!'

'Alexis! What are you doing here?' Ed frowned at her, and at Lloyd in the driving seat.

'I'm helping you, of course! I heard all about your accident, you poor thing.'

'I don't need any help, thank you. My legs are perfectly fine.'

Under Jo's raised eyebrows, Alexis helped Ed like a

wounded soldier to the front seat of the car, stretching her succulent body over him to fasten his seat belt.

'Have a good time!' Lyn said.

'Don't worry,' said Lloyd, 'we'll look after him, Mrs G.'

Conscious of her dishevelled hair and scruffy jeans, Jo responded to Ed's little wave with a curt nod. Her heart hammered so hard, she thought she'd be sick. Two blokes, two girls, out for the night. And her, the employee, pushing a motorbike about. The employee. Don't forget that. Barely worthy of friend status, it seemed. Her 'no funny business' proclamation rang in her ears. He was only playing by her rules. She glared down at the bike, fighting the urge to cry and give it a good kicking.

'Bastard,' she muttered, under her breath, without a clear idea who she was directing the curse at, standing the bike upright without a second thought.

'Oh, well done,' called Lyn. 'That's the spirit.'

Anger flowed through Jo's veins as she gripped the bars and wheeled the bike around the makeshift course.

'What next?' She tried not to growl at Lyn. It wasn't her fault that her son was so annoyingly handsome, fickle, gorgeous, unreliable, lovable and hateful all at the same time.

'Go round a few times and we'll try something bigger. I think you've sussed it now. It's all about confidence.'

By the end of the evening, Jo had mastered the biggest bike there, picking it up several times, and Lyn was delighted with her. She should be feeling thrilled with herself. Instead, a black cloud had descended on her and she was furious. With Ed, and with herself. She could have hurled that big bike across the horizon.

Really. What had she expected? That he'd become a monk, because she'd put herself off limits? Maybe, she admitted. But she definitely hadn't expected Alexis to be back on the scene. And for Ed to just meekly swan off with her? Oh, she could spit. But she was the one who'd made the 'No Funny Business' Rule, when he'd shown every sign of wanting the exact opposite. She could hardly blame him for going out and having a bit of fun. Also, she'd ripped him off a strip with the 'Daddy' thing. And now, she'd volunteered to spend an entire weekend with him at this bike show. Which she'd been looking forward to – until now.

She could cancel. Except Lyn was so delighted with her, telling Griff what a perfect pupil she was. She liked them. She liked Ed. She swallowed. Okay, she loved Ed. She knew she did. She was jealous. Jealous of all the women who came into the Bike Palace with their bikes. She noticed their eyes wandering over his tight muscles and gazing into his sea-green eyes as he told them what was wrong with their bikes.

He was never anything but matey with them. Never flirted. He didn't have to. They'd glance over at her and Liam, and she could see them assessing the relationship. She'd never admitted to herself until now, how much she wanted to say, 'I'll ask my boyfriend/husband to check your bike,' to them because until now, she and he had been mates. Friends. It had felt like a privileged position – no awkward relationship issues based on sex and jealousy. She could trust her 'friend' responses – the easy banter and joshing, with Liam as the focus of both their attentions. In that bubble of security, everything was fine. He was hers, and she didn't have to give everything of herself over, could choose the bits that she revealed. Hadn't had to open up that Pandora's box of her past and expose it to him – watch his disgust and repulsion as the lies and realities flew out. It would be her secret forever and ever, and the price for keeping that secret was lying to the people she grew to love and sacrificing any chance of a life with a man who loved and knew her.

For a moment, she thought about telling Ed her secret. Maybe he'd understand. In that instant, she thought about being diminished in his eyes and couldn't bear it. He thought she was amazing, strong. A tragic heroine. He didn't have a clue about the many lies upon lies. The truth was buried deep, even though it pierced her dreams still after all these years.

Her pity party for one was interrupted by Lyn.

'How about learning to ride, Jo? You don't need to pass your test to ride in the showground, and it would save you having to push the bikes around so much.'

Liam, swinging on the gate and watching, bobbed up and down with excitement.

'Mummy! Ride a moker bike!'

'*Oh*, why not?' Jo was astounded to hear her voice say. In her current mood, she didn't give a flying feather about anything. Couldn't have cared less if she rode straight into a wall. Except that would make Liam an orphan. Huffing a long breath, she squared her shoulders. 'Lead me to it.'

Sipping tea in the kitchen with Lyn and Griff and Liam an hour or so later, Jo had a very different head on. She couldn't believe it had been that easy. It was as if her 'don't give a shit' attitude had taken all her nerves away, and sharpened her brain. Or perhaps Lyn was a top teacher.

Either way, she'd flung a long leg over the dirt bike, popped it into gear, and ridden away on it. Easy peasy. What was all the fuss about? Perhaps it was her cycling background. Perhaps it was that the bike was skinny and lightweight and it felt familiar after spending an hour pushing it around. Perhaps it was that if she dropped it, she knew how to pick it up – but whatever it was, it felt like the most natural thing in the world.

And she couldn't wait to do it again. She decided not to tell Ed. Serve him right to be surprised when she casually rode the bikes into position.

'Can I have a go?' Liam wanted to know.

'Daisy has a little bike that you could ride in a few years,' Lyn said.

'A few years?' Liam pouted. 'But I'll be really old by then.'

'You'll need to kick-start the classic bikes, Jo, and it's a bit of a knack,' Griff pointed out. 'But you've got strong legs. You'll be fine.'

'You'll need long boots though,' Lyn said. 'That kick-start lever has a nasty habit of flicking back and catching you on the shin.'

'That'll look nice with my frock.' Jo laughed at Lyn's dubious face. 'It'll be fine, don't worry. I'll manage.'

'I hope Ed knows how lucky he is to have you,' Lyn said.

Lloyd drove them to Rhossili and Ed sat in the café, looking out over the fabulous view wishing he was anywhere but there. He'd thought this was meant to be a mates only, casual brunch meet up, and he really wanted a chat with Cled about the 'he called you daddy' thing. He didn't want to be sitting with Alexis, treating him like a wounded soldier, and cutting up his hash browns and sausages. What was her game? She'd made her feelings about him perfectly clear before.

He'd felt completely useless earlier, watching through the window as Jo wrestled the bikes. She wasn't doing too well, and he fought the urge to go out there and show her himself, but realised that would undermine both her and his mum. Best to leave them to it. He heard Lloyd's motor arrive and opened the front door as he parked outside.

His stomach sank into his boots as Alexis tottered towards him, dressed in one of her second skin outfits and shoes she couldn't walk in. Whatever had he seen in her? He flicked a glance at Jo, tall and strong, her springy cloud of dark hair mirroring her energy, just as the bike over-balanced and crashed to the ground. Pretending he hadn't noticed to save her embarrassment, he looked away and hurried into the car.

Her face was set like stone as he left. But he knew how determined she was when she wanted to do something, so he gave her a little wave and left her to it.

Cled arrived late, with his heavily pregnant wife. Ed stared at her blooming vitality, as she shoehorned her bulk behind the table, and managed a weak smile before looking out of the window, pretending to admire the view.

'I thought you might have brought Jo with you,' Cled said, after he'd ordered for them.

'She was busy throwing bikes around when we left,' said Alexis, with a smirk. 'Shocking potty mouth, too.'

'She sounds fab,' said Cled's wife, with a grin. 'I'm surprised that you're *here* then Ed!'

'Jo's my saviour. She's driving the bikes up for the Bike Show, and doing the stand with me. Her and Liam.' Ed didn't want to say that he hadn't known it was a couples thing, for fear of insulting the other girls.

'*Wow*,' Cled said, licking his lips as his food arrived. 'All the more reason to have brought her, mate. I can't wait to meet her.'

Alexis huffed and turned to talk to Lloyd's girlfriend. Ed made a point of getting up and sitting next to Cled and Clara.

'How long now?' he asked her.

'Any day! I just want my body back now.' Clara smiled, and Cled rubbed her back.

'How did your day out with the lad go, then?' Cled asked.

'Oh, brilliant, except for my dislocating my shoulder.' Ed filled them in and they both chuckled.

'Poor you,' Clara was sympathetic. 'Kids can break you.'

'He called me daddy.'

Clara and Cled exchanged a glance. 'Uh-oh. That's a biggie,' said Cled. 'What did Jo think of that?'

'She wasn't happy.' Ed fiddled with the salt cellar.

'I'm not surprised!' Clara's eyebrows were almost at her hairline. 'She's spent, what, five years carrying and bringing up that little boy, and you rock up and in the wink of an eye, he's calling *you* Daddy? I would've been bloody furious.'

Cled gazed at her with pride. 'Don't mince your words, sweetheart.' He grinned. 'Say what you mean!'

'Sorry,' said Clara, not looking at all sorry. 'But really, what did you expect? And with your reputation …'

'*Oh!*' Ed heaved a noisy sigh. 'Is that what everyone thinks of me? That I'm just a … a *playboy*?'

'Yes,' said Lloyd, from the other end of the table. 'What? You did ask …'

Chapter Twenty-Five

Jo was deep in thought as she drove the van containing six motorbikes, bits of motorbikes, Ed and Liam up to the Classic Bike Show.

There was an awkwardness between her and Ed that had never existed before and she was finding it exhausting trying to keep up the bright chatter which focussed on Liam. It was torture. Having admitted to herself her feelings for Ed, she now noticed every single thing about him. His smell, his skin, the inflexions of his voice, his body language. It was driving her insane. She was only glad that he was on the other side of Liam or she'd have been too distracted to drive. He, in turn, was being excessively polite and appreciative. She much preferred the old Ed who teased and joshed her.

How was she going to manage for a whole weekend? Did it mean that he was going back out with Alexis? She couldn't ask, couldn't trust her reactions if he said yes. Maybe it was the other girl in the car. Another blonde bimbo type, she decided, savagely dismissing her. That would be just right for Ed. He probably didn't want to be seen with some weird skinny bird in shorts, mad curly hair, no make-up and a kid in tow.

Well. He was going to get a surprise this weekend, because that was exactly the opposite of what she was going to look like. Apart from the kid. It dawned on her that she was already thinking about staking her claim. Fighting for him. Oh God, was that a good thing? All the things she'd decided about him were turned upside down. Did she only want him because someone else had her claws in him?

She glanced down at Liam beside her, remembering his dress rehearsal with Beryl in the week. He looked as if he'd stepped out of an old newsreel from the forties. Particularly since Beryl had run a pair of hair clippers over his head, under Jo's anxious gaze.

'Not too short!' she'd squeaked.

'It'll grow back quick as you like,' Beryl had reassured her, getting out her smart phone and clicking off some photos. 'Look! Totally authentic now. And nice and cool for the summer.'

As they neared the showground, Ed fished out his mobile and calls and texts flashed back and forth. Jo understood why, when people materialised from everywhere as she parked as close as possible, and stretched her shoulders as willing hands wheeled the bikes out, carried the gazebo and began unloading all the stock that had been loaded by all his mates at the other end.

'Strange not to have your folks here, young Ed,' said a wiry old chap, corded forearms straining as he hefted box after box. 'Sorry to hear about Griff. He had a lucky escape.'

'*Mm*. Thanks to Jo here.' Ed nodded. 'Saved his life.'

'Wow. Good on yer, missus. Keep 'er in the family, eh?' The old man chuckled. 'What happened to you, anyway?'

'I fell on him,' Liam piped up, carrying little boxes in and out and scaring Jo by threading his way in and out of everyone.

There was a resounding ripple of laughter and Ed joined in.

'Better than the other way round,' he said, winking at Jo.

A warm glow spread over Jo. This was more like it.

'I'll take this one,' she said, sitting on an Ariel and kick-starting it with ease. 'Where do you want it?' She barely glanced back at Ed, satisfied that his mouth was hanging open, as she cruised away, hair bouncing in the draught. Ha ha. That was definitely a reee-sult. See Alexis doing that! Not that she was in competition, of course. Perish the thought. She chuckled loudly as soon as she was out of earshot.

As she let Liam into their hotel room later and waved a 'bye, laters,' at Ed, Jo felt as if she was on some kind of a chemical high. She hadn't known what to expect, and it had been completely bonkers, and fun. Everyone seemed to know everyone else, there was laughter and banging from stand building and shocking draughts with the huge shutter doors open and bikes zipping about and Liam getting in the way of everything and Jo had the worst headache ever right now from keeping her eyes on the little boy and making sure he wasn't run over. It was nothing a decent cuppa couldn't cure. And a shower, and some food. And an early night.

Ed had told them they had to be on the stand by eight a.m. and had to be up at sparrow-fart, and, after an attack of the giggles, Liam had said that in that case, he wasn't going to bed.

It was nicer than the no frills hotel she'd expected. Liam was in heaven, trying out the big double and single in turn and opening all the drawers.

'There's wine in here!' he shrieked. 'Aunty Beryl would love it!'

Jo laughed. 'Shall we Facetime her and you can show her? I'm going to jump in the shower.'

She smiled as she listened from the bathroom to Liam and Beryl loudly exchanging news of their days, and abandoned herself to the pleasure of the smart shower cubicle, sniffing the free shower gel and shampoo. She had never stayed in a hotel. This was luxury to her.

'Mummy! There's someone at the door!' Liam yelled.

'I'm in the shower!'

'They're still there!'

'Don't open it – I'm coming now.'

238

Shrouded in a bath towel, Jo opened the door a crack, expecting it to be Ed. There was nobody there. The tapping persisted.

'It's coming from here, Mummy!'

'That's a wardrobe. Isn't it?' She tussled with the handle until it clicked open. Ed stood there. Behind him, was not Narnia at the back of the wardrobe, or the corridor. It was his room, a mirror of Jo's. A linked room. How had Jo not realised? She'd stood back at the check-in desk, had assumed his room was on the same floor, along a bit. Not actually attached. By just a door. Had he told her that? Which side had the lock? Was it weird, or cute?

'Sorry to disturb you,' he said, pointedly not looking at her, scantily clad in a not quite big enough towel. 'Hungry?'

'Yes!' shouted Liam. 'There's wine here, look! It's free! Have you got wine?'

'It's not free, Liam, you have to … oh, never mind. Yes. I'm starving, now you mention it. What are you thinking of?' *I'm still thinking about that linked door. And that I'm in a bath towel.*

'Sit down, or takeaway?'

'It's early still. We could do sit down.'

'There's a restaurant here … or there's these.' He fanned a selection of leaflets at her. 'I asked the receptionist.'

'It's been a long day. I don't think I can face driving any more tonight. And I'd really like a glass of wine. Can we do the restaurant here?'

'No problem. Meet you in reception in half an hour?'

Oh, it was back to formality again, grieved Jo inside. He hadn't lasciviously cocked an eyebrow at her bath towel, or made a comment. Ed being polite was worse than any amount of anyone shouting at her. It had all been a front earlier, then. He'd bantered with the other guys, not her. She wanted to curl up on the big bed and cry herself to sleep.

Wearily, she unpacked, decanted her beautiful dress onto a hanger, and stowed their clothes. Liam had already unpacked his little rucksack and arranged his few possessions into 'his' drawers.

'Can I wear my boots tonight, Mummy? Please, Mummy?' He dangled one of the now polished vintage boots at her, head on one side

'They're not really ...' Jo began. 'Oh. Okay.' He'd run rings round her this weekend, she could see it now. But she'd learned to pick her fights. Otherwise you spent your whole time saying no to everything. Pulling on her smarter jeans, a smaller white vest she'd unearthed, and the black jacket, she fluffed her hair and yanked out the little make-up kit she'd bought from Marjorie and had been practicing with every night since.

'You look pretty, Mummy.'

'Thank you, darling. You look very grown up.' He looked cute in his cargo pants and hobnail boots, hooded sweatshirt and severe haircut. Foreign, somehow. Like a magazine shoot.

Ed was draped over a long sofa in the reception in a fetching navy sweater. Jo was jolted again by his utter beauty. The receptionist was too, judging by the cow eyes she kept making in his direction.

It was probably best that they weren't a couple. Jo might have to kill any woman she saw anywhere near him.

'Steak for me, I think,' Ed said, flicking his eyes over a menu that made Jo wince. She could feed both of them for a week on the cost of this meal.

'Can I have a steak?' Liam asked.

'No,' said Jo.

'Yes,' said Ed.

'How do you know about steak? You've never had a steak,' Jo said, sending a look at Ed and a shake of her head.

'I know. But can't I try one?'

'How about you try some of mine instead?' Ed said. 'And that way, if you like it, you can have it tomorrow.'

'Okay.' Liam nodded. 'Do they do chicken nuggets?'

'Well,' Ed said, after they'd ordered. 'Well done, everyone, for all your hard work today. It's all fun from here. And Jo,' he clinked his glass to hers, 'you're a dark horse. You drive us here, and then,' he took a long gulp of his wine, 'and then you kick-start a bike, and ride it away! Is there anything you can't do?' He shook his head. 'You never cease to amaze me.'

You want to bet? She forced a smile. 'I wanted to surprise you.'

'You always do. Just when I think you couldn't get any better, you do.'

'Employee of the month?' she said, deliberately making the distinction between friend and worker. Ed didn't seem to get the memo though.

'You're a bloody … er, *blimmin'* … star. You put me to shame.'

'I do not. I'm not that great. Really I'm not.'

'She is, isn't she, Liam? A tough act to follow, your mum!'

I don't want to be followed. Who are you planning on following me with? I want to be alongside you! But I don't know how to get off this pedestal you've put me on without crashing and burning and falling out of your life forever! her head screamed.

'We'll get a bottle, I think,' he said, nodding at her empty glass. 'We deserve it. Correction. You deserve it.'

A weak smile slid over her face. *I so do not. I'm a liar. I'm a …*

'I just can't manage without you, Jo,' Ed said, as their food arrived.

Her heart leapt. Ed gazed at her for a long moment, then he swallowed. 'Could you cut my steak up for me?'

Chapter Twenty-Six

When the linked door was tapped early the following morning, Liam opened it.

'Hey!' Ed said. 'Look at you, cool dude!'

'You're too early! I'm not ready!' yelled Jo, diving into the bathroom.

'Me neither!' shouted Ed. 'I ... *er* ... I need some help here.'

'Can't Liam do it?'

There was a pause. Jo, tights halfway, hair a froth of frizz, face naked of make-up, stared at herself in the mirror in despair. She'd wanted to appear dazzling. Fully loaded. And later, she decided, she was going to tell him her secret.

Maybe.

'I'd rather not ...'

'Oh, for goodness' sakes. Give me a minute!' Carefully, she thumbed the tights up and wiggled them comfortable. She strode out. 'Right. What's the problem?'

'Wow. You look ...'

'... unfinished,' Jo cut him off with her stern, mummy face. 'What's the matter?'

'I ... I can't do up my bloody ... *blimmin'* trousers!' Ed held them together at the top, his face a mixture of pleading and exasperation. 'I can't ask Liam to do it! Come on ... that would be totally weird and I'd get arrested or something. And there are these stupid things. I can't do them, either!' He flapped a pair of skinny brown belts that Jo finally identified as braces. 'They're supposed to button here ... and the flies are buttons, and with this stupid basta—, *blimmin'* shoulder, I Just Can't *Flipping* Do It!'

'I can do it!' Liam advanced and Ed jackknifed away from him.

242

'Maybe not, Liam,' Jo said, barely stifling her laughter. She fastened the braces to the trousers, and struggled not to notice what she was doing as she bent to button his flies. Did she meet his eye, and just do it by feel? Or should she bend, with her head at crotch level? She could feel the heat from his body. Her fingers could just unbutton this one instead, and then this one, and …

'And the tie. Please.'

She obliged, meeting his eye as she snugged it up to his neck.

'Do you need the shirt tucking in?'

'I'll manage.' His voice was a squeak. 'Ta. See you in a bit. Breakfast at the show. Don't rush. Bags of time.' Clearing his throat, he closed the door on her. 'You look very nice,' she heard him call through the door as mirth overtook her.

Even the hotel receptionist goggled at them as she and Liam swung through the lobby. Jo felt a million dollars in the Rita Hayworth dress, heels, the nipped in velvet jacket slung over her shoulders, her hair coiffed and her lips glossed. Liam trotted beside her, revelling in the clicketty click of his hobnail boots, and clearly pleased with himself in his tweed hat and jacket.

Ed unfolded with languid grace from the sofa, and Jo caught her breath as he lifted his hat to her and held out an elbow for her to take. With his dark hair brushed just so, he looked nothing short of film star glamorous, and her stomach somersaulted. Cary Grant to a tee. His lean body perfectly complemented the sharp suit with its padded shoulders, and the gleaming shoes.

'You look fantastic, Jo.'

'You've scrubbed up alright yourself. No sling?'

'It's in my pocket. But you never get a second chance to make a first impression, huh?'

Their eyes met and he squeezed her hand with his arm. The warm glow was back.

'Come on team,' he said. 'Let's go smash it.'

Arriving in the enormous van and breakfasting on bacon rolls didn't exactly go with the image. Only the hardiest customers were there that early, but there were enough wolf whistles to put a smile on Jo's face, and Liam was loving it.

As Jo arranged the tables with the sales stock, checked the price tickets and set out the photo book she'd designed, she felt a swell of pride at everything she'd achieved in such a short space of time.

She'd driven them there, learned to ride a bike, and she looked stunning. She was not the person she'd been just a few weeks ago. She was almost shocked at herself.

Wrestling with her emotions had no place at this show, she decided. She'd done a good job, and whatever happened between her and Ed was in the lap of the gods. She was just going to enjoy herself. Be more like Liam, and live in the moment.

There was a fast trade in bits and bobs and banter as customers hunted down the parts they needed before anyone else got them. Liam trotted between their stand and the stands on either side, one of which was run by an elderly couple showing their sidecar outfits, complete with camping kits. They seemed to have endless biscuits and a bottomless thermos.

'We've been doing this show for years,' the old lady confided to Jo. 'Never missed one. It's like seeing our family.'

There was a lull at lunchtime, which meant a chance to eat. Jo was sipping a watery coffee in a wobbly plastic cup, which threatened to give way over her beautiful dress when she heard, 'Can you ask your dad how much the BSA is?'

Before Jo could blink, Liam yelled over at Ed, chatting to the standholder adjacent to them.

'Dad! This man wants to know how much the B—?' He fizzled out.

'—SA is,' supplied Jo, with a grin. She surprised herself. It had only been a short time ago that she'd thrown a wobbly about Liam calling Ed 'Dad'. They were already dressed up as a 1940s family, who could blame the customers for assuming that's what they were. 'It's a 1958 BSA 500cc DBD34 Gold Star. Fully restored and in mint condition. Twenty one thousand, five hundred pounds.'

'It's gorgeous.'

'It is,' Jo agreed, standing alongside it as Ed strolled over. 'It's my favourite. Always gets a polish as I pass.'

'It would look great in my collection. What's your best price?'

'What are you thinking of?' Ed said.

'That is the best price,' Jo said. 'There's nothing else like it here. I've checked.'

Ed looked at her in surprise and Jo sent him a tiny raised eyebrow. *I'm in charge.*

'We've already had two enquiries,' she said, flicking through her little notebook. 'Better not leave it too long.'

She left Ed chatting over the finer points of the bike and served customers at the busy parts section.

'He didn't bite,' Ed said at her elbow a few minutes later. 'I gave him a card though.'

'He'll be back.'

'What makes you say that?'

'He's over there, on his phone.' She cocked her head without looking. 'I bet he's checking out the prices. You know it's a good price. And he's a collector, he said so.'

'Have you really had two enquiries? You haven't said.'

245

Jo opened her notebook and showed him. He peered over at the pages, decorated with scribbles and Mr Men stickers.

'It doesn't mention anything here about the BSA.'

'No. But he doesn't know that.'

'*Oka-ay* ...' Ed's expression was doubtful.

'*Classic Bike* magazine,' said a voice behind them. 'Loving the period costumes, guys. Mind if I take some photos for the mag?'

'Fine,' said Ed as Jo's mouth opened to say 'no'. She stopped. No one would recognise her in this get up. Where was the harm in it?

'Take one on my phone for me, would you?' Ed held out his mobile. 'So I can send it to my mum and dad. This is usually their thing, to be honest. We're just standing in.'

'Interesting,' said the photographer, scribbling in his notebook. 'Who are your parents? And your names? You and your wife and little boy?'

'Oh, we're not ...' Jo and Ed said together, tailing off in embarrassment.

Jo let the photographer take a few shots of her and Liam and then sidled away towards a scruffy couple in anoraks who were scrutinising every item carefully on the sales table. The neighbouring stands had warned them about pilfering, and she wanted to keep a lookout. A glance over her shoulder revealed Liam perched on Ed's knee, looking exactly like models for *Classic Bike* magazine. Shot in sepia, they could be time travellers.

The sales racked up during the busy day, and Jo was relieved she'd brought along the flat leather bowling shoes instead of wearing the heels all day. Two of the cheaper motorbikes on the stand sold, but the Gold Star remained gleamingly unsold, and Jo hadn't seen the buyer from earlier for hours. It was a huge show though, with stands outside, and displays during the day of stunt riders and suchlike that

Liam was desperate to see. The buyer might still be here. Jo hoped so. She was beginning to regret her earlier confidence, and worried that she'd scared him off.

By four o'clock, Liam was wilting and Jo wondered what to do with him. It was a dreadfully long day for a small boy.

'I could take him back to the hotel and he could have a sleep. I'll bring him back to collect you,' she suggested to Ed, who had had his sling on for a few hours, and was also looking wan.

'He can have a nap under here, if you like?' called the older lady on the stand next door. She indicated an inflatable mattress towards the back of the stand, inside the tiniest tent, complete with hospital style aertex blankets and inflatable pillows. 'We'll keep an eye on him, don't you worry.'

'Aren't you hoping to sell that?'

'Oh, not really, it's what we used to go camping in. They're just to show how much you can take. We take orders for the sidecars now. They're just like they always were, except they're made in India now.' She sighed, and Jo did a double take and looked again at the sidecars, realising they were, in fact, brand new.

'Oh. If you're sure, that would be really kind, thank you.' Removing Liam's hat and boots, she bent awkwardly in the dress and slid him into the little tent, with a promise that she'd only be just here, and that they wouldn't go off and leave him. His eyes closed immediately, despite the noise and bustle and intercom announcements. As she backed out and straightened up, a voice said, 'How many offers now?'

The buyer was back. He cast an appreciative eye over Jo and she reddened, even more determined to hold her line on the price.

'There's someone coming back to give us cash,' she lied, brazenly, glancing around for Ed.

The man laughed, revealing perfect white teeth. 'I like to

enjoy spending my money,' he said. 'And you have the cheek of Old Nick himself.'

It was the sort of thing her dad used to say.

'Yeah. Sorry. Blame my background.' Jo grinned. 'So, what are you thinking?'

'Your man has done a fantastic job there. He's very talented. Just about everyone at this show has heard of him and his father.'

Jo glowed with pride. It had been wonderful to see Ed chatting to people at the show, and she had noticed how deferential they were to him, popping over to ask his opinion throughout the day. He really was wasted as 'just a bike mechanic'. She was glad she'd spent so long boning up on the stock. She hadn't wanted to let him down.

'I would really like it. But there needs to be some movement on the price. I'm not a bottomless pit.'

'Do you have a classic bike already?' If she could just keep him talking. He listed them on his fingers. She recognised only some, but it was a long list.

'Goodness me. Do you live in a stately home or something?' Where had Ed gone? She was running out of knowledge at a frightening rate here. Except ... did she need knowledge? She knew how to sell. This man knew that he wanted it. It was just the price that was the tricky bit.

'I do, actually. We have a vintage bike collection. I don't suppose I should have told you that.'

'Not if you want me to feel sorry for you and lower the price,' Jo said, with an impish grin. 'I know you want it, you know you want it. Buy it. It's beautiful. The most beautiful thing in this show.'

'Oh, I don't know about that.' The man raked her from head to foot with a hungry glance and Jo felt hot.

'So, am I arranging a delivery?' said Ed, suddenly beside her.

'I believe you are,' said the man. 'Very capable young lady, your wife. Don't leave her around anywhere. She'll be snapped up.' His long look indicated *by me.*

Jo felt her hand being squeezed briefly by Ed, who managed to position himself between her and the buyer.

'Can I get you a coffee, Mr—?' he said, suave in his sharp suit, and every inch in charge now.

She stepped back under the pretence of checking on Liam, feeling suddenly flustered and euphoric at the same time, and rather wishing she was still holding Ed's hand. Wow. Had she actually closed that huge sale? Liam was snoring gustily in his tent, and she took a moment to compose herself, not wanting to go back to their stand until the buyer had gone.

'Customers, love,' the elderly lady nodded at the queue and Jo reluctantly returned as Ed walked away with the buyer.

As the tannoy announced the close of the show for the day, Ed yawned. His mobile had been clamped to his ear almost all day, and his brain was in over-drive from customers calling him for prices, questions about renovations and wanting to sell him bikes. They'd done well. Jo had been nothing short of utterly fantastic, from driving them in the huge van, to riding that bike, and reeling in the biggest sale of the show! She'd completely exceeded his expectations.

He'd been on pins ever since that brunch at Rhossili, rehearsing what he was going to tell her. He'd so nearly blurted it out at dinner the night before, and then lost his nerve, making some stupid joke about her cutting up his steak. He really was an idiot.

'We should have brought more stock,' he said, as they checked they'd got everything they didn't want to leave on the stand, and collected their belongings.

'Better than still having everything,' said Jo. She still looked stunning in that dress. He could hardly take his eyes off her.

He laughed. 'I should say. High five, Liam! Let's go get some food! Caviar and champagne?'

'Does this mean what I think it means?' said Jo, her eyes alight with excitement.

'Saleswoman of the Year.' Ed nodded, holding her gaze. To think he'd doubted her earlier, with her notebook full of Liam's stickers.

'Wow. For the full price?'

'Yep. Although, I think he wants you to deliver it ...' He smiled, although he'd been surprised by his protective instinct as he'd spotted the buyer eyeing Jo up.

'I got that impression. Glad you turned up when you did!' Jo snorted a laugh. 'I need to get out of this gear.'

'I think he had that in mind, too. Come to think of it, I might have got some more money out of him ...' Ed waggled his eyebrows at her and she elbowed him gently.

'Remember who's driving you home.'

'It's the drugs. I don't know what I'm saying.'

They laughed, easy together, arm in arm, threading their way past the stands and calling their goodnights. Ed's phone rang as they swung into the van seats. It was Lucy, requesting a video call. He pressed accept, and Lucy's smiling face filled the little screen.

'Two of my favourite people! What are you up to?'

'We're in fancy dress!' shouted Liam. 'And we're in a hotel!'

'Hi, Liam! That makes three of my favourite people then!'

'What happened after the yard of ale thing? You didn't do it, did you?' Ed asked.

Lucy groaned. 'Of course I did it! But I was sick as a dog the next day, and I couldn't ride my bike.' She pulled a rueful face.

'I *told* you! So what happened? You're on a schedule, aren't you?'

'Well, er, one of the crew had to ride it. He's short, and he wore my jacket, so hopefully no one will notice. The painting bit wasn't too bad, but I might have to go back that way and do some more shots. They weren't happy with me.'

'It was their fault though!' Jo said, concentrating on the traffic.

'It would be nice to think so,' Lucy's voice crackled over the speakers. 'But they didn't exactly pour it down my neck.'

'What did Ash think?'

'Oh, I was in the doghouse there too, for a bit …' Lucy pressed some buttons and her face turned into a fire breathing dragon and then a cute bunny, with whiskers. Liam pealed with laughter. 'We're all good now. So how's the show going?'

Ed told her about Jo clinching the sale of their trophy bike.

'Wow, that's fantastic, well done, Jo! Listen, I've been doing a bit of blogging and, get me, *vlogging*, about how proud I am of the Art Café, and my wonderful staff, running the place without me. I'd love to put a bit in about your bike show, guys. Would that be okay? I can link the Bike Palace in it.'

'Well, that would be fab, Luce, but I don't have a website. Yet. It's on my list.' It hadn't been, until then, but he remembered that Jo had asked him about it too.

'Never mind. You really should though. Everything is online these days. Send me some photos of your stand, and you two dressed up.' She brought her face close to the screen. 'And don't try telling me you aren't dressed up, because Liam told me, and I can see it from here.' They laughed, and after some back and forth banter, she ended the call saying, 'I'll be home in a few days. Can't wait to see everyone.'

'*Awww*. I miss Lucy.' Jo sighed. 'She's such fun. We all miss her.'

'I bet Ash and Daisy miss her more,' Ed said, remembering his friend when they'd split up when their relationship was still new, due to the spiteful actions of a family member. He understood his misery now. 'What do you want to eat tonight?' he continued as they arrived at the hotel, watching in admiration as Jo reversed neatly into a parking space.

'Oh, let's celebrate!' she said. 'Fish and chips? Pizza? I think Liam will need an early night if he's going to manage another long day. Me too, come to that.'

'Pizza!' Liam's eyes lit up.

'There's a pizza place a few minutes walk along the canal. I googled it,' Ed said. 'How does that sound? It's eat in or takeaway.'

'A walk sounds nice, actually. I'm thinking takeaway might be kinder to Liam. We've never had takeaway pizza. Way too expensive. Can we pick up a bottle of wine too?'

'Your wish is my command, my lady. Let's regroup in half an hour. I'll knock for you.'

'It sounds like we're in school.' Jo sniggered. 'I just need a quick shower and change, and I'll be ready.'

The golden evening light threw long purplish shadows as they strolled onto a path alongside a lazy canal, reflecting the turquoise sky. Ed walked behind as Jo ran ahead with Liam, sending the ducks quacking and flapping.

'First one to the bench!' she yelled at the little boy. 'Go!' She made it a dead tie, catching him and throwing him up in the air as he shrieked with laughter. They sat on the bench, swinging their legs and waiting for Ed to catch up, awkward in his sling.

'You two are a picture,' he said, with a wide smile, putting his phone away. 'I've ordered a selection of pizzas. They'll be ready in fifteen minutes. So let's go find somewhere to get a bottle of wine, pick up the pizzas and head back to the hotel. I'm starving.' He was hungry but also his shoulder hurt more than he was letting on, and he hadn't slept very well.

'Fine by me,' Jo replied.

Sneaking guiltily past Reception with their booty, which included wine and chocolate and snacks for the following day, they spread the pizza boxes over Ed's big double bed, licking their fingers and smacking their lips.

'This is a picker-nicker,' said Liam, drumming his legs against the bed. 'Only indoors.'

Despite his enthusiasm, the little boy was drooping over his food before too long.

'Time for bed for this young man, I think,' Jo murmured. 'He can have a shower in the morning.'

Liam barely protested, and didn't even ask for a story. Ed listened to the cursory teeth cleaning ritual with a smile. She wedged the adjoining door open with her case, and tiptoed back to Ed's room. They heard his breathing turn into snuffly snores almost instantly.

'I can relax now,' she said, topping up her wine, and sinking back against the pillows. 'He went out like a light. I won't be long after, that's for sure.'

Although it was covered in four different types of pizza, wine bottles and chocolate, Ed could feel every hair on his body standing to attention at her proximity on his bed.

'Jo.' He picked up a slice of pizza and then put it down again, fixing her with an intense gaze. 'Jo, thank you so much for this weekend. I can't tell you what it's meant to me.'

'Oh, I've enjoyed it. I've learned so much! I actually even quite like bikes now!'

'I need to tell you something.' He took a deep breath, and alerted, she fixed him with a look, wine halfway to her mouth.

'Is this about Alexis? You're going back out with her?'

'What? No. What?'

'From the other day, when your mum was teaching me to—'

'God, no. She just turned up. I think Lloyd's missus brought her along. No. There's nothing between me and Alexis.' He was a bit taken aback. It hadn't occurred to him that she'd be worried about something like that. He should've said something before. No wonder she'd been a bit off with him earlier.

'*Oh*.' She took a big mouthful of wine. 'What then?'

He tried to sit up a bit straighter, to give his statement the full import, but ended up struggling like an upturned beetle. *Just say it*.

'I ... I really, really like you, Jo. A lot.' That hadn't come out quite the way he intended it. It was never like this in the films.

She was still, wary. 'But ...'

'But I know,' he gulped, 'I know that I haven't got a very good track record with women, and so you've probably been warned off me by everyone.' He watched her wrestle with her expression. She didn't contradict him, and he hurried on, 'And I don't blame you. But there's a reason for it. I've never told anyone else.'

Jo's eyes were fixed on his face.

'I ... I had cancer when I was younger. And ... er ... basically, I ...' His voice shook slightly and he cleared his throat. 'I had cancer when I was a teenager, and ... I'm infertile.' He let out a long breath. He'd been holding it all in for so long, and now it was out there, it didn't seem so bad. 'I can't have children.'

'Thank God!' Jo blurted.

'What?'

'I mean't, sorry, Ed, I thought you were going to tell me you were going to die!'

'Why would I die?' This wasn't going to plan at all.

'Er, look, I saw some photos of you on your laptop. You looked ... okay, you looked terrible. I thought you must have

254

some kind of …' Jo flapped her hand. 'Sorry, I interrupted you. Carry on. Sorry.'

'So … er, I'm infertile,' Ed continued in a rush, eyeing her, 'and that means I can't have children of my own. I'm not planning on dying any time soon, if that helps.'

Jo stared at him. After a long pause, she said, 'Okay, it's beginning to make sense. So … you either pick girls who are not really into having children anyway …'

He nodded, his stomach squeezing into a hard knot.

'… Or at the point where the ones start to get serious about you – you dump them so as not to have to tell them?'

He nodded again, his eyes downcast. 'Yeah. Got it in one. Or I encourage them to dump me, just to ring the changes. I'm not proud of it. But I always wanted children! And if I wanted them, well, wouldn't my wife? How could I deny her that? It made me feel … useless. Lacking. And I wouldn't want to be with someone who didn't like children, so …' He shrugged, his eyes appealing for understanding. 'Men who can't make babies – it's always a bit of a joke. Firing blanks, that sort of thing. But it's a failing, isn't it?'

There was a long silence while Jo digested his words. He could see tears sitting on her bottom lid. He said, 'I didn't tell you to make you feel sorry for me, Jo. I wanted you to understand why I've … why I …' He gulped. 'I'm not excusing my behaviour. I could have said something before. But, blokes can be so cruel – they make jokes, y'know, it's their way of dealing with things. I didn't want to be the butt of their jokes, day in, day out. It's what happens.' He tailed off, watching her. 'When women can't conceive, everyone feels sorry for them. But when it's blokes … we're not allowed to feel sad.'

Jo cuffed her eyes, plucking a tissue from the box beside the bed. 'That's absolutely tragic for you, Ed, and so unfair. I'm so sorry. I totally understand why you wouldn't want to make it public knowledge. But ... *er* ... why are you telling me?'

'Jo! Isn't it obvious?'

'You've been really weird with me this weekend. Nothing is obvious!'

'I have been weird. I know. I've had a lot to think about. I wanted to tell you because for the first time in my life, I've found someone I want to be with. No matter what. And I didn't want there to be this huge secret between us.'

'Someone you want to be with?' She frowned.

'You!' Ed swept the pizza boxes to one side. 'I'm making a hash of this, aren't I? You, Jo! I want to be with you! And I'm hoping that you want to be with me?' He reached over and took her hand, and the feeling of her small hand inside his made his heart beat faster. 'And I have no idea whether you might want more children, because you're a great mum, and Liam is just fantastic ... and ...' He paused for a long breath. 'I'm sorry. I've sprung this on you. It's all I've thought about for days, and now I've totally cocked it up.'

'No! No, you really haven't. But,' she swallowed, staring down at their hands, 'I've got to ask. Is this because of Liam?'

He frowned. 'Liam?'

'A ready-made family?' Her voice was tiny.

'You can't believe that.' It was clear from her face that she did, though.

'I'm scared to believe it's just me.' She looked away from him and he had to strain to catch her words. 'I'm not as perfect as you think I am.'

'You're perfect to me, Jo.' She still looked unconvinced. He squeezed her hand. 'It's you, Jo. Trust me. It's you. I love Liam, of course I do, and I don't want to get into some childish game of which one do you love most.' He tipped her chin up and looked into her eyes. 'I love you. I want us to be together forever.'

'Forever?'

'Forever and ever.'

'And this isn't what you tell all the girls you take away to Bike Shows and make them work their butts off for?'

'*Oh*. You've found me out.' He smiled, pulling her hand towards him and wishing with every bone in his body that his shoulder wasn't killing him. She shuffled closer, her eyes on his, and somehow, despite the food littering the bed, their limbs tangled, melding, heat fusing their bodies together. He never wanted to take his lips away from hers. She lay half across him and he groaned as her cool hand slipped inside his shirt.

'*Ouch*, my shoulder!'

'Sorry!'

'No, it's fine. Carry on …'

She did.

'Jo, is Liam …?'

'I'll check.'

She skipped off the bed, returning with a smile on her face.

'A brass band wouldn't wake him,' she reported, kneeling astride him, and yanking his shirt loose from his jeans. 'I'll just help you with these buttons, you with your bad shoulder and all.'

'I can do the zip …'

'Don't worry. I've done it. Goodness me. Look at *that* …'

His shoulder didn't seem to hurt much from then on.

Much later, nestled in the crook of his neck on his good side, Jo chuckled.

'Do you have any idea how much I wanted to undo those buttons this morning?'

'Do you have any idea how much I wanted you to?'

'I think I do, yes. I could have cooked a burger on the heat coming off your crotch.'

'You have to keep that dress.'

'*Oh*, it's just about the dress, is it?' She propped herself up on her elbow, facing him, allowing the sheet to drop off her. 'Am I allowed to go back to my shorts after the show?'

'*Oh* dear. Those shorts. Now look what you've done to me!'

'Can't have that going to waste, can we ...'

Chapter Twenty-Seven

The adjoining door was propped open that morning as they prepared for another day at the show.

Ed's enthusiastic appreciation of Jo's body made it more difficult to get dressed but was luckily lost on Liam, who was just happy that they were happy, exploring both rooms and running in and out of the adjoining door to surprise them.

Buttoning Ed's fly that morning took a surprisingly long time, and then Jo needed help zipping her dress, which entailed the TV going on for Liam and a visit to the bathroom.

She may have looked slightly less groomed than the previous morning, but there was an unmistakeable bounce in Jo's step as the three of them checked out. He loved her! She'd tell him her secret. She would ... after the show. She'd sit him down, and explain. It wouldn't seem so bad. He loved her for what she was now – and she'd worked so hard to expunge the Sojourner of old. She'd evened up the score, surely. It would make them stronger. Wouldn't it?

Working the stand that day felt like a party. Liam took a couple of packets of biscuits to the elderly couple next door with the side-cars to say thank you for letting him sleep in their tent.

The beautiful BSA Gold Star had a smart SOLD card on it. Ed cheerily gave discounts to people 'because we don't want to have to take it all back!' and sold parts by the bucketload.

Jo, in her slightly too short tea dress that had been thoroughly examined by Ed that morning, felt as if she belonged somewhere, for the first time in her life. How her dad would have loved it. She swallowed a lump in her throat, looking around her. She'd spent her teenage years in a garage, eating biscuits with her dad while he tinkered and mended, and here she was, looking super-glam – and, actually, exactly how her mother wanted her to look all those years ago – and amongst all the oily bits of engine things that felt so utterly familiar. But this time, with the most film star handsome man who loved her and whom she loved with all her heart. And her perfect, beautiful son. It was all going to be fine. And he'd said, 'Forever', hadn't he? Did that mean what she thought it meant? Would he propose to her? Maybe here, at the show? Or had that been the proposal?

She laughed. Getting a bit ahead of herself now, she thought. She couldn't wait to tell Beryl.

'Dad! How much for this?' Liam yelled, in response to another, 'Ask yer Dad,' query.

Ed flicked a grin at her, with a raised eyebrow, and she responded with a wide smile and a nod. She remembered how confused she'd been about her reactions at the hospital. She'd just needed time to adjust. He was the perfect father for Liam, and Liam adored him. They would be a family! It would have been wonderful to have had a child with Ed, but they'd have Liam. Maybe they could adopt. At least they could talk about it, now it was out in the open.

'Do you want to stay over tonight?' Jo asked on the way home.

At the end of that exhausting day, they'd packed up, exchanged numbers with other stallholders, and they still had a long journey. Liam would be good for nothing tomorrow, and she wondered about giving him the day off school, which was awkward, as she was working in the café. He'd been asleep for ages though, and he was robust. He'd probably be fine. She still had energy to spend though, she thought, pressing her thighs together and remembering the exquisite pleasure that Ed had given her only that morning. They'd barely kept their hands off each other all day. It seemed so natural to hug him as she passed, to stand close to him, to rest a hand on his arm.

'Or you could come to mine?' Ed waggled his eyebrows at her over Liam's sleeping head.

'Easier at mine,' said Jo. 'Otherwise I've got to pack all Liam's stuff together for school.'

'Can't sleep in that teeny bed with my bad shoulder.'

'Won't be in it long. Seagull Cottage must be nearly finished.' She sounded desperate even to her own ears. Her body longed for his.

'*Hmm*. That's something to think about.'

'What?'

'Us. Living together. More space. Garden for Liam. Allotment for you. Workshops for me.'

Jo blinked. Even she hadn't got that far. He really was serious! She'd only just got used to being all together at last.

'Not Seagull Cottage then?'

'Bigger.'

Jo could barely trust herself to reply. She was so happy. Surely this couldn't be happening to her? But the insistent little voice inside her head was still nagging. Tell him. Her stomach churned. Maybe if she told Beryl first, she could work out a way of telling Ed. That would do it. Wouldn't it?

'Are we unloading the van tonight?' she said instead.

'No. We'll leave it in the compound. Take the truck home. The BSA has gone, if anyone wants to nick the rest, they're welcome to it all. I'm knackered.'

'Really knackered?' She sent him a sideways glance.

'*We-ell*.' He grinned. 'Maybe I will stay at yours, after all. It's too late to tell Mum and Dad the good news, anyway.'

'About … us?' she ventured.

'About the BSA!' His straight face made her stomach leap with fear, until he added, 'Of course about us! I already told them about the BSA.'

'I'm working tomorrow, at the café. Do I get the evening shift off?'

'Get lost, woman! I'll have to dock your pay.'

'I'll make up for it …'

'I should say you will. Just because you're sleeping with the boss now …'

'And my landlord …'

'Hussy!'

They laughed, and Liam stirred with a grumble, changed position, and slept on.

By the time they'd dropped the van off, transferred the still sleeping Liam and their bags into the Nissan, it was really late. Jo ached from the unaccustomed drive, and had to be content with a long and luxuriantly ardent kiss from Ed at his door, and a promise to catch up the following day. It was almost the following day already, as she let herself silently into the caravan, snuggling Liam into his bed after a stand-up-half-asleep wee. There was no sign of life from Beryl's cottage, and Jo fell asleep instantly, her cup of tea cooling, undrunk, on the bedside table.

She was awoken by the sound of banging the following morning. Liam was up too, hair sticking out, fuzzy with sleep.

'There are men! In the garden! I can see them out of my window!'

'I expect it's the builders, darling. Let's go and have a look.' She twitched the blinds and peeped out. Two young men, not the usual builders, were unpacking the flat pack shed thing that had been delivered with the caravan. What on earth was it? Surely it wasn't an actual shed. It seemed much too small. Perhaps it really was a potting shed. Or a greenhouse. Without any glass though?

Pulling on her shorts and flipping a band around her corkscrew curls, she went over to them.

'It's a surprise,' they told her. 'Ask Ed. He's arranged it.'

There was no time to wonder, with school and work to get to. Liam seemed none the worse for his busy weekend.

'When are we doing it again? Can I go out on my bike? Can we have pizza again?'

She was grateful to still have the Nissan as she fitted him into his school uniform and velcro-ed his trainers. She'd be getting fat at this rate, driving everywhere, she reminded herself. And Ed would go off her. At the thought of Ed, her heart sang.

Men in my garden, making something. What is it? she texted him when she arrived at the Art Café.

It's a surprise, he texted back. See you later xxxxxxxxxxxxxxx

She'd have to be patient.

The Art Café felt strange, after the show. Lucy had returned from filming, full of stories about her adventures, but hopeful that the project would be well received and get the backing for a full series. Jo told her and Richard about the bike show – in between customers and baking – until Richard stopped and fixed her with a long look.

'So ... you and Ed are—?'

She beamed and nodded.

Lucy screamed and ran over to give her a hug.

'What happened to "*I don't need a boyfriend*?"' Richard asked.

'It turns out that I do need a boyfriend.'

'Well. I'm pleased for you. Just ... be careful.'

Jo nodded, still beaming. She wasn't about to divulge Ed's secret. Nobody else needed to know, did they? It was no one else's business but theirs. Sunshine streamed through the floor to ceiling windows, and straight into her heart. She skipped away to clear tables, sweep crumbs off the floor and tackle the mountain of washing-up.

The busy weekend caught up with her as she and Liam fell

back through the caravan door after school. Flicking on the kettle, and fixing Liam's tea on autopilot, she was nonetheless delighted to see Beryl at the door.

'How did it go? I want to know everything.'

'Oh, Beryl!'

'You shagged him! Thank the bloody lord for that. I thought you two were never going to get it together!'

'Beryl!' Jo giggled, sending a glance towards Liam, busily shovelling fish fingers and potato smiles into his face.

'I made a lasagne. Do you want some?'

'Yes, please! I haven't even thought about what I was going to eat. I've got the wine, for a change.' Jo nodded.

'It's a lovely evening – we could put a table in the garden and eat. Pretend we're in Greece.'

'Pikker Nikker!' Liam said, with his mouth full. 'Can I come too?'

'Interesting erection out there,' Beryl said, a sly grin on her face.

'It's a surprise from Ed.' Jo pretended not to catch the innuendo. 'No idea. He's coming over in a bit. The surprise will be revealed.'

'I bet it will …'

'Beryl! Stop it!' They both laughed. Jo reaffirmed her promise to herself to tell Beryl her secret. Surely, nothing could faze her.

Picnic in the garden if you fancy it, she texted to Ed.

Be there now in a minute, he sent back. *I've got a lift.*

'I'll put some garlic bread in the oven. I haven't got anything else,' Jo said to Beryl, peering into the cupboards. She'd never been this disorganised. She'd never had a weekend away before though, to be fair. 'There's a fruit cake. And wine. Does that sound okay?'

'Splendid. Now quick, before Ed gets here. Tell me all.'

Beryl was the perfect audience, not interrupting once as

Jo gave her an admittedly PG version of the weekend, while Liam zoomed back and forth in the garden on his new BMX – now complete with stabilisers that Ed had put on – demanding their attention.

'Well,' Beryl said, sipping red wine from her favourite Spider-Man tumbler. 'Well, well, well.'

'Is that it?' demanded Jo.

'I'm going to miss you.'

'Oh, Beryl. I haven't gone anywhere!' *Yet.*

The sound of a car pulling up and driving away again alerted them.

'Helllooo!' Ed appeared around the side of the van. He was carrying a shoebox in both hands.

'Ed!' Jo tried not to squeak, but she couldn't help herself. Today had seemed the longest day, without seeing him. She blushed with pleasure as he planted a fat kiss on her mouth.

'Hiya, gorgeous!'

'Ed!' Liam yelled, his legs a blur on his bike.

'Evening, Ed,' said Beryl, smiling as he kissed her presented cheek.

'What's that?' Rushing over, Liam was all agog, standing on tiptoe to see into the box. 'It's moving! I can hear it moving! Is it a puppy? Is it for me? Is it for Mummy? Is it for Beryl?'

'Careful.' Ed hooked a chair with his foot, and put the box onto it. As they all peered at it, he prised off the lid. Packed tightly inside, was a layer of yellow fluff. With beaks and black dots for eyes. 'Day old chicks!'

'Chicks!' Liam was ecstatic. 'Can I hold one?'

'Chicks?' Jo stared into the box in dismay.

'*Chwks!*' Beryl smiled. 'I used to keep *chwks*. How lovely.'

'Where are we supposed to put them?' Jo said, still peering

in. The yellow fluff peered back up at her. She could see their broken homes in the bottom. 'Oh. Hang on. So that's not a potting shed then …?'

'… they'll need a heat lamp for a while. And straw and an old sheet to stand on, but kitchen roll or an old tea towel for now …' Beryl seemed to be the only one listening to Ed's chick-rearing instructions.

Jo began to laugh.

'So, most blokes give their girlfriends jewellery or something. You bring me a shoe-box of chickens.' She looked more closely. 'And one of them seems to be dead …'

'*Oops*,' said Ed, reaching in and fishing it out so Liam couldn't see. 'Bound to be a few casualties. But think of all the fresh eggs!'

'How old are they when they lay?' Jo said. She couldn't stop looking at them. They were cute, she conceded. Nothing at all like actual chickens. She'd often fancied keeping chickens, but hadn't a clue how to go about it. And she'd only ever thought of grown up chickens. That laid actual eggs.

'About six months,' said Beryl.

'Six *months*?' said Jo.

'It will fly by.' Ed took one out carefully and placed it on Liam's flattened palm, sealing the deal. 'You have to handle them to make them tame, but you have to be really, really gentle. They're just tiny babies.'

Jo's heart melted as she watched her little boy and her tall, strong, handsome lover bent over the fluffy, diminutive lives. Her mind ran back over his instructions.

'I haven't got a heat lamp.'

'You have now,' said Ed. 'Well, you've got a brooder. Much better. Keep them indoors for a bit. And it's nearly summer. They'll be fine.'

'What do they eat?' Jo asked, faintly.

'They can have my Rice Krispies,' said Liam, gazing at the little chick on his hand.

'Chick Crumb. I brought a bag with me. Look, we have to teach them to drink, Liam, because their mummies aren't here to show them.'

'Where are their mummies?' Liam's face collapsed.

'They have far too many babies to look after,' Beryl told the stricken child. 'So Ed has brought these to you to look after.'

Jo let out a long breath. Honestly. Whatever had Ed been thinking of? He was absurd. And lovely, she thought, watching him show Liam how to handle the tiny scraps of fluff. She'd never considered getting Liam a pet, what with their itinerant lifestyles and lack of money.

They trooped over to the chicken shed, which Jo knew would be The Potting Shed from now on. She'd make a sign for it. Even the brooder looked like something that she'd grow seedlings from. There was a little water dish, and feed dish. The bag of chick crumb looked like shredded breakfast cereal.

'... but they should stay in the caravan for a while, till they're a bit bigger,' Ed was saying, as she tuned back into him.

'In the van?' Jo said. 'Not in The Potting Shed?'

'They're in the brooder. They can't get out,' said Ed, smiling. 'So you can keep an eye on them. Make sure they've not drowned in their water or something.'

Jo looked around at the three pairs of eyes.

'It sounds a bit complicated ...' *There'll be poo. And they'll smell, and die, and Liam will get upset. And so will I.*

'They're not really. I can keep an eye on them when you're not here,' Beryl said. 'And it's good to teach Liam to care for little lives.'

'Can they stay in my room, Mummy? Please Mummy please Mummy please ...'

'Okay,' said Jo. 'But maybe not in your bedroom, Liam. In case you accidentally knock into them? When you're practising headstands?'

Liam nodded vigorously.

It could have been worse. It could have been a mini motorbike or something. Oh God. Now she'd thought about it, it was bound to happen. After all, Ed had learned as a child, hadn't he?

Chapter Twenty-Eight

'I want to tell Mum and Dad about us,' Ed said as they tidied up the Vintage Bike Palace before locking up for the day. It was cool inside the shade of the workshop, but heat shimmered off the tarmac compound. The world seemed to be at the beach. It felt like it had been the hottest summer ever, and the forecast showed fine for ages to come.

A big End of Season Party was being planned in front of the Art Café in a couple of weeks. Jo was hoping to be able to enjoy some of it, but she had a sneaking suspicion that all Art Café hands would be needed serving food and clearing up.

'You mean your Mum and Dad haven't guessed about us?' Jo shimmied up behind him and ran her hands inside his tatty T-shirt as she pressed the length of her body against him. They were alone in the building. Liam was with Beryl, checking on his chicks. Now teenagers with proper feathers, well past the tiny yellow stage, they'd been named and were living in The Potting Shed as it had been so warm. Liam loved his *chwk-chwks*, as he and Beryl called them. Jo only hoped that they were indeed all girl chicks, as she couldn't imagine eating any of them now. Liam would be devastated. They'd probably own the oldest cockerels in history as pets if he had anything to do with it.

'Oh, you're mean to me.' He showed her his oily hands and groaned as her fingers slipped inside his belted jeans. 'Yes, of course they know about us being together, now. The whole world knows we're together, don't they? But, I mean, *er* ...' His breath caught as her fingers encircled him, lazily. 'I mean, *er* ...'

'What?'

'Nothing.'

'Ed!'

He shook his head. He was maddening, he really was. She'd hardly dared to hope that there would be a marriage proposal. These days, people lived happily together for ever with no mention of marriage. Did she have a right to that security? That ring on her finger, that change of name, that final adoption of Liam in his name? She yearned for it. But still there was that unspoken secret, dirtying her happiness. It was time. Way past time.

'Ed.'

'*Aw*. Don't stop!'

'Ed. I …' She gulped. 'I have to tell you something.' The words were out before she could stop them.

'*Uh-oh*. This sounds serious. At least I know you're not going to tell me you're pregnant.'

She squeezed his arm. At least he was able to talk about it now, and it was the exact springboard she needed.

'You know how you carried that secret around for years before finally telling me? How much it hurt you inside?'

He nodded, watchful.

'And you know how I've told you so many times, that I'm not as perfect as you think I am?'

'Jo … don't do yourself down.' He reached out for her. 'You're perfect to me.'

'Don't stop me.' Taking a small step back, she shook her head and took a deep breath. 'I can't hold it in any longer, and I can't bear that you might find out before I tell you myself. So, before you tell your parents about us, I need to tell you something.' She'd understood his meaning. Knew it meant that their relationship would go onto the next level. She loved him so much that she needed to tell him now so that he could make the decision that would destroy her. If he wanted to. She couldn't start their lives on a lie. Her hands shook.

'When I was young,' she said, her voice a whisper, 'something happened. Something terrible. Really awful. I still have nightmares about it.'

'Okay.' He nodded, his eyes willing her to go on.

'My dad died. He had a heart attack, while he was driving. And crashed the car.' She could picture it still. 'I was in the car at the time.'

'*Oh*, Jo. That's terrible for you.' Ed reached out to hug her, holding his dirty hands away from her. 'But you did tell me when we first met that there'd been a car crash.'

Jo pulled a big tin of hand cleaner towards her, and opened the lid for him. 'People never asked anything else once I told them that. That car crash – it was the start of everything going wrong.' She sighed. 'After the crash, I had a really bad time. And I ... kind of went off the rails. Got in with the wrong crowd. Had piercings, goth outfits, attitude ...'

Picking up a blob of Swarfega, he scrubbed his hands together. 'I can't imagine you like that!'

She watched his fingers working the green gloop into his palms and fingernails, visualised those hands moving over her body. She should stop now. Not tell him. Make something up, save herself. No. She had to tell him. Whatever happened next, she owed him that.

'I know. I was so unhappy.' She hesitated. 'And this one evening, there was a bunch of us, like there often was. I didn't know everyone. People came and went.' She shrugged. 'It's how things were then. We'd got on a bus for a laugh. The guys were being total twats – we all were, I suppose, by connection. The driver kicked us off. We laughed. We didn't care. We were drinking, cans, bottles, whatever people had brought with them. Smoking ... stuff.' She pulled a face at the memory. 'We didn't want to hang round in the street, in case people called the cops on us. So, we climbed over a fence. Into this field. Out of the way.' Tears began to fall, unchecked. 'Fooled about, like you do. You know?'

He nodded slowly, his eyes never leaving hers. She looked away, not able to bear the disappointment or worse that would surely be his next expression.

'We were so stupid. I don't know, high, probably. Got right in the middle of this huge field. We hadn't even checked for animals. It was all that fake bravado stuff.' Her eyes drifted off, remembering. 'Stamping down the crops. We danced around on it. Someone had a boom box, and rave music. Stupid stupid stupid, but it felt harmless enough. It went a bit quiet, I remember. Usually, we'd just sit about after something like that. Talking, about rubbish mostly. But next thing, there was all this shouting. I could smell smoke. And there was this terrible noise ...'

She gulped for breath, her chest tightening. The memories she'd tried to push away for years finally popped right up to the surface, demanding attention. Big, fat bubbles on a stinking, stagnant pond.

'The whole field went up in flames. It hadn't rained for ages. It was dry as anything. It was so quick. Terrifying.'

'God ...' Ed was still, focussed on her. She was almost talking to herself now, the memory demanding to be told aloud.

'The fire made this terrible noise, like an animal. I was running, I didn't know where – it was pitch black. Except for the fire. It went everywhere. Not in one place. It just ... ran.' Tears and snot poured unchecked as she sobbed, remembering.

Ed handed her the big blue roll of cleaning paper he'd just dried his hands on and she blew gustily, leaning against the counter. Her legs felt rubbery. She could almost smell the smoke, even now, visualise the leaping flames and terror, remembered running as fast as she could. She glanced up at Ed, and then away.

'Must've been really scary,' said Ed, putting a hand on her arm. She felt the warmth on her icy skin and longed to burrow into his chest. 'And a lot of money in crops, I guess. But ...' He shrugged, brow furrowed, watching her closely.

Jo put her hands over her face. She couldn't bear to tell him. She could stop now, couldn't she? He need never know.

She couldn't.

'There was an old man,' she said, through her fingers. 'In the field. Sleeping rough.'

'*Oh* ...'

'And ... and ...' She sobbed, her body shaking. 'He ... he died.' Her voice was a ragged whisper. 'We killed him.'

She scrubbed at her face with the tissue, repulsed by herself all over again, unable to look at Ed. His stillness was enough. His hands hung by his sides. She felt sick.

Ed's voice was flat. 'What happened then?'

'We didn't know he was in there. The fire ... he couldn't get away ... they said he was asleep, drunk probably, whatever. It doesn't excuse us. They caught us, of course. It went to court.' Now she'd told it all, the awfulness of it turned her legs to jelly and she flopped onto a stool, her ears ringing. 'I hadn't actually started the fires, and the others ... they pleaded guilty.'

He was silent, listening intently.

'I had a reparation order. I worked on the farm that owned the field. Lived in a farm worker's hostel there. ' Her eyes darted around the Bike Palace, unseeing, just remembering. 'It was tough, hard labour, and I wasn't used to it. But I learned how to work. How to eat properly. How to plant vegetables.' She sat up straight then, and raised her eyes to his. 'How to drive.'

'Tractors and trucks?'

She nodded.

'I was supposed to be the one helping them, but in actual

273

fact they taught me so much. I was a different person by the time I left them.'

'So … you didn't actually kill him, this old man, then.' His words came out as a whoosh. It wasn't a question. She heard his relief. She couldn't forgive herself nearly as quickly.

'But … I was there! I might not have actually set light to the field, but I was there, and if I'd known what they were going to do, I would've stopped them. That poor man. What a terrible way to die.' Fresh tears tracked over cheeks rubbed raw with the harsh tissue. 'I dream about it still. Running away from the flames. They'd been laughing.' She hiccuped, shaking her head. 'And then there were just screams.'

She couldn't bear to sit before him any more, awaiting his pronouncement. Wobbly with emotion still, she pushed herself off the stool and paced.

'But, Jo.' He stood before her, taking her hand. 'It wasn't your fault. It was terrible. But not your fault.'

'I can't accept that. We were all responsible. I might have got away with it in court,' she stared up at his face, 'but I have never got away with it in here.' Her free hand heeled into her chest, and she rubbed at her breastbone, trying to push the lump in her throat away. 'It's on my conscience all the time. If I'd only stopped them. If I'd seen him, I could've helped. He was old, he couldn't have run as fast as us. I live with that guilt,' she whispered. 'I even changed my name, so no one could find out about it. People judge. What would Liam say?'

Sinking back onto the stool, she rocked with her arms folded about her, sobbing, until her eyes were sore and dry. This was it. It was out there. They say confession is good for the soul, she thought, and she felt strangely calm, although terror gripped her heart as she tried to guess how he might judge her now.

'Sweetheart.' He knelt in front of her, holding her hands,

trying to make her look at him. 'Listen to me. You made a mistake. We all make mistakes. We're only human. I can't imagine having that on my conscience, but to be honest, I think that the fact that you haven't just dismissed it and moved on has made you the person you are. It's what you make of it now. I can't make that memory go away. But it belongs in the past.' He gathered her hands in his. 'Look at what you've achieved since. You're a fantastic mum to Liam. God … you saved my dad's life! You're clever, and talented, and people love you.' He pulled her up and into his arms, smoothing her mop of curly hair, damp with tears, off her face. 'I love you.'

'I love you too. That's why I had to tell you.'

'It was very brave of you.' He squeezed her. 'What would you have done if I'd chucked you?'

'I didn't have a back-up plan. But I couldn't start our lives on a lie.'

'I'm glad I told you my secret first,' Ed said into her ear. 'In case you were wanting a whole brood of children.'

She cried again then, knowing how much that was what he'd always wanted.

'We could adopt, Ed. Or foster, maybe. There are always children who need love.'

'That's true.' He hushed her, smoothing her back. 'No more secrets, now.'

She sniffed into his shoulder. No more secrets. Well. Everyone had some secrets, didn't they? People didn't need to know everything about you. There would always be things that you had no control over, that happened, and no one needed to know about those things. That was just life. She'd told him about the worst thing, and he'd accepted it. The other things were just … stuff.

Chapter Twenty-Nine

'Seagull Cottage will be ready to move into soon,' Ed said late one still, hot afternoon as they made sandcastles at the tide's edge with Liam. The sea shimmered seamlessly against a colourless sky.

'*Ooh!*' Jo had been waiting for this proclamation, and still wasn't sure how she felt about it. She was excited about putting her stamp on the cottage, but she'd become used to the cosy caravan. It represented such big changes in her life.

'It's taken a lot longer than I thought it would.' Ed drew the castle layout in the sand, and Liam improved on it with his bare feet. 'That's the trouble with old buildings. All the underpinning took so much time.'

'It's been fun,' Jo said, meaning it. A sudden memory of that first night in the van made her smile. What a wonderful friendship she and Beryl had now ... and all because she'd moved into a temporary home. It would always have a special place in her heart – and the glorious summer made her feel as if she'd had a never-ending holiday. Even though she'd been planning Seagull Cottage's decor in her head, it still seemed unreal.

Her relationship with Ed ping-ponged between his cottage and the caravan and made her feel young and exciting. Just like a wonderful holiday romance, she conceded, still finding it difficult to trust that their infant relationship could survive. Besides, living in a house was what grown-ups did, and she'd been grown up for too long. She smacked a plastic starfish mould sharply on the base, cheering at the perfect sandy shape beneath.

'Better start packing then!' she said to Liam's emerging sandcastle.

'Or, you could both move in with me,' Ed said it nonchalantly. As if she could take it as a joke if she decided to.

She thought about it, watching him digging the packed sand just below Liam's bottom, so that he'd subside into the resultant hole. Liam was pretending not to notice. It was a game they never tired of.

'What about the chickens?' To her surprise, the balls of yellow fluff had survived, and were now leggy, squawking, squabbling teenagers with attitude. Liam adored them, and never minded their attempts to peck at him as he picked them up and petted them. They needed space, and Ed's pocket handkerchief garden couldn't provide that. 'And the allotment?'

'Yeah, okay,' conceded Ed. 'I tell you what, you stay in the caravan, and we'll rent out Seagull Cottage as well.' He ducked as Jo threw a plastic spade at him. Liam toppled dramatically into the excavated hole with a pretend shriek, which turned real as an incoming wave filled his moat unexpectedly and soaked them all. As the three of them tumbled like puppies together, Jo couldn't help wondering what this move might mean for them all.

It was hot and airless inside the caravan, even with all the windows open. Jo showered her sandy, salty son in tepid water to cool him while he complained about having to go to bed when it was still light. She propped open the van door to encourage a flow of air and told him she was just outside with Aunty Beryl.

'I hope you're not going to laugh and keep me awake,' he'd grumbled, pompously, his eyelids already closing. Jo and Beryl guffawed silently behind their hands, knowing that the little boy would be asleep in moments.

'What are you going to wear for the big party, Beryl?'

Slicing a loaf of walnut and parmesan bread, Jo put out mozzarella, basil and home grown tomatoes and lettuce for them to help themselves. Dappled shadows danced over the checked tablecloth and mismatched crockery.

'*Ooh*, the End of Season Beach Party? I'm going back to see Marjorie at Vintage Rose,' said Beryl, swirling her chilled rosé in her glass. She speared an olive from the dish that she'd brought over. 'I loved those dresses. I can't wait to go shopping in there again.'

'Perfect,' Jo said. 'Ed's Mum is going there too. We're all going to look like something from *Saturday Night Fever*!' She had a sudden vision of Ed dressed up like a young John Travolta and blushed. With his black hair and lithe body, he could definitely carry that role off. He was out with his mates tonight. She didn't mind. Sometimes she went with him, if Beryl or his parents babysat, but the lure of the peaceful garden and a chilled glass of wine appealed more tonight than a hot and sticky bar.

'There's going to be an outdoor cinema, isn't there?' Beryl said. 'What will they be showing?'

'I'm not entirely sure. Summer-feel movies, the posters say. There is a main committee who are organising it, and a whole set of sub-committees.' Jo pulled her T-shirt away from her sticky skin. 'It started off as a bit of a beach barbecue and some music, and it's just evolved.'

'I hope *Mamma Mia!* is on the list!'

'I hope so too! I'd just have that on a loop!' She laughed. 'I believe it'll be feel-good retro stuff, surfing films, *Grease*, *Dirty Dancing*, that sort of thing. I suppose there'll be time to show a few, and have them on in the background with the music going. It's going to be such fun!'

'What's the Art Café going to be doing? Talk me through it.' Beryl leaned back, propping her feet on another chair and sipping her wine.

'There'll be mini versions of the usual stuff, like an advert for the café – mini scones with strawberries, mini toasties, wraps, mini muffins. Teas and coffees, Pimms and summer cocktails. We've got a temporary licence. The car park has been rented out to other food producers, to make it more interesting.' She ticked them off on her fingers. 'There's a fish and chip stand with a difference because it sells lobster, a hog roast, burgers, a vegan stand with that guy off the telly.' Pulling a creamy chunk from a ball of mozzarella, she squashed it onto a thick slice of tomato, topped it with a few leaves of basil swirled in olive oil and popped it into her mouth. It was like summer in a bite, and a very long way from the cheapest bread and cheese that she'd survived on for so long when Liam was a baby.

'Goodness me. It's beginning to sound like a mini Food Festival.'

Jo licked her fingers. 'It is. Loads of people have been in touch, wanting space to sell their stuff. And not just food either. I reckon if it goes well, it could be huge next year. They've had to hire portable loos.'

'What's the plan if it rains?'

'It's. Not. Going. To. Rain.' Jo fixed her neighbor with a determined eye.

Beryl laughed, sipping her wine. 'How long have you lived in Wales?'

Jo grinned. 'Yeah, I know. Well, there are huge marquees for the food and the bar – practically the whole car park will be covered. There'll be another one on the actual beach. The projector has to be out of any rain, but it doesn't matter about the screen, that's weatherproof. We'll all dance with umbrellas. Someone knows someone who can lay their hands on hundreds of cheap ponchos. It'll be fine. It really will. We'll be so busy having fun that a bit of rain won't matter, and look, we're all used to the rain, aren't we? If you didn't go out in the rain here, you'd never go out at all, would you?'

Beryl chuckled her agreement. 'Will you have time to enjoy the party? Sounds as if you're going to be busy.'

'I'm working all the days leading up to it, so I've got the evening off.' Jo nodded. 'There are lots of temporary staff lined up. Although I've got to say, I wouldn't feel right leaving them all to it, so I'm bound to be helping out in the beginning. Richard and Lucy have been so good to me, letting me shuffle my shifts around. Liam's coming too, of course. If he has a nap during the day, he'll be fine for a few hours. And you know what little ones are like, he'll either outlast us all, or fall asleep in the middle of all the action. Lyn and Griff have said they will take him back for a sleepover at theirs. I think Lyn would dance all night, but Griff is not quite up to that yet. They're using Liam as an excuse to leave early. I won't be drinking, so I can run you home if you want to leave early, Beryl.'

Beryl snorted. 'Me? Leave a party early? Wash your mouth out, young lady!'

Her eyes twinkled and Jo sat back with a sigh of happiness. At last, she felt as if she belonged. She had friends – she'd sorted some dates for First Aid courses to run at Liam's school and the café, all of which were fully booked … and she had a busy life, and a bit more cash to enjoy it with, even if she had to work her socks off for it, which she didn't mind at all. She had found a family – Beryl was like the mother she'd never had, and Lyn and Griff treated her just like a daughter, collecting Liam and taking him for days out during the long school holidays. And lastly, of course, she had Ed. He was so steadfast, that she could barely credit how much she'd mistrusted him all through those earlier months. She leaned across the table.

'I've got something for Ed,' she told Beryl, in a conspiratorial tone. She didn't want Liam spoiling the secret.

Beryl was all ears. 'What?'

'You remember that old motorbike that Liam found and we bought for Ed?'

'That rusty old thing that was in bits?' Beryl nodded.

'Well,' Jo hugged herself with delight, 'I got a phone call in the week and the girl that showed us round – Kirsty – she's found the tank for it! It was in the attic, wrapped up in blankets.'

Beryl tried to look interested but Jo could see she wasn't following at all. 'What does that actually mean?'

Jo could feel her mouth curving into an enormous grin. 'It confirms the make of the bike ... and makes it so much more valuable. I've been on the internet and one sold at auction recently for ... are you ready for this?'

Beryl leaned forward. 'Go on ...'

'Three hundred and fifteen thousand pounds!' Jo squeaked, beside herself with glee. She glanced into the caravan to make sure Liam was still asleep. Beryl gave a long, low whistle, lifted her glass and chinked it against Jo's. Her expression said it all.

'So – what are you waiting for?'

Jo said, 'I'm going to give it to him as a Thank You for doing Seagull Cottage up so beautifully for us.'

'That's a hell of a gift,' Beryl said, nodding. 'Very big-hearted of you.' She looked into her glass. 'I'm so glad to have met you, Jo. You're a very special lady.'

Jo's eyes filled with tears.

'Oh, Beryl, I owe so much of my happiness to you. I'm glad I met you, too!'

'Ed had better do the right thing by you,' Beryl said, beetling her brows. 'Or he'll have me to answer to! Is he going to be moving in with you?'

'He asked if we would move in with him ...'

Beryl was silent for a moment.

'Wouldn't it be a convenient thing to do?'

'I suppose. But it feels a bit too convenient, somehow. Like,' Jo stared up into the blossom heavy trees, 'I know it's early days, but moving in together feels like we've missed a step out. I still can't help feeling like it's a holiday romance.'

'Very old-fashioned way to look at it ...'

'I am old-fashioned! You're the trendy one, Beryl. Remember how you wanted to rip my jeans?' They laughed.

'Talking of which,' Beryl levered herself out of the garden chair. 'I bought some of those frozen mojitos. Shall we test them out?'

'It would be rude not to.'

Chapter Thirty

Time telescoped over the next few weeks. Jo thrived on each new challenge as the tasks in the café mounted. Liam adored his surrogate family, and although Jo's heart bled sometimes when she watched him pottering round her allotment with Griff, she felt her dad smiling down at them all from wherever he was.

They really were camping out in the caravan now, with a move date back into Seagull Cottage the day after the Summer Party. Jo worried that they might all be worse for wear, but Ed insisted and as he was still her landlord, she'd deferred to him. She'd been packing things away for ages, only to have to unpack to locate something they needed. It was frustrating and she began to crave the permanence that Seagull Cottage offered. Her notebook of ideas for decorating the cottage was bulging, and she was keen to put her stamp on the blank shell. She'd also missed her upcycling – still packed away in a temporary shed. The current stock was all sold and her eBay shop was looking a bit sad and empty. It was time for some normality to return. Although, she wouldn't be going back to exactly where they were before, because now she and Ed were together. Where would she be in a year's time? Still not quite willing to believe her good luck, she decided not to think about it in case she jinxed it somehow.

Anticipation fizzed in the air, as the enormous marquees went up in the car park during the morning of the big Summer Party. There'd been a few grumblings from customers not able to park, but Richard gave them a free cup of tea or coffee and kept them sweet. A torrential downpour lasting for two days had scared them all into making wet weather contingency plans, but the air was fresher now, with just the barest hint of autumn.

Ed's family was sponsoring the open-air cinema, and Ed himself was on the beach lending muscle wherever he could and setting up the generators. Jo couldn't help peeping out over the café terrace whenever she could to catch sight of him, tanned and buff in his beach shorts. Liam had been with Beryl all day. She'd kept him busy and had then texted Jo to tell her that he had actually fallen asleep for a good hour in front of a Disney movie, which was a relief, and would have topped up his little boy batteries for a later night than usual. The Art Café kitchen was groaning with supplies, there were hired freezers, and Jo had her fingers crossed that all the food would be eaten. Lucy flew in and out as she always did, with a smile and a hug for everyone, and Jo thought again how lucky she'd been with her employers.

The food trailers arrived and set up their gas canisters for cooking. Four of Ed's mates were being paid as security to patrol the car park and beach overnight, after the party. All burly rugby players. Despite their ready smiles, they were determined to take their roles seriously and Jo pitied anyone who dared to tackle them.

Local customers caught up in the excitement were pressed into service, stringing up bunting or solar fairy lights which Lucy had bought by the mile, or so it seemed, their batteries already fully charged by the relentless sunlight. Health and Safety was taking a back seat – it was almost impossible to keep friends out of the way – everyone wanted to help.

A bouncy castle was wobbling its way to inflation on the beach, and a candy floss booth had just arrived. The party had begun already and if it hadn't been that Jo wanted to wear her Rita Hayworth dress – bare legs and flip flops this time – and do her hair and face, she would have stayed as the crowds would begin to arrive from five o'clock. Tugging off her apron, she skipped onto the beach to find Ed. Stripped to the waist, and wearing knee length board shorts and flip flops, he was slick with sweat and Jo's stomach leapt. He was truly film star gorgeous, and she was so lucky.

'Are you ready to leave?' His lips felt cool on hers.

'Nearly,' he said, pushing a curl of hair behind her ears and following his fingers with his lips. 'But those big feather flags and the screen need properly tethering down. There's a bit of a breeze blowing up.'

'I'll go, bring back Liam and Beryl, and you can have the truck to nip home, shower and change.' She traced his chest hair, smoothed by sweat. 'Although I like you just like this ...'

'Unhand me, woman!' He crushed her to him, deliberately pushing her face near his armpit as she squealed. 'I stink! You, however, are always fragrant and cool.' Sniffing her neck, he wrinkled his nose. 'Except for now ...'

'I've been working!' She giggled, wriggling away from him. 'I won't be long. See you later. Love you!'

Jo sang all the way home with the windows open on the truck, and leapt into a cool shower, pausing only long enough to rap on Beryl's window and call that she was back.

She was putting the finishing touches to her make-up as Beryl appeared in the open doorway, with Liam.

'Wow! You look amazing!' they said to each other in unison. Pleased, Beryl did a little pirouette, showing off a neat figure in a floral sundress in turquoise and pinks, a white cotton cardigan slung around her shoulders. She carried a floppy wide-brimmed sun hat and oversized sunglasses, and her feet sparkled in jewelled flip flops.

'Very Audrey Hepburn,' said Jo. 'I went for blingy flip flops too – I can't do heels on the beach!'

'Do I look nice too, Mummy?' Liam asked, imitating Beryl's twirl in his mini-me Ed-style board shorts and T-shirt.

'You look like a proper beach boy.' Jo hugged him. 'Very

grown up.' She stuffed his hoody into his Jack Wolfskin rucksack, along with his pyjamas, toothbrush, a bottle of water and some sensible snacks in case there was nothing he wanted to eat there. He'd begun to recognise the connection between his chickens and the breadcrumb coated nuggets that he loved, and had become quite picky about what he ate. Although pleased to wean him off the processed food, Jo wasn't entirely sure how to address the eating chicken issue, so for the time being she simply made sure he ate a varied diet with plenty of fruit and veg, nuts and seeds, dairy and fish.

He still ate eggs, although it had taken some persuading by Beryl to assure him that he wasn't murdering a baby chick in its home.

'They're vacant homes,' she'd told him. 'Empty. No babies. There's no one in them.'

'Like Seagull Cottage?' he'd asked, to everyone's relief, and carried on enjoying his egg and soldiers.

A final glance in the mirror satisfied Jo that she was ready for the fray. The little make-up set purchased in Vintage Rose had been supplemented since by a lipstick in a soft rose that matched her dress, and even she had to agree that it improved her. Even sun-kissed and freckled, she looked like a much more complete version of her old self these days. Her messy up-do of cascading tendrils enhanced her long neck and the cleavage created by the Wonder-Bra that Beryl had bullied, no, *persuaded* her into buying.

Leaving now xx she texted to Ed, as they climbed into the cab of the Nissan.

They could hear *Grease* the musical playing as they arrived. Jo parked in their reserved spot beside the café, and followed Liam as he skipped inside. Several of the marquee sides had been unlaced and hooked up, allowing the freshening breeze to cool the air. A few fluffy clouds dotted the cobalt sky, and there was a tang of mouthwatering scents in the air from the food tents.

'Goodness me, you've all worked so hard!' Beryl said, keeping a tight hold of Liam's hand as Jo stowed his rucksack in her locker and retrieved her black pinny. Flags fluttered and as early as it was, there were dozens of people already gathering at the beach.

'We have, Beryl!' Ed said, strolling through the big glass doors from the terrace. 'And don't you look the part!' He kissed her blushing cheek, high-fived Liam, kissed Jo and pocketed the truck keys in one fluid motion. 'I'm outta here! Back in an hour or so. Liam, you're in charge.'

'I'm in charge, Mummy!' The little boy puffed his chest out. 'What am I in charge of?'

'Having a good time!' Beryl held out her hand to him, 'and making sure I don't get lost. Shall we go and check out the stands while Mummy gets to work in the café? I believe Mummy has given me some pocket money for you to spend too!'

'Okay,' he nodded, importantly. 'Come on, Aunty Beryl. If you get lost, you have to come back to here, 'kay?'

Jo chuckled as she watched them leave, tying the black pinny over the beautiful dress and presenting herself to Richard.

'You really didn't have to come and help,' said Richard, his gaze appraising her from head to toe with a smile. 'But I'm glad you did. Three of the students haven't turned up! And you scrub up nicely!'

'Thanks!' Jo grinned at him. ' But look, they might just be delayed, let's not worry about it yet. What do you want me to do?'

'In that dress?' Richard looked doubtful.

'Is there something clean that I could do?'

'Yeah. The till. I want someone I can trust until we see how many of the slackers turn up.'

It was Jo's turn to appraise him. He looked frazzled. 'Richard. Let me make you a pot of tea. Put your feet up and take ten. Take twenty! It's early. We'll cope.'

Richard waggled his head, undecided, as Jo made up a tray for him. 'Okay. Good plan,' he said at last. 'I'll be on the terrace, if you need me.'

'We won't. Go on and chill for a bit. You've done all the hard work.' Jo took the tray of teapot, mini scones and pasties out of his reach and put them on the table with the best view of the bay. 'Sit,' she commanded, with a smile. 'Enjoy. And don't come in for at least twenty minutes.'

With the other regulars, she tidied and finished anything they could see that needed doing, as two of the temporary staff wandered in, all long bare legs and flip flops and casual air. Jo was sharp with them until their off-hand facade receded and then she felt a bit sorry for them. It was so hard to be young.

By the time Ed returned looking fresh and cool in stone linen trousers and a patterned blue shirt, *Grease* the musical was halfway through and the evening was in full swing. Beryl and Liam had eaten their way round the marquee, and were currently on the beach, dancing with his school chums and their parents, all doing the moves from 'Greased Lightning' to every tune.

'Go!' Richard shooed her away. 'We're sorted. Go and enjoy yourselves.'

'If you're sure – thank you!' Jo glanced longingly onto the beach, already untying her apron. Hurrying down the terrace steps, she peered over the throng for Ed, locating him deep in conversation in the beach marquee with a clutch of his mates. They grinned and nodded at her.

'Everything alright?' she said, slipping her arm into his and smiling round at everyone. He jumped, his expression a little flustered. Or had she imagined it?

'Yes! I was just …' He bent and kissed her, steering her towards the tent exit. 'Has Richard let you go now?'

'I'm all yours!'

'Shall we go and have a wander? See what's going on?' He nodded to his friends and arm in arm, they sauntered out to the strains of the final scenes of *Grease*, almost drowned out by people singing lustily.

'The bins are filling up already!' Jo pointed in dismay to an overflowing bin liner, surrounded by plastic beer glasses. 'I'll have to go and find some more rubbish bags.'

'Stop worrying, Jo! Look, someone's doing it already. Come on, let's go and get some food before it all goes. I'm fancying lobster from that shack that catches them in West Wales. And a beer.'

'I'm not drinking – I'm driving Beryl back.'

'You are not. I've arranged a lift for her. And us.'

'But … I'm moving house tomorrow!'

'Yes, and your landlord is a nasty piece of work, I've heard.' Pulling her into him, he smiled down at her. 'Chill, Jo. You've worked hard. Let's enjoy it, shall we?'

She relaxed, at last. 'You're right. Thanks, Ed. Lead the way.' With a last glance over her shoulder to check that the bin really was being emptied, Jo allowed herself to be led away. Shoulder to shoulder on the low wall around the café, they watched the pulsating crowd singing to the final *Grease* track, and devouring their lobster rolls.

'That was utterly delicious,' Jo announced, sucking the juices off her fingers. 'I've never had lobster before.'

'I'm really broadening your life experiences, aren't I?' Ed nudged her with his shoulder, wiping his sticky fingers. 'Let's go and join Liam and Beryl, shall we?'

Liam's hair was plastered to his head, but his grin reached from one ear to the other.

'Mummy! It's finished now. I danced to it. Did you see me

dancing?' On the fringe of the main crush, Beryl had found some chairs and was chatting to Lyn and Griff, looking out over the beach, which had never looked more beautiful. At its furthest reach, a turquoise sea reflected the molten sun. *Grease* faded away. A huge grin split Jo's face as she heard the familiar opening refrain to her favourite movie of all time.

'Oh! *Mamma Mia!*' She turned to Ed. 'Did you arrange this?'

'*We-ll* …' He grinned, shamefaced.

Liam was already jigging about, laughing at the screen, anticipating the comedy moments.

'Thank you. It's perfect.' She reached up and kissed him, shrieking as he caught her and pulled her close to him, whirling her away and back again, her full skirted dress swishing around her bare legs.

Jo knew she would remember this night forever, as the crowd sang and danced to the joyous tunes, and the film threw its saturated colours across the throng.

'Back in a mo!' Ed said, after twirling Beryl rather more gently. 'More drinks, everyone?'

'Can I go on the bouncy castle, Mummy?'

'Let's go and see how busy it is first.' Mindful of the swelling masses, Jo took the little boy's hand and threaded her way to where a small funfair had been set up. Smiling faces turned her way as they passed, and Jo felt proud that she now knew so many people. A summer of change. For the better. The bored looking teenage boy in charge of the bouncy castle was being chatted up by a cluster of giggling girls, all with identical shoulder length blonde hair and Super Dry vest tops over their skimpy cut off denim shorts. Accordingly, there was already a fair bit of alchohol being taken onto the inflatable. She felt cross with the boy who was meant to be in charge, and then relented. It wasn't exclusively a children's party, after all.

'*Um*, no, sweetie. There aren't any children on it any more … you'll get squashed by all the grown-ups.' His face fell, and she added gently, 'And it's getting dark, and I wouldn't be able to see you getting squashed either.' She bent and hugged him. 'You'll be leaving soon, with Auntie Lyn and Uncle Griff and having a sleepover. That'll be fun, won't it?'

Liam pouted. 'What *can* I play on then? I'm not a bit tired.'

Jo checked her watch and craned her neck to see if she could spot Ed on his way back with their drinks. Beryl was making her way towards her, a tall young man in her wake who looked familiar.

Familiar, that is, from a very long time ago. A face that Jo thought she would never clap eyes on again. The gap closed.

'This young man has been looking for you, Jo,' Beryl said. 'Someone you know, I believe.' Beryl stood beside the young man, her face wreathed in smiles. 'A blast from the past, as I understand it?'

'Hi, Jo.'

'Will!' Jo stepped back, her stomach in free-fall. 'What … what are you doing here?'

Chapter Thirty-One

'I wondered if you'd remember me. And … I thought, since …'

'Since what? Why are you here, Will?' Jo could hear the sharp edge in her voice. Pins and needles tingled in her fingers.

'I recognised you from an article in *Classic Bike* magazine. Read that you'd been a bit of a hero.' Will lifted a hand to touch her arm and dropped it as she stepped smartly out of reach. 'You look … stunning. Quite a change!'

'How did you find me here?' How the hell had he recognised her from that photo? She'd barely recognised herself!

'Internet, of course. I'm sorry, I thought you'd be pleased to see me.' Will's gaze raked her from head to toe. 'Only … you just left, all those years ago, and I always wondered what had happened to you.'

'It doesn't matter any more. You … you can't stay.' Gripping Liam's hand, she pushed him behind her. Over Will's shoulder she saw Ed approaching, and her jaw dropped as she saw what he was wearing. 'What on earth? Go away, Will! Just … go!'

Beryl's confusion was replaced by open-mouthed admiration as she followed Jo's gaze.

'Tracked you down!' Ed said, resplendently bare chested in a spangled, one piece blue satin suit complete with flares. '*Ta-daaah!* What do you think?' He grinned at her expression. 'Pierce Brosnan?' he prompted. '*Mamma Mia!*? At the end?' His grin faded as he looked round at the little gathering. 'What? What have I missed?'

Beryl was the first to gather her wits. '*Er* … very nice, Ed. *Er* … this is Will. He told me he's an old friend of Jo's, but …'

'Hi.' Ed nodded to Will with an abashed expression. 'Pleased to meet you. Fancy dress. Bit of a laugh, I thought, you know, to go with the film ...'

'He's not staying.' Jo stepped back onto Liam's foot, making him squeal. '*Oh*, I'm sorry, Liam, sweetie!'

'*Ow! Mum-my!*' Liam's over-tired voice whined.

Will stared down at the little boy.

'I didn't come to cause trouble, but I've come all this way and ... I have to know. I've done the maths. He's mine, isn't he?'

'He's what?' Ed and Beryl said together.

'No!' Jo shouted. 'No, he is not. Leave us alone, Will!'

'You called him after me, Jo.'

'What's this?' Ed turned to Jo. 'What's he talking about?'

'I'm Will. William. He's Liam. I'm right, aren't I, Jo?'

'No!' Gripping Liam's hand, Jo edged backwards in a panic. 'Take us home, Ed, please!'

'I don't know who you are, mate,' Ed stood between Jo and Will, 'but you're upsetting my missus. She wants you to leave her alone. So, off you trot.'

'I don't want to upset anyone. But I've checked and, as I said, the dates are right,' Will persisted. 'And look here.' He flicked open a black leather wallet style phone case, and thumbed out a photograph. Illuminating it with his phone, he turned it round to show them a schoolboy of about five years old, with a 'beginning of term' haircut and a gappy smile. 'This is me.' He clicked the home button on the phone to show a photo of Liam in his 1940s fancy dress, short back and sides, and gappy grin. Horrified, Jo slapped her hands over her eyes, but failed to block out the likeness. They were almost identical.

'What?' Beryl frowned.

'And here.' Will scrolled to the photo that the magazine had taken, and which Lucy had shared to the Art Café page, and goodness only knew where else.

'I don't understand.' Ed squinted at the two photographs. 'Jo? You told me Liam's father was dead. What happened to, "They all died in a car accident?"'

Panic made lumps in Jo's voice. She backed away, holding her hands up.

'I lied, okay?' she said. 'What was I supposed to say? That I had a schoolgirl crush on the rich boy, had a one night stand, and then found I was pregnant and he'd already gone off to pursue his glittering career?'

'What did you do to her?' Ed stood eyeball to eyeball with Will. 'I think it's time you left …'

'I did nothing to her! Well, only … y'know …' Will lifted his hands. 'One minute she was there … the next she was gone! I didn't even know she was pregnant!' He turned to Jo. 'You have to believe me. I went to look for you. Your mother made it clear I wasn't welcome in your house.'

Jo laughed harshly. '*Hah! Your* mother told me not to go after you … she told me I was a slut and I'd ruin your life, because "you were going places, and I was bad for you. That I'd hold you back."' She drew in a ragged breath, her heart pounding. 'It was always all about you, Will, "the golden boy". She gave me money to, to …' She stuttered to a halt. 'I can't talk about it here. Not in front of …' She pulled Liam into her, frightened and aware suddenly that he was listening to every word. 'I can't talk about it. You're spoiling everything. We'll have to leave, now. You've ruined everything. Everyone will know. Please, Ed … let's just go. Now. Please.'

'Your mother?' Ed's expression was wooden. 'So … is she not dead either?'

'My mother doesn't deserve to be alive.' Jo's voice was a flat whisper. Tears poured down her cheeks. 'She, she—'

'Let me take Liam,' Beryl interrupted. 'He doesn't need to hear all this.' She held out her hand and after an anguished moment, Jo let him go. 'Shall we go and see if there's a ride free on the fairground, sweetheart?'

'Maybe the bouncy castle?' Liam's voice was hopeful.

'Maybe,' said Beryl. Jo met her look of distress with a bleak stare.

'Jo ... I don't understand.' Ed ran a hand through his hair. 'Is he Liam's father or what? I thought you said Liam's father was dead too. You're making me look a right idiot here.'

'You're doing a good job of that all by yourself, mate,' Will said, looking him up and down.

'No one asked you!' Ed stepped up to him again.

'Ed, no!' Jo spread her hands, pleading with them. 'Will. Go. Please.'

'All these secrets, Jo.' Ed shook his head. 'I thought ... I thought we'd agreed ...'

'Ed ... I don't expect you to understand.' She stared at her feet, tapping her thigh with nervous fingers. 'The only person I could rely on was myself. And then, there was you. And suddenly I didn't want to be by myself. I wanted to be with you. But your life is so perfect and blameless and I thought you wouldn't love me if you knew what a train wreck my life had been. Your parents ... they're wonderful. They support you in everything you do. Mine ...' She shook her head. 'I can't ...'

'What? Tell me!' He thrust his hands out to her, palms upward. Pleading.

'After ... after I saw Will's mother I went home to my mum. I didn't know where else to go. I was desperate. I had nowhere else. She wasn't there.' Jo stared at them, unseeing. 'But ... her boyfriend was. Oh, he pretended to be so helpful.' She spat the words out. 'But,' her voice rose in her anguish, 'he tried to rape me! I told my mum ... and she said I was lying. She said I'd tried it on with *him!* She said I was a slut and told me never to come back.' Covering her face, she sobbed. 'My "biological" father was just a shag in the pub. My mother was the slut. Not me.'

'Oh, Jo ... so the dad you've talked about – he was ...' Ed was still struggling to make sense of it, she could see.

'He wasn't my biological father. He wasn't the sperm donor. Okay? But he brought me up!'

Ed lifted his hands. 'At least she picked someone decent to be your pretend dad.'

'She didn't pick him!' Jo sobbed. 'He picked her! Because he loved her and he told her he'd look after me. She only stayed with him because he had money!' Ed looked as if she'd struck him. His shoulders sagged, and she reached out for him. 'That's not why I'm ... No, please, Ed, you can't think that!'

'I don't know what to believe right now. You could have told me,' said Ed, his face in shadow. 'You didn't even give me the chance to understand. You just lied about it all. I trusted you. I thought Liam would be my ... That we would be a family ... You knew how much that meant to me.' He swallowed, backing away from her, his eyes too bright. 'I can't do this. I've ... er, I've just got to, er ...'

'No, Ed! Don't go! Don't leave me!' She hurried after him, pulling at the silky fabric of the blue jumpsuit, but he sloughed her off, running into the dark crowd. People were looking at her, whispering, pointing. She couldn't look at them.

'I've got to go after him. I can't be here.' Stricken, she stared around, seeing Will behind her. 'Why? Why did you come here, Will? You've ruined everything! My life's over. It's all over. I've got to find Liam. I can't stay here.' She couldn't catch her breath. What a fool she'd been, allowing those photos to be used. Everyone had seen them. Social media went all round the world. She'd assumed that no one would recognise her. That she'd changed so much. She'd lost Ed now, the best thing that had ever happened to her. He was never going to trust her again. No one here would trust her. She'd blown it.

She started towards the fairground with no thought in her head except to find her son and get away, but Will gripped her arm.

'I still don't understand why you didn't try to find me?' He shook his head. 'I would have stood by you. I really liked you. I thought you liked me.'

'*Oh*, Will.' She sighed, her inward breath hiccuping. 'You still don't get it, do you? Your life was nothing like mine. I did like you. You were the rich boy – you had everything in front of you.' She took a deep breath. 'But your mother. She told me to "get it aborted". Her words. She gave me money to do it. Her own grandchild. Nothing more than "it" in her eyes. Told me to leave you alone, that I would ruin your life.'

'She wouldn't do that.' His expression was set.

'*Oh*, she did. And I hated myself in any case, thought I didn't deserve any better anyway. So I ended up with no one. I was terrified.' She looked up at him. 'I used that money to run away. There was just me and the baby. I bet you don't have the first idea what that was like.'

He shook his head. 'I'm so sorry. But when I saw that photo …' He hesitated, then said, 'Was that your husband?'

Jo choked on a sob, shaking her head. 'We're not married, and now … you've ruined everything.'

'You shouldn't have lied.'

'That's easy for you to say. You don't have anything to lie about. I couldn't bear to have to keep explaining to people. They go on and on, have to know everything. It was easier to just say everyone was dead. Then no one asks questions.'

'When were you going to tell my son about me?'

'He's *my* son!' She shrugged then, bleak and defeated. 'Maybe never.'

Will straightened up, frowning. 'Maybe you're more like your mother than you think you are. A quick shag and then find some bloke to take you on.'

'Oh, you bastard! How dare you! Most blokes would be only too keen to get away with an unwanted pregnancy. What makes you so high and fucking mighty?' She whirled away from him. 'Get away from me!' she shrieked. 'Who do you think you are, just turning up like this? You are not welcome in our lives. Just go.'

She ran towards the fairground, pushing into the crowd, disappearing. Hiding again. From Ed. And Will. And from herself, from the guilt and shame. Head down, glad of the dark, she trudged towards the cheerful lights of the fair, no clear idea of what to do next. Just the need to get herself and Liam away from there. Away from the whispers. She had to explain to Ed. Somehow.

Beryl stood between the fairground booths, looking agitated.

'Jo, have you—'

'Beryl. I'm sorry, I should have—'

'—have you got Liam?'

'What? No! What do you mean?'

'He was here, just now! I thought he must have seen you?'

'I didn't see him! Oh God, no, no, no, no …' Jo stared around her, frantic already, her chest clutching in spasms. 'Liam! Liam!' she called out, her voice harsh with panic. 'Which way did he go?'

'I don't know! I had his hand, and then he twisted away and I saw you and I thought he must have run to you … he can't be far … but it's so dark here away from the lights …'

Bile rose into Jo's mouth as her brain echoed: so dark here away from the lights … He could be anywhere. Anyone could have taken him.

'Help! We need lights here!' She screamed. 'Liam! Where are you?'

The soft sand dragged at Ed's feet as he plodded up the beach, shoulders hunched, head low. The ridiculous satin blue jumpsuit glinted jauntily in the lights. He'd had such plans for tonight. Now they lay in tatters.

His own words 'pretend dad' scorched into his brain and he kicked viciously at the sand, nearly tripping over the stupidly wide flares. Why hadn't she told him? Why hadn't she told him when she'd confessed her other 'big secret'? That hadn't meant nearly as much as this did. It made no sense. Had she thought it wasn't important? Clearly, she'd thought that he would never find out ... he could see that it had rocked her to the core. But ... another lie when he'd specifically asked her if there was anything else.

How could he trust her now? Why did she think she couldn't tell him? Didn't she trust him?

The 'whys' tumbled over and over in his brain. He couldn't get his head round it. Yes, she'd had a tough life, but that was all behind her now. Or was it? How many other things might surface to make a fool of him? Was it all just a sham? A pretend face? Did she even really love him, or was it all about security and money?

He grieved for her past, and she was right, he couldn't understand parents that behaved like that. He could barely credit that she'd been told to abort her baby – by that child's own grandmother.

He shook his head, his mind whirling over the times that he'd despaired at his inability to have children. To give the joy of grandchildren to his parents, who had given him such a wonderful childhood. In Jo and Liam, he'd seen the possibility of that happiness, felt his heart gladden, watching his parents delight in the little boy. Accepted a future without his own children and imagined that they could be a family. But, what did it mean to be a 'pretend' family?

His mobile rang, buzzing against his thigh in the thin jumpsuit. Wearily, he pulled it out and stared at the name on the screen, hesitated and then clicked Accept with a sigh.

'Beryl.'

'Liam is missing!' Her voice broke. 'He was at the fairground with me and then … and it's dark and … Jo …'

'Where are you now? What's he wearing? No, I know, the orange hoody and blue board shorts. Have you rung the police? Ring them now. I'll get lights sorted. And the PA system.'

Hanging up, he ran full pelt to the café, relieved to see Richard and Nicola, Lucy and Ash relaxing with their feet up, the crowd more interested in the bar than the café now.

'WooHoo! Nice get up!' Richard whistled.

'Liam has gone missing. We need lights on the beach – can you turn everything on?'

Ash was on his feet in an instant. 'I'll ring the boys …'

Ed raced out, not waiting to hear the rest. As he sprinted to the marquee housing the PA system, he told anyone he saw that he knew, 'Liam's missing.' Everyone knew Liam – he couldn't go far, surely. He tried not to think about the caves, and the incoming tide, and the traffic, and abductions …

The film halted abruptly, plunging the beach into pitch black. There were a few screams, and then laughter.

'Turn it back on!' yelled Ed. 'Just pause it! We need the light.' He panted out his message to the DJ, who promptly relayed it across the beach.

'… he's nearly five, brown hair going blonde, grey eyes, wearing …' The message repeated over and over. 'Please check inside tents, sleeping bags, anything he might have crawled into …'

Chapter Thirty-Two

There was no point looking for Jo, Ed decided. He needed to focus on Liam. She had Beryl with her anyway. And probably that Will. He'd only make things worse. The beach was alive with partygoers scattering in search and calling out Liam's name, and he saw the blue lights of approaching police.

Please, please don't let Liam be another statistic. Not another beautiful, chubby-cheeked child on the front pages of a newspaper. His heart hammered. Somewhere deep down, he didn't really blame Will for wanting to claim his son. He would have, wouldn't he? Oh God, what if he took them away? Wanted custody? Could he do that?

'Liam!' he yelled over and over, searching behind the marquee in the car park. He remembered the little boy squeezing into the hidden room in the barn where he'd found the motorbike that Jo then bought him. Visualising rock fissures they'd explored in the summer, caves as the tide came in, dread swept over him. He'd never be able to forgive himself if …

He ran to the nearby cars, abandoned haphazardly, and began hunting beneath them, calling, and checking his mobile, praying for the message that would tell him Liam was safe. The screen remained blank. He couldn't begin to imagine the terror Jo was feeling right now.

His truck was parked furthest away, near to the café. He hurried towards it, thinking to broaden the search, along the roads. Something. Anything. He was completely blocked in. Frustrated, he whacked the bonnet, and propped his hands on the cab, scanning the area and thinking.

Where would he go? It wasn't like him to just wander off. He was a good kid. He began to think back over the evening. He'd been there, when Will had arrived, making all those claims. What had Liam understood from that? He might only be little, but he was bright, and Ed had often been surprised by the connections he made.

Like a film on fast forward, his memory travelled over the summer, the fun they'd had, the Classic Bike show, each scene lit in technicolour. Just like that blasted *Mamma Mia!* movie, frozen now in mid-song on the colossal screen. How much they'd come to mean to him. The thought of losing them both was ripping him apart.

There was a snuffle. An unmistakeable sniff. Close by.

'Liam?' he called quietly, hardly daring to hope. Why hadn't he thought to look here first? Please let it be him and not some couple snogging. Treading softly, he crept around the truck. 'Liam? It's Ed. It's okay, you can come out. No one will tell you off. There's just me here.'

The tarpaulin moved and Ed tugged it back, holding his breath, hearing his heart pounding in his ears. Hunched amongst the clutter that lived in there, was a small boy in an orange hoody and blue board shorts.

'*Oh*, thank God. Liam ...' Ed pulled the tarpaulin back further and clambered in, hunkering down beside him. 'I'll just let Mummy know you're okay.'

Liam leaned into him, his little body hiccuping from crying, his arms snaking up around Ed's neck. Choking back a sob himself, Ed rang Jo's mobile. 'He's safe. I've got him.' Jo's screams of relief rang down the phone. 'We're in the truck. Shall I come to you? Okay. We'll wait here.' He texted Ash next, watching as the message was read.

Pulling Liam closer and smoothing his back, Ed said quietly into his hair, 'How did you get in here?'

'I c-climbed up the wheel,' Liam stuttered.

Ed made a mental note to lash the cover down more securely in future. Except that it had at least given the little boy a safe hideyhole. 'Where were you going?'

'H-h-home. On my bike.'

Horrified at the idea of him cycling home in the dark through the busy roads, Ed gulped.

'But I couldn't get it out of the truck.' The little boy tightened his grip on Ed's neck. 'It was too h-heavy.'

'Weren't you scared?'

Liam shook his head. 'I've got my torch,' he said in a small voice.

'What were you going to do at home?'

'I was going to talk to my *chwk-chwks*.'

'Oh. I see.' Ed didn't see at all. It was the last thing he'd been expecting. God, the responsibility. He'd given Liam the pedal cycle, and the bloody chickens. This was all his fault. 'What were you going to tell them?'

'I was going to tell them that I was sad.'

Ed was silent. He had no idea what to say next. He went for a wise sounding,

'*Ah.*'

'Aunty Beryl told me,' Liam carried on, his voice racked with dry sobs, 'that when she was a little girl, they had bees. And her daddy told her that she had to tell the bees all the news, 'specially if she was sad about something.' He nodded for emphasis. 'But we haven't got any bees. So, she said to tell the chickens all the news.'

'Okay.' Taking a long, silent breath, Ed said, 'What were you sad about?'

Liam's voice was muffled against Ed's shoulder. 'I was sad because everyone was sad. You were sad, Mummy was sad, and Aunty Beryl was sad. And Mummy was crying. Like I do when I fall over, only she hadn't fallen over. And everyone kept saying my name … Was it my fault? Have I been naughty?'

'*Oh*, mate. Come here.' Ed scooped him closer, thinking carefully about what he said next. 'It wasn't your fault at all. You mustn't think that. There was a lot of shouting, and grown-ups do that sometimes. Don't you and your friends sometimes shout at each other?'

Liam sniffed and nodded. 'And Mummy … she did a bit of a silly thing, and she didn't tell me something she should have.' He sighed, a long, ragged sigh. 'But, you know, I think she might have done it to protect you and me.' He paused. Explaining it to Liam gave him a piercing clarity into Jo's reasons. He took a deep breath, closing his mouth on the words, *So that I could be your daddy and not have to share you with anyone else, except Mummy.* Family was about more than DNA. He wanted to cry just like Liam. Big boys didn't cry though, did they? And wasn't that half the problem?

He said instead, 'So even though it's been very upsetting, it wasn't anything to do with you being naughty. Please don't think that. Mummy loves you. And so does Beryl, and so do I. And another thing. Even though we know you're a big, grown-up boy, you mustn't ever go anywhere on your bike without me or Mummy, okay? Because the cars go really fast and they wouldn't be looking for you down here on your bike.' His hand waved, palm down, a foot off the floor, and Liam nodded earnestly.

'I'm not that little, you know. I am a big boy. I'm nearly five!'

'Look! Here's Mummy. Shall we get down now?' He clambered out of the back of the truck with Liam clinging to him koala-style. Flanked by Beryl, Lyn, Griff, Will and a policeman and woman, who glanced over his outfit but made no comment. Jo looked dreadful, her eyes red and raw, her make-up smeared. She ran towards him, but stopped short, her eyes pleading.

'Liam …?' He submitted to a head down hug but remained resolutely in Ed's arms. 'I'm sorry,' she mouthed at Ed, her eyes brimming with tears again.

The policeman cleared his throat, holding out his

clipboard. Ed didn't recognise him, and looked around for Ash, pleased to see him climbing the steps towards them.

'So, this is Liam, then? No injuries or anything?'

Jo nodded, her hand on her son's back.

'He's not hurt,' said Ed, nodding to Ash as he joined them.

'Alright, mate?' Ash shook his hand.

'*Mmm.*'

The policeman acknowledged Ash with nod. 'Cancel the troops, please, Gwynneth,' he told the policewoman, who moved away a little, talking urgently into her radio. 'I just need a word here so we can wrap this up.' He began to check through the form. 'Right. So, you're his mother …'

Jo nodded, her lip still wobbling.

'… and,' he looked at the men present in turn, 'is his father here?'

Ed saw Will open his mouth to answer.

'I am,' he said, interrupting firmly, and feeling Liam's hot and damp face in his neck. He turned to Jo. 'That's … if the job is still vacant?'

'*Oh*, Ed!' She ran into his spare arm, hugging them both tightly. 'Are you sure, after everything I—? I thought you would … I mean, yes, of course!'

'No more secrets? Nothing else I ought to know?'

She shook her head. 'Nothing. You know everything there is to know about me. That's everything.'

'I think I understand,' Ed said, carefully, his eyes travelling over the faces of his parents. 'Nothing is ever straightforward … and I know that you'd always do the best for Liam – and I believe, for me …'

'*Oh* … Ed.' Jo burst into tears again. 'I would. It was stupid of me. I should have told you everything so long ago. I was only trying to protect you … and I thought you'd hate me …'

Lyn and Beryl blew their noses simultaneously.

'Well, *I've* got a secret.' Ed set Liam carefully on his feet, his chest swelling with a sense of fierce protectiveness as he felt the little boy wrap his arms around his legs. It was now or never. 'And Jo, even though you've done your level best to ruin it, I'm going through with it. God, I had this all organised, you wretched woman! Oh, but at least the music is back on!' *Mamma Mia!* stuttered into life where it had left off, and there were cheers from the crowd. Fishing in his pocket with suddenly trembling hands, he brought out a small, velvet box, hitched up the skimpy outfit, and getting to one knee, opened it to show her.

'You're the best thing that has ever happened to me, Jo. And this has only made me realise that I can't lose you. Either of you. I love you – both of you.' He took a deep breath, trying to steady his shaking hands. 'Jo, would you do me the honour of marrying me?'

'*Aaah!*' said Beryl, Lyn and the policeman together, as the solitaire diamond winked and sparkled in the dazzling lights.

Tears streamed again down Jo's face.

'That's a yes, right?' Ed looked up at her. 'Only this outfit is giving me a terrible wedgie …'

She nodded, reaching out to touch the beautiful ring. '*Oh*, yes.' She sighed over it. 'It's stunning.'

'It's Welsh gold,' Ed said, pulling himself to his feet and tugging the blue satin straight. 'Well, platinum, actually. Only the best for you.'

'Can I wear it?' Jo touched the bright metal with reverence.

'Of course you can! If it doesn't fit, we can have it altered …' Ed held her hand and slid the ring onto her slender finger.

'Congratulations!' chorused the little group. Lucy hurried over to join them, and Ash pulled her into a hug, whispering in her ear. She let out a little squeal.

'Congratulations, you two! How lovely!'

'I absolutely love it,' Jo said, still staring at the ring. She looked up at Ed, her eyes bright. 'I've got something for you, too …' Giving the ring box safely to Beryl, she put one foot on the wheel hub of the truck and levered herself into the back.

'That's how I got in,' Liam said, pointing.

Jo reappeared carrying something bulky swathed in an ancient pink candlewick bedspread.

'If you can guess what it is, you can keep it.' She handed it to Ed.

His fingers probed the object within, and a grin lit his face.

'*Oh*, you beauty! Is this what I think it is?'

'What do you think it is?'

Kneeling, he set the thing on the ground and everyone leaned over to see.

'Nicely wrapped,' he nodded approvingly and Jo laughed shakily. Layer after layer of bubble-wrap peeled away to reveal a silver, teardrop shaped tank.

'What is it?' Will leaned in to get a better view. He wasn't giving up easily, Ed thought. But then, neither would he.

'It's the petrol tank for a classic motorbike. But not just any motorbike. A Brough Superior. The same model that Lawrence of Arabia rode. Now it's got a tank it's worth hundreds of thousands of pounds.' He picked it up reverently, inspecting it under the floodlights. 'And do you know who found it?'

'I did!' said Liam, his face split with glee.

'You did, you clever boy!' Ed hunkered down and gave him a hug. 'Thank you.'

Will was still hovering in the background. He stepped forward.

'Well. I suppose I should congratulate you too.' He nodded, his mouth a straight line as he shook Ed's hand with a firm grip. 'But … *er*, I'd still like to share a part of Liam's life. Would that be okay? Even if it's just a bit. I'd like to contribute towards him. I'm a pilot, with a big airline. I don't want to take him away from you, I can see how well you get on, and I suppose I ought to be grateful for that. Maybe … a day out, and then perhaps holidays or something?'

Jo looked taken aback.

'Wow, so you did turn out to be the golden boy after all! Thank you, Will. I'm so sorry, I haven't handled it at all well.'

He gave her a thick white business card. 'Would you ring me? Keep in touch?'

They nodded.

'Yes, of course,' Jo said. 'I owe it to you. Are you staying somewhere nearby? Maybe we could meet up tomorrow, and properly talk everything through. And you can meet Liam without all this drama.'

Ed blinked at her. This was a very different Jo. A calm, collected Jo, despite her tear-stained face and wayward curls. As if a huge weight had been lifted from her. He realised the enormity of the burden she'd been carrying about for so long. Jo had adored the man who'd turned out not to be her biological father. He'd been the man who'd made the most impression on her. He was sad that he'd never met him.

Ed was determined to be the father that Liam needed. It didn't matter that they weren't blood related, did it? He had what he'd always wanted – a family to love. He could afford to be generous.

'Of course, you two will have a lot to catch up on.' He lifted his hands, palm up, indicating that he trusted her enough to leave them together.

'I'd like you there too, Ed,' Jo said. 'No more secrets. Okay with you, Will?'

Ed could see Will wrestling with his emotions, but with a glance at Liam, he nodded and held a hand out to Ed. 'Agreed. Maybe, you could – both, or all of you – meet me at the Art Café for brunch, tomorrow? If that's okay?'

They nodded.

'Brunch?' said Liam. 'I know what that is. Too late for breakfast and too early for lunch, right?'

'Well done, sweetheart,' said Beryl with a smile of pride.

'Can I have pancakes then?' he said, to laughter.

'As many as you like.' Will smiled down at him, and then saw Ed's expression. 'Until your mum tells you that's enough,' he added quickly. 'Well, I'm calling it a day. I'll see you all tomorrow morning.' He backed away with an awkward wave, and then turned and strode across the car park.

'I need to get out of this outfit,' Ed said in an aside to Jo. 'I feel a right twa—, er, idiot in it.'

'Shame,' Jo shuffled her eyebrows and surreptitiously stroked his silky thigh, admiring the winking diamond on her finger. 'I could get used it. It's quite … manly, really …'

'No.'

'What were you going to do in it, anyway?' she said, her eyes laughing up at him.

Ed stared across the beach. The silver moon gilded the surf and the remaining partygoers.

'It'll keep,' he said at last, with a straight face. 'Right! Got to get Mum and Dad home. And Liam.'

'And Beryl,' said Beryl. 'All I want right now is a nice pot of tea. With a good slosh of brandy in it.'

'We'll drop you off,' said his mum. 'Bye you lovely pair. Congratulations again. Come on, Liam. Time for some stories. And hot chocolate.' The little boy beamed, and went willingly enough. There were kisses and hugs all round as they left.

'And we have to be up early to move into Seagull Cottage tomorrow,' Jo said, watching them leave. 'There's a lot to do. And with brunch now, in the middle of it.'

'*Ah*. That's something else I suppose I should tell you.' Ed pulled her into his side, feeling her warmth through the thin fabric of his outfit.

'What? Isn't it ready? Oh well … I suppose I could bear a bit longer in the caravan.'

'No, it isn't that … I was going to wait until tomorrow and surprise you.'

'Ed. I've had more surprises than I can cope with tonight. Tell me now!'

'*We-ell.*' He turned to face her, smoothing the tousled curls behind her ears. 'You remember that farmhouse where Liam found the bike?'

'*Ye-es …*'

'I've bought it.'

Jo shook her head, blinking. 'I'm confused … Kirsty said it was sold, but she didn't say it was to you …'

'*Ye-aah* – looks like you're not the only one with secrets …' Ed looked apologetic.

'For us? You and me and Liam?' Her jaw dropped. 'With all those workshops?'

He nodded. 'Yes! You could have your upcycling business there!'

'Oh, my goodness. Ed! And your bikes!' Her face split into a huge beam and then fell. 'I'll miss Beryl …'

'I thought about that. A girl needs her mum. There's enough space to make a granny annexe, if she wanted that.'

'I don't think she'd be keen on the idea of being called "granny".' Jo chuckled. 'But that's a lovely idea.'

'Yep. Except it needs some doing up, and …'

'… and we have to live in the caravan for a bit longer?'

'Yes. Only there, instead of Seagull Cottage.'

She laughed. 'I reckon we could cope with that.'

'That was a good surprise, right?' He snuggled her closer.

'Yes. Wonderful.' She held her left hand up, turning it to catch the light. 'No more secrets though, from now on.'

'A few,' Ed conceded. 'Just the good ones. Christmas presents. Birthdays. Wedding plans don't need to be secret though … or, I wondered … a Greek honeymoon, with Liam?'

Thank You

Dear Reader,

Thank you for reading my second novel, *Meet Me at the Art Café*. I do hope you enjoyed meeting my characters and following their story.

Jo and Ed walked into the spotlight from *Summer at the Art Café*, and made me laugh and cry as their lives unfolded. I found myself browsing for children's clothes for Liam in a supermarket once before I caught myself doing it, and I would absolutely love to go on holiday with Beryl, although I'm not sure my liver would keep up.

It's exciting and terrifying in equal measure to share them with the world. I would be thrilled if you took the time to leave a review on the retail site where you made your purchase. Reviews really do help to improve a book's profile and sales and are very much appreciated.

My contact details are given at the end of my author profile, and if I've encouraged you to learn to ride a motorbike, details of how to do that are there too!

Much love,
Sue

About the Author

Sue McDonagh's career as a policewoman for Essex Police was cut short when she was diagnosed at the age of twenty-four with ovarian cancer. After a successful recovery and a stint working as a Press Officer she moved to Wales.

In Wales her love of art evolved into a full-time occupation and she made a living teaching and sketching portraits at shows. In 2014 she was a regional finalist for the Sky Arts Portrait Artist of the Year. She now works exclusively to commissions from her art gallery.

In 2009 she learned to ride a motorbike, and now helps run Curvy Riders, a national, women only, motorbike club. Her joy of motorbikes and her love of writing inspired her to write the Art Café series.

Sue is a proud mum and granny in the gloriously blended family she is honoured to be part of. She lives a mile from the sea in Wales and can often be found with her border terrier, Scribbles, at her art gallery. Scribble thinks the customers only come in to see him. Sometimes, Sue thinks that too.

When she's not painting, she's writing or on her motorbike. She belongs to a local writing group and the Romantic Novelist's Association.

You can find more about Sue here:
Website: http://suemcdonagh.co.uk/
Facebook: https://www.facebook.com/SueMcDonaghWriter/
Twitter: https://twitter.com/SueMcDonaghLit

More Choc Lit

From Sue McDonagh

Summer at the Art Café

From watercolours and cupcakes to leather jackets and freedom …

If you won a gorgeous purple motorbike, and your domineering husband said you were too fat for leathers and should sell it, would you do as you were told – or learn to ride it in secret?

Artist and café owner Lucy Daumier intends to do just that – but learning to ride is far from easy, especially under the critical eye of prickly motorcycle instructor, Ash Connor.

But gradually she gets the hang of it, and in the process re-discovers the girl she used to be. So starts an exciting summer of new friendship and fun – as well as a realisation that there is more to Ash than meets the eye when she is introduced to his seven-year-old daughter, Daisy.

But can Lucy's new-found happiness last when a spiteful family member wants to see her fail?

Available in paperback from all good bookshops and online stores. Visit www.choc-lit.com for details.

Introducing Choc Lit

We're an independent publisher creating
a delicious selection of fiction.
Where heroes are like chocolate – irresistible!
Quality stories with a romance at the heart.

See our selection here:
www.choc-lit.com

We'd love to hear how you enjoyed *Meet Me at the Art
Café*. Please visit **www.choc-lit.com** and give your feedback
or leave a review where you purchased this novel.

Choc Lit novels are selected by genuine readers like yourself.
We only publish stories our Choc Lit Tasting Panel want to
see in print. Our reviews and awards speak for themselves.

Could you be a Star Selector and join our Tasting Panel?
Would you like to play a role in choosing which novels
we decide to publish? Do you enjoy reading women's
fiction? Then you could be perfect for our Tasting Panel.

Visit here for more details…
www.choc-lit.com/join-the-choc-lit-tasting-panel

Keep in touch:
Sign up for our monthly newsletter Spread for all the latest
news and offers: www.spread.choc-lit.com. Follow us
on Twitter: @ChocLituk and Facebook: Choc Lit.

Where heroes are like chocolate – irresistible!